Unconditional LOVE

A NOVEL

CAROL ANN IACIOFANO

The EC Publishing LLC books may be ordered
through booksellers or by contacting:

EC Publishing LLC
116 South Magnolia Ave.
Suite 3, Unit F
Ocala, FL 34471, USA
Direct Line: +1 (352) 644-6538
Fax: +1 (800) 483-1813
http://www.ecpublishingllc.com/

Ordering Information:
Quantity sales. Special discounts are available on quantity purchases by corporations, associations, and others. For
details, contact the publisher at the address above.

Printed in the United States of America

Thank you to my family and friends for the your endless love and support. This novel has been playing around in my head for a while. The start of the novel came to me in a dream and I woke up and wrote chapter 1. My characters create their own adventures. I am always amazed at where they take me...

Rosemary –

The world is a better
place because of you!

To the reader, thank you for supporting me. I love creating stories about a lot of characters. I try to limit how many character share parts in my novels. I write with humor and make myself laugh when I write. And or cry. I hope when you read it, you sense my humor. Thank you again! Big hugs and much love to you!

Lots of love to you
always –
Carol Ann Jackson

Chapter 1

"Sebastian Timely!" A man's voice booms. "I am looking for Sebastian Timely."

"I am Sebastian." I say.

The man looks at me. He takes into account that I am one a woman, two that I am in a wheelchair, and three I don't fit the profile of the person that he was expecting. "Come with me." He says.

"Sure."

He turns and walks quickly down a hallway. He turns back to see that I am following him. He looks ahead and then walks to a door on the left side of the hallway and opens it. He goes inside. I follow him. He walks to the table and removes the chair. "Make yourself comfortable, your lawyer will be right with you."

"My what?" I choke. "I thought I was here to pay a traffic ticket."

He looks at the file that he holds in his hand. He opens it and reads the material inside. He puts the file on the table. "Like I said, your lawyer will be right with you." He walks to the door, opens it and leaves the room.

I sit in the room at a large table. The room is bright. The lights shine down on me and make me hot. I feel my heart beating in my chest and hear it pounding in my ears. I am a good person. I live in the same house that I was raised in. I have a job that I love and have had for six years. I am a school teacher. I teach third grade. Its my favorite grade because the children are not babies any more but not yet old enough to not need help.

The door opening jars me back to the situation I find myself in. A man walks in. He looks up at the lights in the ceiling and turns the knob making the lights dimmer.

I look at him. I can't take my eyes off of him. I want to stop staring but there is nothing better to look at and he has captured my attention.

He crosses the room, takes the chair and pulls it away from the table. He sits down, lifts the file and reads the contents. He stands and leaves the room. He opens the door and says, "Excuse me, I will be right back." He closes the door before I can answer.

I look at my watch. I am glad that there is no school today. I am supposed to be at work for a workshop that I am missing. I am curious to know what is in the file but don't have the nerve to reach across the table and read it. I feel like I am being watched.

My phone rings and I just let it. My purse is buckled into the seatbelt that I use because safety always comes first. I hear the ping and know that some one has left me a message.

The door opens again. A woman enters the room followed by the man who has captured my attention yet again. She walks over to the table, opens the file, closes it and then says. "Do you have your identification with you?"

"Of course." I say. I open my purse and hand her my ID.

"Why are you here?" She asks.

"I am here to pay a traffic ticket."

They both look at me.

"Is something wrong?" I ask.

"You drive?" The woman asks.

"Yes. I love my car."

"What bank do you use?" The man asks. His voice is so soothing.

"Bank? Is this about my stolen ATM card?"

"Stolen ATM card?" She asks. "When did that happen?"

"Three weeks ago. I went to Beyond Education to get material for my class. I dropped my purse and someone helped me pick it up. I thought at the time that I had all my stuff. When I went to go pay, I had no ATM card or credit cards. My wallet was at the bottom of my purse.

"Empty your purse." The man says.

I push back from the table. Unbuckle my seatbelt and get my purse. I put it on the table. He grabs it, unzips it and dumps out all the contents. He takes my wallet and opens it. Ten dollars floats to the table and falls to the floor. He takes my purse and looks for pockets. There is one that is zipped. He unzips it and the zipper comes off. "How is it you can afford a purse this expensive?"

"I work." I snap.

"Don't raise your voice."

"I came here to pay a traffic ticket." I say quietly.

"With what money? You have no money in this purse."

I put my hand on my shoulder and reach in my shirt. They both look at me and watch to see what I am doing. I pull a credit card out of my bra strap and put it on the table.

"The one that got away?" He says sarcastically.

"Um, no. It's the one that I got as a replacement." I look at both of them. "Are one of you my lawyer? Or are you both police officers?" I look at everything that I have in my purse and the one thing that embarrasses me the most is the torn picture. I reach over and take the pieces in my fingers.

"What are you hiding?" He asks.

"I am not hiding anything. You have dumped my purse out on the table. What else is there to hide?"

"What did you take off the table?" The woman asks. "I am a police officer." She looks at Mr. Tall and handsome. "This is your lawyer Justin Case."

I am struck by a fit of laughter. I can't help it. I put my head on the table and laugh until I cry.

He storms out of the room and slams the door when he goes.

I am finally allowed to leave the room. I go into a waiting area and wait for the man who first had me follow him into a room. He comes out from behind a wall and looks into the waiting room.

There are only three people in there. There are two men. One is short and looks like he has worked a full day outside in the heat of Florida. He looks at me once and then back to his phone which is playing a Schwarzenegger movie. Its low but I can still hear the fighting and guns going off. The other man is tall. He has the body of a bodybuilder. He is dressed in a suit. He also has his phone in his hand and he types and reads on and off.

The shorter man looks at me and smiles. Gold teeth fill his mouth. "My movie bothering you?" He asks.

No the smell of you is I think. I smile back. "Not at all." I say. I look around the room and see the man that lead me to the room where I sat for hours. "I have to go the lady's room." I say to him.

"Of course." He says. "Follow me."

I do. He walks down a short hallway and opens the door to a bathroom. "Thank you." I say.

"I will wait for you out here."

"Do you know when I can leave? I have to get to my second job."

"A second job?" He asks. "Did you miss a day of work being here?"

"I am a teacher."

"There was no school today. My children made sure to tell that to me when I went to wake them up this morning."

"There was no school for them. I am a teacher, there was work for me. I did miss the whole day." I look at my watch. "I do have to be at my next job at three-thirty." I close the door and do what I need to. I look at myself in the mirror. I take the torn picture and hold up the two pieces. I blink away the tears.

"Miss Timely?"

I wash my hands and open the door.

"Follow me." He says.

When we go down the hallway, I feel someone watching me. I hear that soothing voice again. "Miss Timely." He says

"What?" I ask.

"Can I talk to you?" Justin asks.

I look at the guy who looks at both me and Justin. "Can I go?"

"You are not under arrest." The man says.

I feel my heart slam against the walls of my chest. I feel like a can't breath. I put my hands over my eyes as the room starts to spin around me. I start shaking uncontrollably. I feel wind rush around me as someone runs down the hallway pushing me. I open my eyes and the brightness makes my eyes hurt. I squeeze them shut and then there is blackness.

When I open my eyes, I don't know where I am. I raise my head. I look at my hand that is being held tight by my mother. I look at here.

"Mom?"

"Hi sweetheart. How are you?"

"Where am I?" I ask.

"You don't know where you are?"

"Am I still at the courthouse?"

She looks at me. "You are in the hospital."

"Is it Monday?"

"Its Thursday." She says.

I look at my mom. She has a great sense of humor. She looks at me with sad eyes. "Its Thursday?"

"Yes."

The door opens. A doctor walks in. "Miss Timely?"

"Yes." I say.

"Do you know why you are here?"

"I think I passed out."

"You do. We have run tests and everything comes back clean."

"That's good right?" My mom asks.

"I would say yes, but it doesn't explain why she passed out and has been out for three days."

"Stress." I say.

"What?" The doctor asks.

"When I get stressed out, I pass out."

"So this has happened before?"

"I haven't missed three days of my life before."

"What kind of stress have you experienced lately?" He asks as he comes to the side fo the bed, he takes a light and shines it in my eyes. "Are you aware that you lost a contact lens?"

"I just woke up." I squint my one eye and then the other. "Well now I do." I say.

"Don't be smart." My mother says.

The doctor looks at her. "She is fine." He listens to my heart beating. "Can you wiggle your fingers?"

I do.

"Can yo wiggle your toes?"

"I can not." I say.

"Right." He says looking at the wheelchair. My wheelchair in the corner of the room. "That is yours."

"It is." I say.

"Tell me what kind of stress you have been experiencing lately." He says after he takes leg in his hands and squeezes it. "Can you feel that?"

"I have feeling, I can not walk." I say "I went to the courthouse to pay a traffic ticket—"

"I always tell her she needs to stop speeding." Mom interrupts me.

"Thank you." I say to my mom. I look back at the doctor. "I was taken into a room and I was interrogated for hours. I used the bathroom and then everything blurred."

"Do you know how you got here?" He asks.

"No."

"Ok, I am going to leave you for a little while, I will be back to check on you."

"So what's wrong with me?"

"Like I said before, all the tests came back normal."

"Can I leave?"

"I need to go consult with a few colleagues before you go."

"Ok." I say. "Can I get out of bed?"

"Yes." He says. "Do you need help getting into your wheelchair?"

"I just need it close to the bed." I say.

He leaves the room and my mom gets my wheelchair for me. I sit up and scoot to the edge of the bed. I stand up and quickly turn and sit in my wheelchair. I go in the bathroom. I use the toilet and then wash my hands.

"Mom, do you have a brush?"

She opens her purse and hands it to me.

"Thanks." I say.

"Do you have a new boyfriend?" She asks looking at me in the mirror.

I brush out my long locks. I look at her in the mirror. "I have two jobs. When do I have time to date?"

"There is a guy who keeps coming to see you. He told the staff that he is your boyfriend."

"Mom, the only guy in my life is Astro."

"Sweetheart how many time do I have to tell you, that dog is not a substitute for a man."

I smile at her in the mirror. She smiles back. "That's my point." I say to her.

She looks at her watch. "I have to go." She says.

I hand her back the brush. "Ok. Thanks for being here."

"I will be back. Keep me posted about what is going on." She kisses the top of my head and gathers her stuff. "I can leave the brush for you."

"No its ok."

"You look beautiful." She says and kisses the top of my head.

I sit in my wheelchair for a while. I look through my purse and everything that I had it when I went to the courthouse is there except the ripped photograph. I feel my heart sink in my chest. I take everything out of my purse and I look for it again. Its not there.

I sit facing the window staring out but I see nothing. The sky is blue. The wind blows the trees but I don't notice it.

The door opens and Justin walks in. I don't hear him even though he is not at all quiet about making his entrance. He looks around the room and sees my purse and all of its contents on the bed like the purse threw up. He walks over to where I am and sits down. He touches my arm and I nearly jump out of my skin. "Hi." He says softly

I look at him and then back out the window.

"How are you doing?"

"I want it back." I say.

"What?"

"I have everything except my picture. I want it back."

"Why do you walk around with a ripped photograph?"

7

I still don't look at him. "That's my business. Why do I need a lawyer if my only crimes are speeding tickets?"

"Did you call the police when your cards were stolen?"

"Yes." I say closing my eyes.

"My name is Justin Case. I am a lawyer but I am not your lawyer. I am helping the police look into why we have information that a Sebastian Timely is wanted for robbing a bank."

I nearly choke. I finally look at him. "I didn't rob a bank." I say to him.

"We know that. We knew that the minute that you were in that room. You don't fit the profile of the person that robbed the bank. Your name does." He looks at me. "Are you going to faint again?"

I look at him. "No."

"Why do you walk around with a torn picture? Who is the picture of?"

"My husband."

"If you were married how can you still be a Miss?"

"I was only married for three days."

"Why?"

"He died."

"Then why is the photograph ripped?"

"His mother ripped it. She wanted to tear my heart out. She ripped it so that I wasn't in it." I turn my head and look out the window again.

I get released from the hospital the next afternoon. I have missed a week of work for not one but two jobs that I have. Plus tutoring jobs that I do for some of my fellow teachers' students that need extra help.

I get home and the love of my life Astro greets me at the door. His tail wagging. He puts his paws on my legs and licks my face.

"Hi Astro. I know, I have missed you too." I tell him. "Ok, get down." I pet his side when he stands next to me. He nudges me and I lean in to him and hug his head. "I love you." I tell him.

I go through the mail. I throw out the junk mail and put the important stuff in a drawer and close it. "We will leave this for later."

I look at Astro. "I am going to take a shower. Do you want to go out before I take care of me?"

He wags his tail.

"Where is your leash?" I go over to the basket that holds his leash. I click it on the collar. I put the handle of the leash in my seatbelt and go outside. Astro stays to the left of my wheelchair. He lifts his leg and pees on everything. We go to the end of the street and he wags his tail as he sits next to me. He sees someone approaching us. I look to see a guy running towards us. "Astro, stay."

The guy stops and slows his approach. He looks at me.

I look at him. I look at Astro. "Turn. Lets go." I say.

"Wait!" Justin says. "Please don't walk away from me."

"Why are you here? I live here. Go away."

"I live here too." He says.

I spin around and look at him. "What?"

"My brother and I just moved into the neighborhood." He looks at Astro. "Who is your friend?"

"This is my dog, Astro."

"He is beautiful." Justin looks at me. "Can I pet him?"

"Yes." I look at Astro. "Sit." I tell Astro. He turns his head up to me and wags his tail.

Justin sits on the grass and pets Astro. Astro throws himself down on the grass. Justin looks at me. "Can I ask you a question?"

"Yes."

"Why are you in a wheelchair?"

"I have cerebral palsy."

"What's that?"

"It translates to brain weakness. I can not balance. I can walk with the aid of a walker."

"Which house is yours?"

"I want my picture back."

He looks at me. "I don't have it." He pets Astro's tummy. Astro rolls into him. "Why were you only married for three days?"

"I told you. He died."

"Was it a sudden death?"

"Yes and no."

"What does that mean?"

"I can't do this." I look at Astro. "Come on, lets go."

"Can I see you again?"

"You live in the neighborhood." I go to my house. Astro lays down in his favorite spot. I give him a treat and then go in my room. I take my clothes off and go in the bathroom. I go in the shower. I sit in the chair that's in there and let the water run on my body.

I take the towel and dry myself. I wrap up in it. I get out and go in my room. I get dressed and pull my long hair into a ponytail. I lower the comforter on the bed. I get on the bed. Astro jumps on the bed with me. I snuggle with him and fall asleep as Moonlight Sonata plays on a endless loop.

My cell phone rings waking me up. I take the phone off the side table and answer it.

"Ms. Timely?" The male voice booms into the phone.

"Yes."

"My name is Donald. I work with Ms. Case."

"Ok." I say.

"We want you to know that we have your ID."

"Why?" I hang up the phone.

My phone rings again.

"Ms. Timely?"

"I am sorry. I just got out of the hospital. Give my ID to Mr. Case. It turns out that he lives close by me."

"I can't do that."

"How do expect me to get it? Without it, I can not drive my car. Do you happen to have my car keys too? They are missing."

"We did find a set of keys. The ones we have has a unicorn."

"Not a unicorn. It's a winged horse."

"We have them."

"Wonderful. Do you have my photograph too?"

"I told you we have your ID."

"No, a ripped photograph?"

"No."

"Ok, well thanks."

"I will ask around for it. If we find it, we will put it with your stuff."

"Thanks."

We hang up.

Chapter 2

I go in the kitchen and open the refrigerator. I go to the grocery store on my way home from work on Wednesdays. I have a dozen eggs and yogurt. I close the doors. I open a drawer and take out my spare keys. I put them on the counter and let out a scream.

I pick up my phone. I dial my friend's number. Savannah and I have been friends since second grade. She cheated off of my spelling test and got an A. That led to a life long friendship. She answers the phone as only she could.

"Where the fuck have you been? Did you go to jail or something?" She laughs.

I burst into tears.

"Holy shit, are you crying?"

I don't answer her.

"I will be right there. I will pick up our favorite eggplant dishes from our favorite place. Do you need anything else?"

"Just you." I say between sobs.

"Did you call Pipes?"

"No."

"Want me to call Pipes?"

She is referring to the last installment of the three musketeers. We are sorority sisters too as we pledged the same one at different colleges. We have been friends since we were seven.

"I will be there in twenty minutes or so."

"Don't speed." I say. We always say that to each other.

"That's your job. I will be right there. Sabby make some good coffee."

"Ok." I say. I end the call. I call Piper. It goes to her voicemail. "Hi its me. Just to let you know, I am home. I was in the hospital. I will tell you all about it. Call me when you get this. Tomorrow. If not, I will see you at church on Sunday. I love you Pipes."

I go in the family room and click the television on. I get my purse and I dump out all of its insides out on the table. I look through everything. I go in my room and into my closet where I have a collection of purses. I get one that I love using, I put the one that I was using in the bottom of the drawer. I am sad that the zipper is broken.

I put all the contents that I carry with me on a daily bases into this purse. It is another designer purse. A designer that I love. I buy a lot of her line because I saw her on an interview where she told the reporter that she never felt pretty. Her father told her that she better get used to the world seeing her as an ugly person. She makes purses that I love. They are fun and artsy.

I put my purse on the hook that is near the front door. I take the garbage outside after I feed Astro. He eats his dry food mixed with a can of wet food. When I open the freezer he wags his tail.

"You want your ice cream?" I ask him. His tail bangs against the cabinets. I open it and he sits with his paws on my leg. "Easy." I say and let him lick the ice cream.

I busy myself until Savannah comes. I set the table for both of us. I put drinks on the table. I see car lights pull into the driveway.

I go to the door to open it and I am surprised when its not her, but Justin Case standing on my door step.

"What do you want?" I ask him.

"Tell me about your three day husband."

"My friend is coming with dinner. It seems like Douglas, your friend has my ID and my car keys."

"The unicorn keys are yours?"

"Oh for Christ sake, it's a winged horse."

"Like Pegasus?"

"Yes."

"Can I come in?" He asks.

Savannah pulls into the driveway. She runs up the front walk. She looks at Justin. She looks at me. "Mr. Case, what are you doing here?" She asks.

"I came to introduce myself to my neighbor."

"You live here?" She asks.

"He doesn't live here." I say.

"I live two streets behind her."

"I brought enough food, would you like to join us?" She asks.

I roll my eyes. He smiles and kisses my cheek as he walks in the door.

"Are you working on a case?" She asks Justin as she takes the food out of the bags.

I glare at him.

"I am. You know I can't talk about my jobs." He smiles at me.

Savannah looks at me. "Tell me about you." She says. "Why were you crying? How was your week? How many jobs are you working now?"

He looks at her with a look that reads 'ok, shut up! Let her answer the questions. I want to know the answers too.'

"Savy, you know how many jobs I have." I say.

"How many?" Justin asks.

Now I glare at Savannah.

"Sabs, don't be mad at me." She says.

I roll my eyes. "I have two jobs."

"What are they?"

"I teach third grade at the local elementary school. I have for six years. I might not have my job after the week that I have had."

"What happened?'

"I passed out at the courthouse." I own up.

"Oh come on, it couldn't have been that stressful. You went for speeding tickets."

Justin opens his mouth to say something but looks at me and closes his mouth.

"What are you both keeping from me?" She asks catching the looks between us.

"Tell her." I say. "I will be right back, I have to go to the bathroom."
I go in my room and close the door. I just sit in my room listening to
what he tells her.

"How do you know her?" She asks him.

"I met her because she came into the courthouse to pay her traffic
tickets, but she was ushered into a room because someone robbed a
bank."

"What does that have to do with her?"

"Her name."

"Sebastian?"

"Why does she have a boy's name?"

"Her dad passed away three months before she was born."

"What happened to her husband?"

"How the hell do you now about him?"

"Why three days?"

"That's all they got." Savannah says.

"Why?"

"Because he wanted to marry her his whole life. She wanted to
make him happy. He was dying. His mother begged them not to do it.
Sabby wouldn't hear it. The doctors told all of us that he only had days
left. She went to church and got the priest. He married them. She stayed
at the hospital with him until he took his last breath."

"What was his name?"

"Craig Harrison." She says sadly.

I come out of my bedroom. I say nothing.

"What is your other job?" He asks.

"I work in an all night bookstore coffee shop."

"When do you sleep?"

"When I visit hospitals." I say sarcastically.

They both look at me.

"What did you bring? I am starving." I say to change the subject.

Savannah stands up and plates the food. She knows her way around
my kitchen. She pats Astro's head as he gets up to see what all the new
smells are. She looks at him. "I brought you something. I always do."
She says leaning in to hug him.

"Do you have a brother?" Justin asks.

"I do not." I say. "My dad died before I was born and my mom has dated since but she never had other children.

"Why do you ask?" Savannah asks him.

Justin looks at me.

"We have no secrets. We have been friends since second grade." I say.

Justin tells us about his theory. That there is a guy who is my brother. He tells us that the thinks that we share more than just DNA, but we have the same name. The only difference is he is a junior. They have him on camera robbing the bank. He didn't do anything to hide his identity. When you got pulled over for a speeding ticket the authorities were then made aware that two people had the same identification.

"To my knowledge I don't have siblings." I say. "My mom always talked about my dad when I was little and told me that he was her hero. They weren't married, but she gave me his last name. She named me after him."

"I am going to look into this." Justin says and cuts a piece of eggplant lasagne. He hands the plate to me before cutting one for Savannah and then himself. "Thank you for having me."

My phone rings. I answer it. "Hi Paul." I say. I don't have him on speaker, he talks so loudly Justin and Savannah hear him.

"How are you feeling?"

"I am ok." I say.

"I am sorry that you were in the hospital. Do you have your planning done for the upcoming week?"

"I just got out of the hospital today."

"I need your plans by Sunday so your sub can have a better week."

"I plan on being back to work on Monday."

"There are rumors going around that you robbed a bank."

"Rumors my ass." Savannah says. "His brother is the top DA."

Justin looks at me. He looks around the kitchen for something.

Savannah looks at him. "What are you looking for?" She asks.

"Paper and something to write with." He says. He puts his finger to his lips to quiet Savannah. He looks at me and extends his hand. He taps on the table. And whispers "Keep him talking."

Savannah walks over to the bookshelf right off the kitchen. She takes a box off the shelf and opens it. She takes out a note pad and pens. He watches her carefully. She walks back over to the table and places the paper and pen on the table.

Justin looks at me. He reaches his hand across the table and takes my hand in his. "Put him on speaker." He whispers.

I put the phone on speaker and set it on the table. "Paul, why are you calling me?" I ask.

We hear him chuckle. "I am calling to tell you that you are suspended until further notice. Unpaid."

"I didn't rob a bank. When it happened, I was on a field trip to Safari South with my third graders and the everyone else." I say.

"I can't have thieves teaching the youth of tomorrow." He says with a snicker

"Thanks for calling." I say.

"You have school stuff at your house. I need it."

"I have nothing that belongs to the school at my house."

"Assignments that your students have turned in and might have needed grading." He snaps.

"I don't take my work with me. I have graded all of their assignments and they are in their folders on the right corner of the file cabinet. When I leave school, I go to my second job where I am at until three in the morning."

"You work in a bar?" He laughs. "I heard that some of my teachers twilight as strippers."

"Paul! I work in the all night bookstore coffee shop. You know that. You come in with your girlfriend at one in the morning and make out until all hours of the morning after you have fought with your wife."

Justin puts his hand to his mouth to silent his laughter. "Shes a fighter." He says quietly.

"If that ever gets out, I will fire your ass so quickly, Astro will think he went to fucking outer space." He yells.

17

Justin clicks the end button on my phone. "That's enough of that shit." He says.

"Paul Dun-in is cheating on his wife?" Savannah asks.

"For years." I say.

I push my plate into the center of the table. "Excuse me." I rush into my room and close the door. I go into the bathroom and close the door. I turn the facet of the sink on and then I scream as loud as I can.

The bathroom door bursts open and Justin comes running in. He takes me in his arms and hugs me while I cry. He kisses the top of my head. He holds me so close to him, I close my eyes and before I know it, I fall asleep.

Justin picks me up and carries me to my bed. He puts me in and before he can leave me, I grab his hand and don't let go. He climbs into bed with me and tries to lay as far away possible. I snuggle into him.

Savannah walks into the room. She looks at the two of us. "Wow, you waisted no time."

"I just hugged her. She fell asleep almost immediately." Justin says.

"Be good to her. I will take Astro out and then lock up."

"Savannah, why didn't you tell me about her?"

"I told you about my friends. There is Piper and Sebastian."

"Why did I always think that Sebastian was a guy?"

"She has a boy's name." She throws at him.

"Keep your voice down."

"Bombs could go off. Once she is asleep its like waking the dead."

He looks at me and kisses my forehead. He looks back at Savannah. "She doesn't know that Mark and I are your brothers?"

"Step brothers." She says. "Twice removed."

"That is hurtful. I always consider you my sister. Your mom will always be my favorite step mother. She is the only one that gets flowers throughout the years."

"Those are from you?" She asks. She puts her hand to her chest.

Justin looks at Savannah. "Just because our parents didn't make it, doesn't mean that I stopped loving you and your mom. The kindness she showed and shared with us will never be forgotten."

"Like I said, be good to her. She is my best friend in this whole fucking world."

"Can I ask you a question?" He says seriously.

"Of course."

"Can one fall in love with someone this quickly?"

Savannah laughs.

She turns and closes the door. She takes Astro for a walk around the neighborhood. Mark walks out of the house that he just moved into. He crosses the street and walks over to Savannah. They hug.

"Well look what the cat dragged to my street." He says smiling.

She punches him the stomach lightly. "Its good to see you too." She says.

"You live here?"

"No, my friend lives here. I am walking her dog and then going home."

"Come in for a drink." Mark says. "Lets catch up."

"Maybe one drink." She says. "Come on Astro." She follows Mark back to the house.

"Astro? Your dogs name is Astro?"

"He is my friend's dog."

"Which friend of yours lives in the neighborhood?"

"My best friend since second grade. Sebastian."

"Sebastian who?'

"Timely?"

"The bank robber?"

"The school teacher." Savannah says.

"That tall guy is a school teacher as well as a bank robber?"

"My Sebastian is a girl." She says. "We have been friends since second grade. This is her dog."

Mark looks at her. "I know your friends. Why don't I know Sebastian?"

"You know her."

"What?"

"She's the one you call Little Mermaid."

"I thought that her name was Ariel." Mark laughs.

"You always say that. My friend's name is Sebastian."

"Did her mother not like her?"

"Her mother named her after her father."

"Did he not like her enough to object?"

"He died before she was born. You have that drink?"

"Come, I will show you the house."

I wake up in the middle of the night and I can not move. I open my eyes and see Justin Case sleeping in my bed. For some reason this doesn't make me nervous, it makes me feel safe. I have always felt safe in my house, but right now, I feel safe and cozy.

Our hands are twined with each other and I raise my hand to my chest, I turn my hand so that the back of his is on my chest. I feel his pulse against my chest.

Justin opens his eyes and sees me looking at him. "I can leave." He says.

"You can stay." I tell him. "How did Savannah know who you are?"

"My dad was married to her mom. Twice."

"How come I have never met you throughout the years?"

"My brother Mark and I lived mostly with our mom. I think you knew Mark throughout the years."

"I don't know for sure." I say. "Without my ID and keys, I won't be able to get to my job tomorrow."

"I can't get them for you until Monday. I can give you a ride to work tomorrow." He looks at me. "Tell me about your husband."

I look at Justin. "I have to sit up." I say.

"Do you need help?"

"I need you to untangle your legs from mine."

He looks down and moves his legs.

I shift my weight to my elbow and push myself up. I sit on my bed. Out of habit, I pat the bed for Astro. He doesn't come. "Where is Astro?"

"Savannah took him out. I don't know. I never heard her come back." He looks at the clock on the night stand. "Should I leave?"

I look at the clock. It reads four-thirty. "No. Let the neighbors talk." I laugh.

"The neighbors would talk?"

"Oh yes. There are three cars in my driveway." I look at the clock again. "Than again, they won't talk. They will think that its Pipes and Sab."

"Tell me about your husband." He says.

I look at Justin. "I knew Craig my whole life. We were in preschool together. Our moms were close friends. They always had us on play dates. My mom would keep Craig for long weekends when his parents traveled. One summer he went to Europe with his parents. Only him and his mom returned. And Craig was never the same since then."

"How old were you?"

"Eleven."

"What happened?"

"He secretly started cutting himself. He stopped eating. His mom, Carla tried everything. He was in therapy for years and nothing seemed to help. When he was around me, he would at least eat. My mom offered to have him with us more and more. Carla refused more and more. She tried keeping me away from him. Thinking that if she punished him he would do what she wanted and in turn get what he wanted. In the end it backfired."

I stop talking.

"Why only three days?" Justin asks softly.

"We would be inseparable in school. As long as I was with him, he couldn't hurt himself. He was depressed beyond anything. His mom sent him to live with his uncles. When he came back to us, he was normal. He looked great. He was handsome. He was strong. We thought that he was back. So his mom rewarded his progress with a car. He crashed it almost immediately."

"On purpose?"

"He left a note. I never told anyone about it until after he was gone. I told my mom. I still have it. I will always have it."

"What did it say?"

"I can't tell you."

"So he died after the car accident?"

"No. He lived for three years after. The insurance proved that there was something wrong with the car. They got him another car. He drove that one off of I-95 overpass just days after our graduation. He was in a coma for months. His mom wouldn't let me go to the hospital. The nursing staff would make her leave and let me come visit him. She caught me. He woke up and they discovered that he was not going to make it. He was dying. From all the injuries he sustained from the crash. He couldn't breath on his own. He kept trying to take the oxygen off." I start crying. "He wanted to die."

"So then why marry him?"

"Because through it all, I loved him. He loved me. I think that he would have killed himself when we were twelve."

"What happened in his life that made him—"

"When they went to Europe he was physically assaulted."

"Did his dad do it?"

I look at Justin. "His dad walked in on it happening."

"What did the letter say?"

"I can't tell you." I get in my wheelchair and go in the bathroom. I go in the kitchen to get a drink.

Justin is in there. He sits at the table. "You didn't eat anything. Are you hungry?"

"I am starving."

Chapter 3

A tall man walks into the bookstore coffee shop at midnight. I am at the front desk grading papers that I am not supposed to have, but my friends who are teachers split my class up so that they were all in good hands and allow me to grade their papers. I am grateful. I look up as he walks into the store.

He smiles at me. I return the smile and then look back to the work I am doing. He walks around for a while. He buys two coffees and walks back over to me and puts the coffee on the counter in front of me.

"For you." He says.

"Thank you, but no."

"You don't drink coffee?"

"I do."

"Well here you go."

"No. Thank you."

He looks at me. "You are going to make me drink both of these?"

"I am not allowed to drink the merchandise."

"What are you doing?"

"Grading papers."

"Why?"

"I teach third grade at the local elementary school."

"Then what the hell are you doing here?"

"I also work here."

"Every night?"

"No. Three days a week."

"Why during the school week?"

"Because weekends are only two days." I smile.

"What kind of books do you like?" He asks.

"Short ones."

He laughs. "Clever."

"What time do you have to be up for work?"

Someone walks into the store and calls out, "Hey Sebastian."

"Hi." We both say.

"Did my collection come in?"

He looks at me. He doesn't know what she is talking about.

"Your collection is behind the shelving. Ask Matt for them."

The man in front of me is still looking at me.

"Do you want something specifically or are you a stalker?"

"I am not a stalker." He says. "Why did that woman call you Sebastian?"

"That's my name."

The door opens and closes and the lights in the place flash. I get my purse, gather my stuff and stick it in my tote.

"What's going on?" The man asks me.

"Shift change. My night is over." I go to the café area and clock out.

Matt who is my manager walks over. "Just so you know, I am docking your pay for tonight."

I look at him. "Why?"

"What's the point of working here if you are going to grade papers and flirt with the customers?"

"Matt, everyone brings stuff with them to keep them busy. I was not flirting with anyone."

"There was a man standing at the counter for over twenty minutes. He bought you coffee. You know the rules."

"I didn't drink the coffee." I say biting back a yawn. I needed that coffee. "You know what, keep the whole thing. You need it more than I do."

"Do you want to keep your job?"

"Before I say something that both of us will regret, I will be in tomorrow."

"I need you here at six."

The man stays where he can hear the entire conversation. He just watches us.

"I can't be here at six. I tutor until nine."

"Tutor here."

"This is an adult place. I tutor children. Children do not belong here."

"Show up or don't come in. You missed a week of work."

"Oh my God, I was in the hospital for a fucking week." I say.

"You should have called and told us."

"I missed out on three days of my life. When was I supposed to call?"

"Not my problem." Matt snaps.

I turn and leave. "Fucking asshole." I say as I go to my car. Just as I am ready to stick the key in the door to unlock it, I see that my window has been smashed. "Oh come on!" I yell.

The man walks out of the store. "Are you alright?"

"Oh just fine." I say. I fight back the tears that are threatening to fall.

One of our regular customers walks over. He looks at me and sees the broken window. "Those bastards got you again?" He says.

"Hey Tony."

"Does Matt know about this?"

"He probably did it." I say under my breath. "No."

"You need to call the police." Tony says.

"I need to do a lot of things."

"Let me run these in and then I will stay with you."

"Its ok really." I say.

"Do you need a ride?" The tall man asks me.

A college girl with bright pink hair walks over. "Sebastian? You ok?" I look at her. "I am ok."

"My dad is on his way." She says. "He heard about the smash and grabs"

"Thanks, Twix."

The man steps closer to me. "I will stay to give you a ride home."

"No need."

"Your car is a crime scene." He says. "Is anything missing?"

"No." I say.

The police come and my car is loaded on a tow truck and taken away. I close my eyes and cringe thinking that this is going to cost me at least a few hundred dollars that I don't have, Paul, the principal of the school, won't let me work until everything is cleared. Matt, my twenty-three year old control freak boss, isn't going to pay me.

Twix looks at me. "I can give you a ride home."

"Thanks Twix, I only live a few blocks. I should have left my car in the driveway at my house and walked to work. It would have saved me all this trouble."

"My little brother is sick with a cold. You don't have to tutor him tomorrow. He hasn't been to school in a week and it will be a waist of time."

"Thanks. Don't tell Matt that. He will be surprised when I show up at five-thirty."

"See you tomorrow."

"Thanks again, Twix." I say.

I push my wheelchair down the surprisingly well lit street. I enter my neighborhood and go to my house. Astro barks loudly. By the time I get home, its after two in the morning. I unlock the door and Astro walks himself outside and does his business on the front lawn.

"Come on." I say.

We go in the house and I set the alarm. I make myself a cup of coffee and sit at the table finishing the grading. I look around the room. I go through the mail doing what I normally do, throw out the junk mail and put the important stuff in the drawer. When I finish the coffee, I put the cup in the dishwasher and turn the lights out.

I go in my room and go to bed. I close my eyes grateful that the day is over.

~~~~~~~~~~

Sebastian Timely Jr. sits at his massive desk in the back of the bank. He holds my ATM card and credit cards in his fingers. He has them all. Not because he stole them, but because when someone came into his bank to withdraw money, the tellers were alerted that the cards were stolen.

Sebastian holds my ATM in his hand. He looks at it. He reads the name over and over. "Sebastian Timely. How is this possible? Why does that beautiful woman have my name?"

A young woman walks in to his office. "Sir, your clients are here."

He tears his gaze from my cards and looks at her. "Right." He says. "Put them in room two. I will be right there."

"I have that information you asked for." She says handing him a yellow envelope.

"Thank you." He says.

"The security team will be here in an hour."

"Right." He says.

When she walks out of his office, Sebastian looks at his reflection in his computer monitor. "There has to be a good explanation." He says aloud.

The assistant who sits just outside his office startles. She looks up and at him. "Did you say something?"

He looks at her. "I am doing some much needed research."

His assistant looks at him. She takes in his good looks and adjusts her top. She looks at the monitor that lets them know that the bank is officially open for business. She knows the truth about the bank robbery. Mr. Timely robbed his own bank.

She looks at Sebastian. "The police are here." She says.

"Let them come in." He says.

She gets up from her desk and walks up to the officers. "How can I help you?"

"We are here to see the owner to of the bank."

"He is in meetings right now, but if you come with me, as soon as he done he will see you."

"Can you answer a question for us?" The taller officer asks.

"If I know the answer I will share it." She says.

"Do you know if one of the patrons of the bank is a Sebastian Timely?"

She looks at him. Sebastian Timely's name is all over the bank. Her boss. There is a picture on the back wall of the bank of Sebastian Timely Jr. "He is not only a patron of the bank, he owns it." She says.

"He? No. Sebastian Timely is a woman."

She laughs. "That's absurd."

Sebastian walks out of his office. "Come into my office officers." He says. "I called you because I have something to give you."

The officer who remained quiet looks at Sebastian. He looks at all the pictures. "What do you have for us?"

They follow him into his office. He closes the door and sits at his massive desk. He opens the drawer. He puts his hand on my cards. He puts them back and then closes the drawer. He opens the drawer closer to his knee and pulls out the USB stick. He rolls it in his fingers.

"I asked you to come today because I have footage of the bank robbery." Sebastian says.

"Everyone knows you robbed the bank." The one officer says.

"Or did I?" He sticks the USB into the computer and turns the screen so that everyone watches the same footage.

Two security guards are not paying attention. He walks right over to both of them and addresses them by name. Sebastian then walks right up to the teller at the first station and demands the money. All the time looking back at the two guards. They do nothing.

"Why are we here?" The other officer asks.

"I didn't get any money. She slipped me a note. The teller slipped me information that there is a woman who has my name." Sebastian looks at the screen again. "Your guards, whom I pay big salaries to dropped the ball here. They allowed someone to come into my bank and open an account using this woman's identity. I want them arrested."

"They didn't break any laws."

"They didn't do their jobs."

"So you want us to arrest security guards because a woman stole your identity and opened an account?"

The two officers get up and leave. One pokes his head in the door. "My advice is to fire them. If they cause you any problems after that, we will arrest them. Until then, there is nothing we can do."

His assistant is busy working. Her phone buzzes and she just answers it. "Hello." She says.

"Its time for lunch." Sebastian says.

"Want me to go get something for you?"

"Yes." He admits.

She stands up. She gets her purse and walks into his office. "What can I get you, sir?"

"Can you go to the Bookstore Coffee shop and get two coffees for me?"

"Of course." She says. "What kind of coffee?"

"Caramel."

"So sugar." She teases.

He looks at her and laughs. "I like it. I had it the other night and it was delicious."

"My son is the barista there."

"Does he know the young woman in the wheelchair that works there?"

"I will ask him." She says. "He never mentions anyone in a wheelchair working there."

"Maybe they are on different shifts." He says.

"So two coffees? Hot or cold?"

"Cold." He says.

"I will be back." She smiles.

When she leaves he takes out his phone and looks at the picture he took of me. He notices that I look like him a bit. He looks at my eyes and sees the green in my eyes match his.

He opens his computer to Google and types in Sebastian Timely. He sees searches that fit his life. He scrolls down and he sees information that fits a woman. Me. He clicks on one and reads a few paragraphs. He prints it out. He finds more of them and prints them too.

He takes a file folder out of his desk drawer and puts the printed information and my credit cards in it. He puts the file in the desk drawer and locks it.

Amanda his assistant returns with the two coffees. "My son made his famous soup and grilled cheese sandwiches."

"Thank you." He says.

"Why did the police officer ask me about a woman with your name?"

"Apparently there is a woman who shares my name."

"That's weird."

"I think my dad is her dad."

"You have a sister with the same name?" Amanda asks.

"I don't know for sure."

"What can I do to help you find out?"

"I don't know yet."

"Eat the lunch while its hot."

"Join me." He says to her. "I hate to eat alone."

They sit in the little luncheonette and share the food. They sit side by side not talking until the food is gone. He stands to clear the table. When his back is to her, she takes the time to admire his back side.

"My son said that he doesn't know anyone who doesn't work the same same shifts as him.

"Thanks for asking." Sebastian says.

"Did you google her?"

"I did."

"What does it say?"

"I didn't read it the information."

"Asher." She says using his middle name. She has known him for many years and knows a lot about him.

He turns and looks at her. "Even her middle name is the same as mine. Sort of."

"What's her middle name?"

"Ashley." He says. "She was definitely named after my dad. She looks kind of like me."

"You have a picture of her?"

"I sort of met her last night at the Bookstore Coffee Shop."

"She works there then?"

"She works two or three jobs."

"What else does she do?"

"She's a teacher."

"Where?"

"The local elementary school."

She looks at him. "Asher, there are ten thousand elementary schools in the area."

He looks back at her. "You can find out for me."

"I will." She says. She takes her phone out of her purse. She punches numbers into the phone and then puts the phone to her ear. "Pauly! How are you?"

Paul Dun-in smiles as he says. "Its my favorite bank teller."

"I am not a bank teller." She snaps at him.

"To what do I deserve this beautiful call?"

"I am calling to ask you a question." She doesn't wait for him to respond she just asks so she can end the call. "Do you have a teacher by the name of Sebastian Timely?"

"I do. I did."

"You did?"

"She is suspended as I have it on good authority that she robbed a bank."

"She did what?"

"She claims that she was on a field trip, but I know the truth."

"Thanks, you answered the questions I have. Listen, are you aware that your account has a negative balance?"

"What?" He yells. "I will look into that."

"We have frozen the account so that it doesn't keep withdrawing money that you don't have." Amanda says smiling.

He yells something that sounds like a string of curse words. "I will look into it." He says. He hangs up the phone.

Amanda smiles. She is proud of herself. "She works at Panther Cove Elementary School." She gets up and leaves the room for a moment. She returns a few minutes later.

"There is nothing wrong with his account." Sebastian says.

"Its going to show that he is negative."

"Why?"

"He suspended her because of the rumors that he heard from his asshole brother that she robbed a bank when he knows damn well that she was on a field trip."

31

Sebastian rubs his neck and runs his fingers through his hair. "Isn't anyone nice to her?"

Amanda pulls my name up on Google on her phone. "It looks like she lives in a nice home. She has a dog." She scrolls and finds my Facebook page. She clicks on the photographs. "She likes to go to concerts. That's not cheap. She's been to Time Square." She clicks on an album. "It looks like she pledged a sorority." She looks at Sebastian. She offers him her phone. "Take a look."

There is a loud noise in the front lobby that gets both of their attentions. They run out of the room and into the lobby. The security guards who had failed to do their jobs just weeks before are both holding Paul Dun-in with his hands behind his back.

"There has to be fucking money in my account. Its my secret account. My wife doesn't know about this one and my girl friend only knows about the one I share with my wife."

Amanda looks at Sebastian. "This is fun. I will take care of this." She smiles leans in and kisses his cheek."

"This is not how we do banking." He says smiling at her.

"It is today." She says and turns to the security guards. "Please show Mr. Dun-in into my office."

~~~~~~~~~~

I sit at the Bookstore Coffee Shop at the front desk. I have Astro with me because no one else is in the store. Our usually customers go about their routines. They can make the coffees that they like on their own. There is self check-out so they can come and go as they please.

Astro lays next to me. When the door opens and the bells ring, he opens his eyes and sits up. I don't pay attention to who comes in and leaves.

Twix comes over. "Do you have an extra pen?" Her normally bright pink hair is now bright orange. She flips her head from side to side.

I laugh at her. I hand her a pen.

"Who was that guy"

I look at her.

"The one from he other night. The one who offered to take you home?"

32

"I don't know." I say.

"He followed you to make sure that you got home safely. Did you know that?"

"No." I say. "What are you working on now?'

"A lot of things." She says. She looks at Astro. "You want me to take him out for you?"

Astro sits and wags his tail when he hears the word "out".

"Thanks." I says.

"Matt doesn't mind that he's here?"

"Matt's the one who told me to bring him to work with me. Its for safety. I am walking home."

"Where is your car?"

"My mom's boyfriend is having it fixed. Its at her house. I can literally walk to all of my jobs so its not like I need a car right now."

"If you make a list of groceries, I will get them for you." She says.

"Twix, you don't have to do that."

"I don't have to. I want to help." She takes Astro's leash from me and walks outside.

Mark Case walks into the door. "Little Mermaid." He says.

"Hi." I say to him.

He looks around. "Where is everyone?"

"I am lone here tonight."

"Why?"

"One night a month, I work here by myself. Everything runs without problems. Customers can make their own coffees or drinks. They can check themselves out. I am just here to make sure no one gets out of control."

"Justin and I moved into your neighborhood." He says leaning on his elbows on the counter top.

"I know." I look at him. "How come I can't remember ever meeting Justin?"

"He's a momma's boy." He laughs. "Seriously, I don't know. It seems like we were always with Savannah and her mom when my dad was married to mom."

"You still call her mom?" I ask.

"I will always call her mom. She was by far the best step mother anyone could ask for. When my dad divorced her the second time and married wife number four, she told us that no matter what she would be there for us. She never missed sport events that we were involved with. She came to our graduations. She came when our mom passed. She held us while we cried for our loss. She cried with us. She will always be mom." He says again. He looks around. "I don't like that you are in here alone."

I look to the back of the store. There are three guys in black tank tops sitting at a table together with computers in front of them. They don't talk much to each other but when I look at them, they look at me.

"Those are security guards. If anything happens, they will take care of it."

"I don't remember security guards ever being here."

"There have been a lot of incidents that have been happening. The security teams just showed up. They get paid by a third party. They report to someone else."

Twix walks back in with Astro who is panting. "Lets get some water." She says and her orange ponytail swings from side to side.

"Did you run him?" I ask.

She turns to me grinning.

"You didn't have to do that."

"I wanted to do it." She says.

Matt looks at me. "What the hell is she?"

"Ready for Halloween." I tease.

"I heard that." She says smiling.

"Twix, what do you do for a living?" I ask.

"I am an art major." She says.

I write on a sheet of paper 'undercover cop' and show it to Matt. He nods. He kisses my forehead. "Don't be a stranger. Come for dinner. Bring the dog. He loves my cat." He kisses my forehead again. "See you later, Little Mermaid."

Chapter 4

I pull my car into the parking lot of the mall. I am excited that I am going to meet Piper and Savannah for a girl's night out. As my wheelchair is lowering from the mechanism on top of my car that houses it while I drive, I get the cushion ready. When the chair meets the ground, I press my hand on one side of it and the seat opens. I set the cushion on top of the nylon seat and get in the chair.

I lock my car and go inside. We are meeting at the mall and then going to one of the restaurants for dinner and drinks. I go over to the Star Bucks. I wait on line to order a drink while I wait. I am early.

There is a woman in front of me with three girls. One, the youngest of the three, is touching everything. The tallest of the three turns and takes the bag of chips out of the little girl's hands.

The little starts to cry.

"Let her hold that." The woman says.

"She's going to open it." The older child says.

"I am going to buy it anyway." The woman snaps.

The middle girl looks at me. She smiles. "Miss Timely?"

I smile at her. "Hi Sara."

"We really miss you." Sara says. She steps around her sisters and hugs me.

"I miss you all too." I tell her.

"When are you coming back?"

"Soon."

Her mother looks at me. "Hi Miss Timely." She says bitterly.

35

The older girl looks at her mom and rolls her eyes. "Mom, you know Miss Timely had nothing to do with what they said she does."

Ginger looks at her daughter. "Hush."

"Ginger, I know what is being said about me. Come on, I didn't do that." I look at Sara. "We were on a field trip to the zoo."

"Mom, you were there with us." Sara says brightly.

"Take your sisters and go wait for me outside." Ginger says.

They run out of the store and go sit on one fluffy chair outside. Sara runs back in and hugs me. She looks at Ginger and points to the cookie that she wants.

"I know." Ginger says smiling at her daughter. She looks at me after Sara runs from the store again. "Has anything turned up?" She asks.

"Has anything turned up? What does that mean? I went to pay a fucking speeding ticket."

She looks at me and taps my forehead, "You have a leadfoot – hand." She laughs.

"We know this." I say.

"Next!" The barista behind the counter says.

"What do you want? Let me buy you coffee." Ginger says. She takes out her phone and pays for the coffee. As we wait for them she sends a text message. She looks at me. "I am sending a message to Jack."

"How is Jack?"

"He is great." She reads the text message. "He will be here in ten minutes for the girls."

I look at her. "You are inviting yourself to join us for girls' night?" I smile at her.

"I am sad that you didn't think to include your sister." Ginger says. She takes the coffees off the counter. She walks outside and hands the girls their drinks. She hands the youngest one the bag of chips.

Jack walks over and kisses Ginger on the lips. The girls say in unison, "oh gross." Jack looks at me. He kisses me on the cheek. "Hi Ashley." He says.

Sara looks at her dad. "That's not her name." She says.

He looks at his daughter. "What?"

"Her name is Miss Timely." She sing-songs.

I smile at her.

Ginger looks at Jack. "You are the only one who calls her Ashley."

"Not the only one." Jack and I say together.

Piper walks over. "Carrot top!" She says and hugs Ginger.

The two of them laugh.

Piper hugs Jack. "Hi stranger. Its good to see you."

"Its good to see you too." He says.

Piper hugs me. "Ash." She says.

"Pipes." I say. "Where have you been?"

"We will talk when littler ears aren't around." She says. She looks at Ginger. "You coming to dinner?"

"I invited myself." Ginger says with a big smile.

"Just like old times." Piper says and they both laugh.

Savannah walks over and hugs everyone. "Hi." She says. She looks at Sara. "That's my favorite cookie ever."

Sara smiles at Savannah. "I know."

"Jack did you want to join us with the girls?" Piper asks.

He looks at his watch. "I can't. I have to get them home and get them fed." He laughs. "Now that their appetites are gone." He looks at Ginger. "My mom is coming over."

She looks at Jack and leans into him kissing him. "Sorry I will miss her." She says.

He laughs. "Be nice."

Meg the older girl looks at her parents. "Get a room."

"You might get another sister or brother if we do." Jack says. He takes Becky's hand. "Come on, grandma is coming for dinner. We are going to pretend to like what she makes for us." He lifts Becky up in his arms and takes his daughters hands in his as they leave.

Ginger goes into the restaurant and requests a table. She comes out where we are. "Its going to be fifteen minutes."

"Its good to be out." I say.

"What's been going on?" Savannah asks. "I haven't seen you since the night that Justin came over."

"Justin who?" Piper asks.

"Case." I say.

"Mark's brother?" Piper asks.

37

"Same one." Savanah says.

"Why was Justin at your house?" Piper asks.

"I will tell you all about it." I say.

The server comes over to us. "Ladies, your table is ready." She says. "Follow me."

We follow her to the table in the back corner of the restaurant. I notice the tall handsome guy from the Bookstore Coffee Shop as we pass by. He looks at me and smiles. I return the smile.

We take our seats at the table. I fill my friends in on what's been going on in my life. We all share a fit of laughter.

"Somehow, I can't believe that you are laughing about it." Ginger says. She hugs me tight.

"If I don't laugh, I will cry."

"So you are still suspended from teaching?" Piper asks.

"Paul says if I step foot on the school grounds he will call the police and have me arrested for trespassing. I miss my kids. I haven't seen them in almost a month. He would do anything to fire me. He still hates me."

"I can't believe that you still work at that school." Savannah says.

"Sav, you know I love the kids." I say. I take a drink of my wine and notice that the man at the table we passed is looking right at me.

"You can teach third grade anywhere." Ginger says.

"I love having Sara in my class."

"Jack and I will pull the girls out of that school so fast, Paul would faint." Ginger says.

When she says faint, we all burst into a fit of laughter again.

"I can't believe you fainted." She laughs.

I take another sip of my wine.

"Do you need work?" Ginger asks seriously. "Jack could always use help. You can help me at work." She says.

"Matt's mom has given me more forced hours. She runs the store and she heard from some one how awful Matt was to me. She's let me work more hours and has cut back on her son's hours." I say. "The security guards watch out for me."

Piper looks at me. "How is your mom?"

"Linda is good. She keeps herself busy. She is traveling right now with her boyfriend Peter. They are in Nashville."

"That's good to hear."

"Peter is really nice." Savannah says.

"I like him. He makes my mom happy. She makes him happy. He fixed my car."

The server comes over with a plate of desserts. "The men at the table over there paid for your dinners and wanted you to have dessert on them."

Piper looks over at the table where Sebastian Timely Jr. sits with a group of men. One is better looking then the next one. "I'd like to have dessert on one of them." She says.

We all laugh.

"The one with the dark hair hasn't taken his eyes off of you." She says to me. "Do you know him?"

"He has come into the store a few times. I don't know him."

The server puts the plate in the middle of the table. She removes the dinner dishes and comes back moments later with little plates.

I push away front the table. I go to the lady's room. When I am on my way back, I pass by the table of men. "Thank you for paying or dinner for my friends and me. That was very nice of you."

"It's the least I could do." Sebastian says to me.

I look at him. I really look at him for the first time. Looking into his eyes is like a mirror to my own.

"Sebastian, who is your friend?" One of the men asks.

I blink. I think back to the night that I first say him. One of my customers walked in and said my name. He and I both answered at the same time.

He looks at me. "This is my friend Ashley."

I stare at him.

"How do you know each other?" Another of the good looking guys asks.

He never takes his eyes off of me. "She's my sister."

I hear the word and I know its true. I tear my eyes off of him and rush back to the table. "I have to go. I am not feeling well." I say.

"Sebastian, what's going on?" Piper asks.

"I am going to be sick." I say and rush out of the restaurant. I get in my car and go home. I drive as fast as I can on the streets that I know my whole life. My car seems to drive itself. I feel like I am in a dream.

I go in the house. Astro greets me like he always does. I let him out in the back yard. I put my stuff on the counter.

My phone rings. It's a number I don't know. "Hello." I say.

"Is this Sebastian Ashley Timely?" A male's voice asks.

"Who wants to know?" I ask.

"Is that your name?"

I hang up the phone. It rings again and I just let it go to my voicemail. The words of the man from the restaurant play in my head. 'This is my friend.' He knows my middle name. No one knows my middle name but my friends. How is that possible? Then he said 'She's my sister.'

There is a knock at the door and I nearly jump out of my skin. I open the door and I am thrilled to see that its Justin.

He looks at me and steps inside taking me in his arms. "Are you ok?"

"I don't know." I say. I feel safe in his arms.

"What happened?" He asks.

"A man at the restaurant I went to with my friends claimed that he's my brother. I don't have a brother."

"I think you do." He holds me tighter. "Why are you shaking?"

"He knew my middle name."

"Its on public records."

"No. Everything says Sebastian A. Timely. Only my friends know my middle name. He knew my middle name."

"Have you spoken to your mom about this?"

"No."

"Why not?"

"She's in Nashville with Peter."

"When will she be back?"

"A few weeks." I tell him.

My phone rings again. It's the same number. I just let it ring. "How did he get my number? I didn't give him my number."

Astro walks over and jumps up on me. He puts his head over my shoulder like he is hugging me. I wrap my arms around his neck.

I look at Justin. "You said a few weeks ago that I didn't match the profile of the person that robbed the bank. Did you have a picture of him?"

"You didn't look in the file?"

"I thought I was being watched. I was scared to do anything but just sit there."

"It was a picture of a tall guy." Justin says.

My phone rings again. I look at it. Its Savannah. "Are you alright?" She asks.

"I think the wine made me feel sick." I tell her.

"Are you feeling better now?"

"A little."

"Drink plenty of water and sleep it off." She pauses. "What are you doing tomorrow?"

"I have no plans." I say.

"I will come over in the late morning."

"Sounds good. I love you."

"I love you too."

Justin and I go into the den. The television is on. Justin walks over to the bookshelves and scans all the movies. He looks at me. "You have a lot of movies."

"I like movies."

"Me too." He says.

"Pick one." I tell him.

He looks through the movies. "They are all chick flicks."

I laugh.

He walks over and kisses me. "Let me go home and get something. I will be right back." He looks at Astro. "I will take him with me and come right back."

Astro goes by the basket and waits for his leash. Justin attaches the the leash to the collar. "We will be right back."

I open the refrigerator and take out a bottle of water. I take a long drink. My phone rings again. It's the same number that I don't know.

"Why do you keep calling me?" I ask when I answer the phone.

"My name is Sebastian Asher Timely Jr." he says.

"What do you want from me?"

"I want to get to know you. I want to know why we share the same name."

"I was named after my father." I say.

"Did your father marry your mother?"

"No."

"Did you ever know him?"

"He died three months before I was born. My mother named me after him. She said that he was her hero."

"Can I see you?"

"Should I come to the bank?" I ask.

"Yes." He says. "Can I ask you a question?"

"Yes."

"How old are you?"

"Twenty-five."

"I am thirty-one." Says.

Justin comes back with Astro. Astro prances himself into the house. He is wearing a cat on his back.

I look at Justin. "We leave the strays outside." I laugh.

"That's my cat." Justin says.

I go over to Astro and pick the cat up. He cuddles in my arms. "What's your name?" I say to the cat.

"His name is Bob Cat."

I look at Justin and laugh. "You named him Bob Cat?"

"No, Mark did."

"What else did you bring from home?"

"Rambo."

I laugh. "I have left overs from dinner if you are hungry." I tell him. I get out of my wheelchair and sit on the couch.

He puts the movie in and then sits next to me. Astro lays on the love seat across from us. And Bob Cat snuggles into my lap.

"He usually doesn't do that." Justin says.

The movie starts playing and I snuggle into Justin. He runs his fingers through my hair and within minutes, I am sleeping. When the movie is over, Justin takes Astro outside. He comes in and lifts me in his arms.

"I love you." I say in my sleep.

"I love you too." He says as he lays in bed with me.

~~~~~~~~~~~~

I get up in the morning and shower. I get dressed and do my hair. Justin is still sleeping in my bed with not only Astro but Bob Cat too.

I go into the kitchen and make a cup of coffee. Thanks to the Keurig I can make a single cup anyway I want. I put half and half in it. My iced coffee is delicious.

I open the freezer and take out frozen pancakes that I made as prep foods so I could grab and go. I set them on the counter to defrost. I take bacon out of the freezer and put it in a skillet.

Bob Cat comes in the kitchen. The cat jumps up on the chair next to the table and meows. I look at him.

"I don't have cat food." I say. I go over and he steps on to my leg. I scoop him up and he purrs. "Maybe your daddy brought you some when he brought you over for a movie." I laugh. "A movie that I slept through."

"Yes you did." Justin says kissing my bare shoulder. "You look nice."

"I have a meeting." I tell him.

He goes over to the counter. His phone is there.l he picks it up and looks at it. He laughs. "I have to call Mark."

"Is he hyperventilating because the cat is not home?" I ask.

"Exactly." He says. "Bob is an indoor cat."

"He is a love." I say.

"Are you burning the bacon?" He asks taking the spatula and flips the bacon over.

"I like burned bacon."

"No one likes burned bacon. Crispy bacon yes. Burned bacon no."

I laugh.

Bob Cat jumps down and rubs all over Astro. Astro allows the cat to do it. He nudges the cat with his nose. They go nose to nose before they lay next to each other.

"Where is your meeting?" Justin asks.

"At the bank."

He looks at me. He takes the pancakes out of the zipped bag that they are in and puts them in the skillet to warm. Justin looks at me again. "Are you going to meet him?"

"Yes."

"Don't you think you should talk to your mom first?"

"I am twenty-five years old. I want to find out what's going on and then talk to her. She won't be home for weeks and I can't wait that long."

"Do you want me to go with you?"

"I think I do." I say. Bob Cat jumps up in my lap. "Won't you miss out on your work? I don't want to keep you."

"I offered. I want to go with you." He plates the food. He puts it on he table.

I feed Astro. I go in the pantry and take out a can of tuna fish. I open it and Bob starts meowing like he has never had food a day in his life. I take out a plastic bowl and drain the tuna. I scoop some of it into the bowl. I put on the floor for Bob.

"Oh my god." Justin says.

"What?"

"You are spoiling my cat."

"I don't have cat food."

"Who needs cat food when one has tuna fish?" He laughs. "What time are you going?"

"I don't have a set time."

He kisses me before he sits to eat our now cooling food. "I will go home, take Bob home, get dressed and come back."

"That sounds good to me." I tell him. I lift my fork and eat my breakfast. I clean up after breakfast while I am waiting for Justin to come back.

Chapter 5

Amanda sits at her desk doing work. She looks over at Sebastian and takes in that he looks nervous. As long as she knows him, she knows him to be confident and sometimes cocky. She notices that he looks worried. She gets up and walks into his office.

"What's going on?"

He tells her about the restaurant.

"How did you know her middle name?" She asks.

"Its on one of her credit cards." He says.

"How do you know that?"

"I have them in my desk." He says. He looks at the clock and then at the monitor that shows all the people in the bank. He taps a button to look at what the camera that over looks the parking lot shows. He sees my car.

"Don't be nervous." Amanda says to him.

"What if she doesn't like me?"

"I am sure she will love you." She looks at the monitor that shows me and Justin coming into the bank. She watches as Justin takes my hand in his and walks next to me. She notices that he stands like a bodyguard completely in protective mode. "She will love you." She says again. She leaves the office. "I will bring her in." She turns to Sebastian. "Hey, Asher, just so you know she brought someone with her."

"Its fine. Show them in." He crosses the room and takes Amanda's arm in his hand. He turns her to him and kisses her on the lips., "Give me strength."

"Always." She says and kisses him back. She leaves the office and finds us in the lobby of the bank. "Hi, I am Amanda. We have been expecting you." She says sweetly.

Justin walks hand in hand with me. Our fingers laced together make me feel safe. We go into the office.

Sebastian takes me in his arms the second I am in his office. He hugs me so tight. When he releases me, there are tears in both of our eyes. Amanda ushers Justin to a chair.

"Please make yourself comfortable." Sebastian says to us.

I look around the office. He has pictures of his family all over the walls. There are pictures of his mom. Pictures of his dad. Pictures of him at all stages. There is one of him when he is young holding a baby.

"Do you have siblings?" I ask him.

"I have two half brothers. Jacob is twenty-four and Seth is twenty-one." He looks at me. "Do you have any siblings?"

"My mom just had me." I look at the picture of him. He looks like he is six or seven years old and he is holding a baby girl. "Can I see that picture?" I ask.

He hands it to me. I look up at him and then at the picture. I know the second that I look closer that the baby girl in the photo is me.

"How is that possible?" I ask.

"What?"

"That's me." I say pointing to the baby.

"That's my cousin." He says.

"No. That's me. My grandma made that outfit for me. It's a one of a kind." I tell him. "She made me a teddy bear out of it after I out grew it."

He goes over to the desk and he calls his mother. "Can I please speak with Charlotte Jensen?" He waits moments. She comes on the line. "Are you busy?" He asks. He waits listening to her talking. "I need you to come to the bank."

Justin looks at him. He stands and crosses the room. He extends his hand. "I am Justin." He looks at me. "I am Sebastian's boyfriend."

I smile at him.

"I know who you are, Mr. Case." Sebastian says.

"Asher, I can't stay." Amanda says. "Your mother doesn't like me."

He walks across the room and hugs Amanda. He kisses her on the lips. "I love you. That's all that matters."

"Let me know how everything goes." She says. "I wish you all well."

Before Amanda gets out of the office, the door opens and a beautiful woman walks in the office. She looks at her son and at me. "Holy shit." She says. "How the hell did you find each other?"

"Why the hell didn't I know about her?" Sebastian asks his mother.

She looks at me. I am still holding the picture of him holding me.

"My mother knew about all of you?" I ask.

"No." Charlotte says.

"Then how am I in this picture?"

"Your grandma brought you."

"You know Grandma Timely?" Sebastian asks me.

"I do. I don't see her a lot but yes I know her. She is the one who made that outfit for me."

Charlotte looks at both of us. "How did you find each other?"

I look at Sebastian. "He robbed a bank and I went to court to pay a traffic ticket. Then everything kind of unraveled."

Charlotte looks at Amanda. "Its nice to see you again."

Amanda looks at Charlotte, "its nice to see you too."

Charlotte looks at Justin. "Who are you?"

"I am Sebastian's—" he looks at me. "I am her boyfriend. I met her when all of this started."

Charlotte looks at her son, "You robbed a bank?"

"No." He says. He goes back over to the desk and opens the drawer. He takes out my credit cards and hands them to me.

"Why do you have my stolen credit cards?"

"Someone came into my bank and tried opening an account with your information. What looked like a bank robbery was actually me talking to the teller. She slipped me information about the stolen identity. She thought it was my cards. Then we noticed that one of them says. Sebastian Ashley Timely. The ATM card was on the bottom of the stack of cards and when I looked at the picture, I knew exactly who you are."

Justin looks at me. "You feeling ok?" He asks.

I look at him. "I am ok."

Charlotte looks at both of us. "What's going on?"

"When I went to pay the traffic ticket, I was taken into a room and interrogated for hours. It was very stressful and I fainted. I spent a week in the hospital." I look at everyone. "I am fine."

"Do you work?" She asks me.

"I teach third grade at Panther Cove Elementary School."

"There is school today."

"Yes. I can not go back to work until this is all straightened out. The principal of the school hates me."

Amanda looks at me. "I am going to fix that." She looks at Sebastian and smiles. "I need to get back to work." She kisses the top of my head. "Good luck with everything." She shakes hand with Justin. "Can I talk to you for a moment?"

He looks at me. He kisses me on the lips. "I will be right back." He says.

Charlotte sits in the chair that Justin was sitting on. "I knew this was coming."

He looks at his mom. "Why didn't you tell me about her?"

"I didn't want to change the way you thought about your dad."

I look at Charlotte. Tears fill in my eyes. "Did my mom sleep with your husband?"

She jumps up and hugs me. "No. We were divorced before you came along. We hadn't been married for two years." She looks at her son and then at me. "I want you to know that he was a great man. He loved you." She says to her son. "And he couldn't wait to meet his little girl. He rescued your mom. Did she tell you?"

"She just always told me that he was her hero. She never said more."

"He literally rescued her. She was in a car accident and the driver that hit her left her. She was stranded. He drove by on his motorcycle and pulled her from her car. He brought her to the hospital and stayed with her. He never left her." She looks at Sebastian. "He was always around for us. He never missed a milestone in your life." She looks at me. "He wished for a girl. When your mom got pregnant and they found out that you were a girl, he was thrilled. His mom was excited. His mom is a rare gem. She never stopped loving me and Asher."

I look at the picture. "I swore to my mom that grandma told me a story about a boy who had a sister and they shared more than just the same dad. My mom told me that I must have made that up. I remember this picture. Once I told my mom about the story the picture disappeared. Grandma stopped coming as often."

"Not because of that. She met a guy. He was a nice person sometimes, but he was jealous of her family and the love that she shared with us. I mean all of us. She loves your mom as much as she loves me. Her husband didn't want her to share her love." Charlotte says. She looks at me. "How is your mom?"

"She is great. She is in Nashville with her boyfriend Peter."

"She lives there?" Sebastian asks me.

"No. They are visiting his family. He has a daughter and son. They live with their mom in Nashville."

"Did your mom ever marry?" Charlotte asks.

"No. She said that she gave her whole heart to one man and although she's dated, she never lets it get that far. Men have asked her to marry but she never did. She didn't want to betray him."

My cell phone rings. I take it out of my purse. Its my mom. I answer it. "Hi."

"I want you to know that I am coming home. I will be there tomorrow. Lets have dinner."

"I look forward to it." I tell her.

"I have a lot to tell you." She tells me.

"I have a lot to tell you. Love you. I will see you tomorrow. I will make dinner."

"Love you too." She says and hangs up.

I look at Sebastian and Charlotte. "Would you like to come to dinner tomorrow?"

Charlotte looks at me and smiles. "Wouldn't you want to tell you mom about what is going on before she gets thrown into all of this?"

"My mom can handle this."

Sebastian looks at me. "If my mom doesn't want to join you for dinner tomorrow, I will come."

49

"You can bring Amanda if you she wants to come."

"Why would you have all of us?" Charlotte asks.

"Its my house, I can invite anyone I want for dinner." I look at Justin. "You and Mark can come too."

"If you leave Bob out, I can't come." He says kissing me.

"Bob can come." I smile. I look at my watch, "We should go." I look at the picture that I am still holding. "Can I get a copy of this?"

"I will bring you a copy tomorrow when I come for dinner." Sebastian says.

I hand him the picture. Justin and I leave. When we get to my car, Justin looks at me. I smile at him. "I will be right back." I Say and rush back inside.

Sebastian meets me in the lobby. "Come in to uninvite us?"

I laugh. "No. Came to see what you like to eat?"

"I like anything."

"Do you have a favorite?'

"Really what's ever easiest for you to make."

"Do you like Swedish meatballs?" I ask.

"I do." He looks at me. "What can I bring?"

"Nothing special." I tell him. "See you tomorrow." I say. I turn and then turn back o him. "Can I hug you?"

He doesn't answer but takes me in his arms and holds me tight.

"I am glad I found you. Or whatever."

"Me too." He says and hugs me tighter. "I always wanted a sister." He steps back. I leave.

Justin and I get back to the neighborhood. I pull into my driveway. I open the door. Justin puts his hand on my hand. "Come see my house." He says.

"I have to take care of Astro."

"I will get him." Justin says. He jumps out of the car and runs to the front door.

From my phone I disarm my alarm system. He opens the door and Astro bolts for the car. Justin opens the door and he jumps in. Justin gets in the car and I drive to his house.

"You and Mark moved into the O'Conner house?"

"You knew the owners?" Justin asks.

"I lived in my house for twenty-five years." I smile. "Should I park on the street?"

He looks at me. "I have a driveway. Pull in the driveway."

"I don't want to block anyone."

"If your car is blocking anything or anyone, I can move it." He kisses me. "What are you going to make for dinner?"

"My grandma's famous Swedish meatballs." I tell him as my wheelchair is lowering to the ground. I get it.

Justin opens the door for Astro. He jumps out and runs to the big tree on the corner of the lawn and lifts his leg. He then swats and does the rest of his business. I go to the passenger side of my car and go in the glovebox. I take out poop bags.

Justin looks at me. "You have those in your car?"

"I bring him with me. I leave some in my car incase I forget to bring some." I say.

Justin walks over and takes the bags from me. He goes over and collects Astrro's mess. He walks to the door and unlocks the door. Astro jots in in front of us. Justin steps behind me and tips my wheelchair back so that we can enter the house going up the step.

Once we are in the house, I turn and look on the wall for a switch. "Still here." I say.

"What?" Justin asks.

I point to the switch. "Flip it." I say.

"Go ahead." He tells me.

I flip the switch. We both watch as a ramp emerges from the step.

"Oh my god, I didn't know that was there."

I flip the switch up. The ramp goes back.

"No, you can leave it. The ramp can stay." He walks over and kisses me. "You are always welcome here."

Mark comes home and walks in the house. He smiles. He walks into the kitchen and punches Justin in the shoulder. He kisses the top of my head.

"Little Mermaid, I see you brought your fleabag with you." He teases.

I laugh. "Hi Mark."

He looks at Justin. "You installed a ramp?"

Justin looks at me as he prepares a salad. "Go show him."

Mark takes my hand. "Where are we going?"

"To the front door." I say. When we get over there, I point to the switch. I flip it up and we watch the ramp go back.

"Oh that's great. I didn't know that was here."

"Mr. O'Conner installed it for me. Him and his wife used to have my mom and I over a lot. When my mom worked nights, they would keep me for her. The ramp is just one thing that he did."

"Leave it. Its something that should always be in use." Mark says. He taps my head. "Show me what else this house secretly has."

Justin joins us. We go room by room. Justin shows me his room. He has the master bedroom.

"Is there anything in this room?' Mark asks.

There is a built in bookshelf on the wall across from the bed. I go over and feel under the middle shelf. There is a button. I push it and the bathroom wall retracts, opening it up wider so that my wheelchair can fit inside with no problems.

Mark and Justin look at each other.

"Anything else?' Justin asks.

I go in the bathroom and they follow. Next to the shower is another switch. "Up and down turns the lights on. Side to side, a grab bar emerges from the wall." I flip it to the left and the bar appears. I put my hand back on the wall to flip it back.

"Leave it." Justin says. "I will leave it just for you." He kisses me.

Mark stands with his back against the wall. "I always thought that you both would make a great couple. When did that happen?"

"It just happened." I say smiling.

"Be good to each other." Mark says.

~~~~~~~~~

I sit at my kitchen table rolling meatballs. When I have rolled the last one, I put them in the skillet and cook them. I made grandma's sauce. I prepare a salad and the pasta. I get everything ready and set the table.

I put a table clothe on the table and set a formal table. As I am folding the napkins in a fancy style there is a knock at the door. I put the napkins on the plate. Astro jumps up from his spot. He wags his tail as he runs to the door.

"Astro, get back." I tell him. I open the door. Sebastian is the first one to arrive. "Do you like dogs?" I ask.

Astro throws himself at Sebastian. "What's his name?"

"Astro."

"I love dogs." Sebastian says as he pets Astro. "It smells good."

"Please come in."

He looks around at all the pictures that I have hanging on the walls. There is one of my mom and dad. It's a big picture that hangs in the center of the wall with photos of my mom and me all around it.

"Where can I put this?" He asks.

I didn't notice that he was holding grocery bags. "On the counter." I tell him. "I have to change, I will be right back." I slip into my room and change my clothes. I pull my hair out of the ponytail and run my fingers through it. I change my shoes to strappy sandals.

When I come out of my room, Sebastian is looking at all the pictures. He is staring at the one of dad and mom. She is wearing a ring on her finger.

He turns and looks at me. "He never married her?"

"No."

"You look really nice. This is a cute house. And dinner smells amazing."

"Thank you. Can I get you anything to drink?"

"I am good for now." He says.

Mom doesn't knock. She thinks she still owns the place. When she walks in she puts her hand to her chest. Sebastian looks just like my dad. "I knew this day would come." She looks at me. "Hi, sweetheart." She hugs me. She looks at Sebastian. "God, you look just like him." She says. She sits down.

I go in the kitchen and get her a bottle of water. I open it and put it in front of her. I hand a bottle of water to Sebastian.

"How is this happening?" Mom asks.

Sebastian sits across the table from mom. He hold his hand out for me to join them. "Linda, I mean you and Sebastian no harm. Someone came into my bank trying to open an account in my name, only it wasn't my identification that they were showing, it was Sebastian's." He gets up from the table and goes into the kitchen. He comes out and hands me a wrapped box. "This is for you." He sits back my mom.

I open it and it's the the picture. Its just as large as the one from his offie. The frame its in reads 'Big Brother & Little Sister'.

"Thank you." I say. When I look up at him, I see that the teddy bear my grandma made for me is on the couch. Next to it is a cat that she made. "You found my stuffed animals."

"The cat." He looks at it and then at us. "That was made from his favorite shirt." He looks at the cat again. "She made me a dog out of the same shirt."

We both embrace. As we are hugging, mom take the picture. She takes one off the wall and hangs the one he gave me in its place.

The rest of my guests arrive. Savanah and Piper. Justin, Mark and Bob Cat. Amanda and Charlotte are the last to arrive. Savannah and Piper get the food and put it out on the table. Astro and Bob lay on the couch curled into each other.

We finish dinner and Sebastian stands and clears the table. "That was so good. That tastes just like Grandma's."

"Its her recipe." I say. "You don't have to clean up."

"You must have worked really hard on this. You made everything so great for all of us." Sebastian says.

"It was no big deal. It's something that I really love to do."

Amanda comes into the kitchen. "Monday morning you can report back to school." She says to me. "You will never have any more problems with Paul." The smile on her face is devious.

"How do you know that?" Justin asks as he steps closer to me.

"He has resigned." She says.

My phone starts pinging with text message notifications. I pick it up and click the buttons to silent the pings.

Justin looks at me. "Are you going to see what that's all about?"

"I will get to it." I say.

Amanda looks at Sebastian and then me. "I am guessing that your co-workers just found out the news about Paul."

Sebastian takes my phone and scrolls through the notifications on the front screen. "Three are like a hundred notifications."

I take the phone back. I look at it. "Oh wow. The school is going to pay me for my time missed."

"You weren't getting paid?" Justin asks.

"No."

"Why didn't you say anything? I am a lawyer." He kisses me.

Piper pulls me into my room. She sits on my bed. "The guy from the restaurant is your brother? This is very interesting." She says.

"Its weird. I really like the idea that I have a brother. I know I have you and Savanah and all my sorority sisters, but I am an only child and throughout the years I have felt very lonely. I am glad that I have a brother. He has two brothers that he told me he is willing to share with me."

"That's so great." She says. "I am happy for you." She hold the stuffed cat on her lap. Throughout the years, its always been her favorite thing. "You and Justin are dating?"

Bob Cat lays across my bed. He stretches and purrs loudly.

"He brings his cat over?"

I laugh. "Yes. I am dating Justin. We have slept together twice."

She squeals.

"Shut up. We literally slept together. He has been here for me since I met him. He has slept with me in my bed twice. He makes me feel safe." I look at Bob and reach out to him. He gets up and walks on my legs. "We bring our pets to each other's houses."

"What?"

"He lives in the O'Conner house."

She smiles. "I think Savanna is in love with Mark."

"When has she not been in love with Mark?"

"What?"

"Her mom and their dad were married to each other twice. Mark used to always be around. I never remember Justin being around."

"I like that he calls you Little Mermaid." She says.

There is a knock on the door. Mark opens it. He comes in and plucks Bob from me.

"Speak of the devil." Piper says.

He looks at both of us. "Little Mermaid, your guests are getting ready to end the evening. Bob and I are going home." He looks at me. "Don't get attached to my cat. Regardless of what Justin tells you about Bob, he is my cat." He holds the cat close to his chest. He kisses the top of my head. "It was good to see you Pipes. You look good."

"Thanks." She says. She gets off the bed and hugs him.

The three of us leave my room. Astro picks up his head when Mark leaves with Bob. He follows him to the door. Savannah puts Astro's leash on. She walks out of the house with Mark and the two animals. Once they are outside she kisses him on the lips.

They walk hand in hand to Mark and Justin's house. Once they get there, they sit on the couch and kiss each other. It starts something that neither of them want to stop. Astro and Bob lay on the couch next to them.

Back at my house, my mom and Charlotte sit on the couch talking about dad. They chat for hours. Mom has pulled out old albums of her and dad. She shares them with Charlotte.

Amanda walks over to me. "Your job is waiting for you." She says.

"I have a feeling that you did something about that."

She kisses me on the cheek. "Thank you for inviting me for dinner. It was delicious. I hope to see you soon."

"I am sure you will."

Chapter 6

I am in my classroom waiting for my children to come in. Ginger walks Sara to the door. When the bell rings, the children come in the class room and run over to me. They line up to hug me. Sara hugs me first and then runs to the end of the line. After all twenty children have hugged me, Sara hugs me again.

Ginger looks at me. "I am going to help you out today."

I smile at her. "Do you think, I forgot how to teach in the last month?"

We both laugh. "I want to stay."

I tell all my students to take their seats. "We have a guest today. I want everyone on your best behavior. Sara's mom is going to stay with us for the day."

"What do you need help with?" Ginger asks me.

Sara runs over to Ginger, "Mommy."

Ginger looks at her daughter and smiles. "What?"

"She is really good at what she does." Sara says.

Ginger looks at the desk that is intended for me to use. It is pushed against a wall and is currently being used at a bookshelf. As I teach lessons to the children, she moves furniture around.

A little boy, Daniel gets up and runs over to Ginger. "Can I help you?" He asks.

She looks at him smiling. "Maybe in a little while." She says.

"I will come back." He says.

He returns to the reading table and picks up a book. I look at him. I know that he struggles to read. He is one of the tallest children in the class. Other teachers didn't want him because of his behavior problems and his need for help.

With all the children busy doing assignments, I make my way over to Daniel. "I have missed you reading to me." I tell him. I look at the book in his hand. "The Ugly Duckling? We have read that one before."

"I like it."

"Go pick another book, please. One that you haven't read."

"You know them all." He tells me.

"Daniel, you know this book forward and backward. I love that. We need to read a book that you don't know. Maybe we can have a new favorite."

Ginger looks over at us.

"Daniel, I really want to listen to you read to me, but it can not be this book. Have you read any books since I have been gone?" I ask.

A little girl with braids looks up from her work. She raises her hand. I look at her.

"Carrie, did you need anything?"

She gets up from her seat and runs over. "The other teachers made him sit in the office until we went to specials and lunch. No one has worked with him." She says throwing her arms around him.

"Thank you for that information." I tell her. "You are a wonderful friend.

She looks at me. "Sara and I would read to him in specials after we got our work done." Carrie says.

I hug her. "Thank you." A bell rings. I look up. "Everyone put all pencils and pens away. I see the pens, girls, away. Lets get ready for Science. Mr. Evans is coming in today to teach science."

Everyone of them cheers. They love science. Mr. Evans coming to my class means we are going outside for an experiment. This makes them happy. This makes me happy. When he knocks on the door, Sonny one of the boys in the class runs to the door. He opens it.

Mr. Evans looks at him. "Close the door. Walk back to your seat. Raise your hand. Start again." He says.

Sonny looks up at him. "I am excited."

"As am I. We must do it right." He says and closes the door.

Sonny drops his head and walks back to his desk. Mr. Evans taps on the door. Sonny raises his hand. I nod my head and he walks quickly to the door and opens it.

"Much better." Mr. Evan says. He enters the room. He walks over to me and kisses my cheek. "I can't wait for lunch." He says in my ear. He sees Ginger. He nods at her. "Ok, I see that we are not ready for our experiment." Mr. Evans says loudly. "Girls, line up in reverse alphabetical order."

Sara smiles as she goes to stand by the door. Behind her is Ruby, Madison, Luna, Lizzie, Lexie, June, Carrie, Beth and Addison.

"Wonderful." Mr. Evans says. "Boys, line up alphabetically."

The boys line up. Alex is first, followed by Brian, Daniel, Derik, John-Paul, Josh, Kyle, Sonny, Tristian and finally Tyler.

"Great. We are going to the playground. Before anyone leaves the room, make sure your hands are behind your backs. Do not touch anyone in front or behind you. When we get to the playground, please sit in the grass and wait for me. Do not run." He opens the door and they walk out of the room. He looks at me. "You and Ginger coming?"

"Yes." I tell him. "I have to use the—"

"Don't be long."

"I will be right there." I tell him. I go into the back corner of the room and open a door. A hidden bathroom. I go inside and come out minutes later. Ginger is waiting for me. "Are you going to stay all day?"

"Are you going to lose your mind over Daniel being isolated?" She asks.

"What do you think?"

"I think his parents should know what kind of teacher you are and that you care so deeply."

"Ginger, its my job."

"Its their jobs too." She holds up her arms and points to the neighboring classrooms. "It seems like they all dropped the ball."

"I will take care of it." I tell Ginger. "I love Zack's experiments." I smile.

"I think he does them because he knows you love them." She says.

We leave the room and head over to the playground.

Mr. Evans is standing at a table with two big water jugs in front of him. One is filled with water and the other looks like it has orange Gatorade in it. "It looks like water." He says pointing to the one with water in it. He takes the top off and pushes it over. All the children jump back.

"Nothing came out." Daniel says.

"You are so stupid." Ruby says.

Daniel looks at her before he picks up a rock.

"Daniel, put it down." I say sternly. "Ruby, do we call our family members stupid?"

"He is too dumb to be in my family." She blurts out. "His favorite book is stupid."

"Enough!" Mr. Evans says. He looks at Daniel. "You are right, nothing came out. Why not?"

"You mixed it with glue." Daniel guesses.

Ruby puts her hand on her hips. "Are you kidding? You are so stupid."

"Ruby, you say one more word and I am calling your mom." I warn her.

She looks at me. "I didn't miss you." She says.

Mr. Ricks walks over. "Ruby, lets take a walk." He says.

She sits among the other children and drops her head. "I don't want to."

"You are wasting everyone's time. Please get up and walk with me."

She does stand up finally and then she kicks my wheelchair on her way. All the boys in the class jump up. They all stand around me.

Mr. Ricks walks over and takes Ruby by the hand. She drags her feet. He puts his hands on her shoulders. He stands behind her. "Mr. Evans continue on." He says.

Daniel and Sara move closer to me. Carrie puts her arm around Daniel's shoulders.

Mr. Evans finishes his experiment and we go back into the coolness of the classroom. He tells everyone to write a report about what they observed.

Daniel puts his head down. I cross the room but Mr. Evans puts his hands up. He walks over. "If you don't have the words, draw me a picture." He tells him.

"Mr. Evans?" Tyler says raising his hand.

"Yes?"

"Are you going to take him with you like you did last week?" Tyler asks.

"No." He answers.

"Can I be your helper this week?" Addison asks.

I look at all of them. "How about, who ever finishes the work first can help Mr. Evans go to his next class."

They all look at their journals in front of them and stop talking. They work on their assignment. They talk quietly with each other. Daniel takes out markers and draws what he saw.

Mr. Evans walks over to me. He sits down with Ginger and me. "I was wondering how I could get out of that."

Alex and Brian throw their hands in the air. Mr. Evans looks at both of them.

"Finished." They say together.

Tyler puts his head down and cries.

The bell rings indicating that its lunch time. I smile. "Saved by the bell." I say loud enough for Mr. Evans to hear me. "Line up for lunch please. Tyler, you can be my line leader. Addison, can you get the basket of books please? Alex, can you hold the door? And Brian, can you bring this envelope down to the cafeteria and give it to the lunch lady where you pay?"

They all smile at me. I normally don't assign them jobs, but I have been away from them for a month. So I am trying to reestablish my class.

Carrie looks at me. "Can I push your wheelchair?"

"No." I tell her. "You can be the line monitor."

She smiles.

"Is someone going to get Ruby?" Beth asks. The two of them are inseparable.

"She is going to rejoin us later." I tell Beth. "Ok, lets go. We are going to play a game on the way to lunch and back from lunch. If I don't have to remind you how to be the adults I know you, we will have a treat before you leave school today."

"You brought your grab bag?" Sonny asks.

"I did. So remind each other how to behave." I tell them. "Lets go. We don't want to be late. Alex, open the door, please."

They walk like tin soldiers down the hallway. They are quiet as mice. I almost laugh. Alex opens the door and they file into the room. The cafeteria is loud with chatter from all the children already there.

"Everyone eyes on me." I tell them.

They all look at me.

"I want you to count to three with me." I hold up my hand. "One. Two. Three." We count together. "Now, run as fast as you can to get in line. Mind your manners." I tell them. I watch them and laugh as the run as fast as they can to lunch line.

Pam, the lunch lady, looks at me and smiles. She takes the envelope from Brian. She smiles at me again. She is the only who knows that I pay for a few of my students to have lunch. While I was out, she would come to the Bookstore Coffee Shop. I would give her the envelope and she would leave like nothing ever happened.

Daniel is the last one to get his lunch. On the tray there is not a lot of food. She looks at him. "Not hungry today?" She asks.

"My dad didn't pay the bill." He says.

"I think you need more to eat. More food makes you smart." She says and steps away from the register for a moment. She takes his tray and puts more food on it. "Go eat your food." She tells him. She hugs him to her. "No matter what anyone says about you, you are smart."

He looks at her. "I can't read." He tells her.

"You can read. You need to practice more." She looks away to blink away tears. "Go enjoy your lunch." She kisses the top of his head and fluffs his hair. She knows that Daniel's dad hasn't paid the bill for lunch in a long time.

I come back into the cafeteria and Pam walks over. She hugs me. "I have to say that I am so glad that womanizing ass-wipe no longer works here." She says about Paul Dun-in." She looks at me. "Did you hear what happened?"

"No." I tell her.

I honestly don't know what caused him to leave his job that he loved. He loved to torment his employees. He truly loved the kids and seeing all their successes and helping them out with their dramas.

"I heard that his bank account was drained." Pam says.

"Drained?"

"Either the wife or the many girl friends found out about his lying ways and drained his bank."

I roll my eyes. Now I understand what happened to his account. My brother's assistant – girlfriend froze the account.

I look at Pam, "I have to get them out of here."

"Drinks later?" She asks.

Zack Evans walks over. He kisses me on the cheek and hugs Pam. "Are we drinking on a school night?"

"You didn't let me answer." I say to both of them. "I can't tonight, I have to work."

"We will catch up." Zack says.

"We will." I tell them. "I get them back to the room."

As we go back to the room, they walk quietly but I notice that Ruby is in the back with us and she intentionally sticks her foot out to try to trip Daniel. Tristian grabs Daniel's shirt to keep him from face-planting into the sidewalk. Tristian shoves Ruby. She cries out.

"Leave your hands off me." Ruby says.

"We didn't have any problems going to lunch." Beth says. She looks at Tristian.

"Ruby tried to trip Danny."

"He's stupid." Ruby says.

"Ruby Jane!" I say her name sternly. "What's the problem?"

"He tripped me." She lies.

"You liar." Beth says.

"You are my best friend." Ruby says to Beth.

"Not today." Beth snaps.

"Enough." I say to them. "Brian can you please open the door. Girls go in first."

When the girls go in the room, Ruby walks over to Beth and yanks her hair.

"Ouch!" Beth yells. She then pulls Ruby's hair.

Ruby cries out.

Brian looks at me. "Miss, they are fighting."

Ginger runs in the room ahead of me. She steps between the two of them. She lifts Ruby and sits her on the counter. She then goes over to Beth. Beth is red faced and holding her head. She is crying.

"She started it." Ruby shouts.

Mr. Ricks walks in the room. He walks over to Beth. He wants to lift his adoptive daughter in his arms and comfort her, but he can't right now. He looks at Ruby.

"What's going on?"

"Beth, your mommy didn't love you enough to keep you." Ruby says.

Beth turns away from Ginger and vomits her entire lunch. She cries harder. Mr. Ricks turns and lifts his adoptive daughter in his arms and runs from the room with her.

I finally come in the room. I call for the janitor. He comes in the room and cleans up the mess. When he finishes he leaves the room.

"It smells in here." Ruby whines. "I am going to be sick."

"Leave the room." I tell her.

"What?"

"If you are going to be sick, leave the room."

"Beth pulled my hair." Ruby stomps her feet.

"Why?" I ask her.

"I don't know."

"Ruby, go sit in the blue chair."

"Am I punished?"

"Yes." I say to her sternly.

"Why?"

"You are wasting everyone's time." I look at the other children. "Everyone go sit at your tables. We are going to work on our journaling. For the next twenty minutes you can do whatever you want in your journal. Draw a picture. Write about a friend. Write about your pets."

"Can we write about sports?" Josh asks.

"Yes." I tell him.

They all get busy and I go over to Ruby. "Come talk to me." I say. I look at Ginger. "They may need help spelling."

"I will deal with it." She says.

I go outside with Ruby. We walk to the playground. She walks to the swings.

"No miss." I say to her. "We didn't come out here so you can have your own recess. We are going to talk. I am going to call your mom and dad."

"You like Daniel better than anyone."

"I don't have favorites." Now I am lying. I do have favorites. Sara is my favorite girl in my class and Daniel is my favorite boy. I know more about him then his classmates do. They are only eight. Daniel is nine. He struggles with reading. When he gets frustrated he acts out. Teachers have put up with him, but they have never given him the time needed to work on his issues.

"Yes you do. You like him better."

"Why do you say that?"

"You give him more time."

"Ruby, he needs more time."

"I want more time."

"You told me that you didn't even miss me. You can't have it both ways." I remind myself that she is only eight.

I take the phone and call her parents. Her mother answers almost right away. I tell her that I need to see both her and her husband. She tells me that they will both come. I tell her briefly that Ruby has been a problem all day.

We go back in the room. I look at all of them. "Who wants to share your journal entry?"

June jumps out of her chair so quickly I have to put my hand over my mouth to hide my laughs.

"Ok June, enlighten us."

She smiles and her whole face lights up like a Christmas tree. She opens her journal and shows a well drawn picture of a cat. "My mom and dad bought me a cat for my birthday." She says excitedly. She drew a picture of a cat blowing out candles.

"What did you name the cat?" Luna asks.

"Monster."

The whole class erupts in laughter.

"That's stupid." Ruby says.

"Ruby, go change your color to black." I tell her.

She throws herself on the floor.

"Ok, whose next?" I ask ignoring her behavior.

"I think Monster cat sounds great." I say.

June closes her journal and sits down.

Brian goes next. He opens his journal. He drew a picture of a soccer field. "I am the goalie on my soccer team." He says. "I didn't allow ten balls to pass."

"Good job." I say to him.

Alex stands up next. "I wrote a poem." He says.

"Ok."

"Roses are red. Violets are blue. Ruby no one likes you." Alex says.

"Alex!" I snap. "Uncalled for. Go change your color to yellow."

He laughs on his way over to the color chart. He takes his out and changes it to yellow. He takes Ruby's name and flips it to black.

"Thank you." I say to him. "Come back and join us." I look at the group. "Whose next?"

Madison stands up. "I wrote that I am glad you are back." She says. She didn't write anything.

"Thank you."

"I drew a heart." She says.

"Wonderful."

Addison jumps up. "I drew a picture of a lizard. My dad lets me keep it in my room."

"What color is it?" Kyle asks her.

"He changes colors from blue to orange." She says.

"You aren't scared of it?" Lexie asks.

"No. We have snakes too."

"Wonderful." I say.

John-Paul jumps up next. "I drew a picture of all the sports I play." He shows his journal to everyone.

I look at the clock. "Ok, gather your stuff together. We will finish up on journals in the morning. Please remember to do your math homework. Also we have a spelling test tomorrow. Please remember that tomorrow we start all over again. It will be a better day."

They line up and wait for the bell to ring.

"Ms. Timely?" Tyler looks at me.

"What?"

"When can we go back to the zoo?"

"I think we have another field trip coming up soon."

"Will everyone get to go?"

"I think so." I say.

The bell rings. They all stand there waiting for me to let them go.

"Have a good day. Do your homework. Everyone who turns it in will get a hundred points extra credit."

They all leave the room.

Sara looks at Ginger. "Can we get ice cream?"

"I have to go get your sisters." Ginger says. "Then we have to go to the store. On our way home we will get ice cream." Ginger hugs me.

I look at her. "What will the report to the school board say?"

She looks at me. "I will be fair."

"Thanks." I say.

"Are you leavening?" Ginger asks.

"No, I have a meeting."

Sara hugs me. "I think the day went well."

I look at her and smile. "I think so too." I hug her back.

Ruby's parents come. Her mom gets upset that her color chart is black. I explain everything that happened. Her dad doesn't talk until the end.

"She is having issues because we are divorcing;." He looks at Ruby's mom. "Also, I am moving out. Not far away but out." He says with sadness. "Also, Beth is no longer allowed to be friends with her."

"She yanked her hair. We are ending friendships over pulled hair." Her mother says.

"It's a lot more than that." I say. "She told Beth that her mother didn't want her anymore."

"What?" Ruby's dad asks. He looks at his wife. "How did she know that Beth is adopted?"

"I was reading a book with Jackson. He was asking about adoption. Ruby asked if we knew anyone that was adopted. I told her that Beth was. I didn't say why."

Mr. Ricks knocks on the door. "My daughter being adopted had nothing to do with her mother not wanting her. My sister died in a car accident. There is nothing more she wanted in life." He looks at me. "The administration and I have decided that Ruby needs to leave us. We can't have her bullying other children.."

Ruby's dad stands up and shakes hands with Mr. Ricks. "I am so sorry. I agree. We will withdraw her immediately."

I look at Mr. Ricks. "Should I gather her belongings?"

"Yes. You know what is hers." He says.

I go to her desk and I open her journal. I take out her purple pen and I write in it.

Ruby,

I am sorry that you are going though such a tough time in your life. I assure you that life will get better. I want you to know that I loved having you in my class. You're a very unique little person. Being eight is hard. I was eight once. My advice for you is to be kind. When you see someone needs help, offer him or her a hand. Be wonderful.

Ms. Timely

I hand her belongings to her her mother. She takes it and they leave. They go with Mr. Ricks to the office.

I go into the office to clock out. Mr. Ricks comes over to me. "Please come with me." He says.

I go into the office with him.

"I know that you work long hours here. I have just been notified that the after school program we offer needs another teacher. The children have all requested you."

"I am flattered." I say. "Can I think about it?"

"I need a reply by Wednesday." He says.

"Great." I leave and go to get in my car.

The windows are all smashed. I take my phone out and call the police. An hour later my car is on a tow truck.

Tears stream down my face as I push my wheelchair to my house. When I get home, I go in the house and cry. Astro comes and licks my cheek.

My phone rings. I wipe the tears away and answer it. "Hello."

"Sweetheart, I am coming over." Mom tells me.

"I can't wait."

"Do you want me to stop for anything on the way?"

"Not for me." I tell her. I sniff.

"Are you crying?" She asks. "I can bring ice cream."

"I will never say no to ice cream."

"What flavor?" She laughs. "I will surprise you. Wipe your tears away, mommy's coming."

I laugh. While I wait for her to come, I take Astro outside. I go back in the house and change my clothes. I go through the mail. Bills are due soon. I sit at the table and organize all the bills. I take out my laptop and pay the bills.

I read emails. I look at my phone and see that I missed text messages from Justin.

Justin: Hello Beautiful, hope you had a nice day back at work. You have been on my mind all day, I couldn't get work done.

Justin:

I was reading a report that is really important but I couldn't stop thinking of you. I went home from work early and Bob Cat was meowing. He misses his new friends too.

I answer him. Me: Hi! I had an ok day. One of my kids was so mean, I will fill you in when I see you. My mom is coming for dinner. I have to admit that you were on my mind all day too.

Justin: Enjoy dinner with y our mom. Call me when you can.

Me: I need a hug.

I send it before I think.

There's a knock at the door. I open it and he takes me in his arms and hugs me tight. He kisses me on the lips. I feel so loved just being in his arms.

"Where have you been my whole life?" He says.

"Looking for you." I tell him.

He kisses me again. "I have to read this report."

"Call me when you are done." I kiss him.

He leaves as my mom pulls in the driveway.

Chapter 7

Mom and I busy ourselves in the kitchen. She brought ice cream for dessert. She puts them in the freezer. I take out the left over Swedish meatball. I put the casserole plate in the oven to warm it up. I make a salad for us. Mom sets the table. She opens the cabinet over the stove.

"Not those." I tell her.

She looks at me. "What plates do you want to use?"

"Not those. The others are in the dishwasher. I didn't empty it yet."

She opens the dishwasher and takes out two dishes for us. She holds them up. "I like these very much."

"Me too. Macy's had a sale on flatwares and I treated myself."

"You sure as hell work hard enough."

I laugh. "Its funny you say that because Mr. Ricks offered me a job in the after school program. Apparently the children requested me."

"So what job will you give up?" She asks taking the food out of the oven and putting it on the table. "You don't have to work as hard as you do." She plates the food. "While I was in Nashville I saw your grandma. She is going to come visit you."

"I look forward to that." I tell her. I tell her about my day and how sad I am that Beth had to be reminded in such a cruel way that she doesn't have a mother.

"Can I ask you a question?" She asks as we go into the family room and she sits on the couch. She puts her coffee cup on the table in front of her. Astro lays on the couch next to mom. She pets him.

"You can ask me anything."

"Are you upset with me?"

"For what?"

"Keeping your brother a secret?"

I look at her "I am not upset with you for anything. I just want to know more about my dad."

"The truth is, I only knew him a short time. I truly loved him. He saved my life. He came into my life just when I needed a knight in shining armor. He was there."

"Why didn't you marry him?"

"He died." She says sadly. "He died three months before you came along. He died three weeks before our wedding. I had the dress. We had a date. He died on May thirty-first. We were to be married on June twenty-first. He was excited to have a daughter."

"What did he do? Did he work?"

She looks at me. "I am sure I told you what he did for a living."

I look at her. "No."

"Sebastian was a successful person. He ran the biggest chain of car dealerships in the state of Florida. He ran them from Miami all the way to Savannah Georgia."

"What happened to all of them?"

"His mother opted to have Sebastian's brother and sister run them, but after long conversations, they didn't want to work that hard. His brother was much younger and planning on colleges he wanted to attend. His sister was a single mom of two children. She took a job in Aspen and met a really nice guy."

"I never knew he had siblings."

"Yes." She says

"Mom, tell me about him."

She takes her coffee off the table and takes a long drink. "He looked like Sebastian. You look like him. He was kind. He would give anyone the shirt off his back." She looks at the pictures of him and her on the wall. "He saved my life. I fell in love with him in seconds. That's all it took. He held my hand and told me that help was on the way to get me out of my car that was flipped over. He held my hand until the first spark of fire. Then he pulled me out of the car and held me until the ambulance came. Sebastian stayed with me in the hospital. My mom and dad were in Europe." She stretches her legs. She stands and fixes her long skirt. She then sits back down on the couch in a yoga position. "It amazes me how you met Sebastian."

"Is it wrong that I want to get to know him?"

"No." Mom says "I think its wonderful."

"Mom, how are you and Peter getting along?"

"He asked me to marry him."

"They all do."

"It's the first time I wanted to say yes."

I look at her excitedly. "Did you say yes?"

"No."

"Mom, I am twenty-five years old. You need to be happy."

"I am happy."

"You know what I mean."

"I want you to be happy." She says. "You need to work less."

I laugh at that. "Three jobs is not a lot. I like to be busy. I like that I an afford to get whatever I want."

"What happened to your favorite purse?" Mom asks about the purse that I was using a month ago.

"The zipper broke."

"Send it back to the company, they will repair it." Mom says and rubs Astro's belly. He rolls on his back and wags his tail. "Tell me about your boyfriend."

"I am dating Justin Case."

"Tell me about him."

"He is a lawyer. He really likes me. He was Savannah's step brother once. Twice actually." I laugh.

"I don't remember ever meeting Justin."

"He stayed with his mom more. Mark was around more."

"Savannah is ok with you dating her brother?"

"He is not her brother."

"The parents divorce, not the children."

"He is not her brother." I say again. I go in the kitchen and make myself an iced coffee. "Do you want another coffee?"

She looks at her watch. "No, I am going to meet Peter for drinks. If you don't mind."

"I don't mind." I tell her. "I have stuff to get ready for tomorrow."

"You aren't going to take the after school job, are you?"

"I really don't think so." I tell her. "I am grateful that the children thought of me, but I don't know if I can be away from Astro that long. It's a long day for him."

"It's a long day for you." Mom says. She kisses the top of my head. "Let me help you clean up."

"It's a coffee cup. No. I got it." I tell her.

"Let me help you unload the dishwasher."

"Mom, no."

Before I can stop her she goes in the kitchen and unloads the entire dishwasher. She reaches to put the plates away in the cabinet that she knows they belong in and sees that there is a whole shelf of dishes. She turns to me. "Where do these go?" She asks.

I take them from her and put them in the lower cabinet.

"Why didn't you tell me that you couldn't reach the the dishes?" She says.

"I wanted new ones."

"Is there anything that I can reach for you while I am here?" She asks.

"The two vases that are above the stove."

She opens the cabinet door above the stove and takes down all the vases that are up there. There is room on the bookshelf so she arranges them on the shelf for me. She looks at her watch. "I have to go." She says.

"I don't want to keep you. I mean I do, but I can share you with Peter." I tease her.

"His kids are going to visit with their mom. They all want to meet you."

"Let me know when."

"I think when Anastasia comes we well have everyone over my house. We can use the clubhouse." Mom says.

"We can use the clubhouse here." I smile at her. "I used to work there."

"Before I go, where is your car?"

"Broken windows again. This time the windshield and the back window."

"Who do you think is doing it?"

"Honestly, I think its Paul. He doesn't like me." I go to the door and she follows. I hand her her purse and then push her out the door. "Go. Peter is waiting."

My phone pings with a text message. I take it off the counter and read it.

Mr. Ricks: Beth and I were talking and she told me that I was being mean when I offered you the after school job.

Me: What? Why? Awe so sweet that she thinks of me

Mr. Ricks: She put her hands on her hips and said, Daddy whatever would she do with Astro? Sorry I didn't know what she was talking about. She then says, she has the best fluffy dog ever.

Me: I was just talking about that with my mom. It's a long day for Astro. I leave him all day. I would have to find a way to come home and let him out during the day.

Mr. Ricks: Beth told me that he is a service dog

Me: Not technically

Mr. Ricks: Bring him in tomorrow with you. If he gets too much, I will keep him my office.

Me: Really?

Mr. Ricks: Really! Have a good night, see you tomorrow.

I look at Astro and smile. "It looks like you have been hired to do a job." He wags his tail and waits for a treat.

I sit on the couch with him and watch television. Monday nights always prove to be entertaining with the latest shows of The Bachelor or The Bachelorette. I snuggle with Astro as we watch the Bachelor. Mondays are my one night that I don't do anything extra but teach.

A loud noise jolts Astro from his sleep and makes me jump. I get in my wheelchair, put Astro's leash on him and we go outside. There is a tow truck in my driveway. The truck backs up and takes the car off the flatbed. The man walks over and hands me the keys.

He hands me a yellow paper. "Mr. Banklet said you might need this for a lawsuit."

I look at the paper. "This says that all the windows were replaced."

"Yes, ma'am. He said his daughter couldn't be without her car."

Astro pulls a bit to get closer to the man. He extends his hands and pets Astro's head.

"Thank you. Let me get you some money." I say.

"No need, ma'am. Everything has been paid for." He looks at his clipboard. "Where did this happen?"

"Panther Cove Elementary School."

"Are there security cameras?"

"Not where I park."

"Don't you park in the front of the school?"

"No."

"Park in the front of the school tomorrow." He says.

"I can't. There is not a ramp in the front of the school. The ramp is on the west side of the building."

The man looks at me. "How much do I owe you?"

"I am sorry."

"I know that you give money for my son to eat lunch."

I look at him. "I don't want the money. He does need to have better hygiene."

"I will work on it."

"Your son is my favorite student. His reading is getting better. He loves math. He does well when he is busy."

"That girl called my boy stupid."

"She will not be a problem any longer. Circumstances have caused her to be removed from the school." I say.

"Enjoy your evening." He says.

"Thanks."

"My name is Eric."

"Sebastian."

"Your name is Sebastian?" He asks. "Did your mom not like you?" He smiles.

"I was named for my dad. He passed away before I was born."

"I am sorry."

"Eric, you are doing a good job with your son. Daniel is doing well."

He walks over to his truck. Then he walks back. "You make a difference in his life. Thank you for all that you do." He bends and kisses me on the cheek. He pets Astro on the head and leaves.

A car pulls in my driveway before I can get back in the house. Mark jumps out of his car. "Are you causing trouble again?" He teases kissing me on the cheek.

"Always."

"Why was Eric here?"

"He was bringing me my car."

"What happened to your car?"

"Windows were smashed again."

"What do you mean again?" Mark asks.

"I am getting bit by every bitch mosquito out here. Come on in." When we go in the house, my phone rings. I answer it. "Hi Peter, thank you so much for fixing my car again."

"Eric brought it back already?"

"Yes. Thank you."

"Listen, we installed cameras in your car. So if it happens again, we will see who is doing it."

"I think I know who is doing it." I say.

"Who?" Mark says.

"You have someone with you?" Peter asks.

"My neighbor stopped by to check on me."

"I am glad you are not alone." Peter says.

"I live alone." I laugh, "Well with Astro. I thought you had a date with my mom."

"I am with her." He says.

"Thanks Peter."

"Sleep well, sweetheart." He says.

"Thanks, you too." I tell him. I click the phone off.

Mark sits at the table.

"Do you want some Swedish meatballs?"

"You still have some?"

"Yes."

"Yes." He says.

I make him a plate.

"Who do you think is smashing your car windows?"

"I think its Paul. He really doesn't like me."

"Why do you think it was him?"

"He came into the Bookstore Coffee Store with a woman who is not his wife. They ran in like they were teenagers on their first date trying to hide their PDA from the world. I saw them. I didn't watch them, I was doing other things. They were all over each other. Matt, my asshole twenty-three year old boss, made a big deal about it. When they were leaving hand-in-hand, Paul was looking around to see that he didn't know anyone. He saw me. He tried to duck his head and they left. When I left the store, my windows were broken."

"Are there cameras that overlook the parking lot?"

"Not from our store. The diner across the street caught it, but its really grainy.

"How many times has this happened?"

"Today makes five."

Mark eats.

"I have salad too if you want that."

"No, this is good." He says. He takes another bite. "Do you feel safe here?"

"Always." I say. "Nothing happens when the car is in the driveway. Its when I am at work or work."

"Why do you have so many jobs? I know this house has to be paid off."

"It was paid off when my mom owned it."

"So its not paid off now?"

"No. She was selling it. I gave her an offer and she accepted."

"She made you buy the house?"

I laugh. "Not really. I am paying off a mortgage. She didn't know it was me. When I made the offer for the house her real estate agent didn't know that mom and I have two different last names. Mom had told the agent that she wanted to meet the owner. The agent brought her here and surprise."

"How did yo have enough money to buy the house?" Mark asks.

"I have been working since I was seventeen years old. I worked at summer camps. I tutored in high school. I saved all the money I earned. My grandma would give me money for my birthdays and Christmas. I never needed anything because my mom and her boyfriends throughout the years made sure I had whatever I wanted and needed. I paid for the house in cash."

"Why do you have a mortgage?" He stands and goes to the sink and washes his plate.

"I did some renovations on the house. Mr. O'Conner did the bathrooms. All I had to do was get the materials. He changed the windows on the house so that I didn't have to do anything if and when a hurricane hits."

"How much do you owe on the mortgage?"

"Its down to ten thousand."

"Why didn't he do the kitchen? There is no way in hell you are reaching anything up here." He opens the cabinet doors above the stove. "Dishes?"

"They are my grandma's dishes. Too good to use on a day-to-day basis. I use them for the holidays."

"How do you reach them?"

"Savannah or Piper."

He looks at his watch. "Justin is working on a big case."

"Its ok. I will see him tomorrow. You too."

He looks around the kitchen. "I could renovate this for you. I could make it so that you can get to everything. The top cabinets could lower so that you can reach everything."

"Mark, you don't have to do that."

"Let me talk to my team. See what we can put together." He kisses me on the check close to my mouth. "You got my wheels turning." He walks to the door. "Come on Astro, lets go out." He says.

Astro jumps up and goes to the door. Mark walks outside and Astro trots next to him. He sniffs a bit and then does his thing. Mark opens the door and lets him in. He steps back inside and kisses me again on the side of my mouth.

"Sleep well." He says.

"Good night." I say.

I wake up in the morning earlier than usual and feed Astro first. While he is enjoying his breakfast, I make a cup of coffee and gather a few toys for Astro and a blanket. I put his leash on him and take him for a walk.

We go around the block. As my neighbors leave the neighborhood, they honk their horns and I wave to them.

An elderly lady honks and pulls the car to the curb. "Hi sweet girl." She says.

"Good Morning Ms. Conley."

"It seems as if we have new neighbors."

"Yes."

"Two men."

"Yes."

"Do you think they are together?"

I laugh. "No."

"How do you know?' She asks.

"Ms. Conley, Mark Case would be insulted that you don't remember him."

"Mark Case?"

"Yes. He and his brother Justin moved into the O'Conner house."

She laughs uncontrollably. "That's right. His brother's name is Justin Case." She laughs again.

A car blows the horn behind her. She looks in her mirror and smiles. She waves.

"Have a nice day, honey."

"You too." I tell her.

As she drives on she calls, "Tell your mom I send my love."

"I will." I say. I look at Astro. "Come on, I can't have you late for your first day of work."

I get to work and I go into the classroom. I set up Astro's blanket on the floor by the desk that I never use. Ms. Rowe comes in the room. She is a help and a snoop. Overall she is really nice.

"Good morning." She says.

"Good morning. I wanted to thank you for all your assistance while I was out."

"Oh sure. Don't mention it." She looks around. "You changed the room around."

"My friend. Sara's mom, Ginger moved stuff around yesterday."

She says nothing but turns the desk. She takes Astro's blanket from me and puts it under the desk. She puts his toys on the floor under the desk.

"Thank you." I say to her.

"Mr. Ricks called us all in for a meeting this morning."

"Shit. I didn't know."

"He didn't want you there." She says. "He told us about Ruby. He told us what she told Beth. Then he told all of us that he is appointing you to after school teacher and that Astro will be a new member of the staff."

We laugh when he wags his tail.

"He has opened it up that other teachers can bring their dogs or cats in as well." She pets Astro's head. "Mr. Smith went home and came back with his dog, Sparky."

Mr. Smith walks in my classroom through Ms. Rowe's room. He has Sparky with him. Astro and Sparky approach each other. He hands me a paper. "I will come for Astro every two hours."

"Thank you." I say. "Who is your friend?"

"This is Sparky." Mr. Smith says.

The dog jumps up in my lap and licks my face. "Hi." I say petting the dog.

"So it looks like Ricks hired both of us for after school." Mr. Smith says.

"He told me about the job yesterday and told me that I have until tomorrow to give an answer if I want it or not."

"Ricks isn't giving you an option." Mr. Smith says. "I was thinking that we can rotate the dogs. I teach outside most of the day. Sparky can stay out with me a lot of the time but not all day."

"Smith, I think that's a great idea." I say.

"I will take him during the day if you want." Ms. Rowe says. "Dogs are therapeutic. I am excited about this. It makes me want to go get a dog."

"I train dogs if you get one." Mr. Smith says. "Sparky, up." He says. The dog stands by his leg and they leave.

"I have to say, I am pretty excited about having the dogs here." Ms. Rowe says smiling.

I look at her and smile. "You should really tell him how you feel about him."

She swats at me. "Stop that."

"Don't beam too brightly, you will blind your children." I tease her.

She leaves and bumps into the wall. We both laugh.

Astro lays on his blanket and closes his eyes. I finish getting ready for the day before the children enter the room.

There is a knock on the door. I go to the door and let Mr. Ricks in. He comes in the room and sits on the floor with Astro. He pets Astro. He doesn't look at me when he talks. "I know I was giving you an option for the after school position yesterday, the truth is, I don't have anyone else. I need you to do this. I also hired Smith because he wouldn't have it any other way."

Astro throws himself on Mr. Ricks.

Mr. Ricks looks at me. "Apparently there is going to be construction going on in the front of the school."

I look at him. "What?"

"The front of the school is going to have some upgrades. One of your students' parent called the school board last night and reamed them out."

I smile to myself.

"The construction will start next week. And we are getting security cameras installed. Apparently the assistant DA called the school board and notified them about cars getting broken into."

I haven't said anything but now I do. "Ricks, you know who did it."

"I know. We don't evidence and we need to get it."

"He hates me."

"Tell me about it."

The bell rings and my heart leaps for joy.

"I will later." I tell him. "Astro, blanket." I say and he gets up and goes to the blanket. He lays with his toys.

"Let me know when I can have him." Mr. Ricks says. "I will let the kids in on my way out."

"Smith is going to take him every two hours or so. We are going to swap dogs."

"Sparky is trained as a therapy dog. Smith takes him to hospitals on the weekends."

"It's going to be a great day." I say.

The children run in the room. I turn the lights off and they all stop what they are doing. They go sit on the floor in a circle. Astro gets up from the blanket and goes in the middle of circle like he has done this a thousand times. I turn the lights back on.

"I have some news to tell you." I put my finger to my lips so they know not to talk. "Ruby is no longer in our class. Her mom and dad are moving and she is going to another school."

I expect Beth to cry. I was not expecting Daniel to drop his head in his lap and cry. Astro jumps up and goes to him. He sits in front of Daniel and puts his paw on his leg.

"She wasn't nice to you." Tristian says. "She was the meanest to you."

Daniel still cries. Beth hugs him and they both cry.

Brian gets up from where he is sitting and walks over to me. He puts his head on my shoulder and he cries.

"I know she wasn't nice. She's a bully, but she was really going through a lot in her life." Luna says. "Her mom and dad are divorcing."

When Luna shares the news, they all burst into tears. Astro goes to each one of them. He throws himself on John-Paul and that makes them all laugh.

Ms. Rowe sticks her head in the room. "There is an assembly for all of third grade in fifteen minutes. Mr. Ricks wants Astro to come too."

"Thank you." I say to her.

She leave the room.

"Ok everyone line up." I say.

"Who gets to walk Astro?" Sonny asks.

"I do." I tell them. I look at Astro. "Blanket." I say and he goes to the blanket and waits for me to put his leash on him. I look at my class. "Everyone who was assigned jobs yesterday, they apply today. Everyone, on Fridays from here on it, I will assign jobs for the week."

They all cheer.

"Ok, you know the rules." I say as we leave the room. I walk them to the cafeteria. We are the first class to get there. We sit in the front at the table that is assigned to us. I push my wheelchair to the head of the table and sit with my students. I click my fingers and Astro lays at my feet.

John-Paul clicks his fingers and Astro sits up. I smile at John-Paul. I point at the floor and Astro lays back down.

Mr. Smith walks in the cafeteria with Sparky and the kids cheer. He sits at the table assigned for Ms. Rowe. When she walks in the cafeteria with her students she glows. I smile at her as she walks past us.

The rest of the third grade files in. As the kids see the dogs they get excited.

Mr. Ricks takes the microphone in his hands. "Ok I have a couple announcements to make. We are going to have two new mascots at our school. Astro and Sparky. I am going to say this one time so please make sure you are paying attention. No one! Let me repeat. No one is to command the dogs without approval."

Chapter 8

When I get home, it is late. I am tired. I have been up since five in the morning and now its past midnight. I have worked all my jobs in one day. I started with my children teaching, then I did after school training so that I can start tomorrow. I have done the training for two weeks. I followed that by tutoring two children until seven thirty, and then I went to the bookstore.

I open the door to my house and Astro runs in and jumps on the couch where he stays for the rest of the night. I am hungry, but I don't have anything that doesn't require cooking. I don't even have yogurt. I open the freezer and there is all that ice cream my mom brought, but I can't force myself to eat it.

I have been working the same schedule for two weeks now. Astro is with me all day long, unless he is outside for physical education with Coach Smith. I feel really good about all the things I am doing.

I haven't spoken to Justin in weeks. I don't have time for that. I turn the lights off. I go over by the couch and hug Astro. "I love you." I tell him.

I climb in my bed. I close my eyes and sink into the mattress. I am so tired. I left my phone in my purse in the kitchen. I didn't set an alarm before I went to bed. By the time I got into bed it was one thirty in the morning. I am supposed to get up at five thirty to get ready for work.

Five thirty comes and I don't get wake up. Astro is sleeping on the couch. He is just as exhausted as I am.

I don't hear the knocking on my front door. Astro does. He jumps off the couch and starts his loud barking. I open my eyes. I lay in my bed listening for a moment before I hear the pounding on the door.

"Sebastian!" Someone is yelling. "Sebastian are you alright?"

I get in my wheelchair and go to the door. I open it. Justin takes me in his arms. He is dressed in a suit for work. He looks so handsome. The gray suit makes his hazel eyes pop. He hugs me and I close my eyes.

I open my eyes and my eyes hurt. I look at my watch. It reads three. I look at it again. That can't be right. I have missed work. I go to sit up but I feel so weak. I hear someone typing. I look around my room.

"Piper?" I say in a whisper.

"Its about time you joined the land of the living." She says. She jumps up from my desk and goes to get water. "If you didn't wake up today, we were going to take you to the hospital." She says.

"How long—"

"Its Saturday." She says.

I sit up even though it hurts. I take a drink of water. "Saturday?"

"We have all been rotating taking care of you and Astro."

"I need to take a shower." I tell her.

"I will make you something to eat."

"I have to call work."

"Honey, it's Saturday. Mr. Ricks knows that you are ill. And the bookstore employees know too."

I go in the bathroom and I take a shower. I let the water run on my body. It feels so good. I open the shower door and Justin stands in front of me holding the towel. He wraps me in the towel and kisses me.

"You have to stop doing that to me." He kisses me again. "Do you need help getting dressed?" He asks.

I smile. "No. I can manage." I tell him.

"I will wait for you in the kitchen." Justin says.

"I will be right there." I get in my wheelchair and go into my room. I put shorts on and t-shirt. I pull my hair into a messy bun. I open my bedroom door and to my surprise my house is full of people.

Sebastian takes me in his arms and holds me tight as only a brother could. When he lets me go, Mark takes me in his arms.

Peter hugs me next. "You gave us a scare." He says. "How are you feeling?"

"I am starving." I say.

Mom looks at me. "I made a lot of food for you. Your refrigerator was empty. You didn't even have yogurt."

I laugh at her. "I normally go shopping on Wednesdays after work, but when I got to the store, it was surrounded by police. I didn't want to go in and I had Astro with me."

Savannah hugs me. "All your mail is in the drawer." She hugs me again.

I look at my dining room table and see children sitting around it. Sara looks over and jumps up. She runs over and hugs me.

"I am glad you are ok." She says.

"Its nice to see you." I tell her.

Her sisters walk over and hug me too.

Daniel is also sitting at my table. I go over to him and he hugs me. "My dad will be here to get me after work." He says.

Before I can ask anything, Peter sits at the table. "I watch Daniel for Eric on the weekends." He says. "I hope you don't mind that I brought him here."

"Of course not." I say.

Piper puts a plate of food on the table for me. I eat some. She puts a bottle of water in front of me. I drink the whole bottle.

Ginger walks over and puts her hand on my forehead. "The fever is gone." She says. "We should leave her."

"No. Stay. All of you. It's nice to see everyone."

"We have been watching movies." Sara says.

"What have you been watching?" I ask.

"Disney movies. You have a lot of them."

"I like them." I tell Sara.

"Can we watch Spider-Man?" Danial asks.

"Of course." I say.

Justin puts Spider-Man on and everyone sits around the room and watches the movie. Daniel sits on the floor with Astro. Bob Cat jumps up on my lap. I look at Justin and smile.

Mark looks at me. "Don't get attached to my cat."

I laugh.

There is a knock on the door. Savannah goes to the door and opens it. Eric stands there with grocery bags full of food. Savannah steps aside and he walks in the kitchen. Eric looks at the television. He puts the groceries away. Then he joins all of us.

"Danny, we have to go."

"Do we have to?" He asks.

"We really do."

"I want to stay."

I look at Daniel. "You can come back any time."

"Really?"

"Yes." Peter says. "I will bring you."

Eric looks at Peter. "Thanks for watching him. I can't tell you what a help it has been."

Daniel goes over by the table and takes a picture out of his backpack. He walks over and hands it to me. "I did this for you." He says.

I look at the picture. Its of me and Astro.

Sara looks at the picture. "That is really good." She says "You should submit that to the art show." She hugs Daniel.

He smiles. Eric takes his hand and they leave.

After they leave, little by little everyone leaves. Ginger is the next one to go with the three girls. My mom and Peter leave shortly after them.

Piper kisses me on the cheek. "I love you. If you need anything, please call me."

"Thanks." I hug her.

"You scared the hell out of all of us. You really have to stop doing that. You need to work less." She tugs my hair at the back of my head. "Love you."

"Love you too." I tell her.

Mark and Savannah sit close to each other. They are on the couch with Astro laying next to them. Bob Cat is on the back of the couch sleeping.

Justin sits at the table with his laptop. He is working. I sit on the couch and fall asleep.

When I wake up in the morning, I am in my bed and Justin is sleeping with me. He doesn't have a shirt on and I take in the sight of him. I want to run my hand up and down his chest and lower, but I don't. I just lay watching him sleep.

He opens his eyes. "Good morning." He says.

"Good morning."

"Like what you see?" He asks.

"I do." I smile.

He kisses me. "What's on your mind?"

"You are." I tell him. I reach my hand up and touch his face. I feel the five o'clock shadow on his face. I move my hand down his neck. His Adam's apple bobs in his throat. I press my hand against his chest and can feel his heat beating under my palm. "You are always on my mind."

"You know, while you were scaring the shit out of all the people who know and love you, Savannah and Piper were chatting about when we were all young. Savannah was talking about the party that she had when she was fourteen which would have made me fifteen or sixteen. She remembers me kissing you."

"She says that, but I know every boy I ever kissed and I don't remember kissing you. She swears that we did."

Bob Cat jumps on the bed and lays on Justin's chest. He kneads with his paws. He purrs loudly.

"She said that she has pictures of us kissing." Justin says.

"She has always said that too but she has never showed them to me. Not one time. Piper hasn't even seen them."

"That's what Piper said." He kisses me. "She really took a liking to Eric."

"Daniel's dad." I say. I smile. "It was strange and great to wake up to a house full of people. Usually its just Savanah and Piper. Every once in a while some of my sorority sisters come if they are in town."

Bob Cat stands and walks in a circle before he goes right back to where he just got up from. He starts the kneading all over again. Justin rubs the cat's head.

"I think I need to go to the doctor." I say.

Justin looks at me.

"I keep losing days of my life. I sleep right through them."

"Sebastian, you don't need a doctor. You need to stop working as hard as you do. You are exhausted.

"What did you do when I fell asleep in your arms?" I ask him.

"I held you in my arms for hours." He kisses my cheek. "I ran my fingers through your hair." He laughs. "I called Mark to come over because I thought that Astro had died."

"What?"

"He was on the couch sleeping. He never moved for two full days. He didn't eat anything. He didn't drink anything. He never moved off the couch. And he was on his back with feet in the air. We thought the worst."

"What made him get up?"

"Ms. Conley drove by and blew the horn. She yelled out the window that she came bearing treats."

I laugh. "That sounds like her."

"Did you know that she thought that Mark and I were—" he laughs.

"A couple?" I ask. I laugh. "She asked me when I saw her. She was excited that we have new neighbors but she was curious to know if you were a gay couple. She has high hopes that a same sex couple will move into the neighborhood."

"What is that all about?"

"Her son is gay. Her daughter dresses like a guy. Her granddaughter doesn't identify female or male."

"How old is she?"

"Twelve."

"Who is the parent?"

"Her daughter is the mom."

"Why don't they move into the neighborhood?"

"Oh my god, Justin, they couldn't wait to get out of the neighborhood. Her son lives in Delray Beach and her daughter lives in SouthWest Ranches. The granddaughter wants to be a cowboy."

"Ok." Justin says.

~~~~~~~~~

I get back into the routine of my life. I have worked all day at the school and now I get in my car which is parked in the front of the school in a well-lit parking lot. Astro gets in the backseat. I stop at a drive-thru on my way to the bookstore.

When I get to the parking lot, I take Astro to the grassy area and he does his business. I pick up his mess and discard it in the waste can. We go inside and I put his food down for him and a bowl of water.

The security guys walk over to me and hug me. The store is full of people. Its an open-mic night for poetry. As people ramble on badly composed poems, I sit at the coffee counter and grade papers. When people come over, I make them coffee.

The chimes ring as the door opens. I look up to see Sebastian coming in with two guys. They look similar to him but not exactly like him. He walks over to me and hugs me.

"Ashley, these are my brothers." He says. "This is Jacob and Seth."

"Its nice to meet both of you." I say I am getting used to him calling me Ashley, Its growing on me.

Jacob looks at me. "She looks like you." He says.

"She's my sister. We have the same dad." He says. He listens to a woman shouting in the mic. "What the hell is that?" He asks.

"Awful." I say.

"That's a great dog. People can bring their dogs here?" Seth asks.

"Its my dog." I click my fingers and Astro trots over to me. "Astro sit."

"His name is Astro?" Jacob asks.

"Yes." I say.

"That's the name of Sebastian's cat."

I look at Sebastian. I smile.

He smiles. "Space cadet didn't fit him at the time."

We all laugh.

"Can I get you anything to drink or eat?" I ask them.

"No." They say almost together.

"What time do you get off work?' Sebastian asks me.

"Two-thirty." I tell him.

"What time do you get off work tomorrow?"

"It's a half day of school. I get out of work at four."

"That's a half day?" Jacob asks.

"I am a teacher and I cover after school too."

"You work three jobs?" Seth asks. He looks at Sebastian. "That's wrong." He looks back at me. "When do you have fun?"

"My work is fun."

We all laugh because someone is reciting a poem that he meant to be serious. The whole store is laughing. It makes me feel bad for the guy who just poured his heart out.

Someone shouts, "Put that to melancholy music and you got yourself a country hit."

More people laugh. There is a commotion and the security guards usher three guys out of the place.

Seth and Sebastian walk outside. Sebastian takes Astro with them. Astro sniffs almost every blade of grass. Seth looks at Sebastian.

"How long have you known that we have a sister?"

Sebastian looks at his younger brother. "I just found out about her."

"Why didn't we know about her?" Seth asks. "She works three jobs. That is crazy."

Sebastian looks at his brother. "I am working on a plan so that she wouldn't have to work, unless she wanted to."

"I thought that your grandma is loaded. Did she know about Ashley?"

"Her name is Sebastian."

"No shit! She has the same name as you. Sebastian Ashley Timely? That is so great."

Sebastian again looks at his younger brother. "You said we have a sister?"

"Anything that is yours is ours too. We always wanted a sister."

Astro barks at a dog approaching. He wags his tail. The other dog doesn't. The other dog shows his teeth. Sebastian and Seth stand on either side of Astro boxing him in. The other dog lunges at Astro. Astro barks but still wags his tail.

I walk out of the store. I look at the guy walking the aggressive dog. Its Paul. Security comes out of the store behind me. One of them stands in front of Paul and his dog. He looks at Sebastian and Seth. "Take them inside."

The alarm on my car starts going off as we hear glass breaking. The security guard takes control of my wheelchair and pushes me in the store.

"That's my car." I say.

"We know."

"I don't have time for this shit." I throw my hands up and slap them down hard on my legs.

Jacob comes and stands next to me. "What's going on?" He asks. He looks at the wall behind the front desk where there are employee pictures hanging on the wall. He reads the name under my picture. "Your name is Sebastian?"

"Yes." I say.

A noise sounds that the back door of the store has opened. Astro comes running over to me and jumps up with his front paws on my shoulders. He puts his head over my shoulder like he is hugging me.

"Its ok. We are ok." I tell him. "Get a drink." I click and point to the bowl. He jumps down and gets a drink.

"Your name is Sebastian?" Jacob asks again.

"Yes." I say again.

"My brother called you Ashley."

"That's my middle name." My cell phone rings. It's a number that I don't know but I answer it anyway. "Hello."

"Sebastian, its Eric. Why is your alarm going off in your car?"

"How do you know that?" I ask.

"Peter set it up that he would get notified. He called me because he is out with your mom."

"Someone smashed my windows again."

"I will be right there." He says and hangs up.

I put my phone on the counter. I look at Jacob. "My name is Sebastian Ashley Timely. I was named after my father."

"Did you know about us?"

"No."

"What do you want from my brother?"

"Nothing." I say honestly. "What do you think I want from him?"

Jacob looks at me. He is like a little bulldog he doesn't back down. "How did you find out about him?"

"I got a traffic ticket and I was taken into a room and interrogated for hours. I was told over and over that I didn't fit the description of the person who robbed a bank."

A lady walks over with a big stack of books. "The self checkout doesn't work. Can someone help me?" She looks at Jacob.

"I will ring you up." I tell her. I go behind the counter and get the scanner. "Are you paying with cash or card?"

"What's ever easiest." She says. She looks at me. "You are one of the teachers at Panther Cove?"

"I am." I tell her.

"What the hell are you doing here this late?"

I smile at her.

"You tutor my nephew and he was telling my husband and I that he needs a dog because its easy to read to a dog."

I smile at her.

"Your dog is a big hit at the school. So is the little dog that coaches PE."

I laugh. "Mr. Smith coaches PE. His dog Sparky is a big hit. We both teach all day and then cover after school care. Its long days for our dogs to be alone. There is a cat who has taken up residency in the library."

"That is really great. My nephew was telling my husband and I that the principal quit."

"He was reassigned." I tell her. I take the cash she gives me for her purchase. I give her change back and a flyer for upcoming events.

"My nephew loves you."

"That's nice to hear." I say. "Enjoy your day." When she leaves I look at Jacob. "What is it that you are accusing me of wanting from your brother?"

"Anyone can be a gold digger." He says.

I push past him and go into the bathroom. When the next person starts shouting into the microphone, I scream as loud as I can. There is a knock on the door.

"Someone is in here." I say.

When I come out of the bathroom, I am happy to see Brady. He is the next one on shift. He looks at me. "There are police all around your car. It's a crime scene again."

"Wonderful." I say. "I guess I am walking home."

Brady looks at me. "You are going to walk home?"

"I live down the street." I tell Brady.

Eric walks in. "Are you done?" He asks me.

"I have to clock out." I say.

"I will drive you home."

I look around for Sebastian and his brothers. They are no where to be seen. I clock out. I gather my stuff and Astro. Before I leave, I go over to Brady. "Did you bring earphones with you?"

He laughs. "When does this end?"

"Whenever you want to shut it down."

Brady laughs again. "You know what's funny about this?"

"No alcohol."

We both laugh.

Brady looks at me. "Do you know the guy who is offering you a ride home?"

I look at Brady and smile. "I do. Thank you."

"You want one of the security guys to take you? That would make me feel better." He bends and scratches Astro's head and ears. "The guy who hired the security guards was in here?"

"What are you talking about?"

"The guy that was here with the two other guys."

"Brady, there are a lot of guys here."

"The one that was outside with Astro when I got here."

"Sebastian."

"What?"

"His name is Sebastian." I say.

"He is the one who hired the security detail so that you are protected while you are here."

"Thanks for the information." I give him a hug. "I suggest you kill the entertainment sooner than later. I think I let it go on too long."

Eric lifts me out of my wheelchair and into his truck. He puts my wheelchair in the bed of the truck. He helps Astro in the truck. He drives me home and takes Astro out first.

"You can let him roam." I say. "He will do is business and then we can go to bed when we go in the house."

Eric takes my wheelchair out of the bed of the truck. He puts it on the driveway and then he lifts me in his arms and puts me in my wheelchair. "Need anything?"

"No. Thank you again."

"What time do you leave for work?"

"Seven thirty."

"I will have your car in the driveway. I will leave the keys in the car. You have a spare set?"

"I do." I tell him.

"There is great footage of who smashed your car windows. The police told me I can't tell you who it is." Eric says.

"Thanks." I hug him.

He hugs me tight. "Sleep well." He waits to leave. He watched Astro and I go in the house. I turn the lights off. He drives away.

I take a shower and put a tank top on with matching shorts. I finish grading papers. I put all the stuff in my bag for the next day. I go through the mail. I throw out the junk mail. I put the bills that I have to pay next month in the drawer.

I turn the lights out in the kitchen and go into my room. I get into my bed and set the alarm. I put the phone on the night stand. I lay in bed and Astro jumps on the bed with me. I hug him and we both fall asleep.

I read to my class The Water Horse. Sparky sits on a chair like he is one of the students. All of them are excited about the book. When I finish reading it, I give them a comprehension test. They all do really well on it.

The bell rings at twelve thirty indicating that the day is over. "Ok everyone, get your stuff together. When the second bell rings, you can all go."

"I wish that everyday was like today." Tyler says.

"What does that mean?"

"We got so much done." He says.

"I wish that everyday were like this too." Addison says. "I get to go be with my mom for the rest of the day."

John-Paul, Daniel and Brian sit on the floor. The three of them go to after school care. Beth, Lizzie and Luna sit on the floor too. When the bell rings all the children leave the room.

The six that are in after school care, line up at the door. Sparky lines up with them. I laugh. "Stay together. You can go to the cafeteria. I will be right there." I tell them.

I go into the cafeteria. There is a guy dressed like a clown juggling. I roll my eyes. The entertainment is here. To his credit he is very entertaining. The kids love him. Surprisingly his show is long. He picks kids at random to help him with tricks.

The children leave at five. We all help clean up. Then I get Astro and we leave.

I go home first. I usually don't do that, but I have time before I have to be at the bookstore. I feed Astro. Then I take him a for a long walk. I bring him back in the house.

I sit at the table and I grade papers. I then go through the mail. I open an envelope. I have a returned check for my mortgage.

"What the fuck?" I ask to no one. I get my phone and I call the bank. I wait through all the automated crap before a person actually is available to talk to me. "Hi my name is Sebastian Timely and I am calling because I just received a returned check in the mail."

"Ms. Timely. Do you have the account number."

I give her the account number.

"Let me look into this for you." She says. "I am going to put you on a quick hold."

"Great." I say. I put the phone on the table and make a second cup of iced coffee.

"Ms. Timely?"

"Yes."

"You said that you received a returned check?"

"Yes. I wrote a check like I always do for my mortgage and I got it back."

"That's correct."

"Was there something wrong with the check?"

"You over paid." She says.

"I owe ten thousand."

"No. You over paid." She pauses. "Is there anything else I can help you with?"

"No. Thank you."

"Have a nice day."

"You as well." I answer her. I look at the check again. I open another envelope. I take the check out and look at it. "I know I didn't overpay my insurance." I look at Astro. "What the fuck is going on here?" I open the others and there are return payments for my car as well.

I go in my room and change my clothes. I put on a business dress. I do my hair. I fix my makeup. I leave my room and grab my purse.

Astro jumps up.

"No, sweetheart, you have to stay for now." I kiss the top of his head. "I will be back. I love you." I leave my house, get in my car and drive away.

I park my car at the bank and go in as fast as I can. Amanda comes into the lobby. She looks at me and notices that I look mad. "Are you ok?" She asks.

"Is he here?"

"No. He is at our other location today."

"Where is that?" I ask.

"Palm Beach." She says.

I look at my watch.

"Can I help you with anything?"

"No." I snap at her.

"I will tell him that you came."

"Please do." I turn and leave. I go to my car. I turn back and go back into the bank. "Where in Palm Beach?"

"Okeechobee boulevard."

"Can you give me directions?" I ask her.

The door opens and she looks past me to see who has entered. Its Sebastian. He looks at her and then at me. "Directions to what?" He asks.

I turn around. I am mad and he sees it.

"Come talk to me." He says and pushes my wheelchair into his office and closes the door. "How are you?"

"I am mad."

"I see that." He says. "Why are you mad?"

"Last night your brother said something and I have been wracking my brain trying to figure out what he meant. I couldn't think of anything."

"Which brother?"

"Jacob."

"What did he say?"

I ignore him and finish my train of thought. "Then I got home early from work and I don't have to tutor or be at the bookstore today. So I went through my mail." I glare at him. "How did you know I had a mortgage?"

"I don't know what you are talking about. And what did Jacob say to you?" He stands up and walks around his desk and sits closer to me. "Why would you have a mortgage if you live in the house that you grew up in?"

"I bought it from my mom." I say absently.

"Your mom made you buy the house from her?" He is angry now.

I blink a few times. "No. Yes. No."

"Which is it?"

"Overall yes. But she put the house up for sale. The real estate agent didn't know that my mom and I have different last names. I made an offer on the house. I paid cash."

"Why do you have a mortgage?"

"I took out a mortgage to do renovations."

"The house wasn't always the way it is now?"

"No."

"Why are you so mad? What did Jacob say to you?"

"I am new in your life. I don't want to ruin your relationship with your brother." I say.

"Ashley!" He yells. "Tell me." He rakes his fingers through his hair. "What did he say to you?"

"I have to go."

"No." Sebastian's yells at me. He walks back to the desk and gets his phone. He dials Jacob's number. He puts the call on speaker.

Jacob answers right away. "I am in a meeting. Can I call you back?"

"Make it quick." Sebastian yells at him.

"Are you alright?"

"Not really."

We hear Jacob talking to people but can't make out what he is saying. "What's going on?"

"What did you say to Ashley last night?"

"We were just talking." Jacob says.

"What were you talking about?"

I go to the door to leave the office. Sebastian crosses the room in record time to stop me. He looks at me and sees tears in my eyes.

"What did you say to her?"

"Why are you asking me this?"

"I want to know."

"Did she run to you and tell you that I called her a gold digger?"

Tears run down my cheeks.

"You did what?" He yells so loud.

Jacob lowers his voice. "She didn't tell you?"

"No." Sebastian says. "She didn't tell me. Why would you do that?"

"Where did she come from? She obviously wants your money."

I can't stop the sob from escaping. "I don't want anything from you." I say to Sebastian.

"She is with you?" Jacob yells into the phone.

"Yes." Sebastian says.

I push the door open and leave as fast as I can. A customer is walking in the bank as I am ready to leave so I run out. I get to my car and I fumble with the keys. I drop them. I unhinge my armrest so that I can lean over to get them, but I can't reach them because they went under my car.

Sebastian runs over and takes me in his arms. He reaches the keys and hands them to me. He then takes me in his arms again. "Come back inside with me." He says.

"I have to go." I tell him.

"Please."

"I didn't know that you existed. I didn't know anything about you."

"I know." He says.

"I don't want anything from you."

"Come talk to me." He stands up and takes my hand. He walks back in the bank with me.

Amanda looks up from her desk. "Is everything alright?"

"Cancel my meetings for the rest of the day." Sebastian says. He walks into his office and closes the door. He walks over to the window that overlooks a canal. He sits down and looks at me.

We sit in silence for a while. The clock is ticking from the wall across the office. We can hear birds chirping outside. Sebastian taps his heals on the floor. Neither of us say anything.

~~~~~~~~~~~~~~~

Justin leaves work and goes to the grocery store. He quickly goes around picking up things for dinner. He gets flowers and dessert. He leaves and drives to the neighborhood. He parks the car in my driveway.

He notices a different car in my driveway. He takes the groceries from the car and comes to the door. He knocks. When I open the door, he bends and kisses me.

"Where is your car?"

"Someone slashed the tires on it when I was at the bank with Sebastian." I say.

"Are you kidding?"

"No." I say.

"Whose car is in your driveway?"

"Peter gave me a loaner car."

Justin looks at me. "Is it adapted for you?"

"No."

"How the hell are you supposed to drive it?" He goes in the kitchen and starts pulling food out of bags. He opens the cabinet next to the stove and takes a frying pan out.

"Eric will be here to take me to work tomorrow. He is going to drive that car. Everyone has a plan."

He kisses me. "Did you have a nice day?"

I tell him about my day. We eat the meal he made for us. We take Astro outside. When we get back to my house, my mom's car is in the driveway. She jumps out of the car when she sees us coming up the walk. She takes me in her arms.

She looks at Justin and smiles. When she sees him she recognizes him. She hugs him.

"This is the one that you kissed when you were fourteen." She says.

We both look at her and then each other.

"I have the picture to prove it." She says.

"Mom, I have all the pictures from my childhood, I don't remember the picture of me kissing anyone."

"I have it." She says. "Savannah has the other picture."

Chapter 9

Halloween is coming soon, I decorate my house with Halloween decorations. My favorite is the witch's cauldron. Mark and Justin came to hang the pumpkin and bat lights over the front door.

My grandma is planning on coming in the middle of October for a visit. She is going to stay through the holidays. We have been communicating a lot more than we have in years. She told me that she was the one who paid off car, my car insurance and also my mortgage.

She told me that there was a trust that was left to me from my dad. She told me that she would tell me more about it when we were all together.

As I get ready for work, my phone rings. I answer it and put it on speaker so that I can do more than one thing at a time. I am really good at multitasking. "Hello."

"Hi sweetheart, its grandma." She always says like I don't know who is calling me.

"Hi grandma."

"I wanted to tell you that I will be arriving earlier than I thought. I am going to stay with Sebastian for a week." I can almost hear her smile through the phone.

"Great." I say.

"Have you spoken to each other?"

"No."

"How long has it been?"

"A couple of weeks."

"When I come, I want to have dinner with both of you."

"I will be there." I tell her. "I have to go, I am getting ready for work."

"Sweetheart, you don't have to work."

"Yes I do. I love my kids."

"They are germs on legs." She says.

I laugh. "I love you."

"I love you too."

I gather my stuff and go out to the car. I put everything in the car and then go back in the house for Astro. We are having an assembly. Its going to be a fun day of school. When I get to the school, Mr. Ricks meets me and gets the stuff out of the car for me.

"Just so you know, I have you assigned to the guest."

I look at him. "Ok."

"Ms. Rowe is going to cover your class until the assembly is over."

"I was going to read to them before we go."

"Our guest will be arriving soon." Mr. Ricks says.

I know that we are having an assembly on careers. It is to encourage the students about what they want to be when they grow up.

Mr. Ricks takes Astro. My big fluffy dog walks the halls like he lives here. He loves going to school with me. The children all love him. The staff all love him as well.

Mr. Smith walks over with Sparky. The two dogs greet each other and stand nose to nose like they are carrying on a conversation. The three of us laugh as we go into the school.

Mark is standing against the wall. He hugs me when he sees me. Justin is standing next to him. He looks so handsome in a suit and tie. The colors in his tie make his eyes darker. Justin kisses me on the lips.

Mr. Ricks clears his throat and we all laugh.

Twix is standing against the wall. Her bright pink hair makes her stand out, but her uniform is what makes me stare at her. She hugs me. She is standing next to two male police officers. Next to them are four firefighters and paramedics.

I go into my classroom and lock up my purse in the desk. Ms. Rowe comes in my room. "Your room looks like a not so haunted house. It looks amazing. I have bats hanging from the ceiling. That's all I did."

"I am jealous. I don't have decorations hanging from the ceiling."

"Leave what you want and Smith will hang them."

"I don't want to bother him."

He walks in the room. He kisses Ms. Rowe. "Karen." He says and kisses her again.

"Parker." She says.

Sparky and Astro lay on the bean-bag chair.

Mr. Smith looks at me. "You know who all the speakers are?" He asks.

I look at him. "Ginger, Sara's mom. There are a couple doctors. A dentist. A lawyer. Firefighters and paramedics." I say.

"A banker." He says. "Have you spoken to Sebastian?"

"Not in a couple of weeks." I say sadly.

"Has he tried to reach out to you?" Karen asks me.

"I have been busy." I say. "I work here all day. I leave here and tutor, and then I am at the all night bookstore."

"Why do you work so hard?" Mr. Smith asks.

"How do you have time to look so good?" Ms. Rowe asks.

My cell phone rings. I answer it. I click it off. I go up to the office. I go into the offie as I was told to. When I get up there Jacob is standing in front of me.

"I work here." I tell him.

"I know you do."

"Please don't bring my personal life to my work."

"I need to talk to you."

"I am working." I tell him.

"Your security guards won't let me come in the bookstore."

"Talk to your brother about it, he hired them." I look at Mr. Ricks, "What time are we getting started?"

"We are going to get started at ten."

Jacob sits on the bench. I look at Mr. Ricks and Jacob. I feel myself getting sick. I can feel bile in my throat. I start to sweat.

I look at Mr. Ricks. "I am going to be sick. I think I caught what Tyler had." I say.

"Whatever you need." Mr. Ricks says.

I rush into the bathroom and lose my breakfast. There is a knock on the door. Justin doesn't give me a chance to let him in, he barges in the bathroom.

"Sebastian? What is going on?"

"I just don't feel well." I tell him.

"What can I do?"

"I am not sure." I say.

I sit in the back of the cafeteria half listening to the speakers talk about their careers. When its all over, I take my class back into the room. When we go back in the room, I give them a math assignment. I give them busy work. I usually don't do that. I usually work with them on most of the activities they do during the day.

When I take them outside for recess, I let them play whatever they want. I keep an eye on them so that no one gets hurt. When we go back in the classroom, its almost time to leave for the day.

I am the teacher who is running the after school care for the day. We take turns calling attendance and running activities. I am really in no mood at all. Mr. Smith comes by just before the bells ring.

"I have talked to Ricks and I am going to take over after school care today. We will just switch it out."

"Thank you." I tell him.

"Are you alright?"

"I have a lot on my mind." I tell him. "I feel like I need to be anywhere but here."

The bells ring and the children leave the room. The six that go to after school care stay and clean up the room. I forgot to have my class clean up after themselves today.

Daniel walks over and hugs me. "I am sorry you are sad." He says.

"I am just having a bad day." I tell him.

"The assembly was really neat."

"I know." I look at him. "What did you like the best?"

"The firefighters."

"Firefighters are exciting."

"They are brave."

"They are brave." I clean up Astro's toys. "What else did you like?"

"The dentist was cool. He brought that big tooth with him. Sharks have big teeth."

"Sharks do have a lot of big teeth." I look around the room. "Its good enough." I tell them. "Lets go to the cafeteria."

They leave the room and I turn the lights off. Astro stays with me. I take him over to the designated area that Mr. Ricks allow the dogs to use. He does his thing. We go into the cafeteria. They run over to the group that they need to be in.

Mr. Ricks walks over to me. "We have decided that you are going to stay up here and check the children out when their parents come."

"Oh thank you."

"There is no school for the next three days. I hope that you will go home and rest."

"I will be better next week."

He kisses the top of my head. Then he leaves the school.

The last child is signed out at seven thirty. Some of the parents got caught up in a traffic jam. They called to let us know about the accident that was keeping them from getting to the school on time.

After the last child, leaves, we clean up the cafeteria. The janitors come and they mop the floors and clean the bathrooms. I go back into my classroom before leaving and grade papers so that I don't have to bring anything home with me. Mr. Smith stays in the room with me.

"Who was the guy who came to see you this morning?" He asks. He sits on the floor with the two dogs. "Is that your boyfriend?"

I look at him. "I am dating Justin Case."

He nods his head. "So who was that guy?"

I pinch the bridge of my nose. "The guy who came this morning is my brother's brother. He thinks that I am a gold digger."

Parker Smith jumps up from the floor and sits at the table with me.

"Does he know that you work non-stop?"

"Yes." I say.

"Does your brother know?"

"He does."

"What does he say?"

"We haven't spoken in a while. Now my grandma is coming and she wants to have all of us together. I don't know if I want to do that."

Parker takes half the stack of papers that need to be put in the folders for each child. He puts their graded works in the folders. "Do you want them on their desks?"

"Oh you don't have to do that." I tell him.

"I am not leaving until you do. So lets get out of here." He says. "Let me help."

Twenty minutes later I finish up what needed to be done. For the first time in a long time, I am not taking anything home with me to work on. Before we walk out of the room, Parker takes the basket of books. He quickly puts them in order.

I look at him.

He laughs. "My mother is a librarian. She always made my sisters and I organize our books."

"Why didn't she come for the assembly?"

"She was supposed to come but my youngest sister is having a baby. It was more important for my mom to be with her." He says. He looks around the room before we leave. "Oh where are your hanging Halloween decorations?"

"I think Karen took them."

"Why?"

"So she could ask you to hang them in the morning."

He goes in her room. He finds the Rubbermaid box with my name on it. He brings it back into my room and he opens it. He hangs all of the ghosts and bats. He hangs the big pumpkin too. And the last thing he does is secures the scarecrow by the reading center.

"Thank you." I say to him.

We finally leave. He walks me to my car and I get in it. He is parked directly across the lot from me. When I get in the car, I send Mr. Ricks a text message stating that I have left the school.

When I get home I see a car on the street. I pull into the driveway and get out. I get Astro out. He trots over to his favorite spots and sniffs around. I watch him. Then I unlock the door from my phone and I go into the house. I close the door and go in the kitchen to give Astro water.

"I feel like we never eat at home anymore." I tell him.

He barks.

"I am glad you agree." I say and hug him. "Drink." I point to the water bowl. I go in my room and take off my clothes. I put on a tank top and shorts. I pull my hair into a messy bun. I go back in the kitchen. I sit at the table going through my mail.

There is a knock on the front door. Astro jumps up and walks with me to the front door. I open it. Justin hugs me.

"Are you mad at me?" He asks.

I stay in his arms as long as he holds me. He pulls back and looks at me. I look up at him.

"Just making sure you didn't pass out again." He teases.

I laugh. "I am tired but not exhausted."

"Why are you home so late?"

"I don't work for the next couple of days and Astro and I are going to the stay in a condo at the beach."

"Can I come?"

"If you want to come."

"I want you to come." He says.

I look at him. "Are you sex talking?" I laugh.

Justin kisses me. "I want you." He sits on the couch and holds his hands out to me.

I get on the couch with him and we start kissing. He runs his hands up my torso. He cups breasts. He kisses me deeper than he has before.

I close my eyes and before I know it, I fall asleep.

In the morning I wake up in my bed. I open my eyes and I am alone. Astro isn't even in bed with me. I stretch my arms above my head. I put my hands over my face and scream.

Justin comes running in the room. He climbs into bed with me. He kisses my hands that are still covering my face.

"Come out. Come out, where ever you are." He says.

"I thought you were gone." I say with my hands over my face.

"I took the day off." He says kissing my fingers. "You are prettier when I can see you without your hands over your face. Is this a knew look for you?"

I lower my hands.

"Oh welcome back." He says.

I laugh.

"Why did you scream?"

"I thought that I did it again."

"We didn't do anything."

I swat at him. He laughs at me.

"Astro was whining to go outside. I took him out. He dragged me to my house so that he could see the fucking cat."

"Bob!" I say.

"What?"

"Not the fucking cat. Bob Cat."

At the mention of his name he jumps up on the bed. He lays on my chest and I pet him. Astro jumps on the bed and puts his head on Justin's shoulder.

"I can't make love to you with a crowded bed." Justin says.

I laugh.

"What time do you have to check in?" He asks.

"Oh it's whenever I get there. I have a timeshare. I have the keys. Whenever I get there."

"You amaze me."

I pack clothes in a small suitcase. When I am ready, I get Astro's toys and the stuff that I will need for him. Then I load up the car. Justin's car is behind my car. He is going to follow me.

We will have today and tonight alone, but then tomorrow Savannah and Piper are going to join us. I sent them text messages that there will be more then just us girls for the long weekend.

I give Justin directions to the condo. He takes Astro with him. I tell him that I am going to stop at the store on the way and pick up the list of groceries that we made. I asked him and my friends what I could get and we all compiled a list.

Justin blows the horn as him and Astro go through the light. Astro sticks his head out of the window and barks.

110

When the light changes, I turn into the parking lot. I park right in the front of the store and go inside. I get a cart.

"Sebastian?" I hear a male voice say.

I look up. I roll my eyes. "Are you following me?" I ask Jacob.

"I live around here. What are you doing here?"

"I have a timeshare condo. This is my weekend to be at the beach."

"How—?"

"How do I afford it?" I snap at him. "I worked for the company that was offering the timeshare. They let us buy into them as part of our packages for selling the packages."

"I was going to say something else." Jacob says.

"Excuse me." I say. "Oh just fuck it. I will go somewhere else." I turn leaving the cart. I go outside and get in my car.

He watches me. There is a woman with him. She looks at Jacob. "What was that?"

He looks at her. "What was what?"

"Who is that?"

"That's Ashley. She is Sebastian's sister."

"What? You don't have a sister."

"I don't. He does. They had the same dad."

"Why did she yell at you?"

"I was trying to be protective of him."

His friend turns to him. "What did you do?"

"I called her a gold digger."

"What? How did she find out about him? Did he know that he had a sister?"

"No. He didn't know about her."

I pull into another grocery store parking lot. I park my car. I get out and go in side. As I reach for a cart, I hear my name.

Charlotte hugs me. "Hi Sebastian." She says.

"Hi Charlotte."

"How are you?"

"I am well thank you. How are you?"

"I am well." She looks at me. "I didn't know you lived close to us."

"I have a timeshare condo and this is my weekend for it."

"How wonderful." She says. "Have you and Sebastian talked lately?"

"No."

"You seem upset is everything alright?"

"Everything is fine." I tell her.

"I live right down the street. The house that looks like it was ripped out of Greece, that one is mine. Come by if you get a chance."

"Thank you."

"Which condo are you staying in?"

"The Beach Cove."

"Oh that's the one that Larry oversees." She says referring to her husband. "If you need anything, please let us know."

"I will. Thank you."

She hugs me. "Tell your mom I send my love."

"I will."

She leaves and I go get the groceries. I pay and get in the car. I drive over to the Beach Cove and pull into the disabled parking spot.

Justin comes over and hugs me. I kiss him. We get the groceries and bring them in. We put the groceries away.

~~~~~~~~~

We go down by the pool. Astro goes with us. I get into the pool and swim. Justin sits on the side of the pool with his legs in the pool watching me.

I sit on the steps of the pool and Justin walks into the pool. He sits on the steps next to me. I stand up. With the support of the water, I can stand on my own. I stand in front of Justin and I kiss him.

We don't notice that there are other guests that have come out to enjoy the pool.

"Um, there are no dogs allowed." A man says.

Justin and I look up at the guy who is standing next to Astro. He reaches for his leash to take him away.

"Leave the dog." I say. "We will get him."

"Too busy sucking faces to notice the sign that says no dogs."

Justin stands and takes me in his arms. He sits me in my wheelchair that is covered with towels. He puts Astro's harness on him. The lawyer

in Justin rears his angry head. "The sign says service dogs are allowed."
He takes my hand and Astro's leach. "Come on, honey." He says to me.

The man runs after us. "I am sorry. I didn't know." He looks at me.
"Are you related to Sebastian Timely?"

"No." I say.

Justin looks at me. I smile.

"Listen, we are having a barbecue later. Everyone is welcome. Just
bring your favorite dish." He looks at Justin and me. "My name is Ken."

"Hi Ken. I am Ashley." I say. "And this is my boyfriend, Justin.
And my dog Astro."

"Its nice to meet all of you. Did you all move in?"

"No. I have a timeshare."

"Oh that's right. My wife and I just moved in."

"This is a beautiful place." Justin says.

"It really is and the people who run this place are amazing. If you
have any problems just call the number that is tacked on the refrigerator.
They send their son."

I roll my eyes.

"Don't let me chase you all away." Ken says.

"We will be back." I tell him. "It was nice meeting you."

"You too, thanks."

Justin and I go into the condo and get changed. We decide to go
for a walk. We hold hands and go across the street to the beach. There
is a wooden pathway so we go. He walks next to me holding my hand.
We go over by the rail and look East to the water. The waves crashing
on the sand is relaxing.

Justin wraps his arms around me and we stay like that for a while.
As we watch the horizon, we notice dark clouds.

"Its raining." I say.

"No."

"Justin, we better go back. Its raining."

We leave. We are in the middle of street when the sky bursts and
we get soaked. When we get on the sidewalk that leads to the Beach
Cove, we kiss in the rain.

We go up the sidewalk that leads to the room that we are staying in. Ken is in a covered hallway he stops us.

"Join us." He says.

"We are going to change." I say. "We will come back out."

I go shower first. Justin takes Astro outside. When he comes back in, he showers. While he is in there, I make dinner for us.

The rain is heavier now and pelts the windows. We sit at the table together and have dinner. Justin lifts me out of my wheelchair and sits on the couch with me on his lap. He puts his hand between my legs.

He pushes my panties to the side and plays with me before he delves his fingers inside of me. I gasp. He slides his fingers in and out. He lays me on the couch and takes my clothes off me. He gets on his knees and starts touching me. This leads to us having mind blowing sex.

He carries me to the bedroom and puts me in the middle of the bed. He covers himself before he gets on the bed.

Within seconds his is on top of me again and inside of me. He pulls back and pushes deep. I cry out with my pained pleasure. He does too.

After we go a third time, we are spent. We wrap in each other and go to sleep. Astro sleeps at the bottom of the bed with us.

Chapter 10

Piper and Savannah sit by the pool on the lounge chairs. Mark and Justin are by the barbecue. They are cooking lunch for all of us. I sit by the pool with Astro at my feet. Ken and his wife are in the pool. They are talking loudly to each other.

"Did you see that beautiful couple last night kissing in the rain?" Ken nearly yells across the pool to his wife.

"I did. You brought them to my attention."

"We invited them to join us, but they never came back out. I think maybe they don't like us." Ken says.

Before I can say anything, Larry walks over. "Ken cut the crap." Larry walks over to me and kisses me on the cheek. "Hi sweetie. How are you doing?"

"I am good." I. Tell him.

"Are you enjoying your condo?"

"I love the condo."

He looks at Savannah and Piper. "Hello ladies."

They both say hello to him.

"Its good to have you three here."

"It's been a long time since we worked for you." Savannah says.

"It hasn't been that long." Piper says. She looks around. "It looks really good."

Larry looks at me. "Can I talk to you?"

"Of course."

Justin watches as I leave the area with Larry. Mark steps closer to Justin. "What's that all about?"

"I don't know." Justin says. He flips the chicken and hamburgers over. "Could you put the mushrooms on the grill?" He asks Mark.

"Sure." Mark puts them on the grill. Mark looks at Savannah. "How long did you work for Larry?"

"Three years." She says.

"Why did you leave?"

"He only wanted college students working for him."

"Weren't you still in college?"

"No. Once we graduated, we moved on to other avenues."

"What do you think they are talking about?" Justin asks. "I wonder if Larry knew that she was related to his step-son?"

Piper's phone rings. She smiles. She answers it. "Hi, how are you?" She gets off the lounge chair and leaves the area.

Mark looks at Savannah. "What's going on with Piper?"

"She has a new boyfriend."

"A new boyfriend?"

"Yes."

Piper comes back. "Eric is going to pick me up. We are going to take Danny to a movie."

"What about girls's weekend?"

Piper looks at Savannah. "Everyone is here with their boyfriends, but me."

I come back and look at my friends. "After the movie, invite Eric back here."

She turns and looks at me.

"You don't mind?"

"I don't."

She looks at me again. "Have you been crying?"

I look away not wanting to lie to my friends. "I am ok."

Eric pulls into the lot and comes running over to the pool. He kisses Piper like none of us are there. He takes her by the hand and they leave.

Larry walks over by the pool. He says goodbye to everyone. Justin stands next to me. He takes my hand.

"What did Larry want?" Savannah asks.

Ken and Diane are still in the pool. They look up.

"He was telling me that this is the last time that the condo will be available. He said that it's the most commonly requested unit."

"You only get it for one weekend." She says.

"Well next year we will have to go somewhere else." I tell her.

Ken pulls Justin and Mark to the side. He looks around to see that no one is within earshot. Ken looks at me.

"No one asks for that unit. No one stays in that unit. He uses it. Him and his wife come all the time." Ken looks at Diane and smiles.

"When did they change it out from timeshare to owning?" Mark asks.

"My wife and I have been here for almost a year. We love this place."

Justin doesn't say anything.

"I wonder what he said to her." Ken says.

"He is her brother's step-father." Mark says.

"Not her step father?"

"No. They share the same dad. They have different moms." Justin says. He shakes hands with Ken and punches Mark in the shoulder. He walks back over to the pool and he lifts me in his arms. He jumps in the pool. He swims down to the bottom of the pool and then comes back to top.

Savannah took a video of us. Mark walks over to her and kisses her. "Who would have thought that after all this time, I would be dating my brother?" She teases him.

He grabs her phone from her. He puts the phone on the table under the umbrella. Then he lifts her in his arms.

"Mark, I just had my hair straightened." She says.

He jumps in the pool with her.

"Mark!" She yell.

"Who I the hell has her hair straightened to go stay on the beach?" He asks her.

"You are not cute."

"I think you think I am." He says. He kisses her.

117

Justin pulls me over by the steps. He sits and pulls me on his lap. "Tell me what was said between you and Larry." He kisses me on the lips.

"The lawyer in you wants to fight my battles?" I ask him.

"The boyfriend in me wants to kick his ass. So tell me why I am not going to kick his ass."

I look over at Savannah. "We will talk when ears can't hear." I tell him.

He stands up with me in his arms. He looks at Mark as he walks out of the pool. "Don't forget to take all that food off the grill. Those Mushrooms should be ready to shrivel up and climb back into the ground. Ashes to ashes." He says.

I laugh.

"We will be back." Justin says.

I bury my face in his chest. "They are going to think that we are going to have sex." I tell him.

"Let them think whatever the fuck they think." He looks over at Astro who is panting. "Astro, come." He says. The three of us go into the condo. Justin sits me on the counter. "Astro, drink." He says. He looks at me. "Spill it."

"Larry told me that I am putting a riff in his family. He told me that he should have put two and two together and figured it out that Sebastian and I are related. He told me that if he would have known that all those years ago, he would have never hired me." I take a deep breath.

"Why were you upset when you got here yesterday with the groceries?"

"When I went into the first grocery store, Jacob was there. When I went to the second, Charlotte was there."

He kisses me.

My phone rings. Justin walks over to the opposite counter and hands me my phone. I look at the call list. I have missed six calls.

"Who called you?"

"I don't know." I say. "I don't recognize these numbers."

"Do you have messages?"

"Yes." I say.

"Listen to them." He looks out the window, "I will get your wheelchair."

"Just don't leave me on the counter." I tell him. "I could fall off."

He lifts me and takes me in the bathroom. He puts me in the shower. I laugh. He kisses me. "I will be back." He reaches behind me and unhooks my bikini top. "Need help talking the bottoms off?"

"No." I scream.

"Enjoy. I will be right back." He says.

I take a shower. When I am done, I open the door and reach for the towel. I wrap up in it and get in my wheelchair. I go into the bedroom and get dressed in shorts and a t-shirt. I pull my hair up in a ponytail.

I go into the kitchen. I sit at the table and listen to my messages.

'Sebastian, its Jacob. I wanted to tell you that I am so sorry. I want you to know that my whole family is mad at me.'

I look at my phone. "Ok, I heard enough. Next."

'Sebastian. This is Seth. I am calling to invite you and your friends to come to the grande opening. Its dress causal. Its Saturday night. Tonight at seven. I hope you come. I will add you and your friends to the guest list. Just mention that you are my— my sister."

I click the phone for the next message.

'Sebastian its Seth again, I am just calling you back to let you know that Jacob will not be coming. He is working a yacht party. The grande opening is at Marina Beach. Again, hope to see you there.'

I click the next message.

'Sebastian, its Charlotte.'

"Do these people have nothing better to do than to bother me? I click the next message. "Mom, left us a message." I tell Astro.

'Hi darling, I know its your girls' weekend. I hope that you have fun with your friends.. I just wanted to let you know that Peter and I will be leaving tomorrow for New Mexico. We won't be gone as long as last time.'

"Have fun." I say out loud.

I click the next message.

"Darling, its mom again. Anastasia wants you to go to dinner. I am going to tell you this because Peter and I were talking and if you don't want to go, you don't have to. I love you. I will let you know when we get to New Mexico.'

I look at my phone. "One more message, Astro. Then we are going back outside with our friends."

'Hi Sebastian its Sebastian. I have to tell you that I truly miss you. I know we just found out about each other but I miss you. Grandma is coming. I don't want you to be pressured into anything. I want to get to know you. I want to explain things to you. I want to apologize for Jacob's comment to you. I do need to tell you that Seth is excited to have you for a sister. He always wanted a sister. He is having a grande opening for his restaurant Marina Beach. He told me that he invited you to his opening. I hope that you will come. Save my number, call me.'

I put my phone on the table and pet Astro's head. "Come lets go out with our friends." I say to him. I put his leash on him.

Justin comes back in. "Tell me again what Larry said to you."
"I told you."
"Tell me again."
"He told me that he wishes he never met me. He told me that I am causing a riff in his family. His sons are not talking to each other because of me. He told me that if he would have put two and two together he would have never hired me or allowed me to get a timeshare so close to his family."

"Anything else?"

"He told me that the contract for the timeshare is up. This is the last year of it."

"Is that what your contract says?"

"My contract is home." I smile. "I have a copy of it in the hidden drawer in the bed."

He kisses me. "What else is in there?"

"A book." I laugh.

"What else?"

"Nothing."

"Can I ask you a question?"

"Sure."

"Whose furniture is this?" Justin looks around and it occurs to him that a lot of the furniture looks the same as what is in my house."

"I furnished it."

"What aren't you telling me?"

"Nothing." I tell him.

I go into the room and flip the comforter up. I take the key and unlock the drawer. I take out the original contract that I purchased the condo to live in it. I also take out the timeshare contract. I hand them both to Justin.

He looks in the drawer. "Is that a vibrator?"

I laugh. I close the drawer and lock it.

"No fair." He says. He goes in the kitchen and reads the contracts.

I go out the back door and walk around the building with Astro so he can do what dogs do best. I wander back by the pool.

Mark kisses me on the cheek. "You doing ok?"

"I am." I say to him. "We have all been invited to Marina Beach's grande opening."

Savannah sits up. "Really?" She asks.

"Sav, you are so awful. I know you were going no matter what." I say.

"Little Mermaid, is this something that you would like to do?" Mark says.

"I would. I have always wanted to go in there."

"Where are we all going?" Piper asks as she and Eric come back.

"We are going to Marina Beach's grande opening." I tell her.

"Oh wow. We always wanted to do that." Piper says. "How are we getting to do that?"

"The owner invited us."

Ken looks at me. "You know Seth?"

Justin opens the door of the condo and runs across the courtyard to the pool. He hands his phone to Mark. Mark reads the phone. He looks at Justin. "You are fucking kidding me! What the fuck?"

Savannah looks at Mark. "Everything ok?"

He looks at her but doesn't answer. He looks at me. "What time is the event?"

"Seven."

He looks at his watch. "We should all get ready."

"What are we supposed to wear?" Piper asks. "I didn't bring anything fancy."

Eric kisses Piper. "Thank you for going to the movies with me and Danny. I am going to go. You and your friends have fun."

I look at Eric. "You are invited to come."

"I wouldn't want to intrude."

"Eric, you are my friend." I say.

"Pipes, your house is ten minutes away. Lets go shopping in your closet." Savannah says.

I look at the two of them. "I brought dresses with me. You want to see if they will work for you both?"

Diane looks at all of us. "If you want, I can do your hair."

I don't want to be rude to her but I know that she and Ken are dying to come into my condo to see what it looks like inside. We don't answer her. Justin gathers all of our stuff and the food that has been on the grill all day. He dumps the food in the trashcan.

He looks at Diane, "That is really nice of you."

She looks at Justin and knows that she is being turned down. "Got it!" She snaps.

Eric, Mark and Justin go into the second bedroom. Savannah, Piper and I go into the main bedroom. Piper showers when we go in the room. I pull out the dresses from the closet. I put them on the covered bench.

"Which one are you going to wear?" Savannah asks me.

"I like the black one."

She looks at all the dresses that I have laid out and laughs. "Sab, they are all black."

"I like all of them." I say. "You and Pipes pick the ones that you want to wear."

Piper steps out of the shower. "That's not how this works. You pick the one that you want to wear. Then we pick the other options."

"Why did you bring so manly dresses?" Savannah asks.

"I am staying for longer than the weekend." I tell them.

"Good for you." Piper says. She towel dries her hair.

We hear the guys in the other room laughing. We don't hear their conversation. We continue getting ready. Savannah showers next.

I put on my favorite black dress that is a ruffle top that lays off the shoulder. I wait for my friends to get dressed. Savannah stands in her bra and underwear drying her hair. She uses the flat iron.

Piper picks a dress and puts it on. She looks good in anything. She pulls her hair back and she looks great.

The three of us sit together and put on our makeup. We sit together and do selfies. Then we take single pictures of each of us. We also do pictures with two of us. We rotate our phones so that we each have the same pictures.

Mark goes in the kitchen and sees the contracts. He looks at Justin.

Eric sits on one of the bar chairs. He looks under the counter and sees that there is a drop countertop. He stands and pulls the counter up and latches it. He sits at one of the other chairs.

"This is a nice feature. Its like the one in Sebastian's kitchen." Justin says.

Mark looks at Justin. "We have one of these in our house too. I guess Mr. O'Conner did this for her."

"If this is only a timeshare, why would she need something like this?" Eric asks.

"I am going to look into it." Justin says. He looks at his watch. He walks to the door and taps on it. "We should get going." He says.

Chapter 11

I open the double bedroom doors and the three of us leave the room together. The three guys stand there with their jaws gaping. Piper spins and the dress twirls around her. She looks so beautiful in my dress. Mark walks over to Savannah and takes her in his arms and kisses her. She giggles

Justin stands back and looks at me. He takes his phone out of his pocket and snaps a picture of me. I look at him. He keeps on snapping.

"Are you ok?" I ask him.

"Out of all the men in the world, you picked me." He says.

Mark takes out his phone and he takes pictures of all of us like we are posing for prom pictures. He laughs. "We should invite Ken or Diane in to take pictures of us."

We all laugh.

"Are we all going together or in separate cars?" Eric asks.

My phone rings. I look at the number that I do not know. "Hello."

"Ms. Timely, your ride is here." A woman says.

"We will be right out." I put my phone in my purse. "Our ride is here."

"What?" Piper asks.

"Sebastian sent a limo for us. Parking is limited and he wasn't sure that the disabled spots would be available or if they are being occupied for the event."

"How did he know to send a car?"

"He sent a text message asking if we were going. I replied with one word, 'yes' which I am sure pissed him off." I let Astro out side. When he is done, he walks back in the condo. I kiss him on the top of his head. "I love you. We will be back soon. Be good."

We leave the unit and I lock the door. We go to the parking lot and get in the car. Eric puts my wheelchair in the trunk and the driver gets in the car. She drives to the Marina Beach. She pulls the car up to the curb. We get out of the car. Justin lifts me into his arms. He puts me in my wheelchair and kisses me on the lips for the first time since I got all dressed up.

Eric steps aside with the driver, "There was no way that she could have gotten out of the car on her own."

"I am sorry." She says. "Its my first night on the job. I didn't mean to upset anyone."

"She's not bringing this to your attention, I am. Please be careful next time." He is really nice about the situation.

"I will." She says. She gives him a card. "Call me when you are all ready to go back."

"Thank you. We will." He takes money out of his pocket and offers it to her.

"No. I can't, your fair has been more than generously paid for."

We stand on the line of people that are waiting to get inside. The line of people stand on a red carpet. When we have reached the front of the line, the bouncer looks at all of us. He looks at me and opens the red ropes.

"Enjoy your evening." He says to us.

"Thank you." I answer.

When we get inside a pretty blonde greets us. "My name is Joy. Please come this way."

Seth walks over to us and greets all of us. He kisses me on the cheek. "Welcome, let me show you around."

Joy leads everyone ahead of him. Everyone follows her.

Seth hugs me, "You coming for my opening is a big deal. Thank you so much."

"Thank you for inviting us."

"I am sorry about what Jacob said to you."

"Its not for you to apologize for him. That's what he thinks. I am glad that's not what you think."

"I heard that my dad threatened you."

I look away from him.

"My mom is livid."

"Your dad told me that I am causing a riff."

"You are not a riff in anything." He hugs me. "You have brought happiness to my brother and me."

"This is beautiful." I tell him.

"Thank you. I am the owner." He looks around and smiles. "Sebastian gave me starter money and I am fortunate that this is my third location."

"Seth this is great."

"Come have a drink at the bar."

At the mention of the bar, I think that the bar is going to be over my head. When we walk over to the bar, it is not high at all. The bar is at a height that I can just pull my wheelchair right up to and feel like I am at a bar.

Joy walks everyone back over and everyone sits with me. Joy takes my phone and takes pictures of us for me. She gets all of us a round of drinks.

Seth kisses the top of my head. "I have to go circulate. I will come find you in a little while. The patio is the only spot that would be difficult for you tonight. Thanks for coming."

We all sit at the bar for a while. Drinks and food are free for all guests for the opening. My friends drink one after another. I look over at Eric because he never has a drink in front of him. Piper on the other hand, keeps drinking. She is a just one drink away from being fall-down drunk.

The server comes over with a tray of drinks. I look at the server. "She is cut off." I say.

Piper looks at me. "What?" She slurs.

"You have had enough."

"Don't judge me."

"I am not judging you." I tell her.

"I can handle myself." She says wagging her finger at me.

"Pipes, you are done." Savannah says.

Piper looks at Savannah. "You too?"

I push away from the bar. Justin gets up. He kisses me. He doesn't taste like anything alcoholic. "Lets go outside." He says.

"You want to leave?"

"No, I want to go outside."

"Ok." I put my hand in his hand.

As we are walking to the entrance, we see the elevator. Joy walks over to us. "Did you want to see the upstairs?"

"I thought that was a private area." I say.

"You are Seth's sister. It is open to you."

"How did you know that I am his sister?" I ask.

Joy pushes the button for the elevator. When the doors open we go in and she taps the button for the second floor. "When Sebastian found out about you, he called Seth and told him to do some research. Seth googled you. He found your Facebook page. We spent hours reading through your FB."

"I didn't know that I was that exciting."

"Why did Sebastian have Seth do the research?" Justin asks.

I look up at him and smile. Always the lawyer. He kisses me.

"He was at work. All the computers at the bank are part of the company. They don't allow outside research to be done. They can look at anyone who has an account in the bank." She looks at me. "You don't bank with your brother?"

I laugh. "If I knew I had brothers I would bank at his bank, but I knew nothing about him. Them." I say.

"Do you know why Jacob is so against having a sister?" Justin asks her.

Joy looks at the elevator doors when they open. She steps out. This room is more beautiful than downstairs. The room has artwork hanging on the walls. I gasp at one of the pictures hanging on a wall of the family graduation photos.

It's a picture of me. I am dressed for my college graduation. No one was there. My mom had forgotten that I was graduating and was in Europe. A professional photographer took pictures of all the graduates.

My pictures went missing. There were also pictures of me as a baby. The picture that is in Sebastian's office hangs on the wall as well.

"This is the family room." Joy says.

"They didn't even know about me. How the hell do they have pictures of me?" I say out loud.

"I provided them." Anastasia says.

"Hi Grandma." I say. "Grandma, this is my boyfriend, Justin."

"Hi." She says.

I look back at the wall where the picture of my college graduation hangs.

Anastasia looks at me. "It was a beautiful graduation. You with all those cords and all those accomplishments needs to hang on walls."

"I sent you an announcement of my graduation, you never sent a reply."

"I told your mom I was coming." She says.

"Why didn't I know that you were there? It would have been nice to know that someone thought I was worthy."

"I broke my ankle on those fucking bleachers." She says. "I was rushing to come down from where I was perched so I didn't miss a thing. I missed the fucking step and landed on my ankle."

I look at her. "I am glad that you were there. I am sorry that you broke your ankle."

"I didn't miss anything that was important to my grandchildren." She says.

The elevator door opens and Larry gets out with Charlotte. When Larry sees me, he gets an annoyed look on his face. He turns around to leave. The elevator door opens again and Seth gets off the elevator.

"If you leave, we are done." Seth says.

Larry looks at his son. "Are you threatening me?"

"No. I am telling you the way that it will be. If you leave my opening, we are done. You threatened her. You have made more money off of her all these years and you know it." Seth says.

Charlotte stands next to her son. She puts her arm around him. "I agree with Seth. If you leave your son's opening, don't just leave here. As a matter of fact, I own that condo."

Larry sits in a chair with his back to me.

When the elevator doors open Jacob steps out. He walks over to me and hugs me tight. He gets on his knees on the side of me and hugs me tighter. "I am so sorry." He says over and over.

"Its ok." I tell him. "You will get to know me. I will get to know you."

Charlotte taps her son on the shoulder and he looks up. "I am glad you came for your brother."

He stands and walks over to Larry. "I thought you were an honorable person. What I learned tonight about you, you make me sick."

Seth stands next to his brother. Jacob looks at him. They both embrace.

Larry stands and walks to the bar. He sits with his back to all of us. Anastasia walks over to Larry. She sits at the bar next to him. He looks at her.

"I have to agree with your son, I thought too that you were an honorable man. What has come to my attention lately makes me extremely upset."

"I don't know that you are talking about." He says.

Justin walks over to me and holds my hand. I look up at him. "Lets go." I say. Justin walks to the elevator. He pushes the bottom and the doors open. Sebastian steps out. He looks at everyone.

"Are you leaving?" He asks me. He shakes hand with Justin. "Please don't leave."

"This is Seth's night. This is a celebration. I don't want to ruin it."

Jacob stands next to Justin, Seth and Sebastian stand around me. Larry looks at his sons and he takes a bottle off the bar and throws it against the wall. It shatters in a million and half pieces. He yells.

"A father trumps a lying bitch." Larry says.

"I didn't lie about anything." I say. "I don't want anything from any of you. I didn't know that you were related to Sebastian. I didn't even know about Sebastian. I don't want anything from you."

Security guards coming running upstairs. They look at the shattered glass and with everyone distracted, I get in the elevator and go downstairs. I go right out the doors and leave.

Sebastian looks out the window and sees me on the sidewalk pushing my wheelchair as fast as I can. He looks at Larry. "If anything happens to her, I will ruin you."

Justin and Sebastian get in the elevator. Seth and Jacob run down the stairs. They run past the bar. Mark and Eric jump up. They all run out of the Marina Beach.

Mark looks at Justin. "Why are we running?"

"Sebastian." Jacob says.

Marina Beach is just over a mile away from the condo. I get there quickly. I go into the Condo and get Astro. He wags his tail. I go to my car and get in it. Astro hops in the car. I start it and wait for my wheelchair to load in the chair-topper that carries my wheelchair when I drive. When its all sealed up, I close the door and put the car in reverse.

I see all of them running in my review mirror. I blink the tears away and drive home. Eric's truck is parked off the street. He gets in the truck. He goes back to the Marina Beach for Savannah and a very drunk Piper. He runs in the building to get them. Piper is passed out at the bar.

Savannah is crying. "She never does this. Something must be wrong." She looks at Eric. "You all left me."

"Something happened with Sebastian." Eric says.

"Its not all about her." Piper slurs.

Eric picks her up like she is a baby and carries her out to his truck. Savannah gets in the truck, Eric puts Piper next to her. He climbs in and then heads to my house.

"Where the hell are you taking us?" Savannah asks.

"Something happened and your best friend went home."

"She went to the condo?"

"No. She went home."

"Did the car come for us?" Piper slurs.

"No." Eric and Savannah say.

"Can you pull over?" Piper asks.

Eric pulls the truck to the side of the road and she gets out quickly and throws up.

I decide not to go to my house. I know that my mom is out of town with Peter. Her house is my hiding place. When I don't want to be found, I go to her house. I haven't disappeared in a while, but now I feel like I have to.

I pull into her driveway. I get out of the car with Astro and I call her. "Don't ask questions, I am going to stay at your house. Can you please take the alarm off?"

She does from her phone. "Sweetheart, I wish I was there. Charlotte let me know a bit of what happened."

"Mom." I choke. "Please. Not now."

"Ok." She agrees.

"If anyone calls you, you don't know where I am. I don't want them coming to your house looking for me."

"How long do you think you need?"

"I don't know. If you don't—"

"Sweetheart, please. You are welcome to stay at my house as long as you need."

"Thank you. I love you."

"I love you too." She says something to Peter in the background. I hear her laughing.

I click the call off. I take my key out of my purse. I unlock the door and we go inside. I go into the guest bedroom which mom has for me. I take my dress off and throw it across the room. I get on the bed and cry. Astro jumps on the bed with me.

They all get to my house. Justin jumps out of Mark's truck. "Are you fucking kidding me? Where the hell is she?"

"Call her phone." Savannah says.

"I did." Sebastian says. "It goes to her voicemail."

"Your dad, is a fucking jerk." Justin says.

"Not my dad."

Savannah goes into the house. They all go into my house. Piper opens the refrigerator and gets out a bottle of water. She sits at the table.

"She went to her mom's." Piper says.

No one really listens to her because they think she is too drunk to know anything. Savanna takes out her phone and calls my phone again. It goes right to my voicemail.

"She hides out at her mom's." Piper says.

"Can you get us to her mom's?" Justin asks.

"Of course I can." Piper says. "I have to go to the bathroom first." She says. She staggers to the guest bathroom." She looks at herself in the mirror and cries. She steps into the shower. She showers quickly and then steps out. She runs into my room and puts on my clothes. She uses my hairbrush and pulls her hair into a ponytail.

She joins everyone in the kitchen. Eric is gone. She sits at the table and cries. "I never drink." She says. "This is why I never drink. He probably hates me. His ex-wife used to drink. She hit someone while she was drunk and is in jail."

Savannah sits at the table next to Piper. "He had to go to the bathroom." She says. "How do you know that she is at her mom's house?"

"When she gets really upset and wants to hide she goes to her mom's." Piper says.

"Should we go now?" Mark asks.

"I think we should go in the morning." Justin says.

Sebastian looks at everyone who has known me practically my whole life. Seth looks around. Jacob does too. Justin looks at all of them.

"Seth, how did you get a picture of her graduation? No one there, but me." Justin says.

Piper snaps her head up. "She always said she thought that you were there."

"Why didn't you tell her you were there?" Sebastian asks.

"I wasn't free to be with her. I was engaged, but I wanted to be there for her." Justin says.

"What happened to your fiancé?" Jacob asks.

"She moved to China and met someone who could give her everything she wanted." He says.

Eric joins them in the kitchen. He looks at Piper. He walks over to her and kisses her. "I have to go home."

She stands and hugs him. "I am so sorry. I never drink."

"Don't worry about it." He kisses her again. "Let me know about Sebastian."

"What time is Danny's baseball game?"

"Its at eleven."

"Ok. I will come." She says.

"If Sebastian needs you, Danny will have other games."

They say goodbye. Everyone leaves my house. Justin makes sure that everything is locked up.

Chapter 12

I sit outside by mom's pool with Astro. I have a book that I am reading. Astro lays by my wheelchair with his head on my feet. We both jump when we hear the gate unlatch. Sebastian walks around to where I am. He hugs me. Seth is next to hug me. Jacob pets Astro's head.

"What are you doing here? How did you know I was here?" I ask.

"Piper told everyone a few days ago where she thought you went."

"Piper was drunk." I say.

"She wasn't that drunk. We were sitting in your kitchen and she told us." Jacob says.

"My kitchen? You went to my house?"

"Yes." Sebastian says.

"Why?" I ask.

"Sebastian, you left all upset. We wanted to make sure that you were alright." Seth says.

"I am sorry that your opening was ruined. It was about you that night not me. I didn't mean for any of this to happen." I say.

"It was about all of us as a family." Seth says.

"How did you get pictures of my graduation? No one was there. My mom forgot about it and was out of town. My friends were graduating themselves. We all met a week later to celebrate our successes. But no one was there."

"Grandma Stacy." Jacob says.

"We call Anastasia Stacy." Seth says.

"It makes sense." I say. I look at all of them. "What do you want from me?"

"We want to get to know you." Sebastian says.

"I am—"

"Worth knowing." Seth says.

"How did you get into the guarded gate?" I ask.

"I went to school with his son. He was excited to hear that our sister lives here." Jacob says.

We go into the house. I make lunch for all of us.

Sebastian looks at me. "Tell us how you met Larry."

"I was with Piper and Savannah on summer vacation. We were in Disney World and we laughing and being silly. Larry couldn't take his eyes off me. It was creepy. He found us at the hotel we were staying at and he offered us jobs. He was excited that they went to different schools than I did because then we could spread the work out between different locations."

"When did you get the timeshare?" Seth asks.

"The summer of my junior year of college. Savannah and Piper had units next to mine. They didn't want to buy into theirs. I bought into mine."

"What do you mean?"

"I had a contract drawn up because I purchased it. I was going to live there. Then I got a notice that it was a timeshare only and I needed to pay for my timeshare straight out."

"How much did he charge you?"

"Off hand I don't know." I say.

"How then did you have money to buy your mom's house?" Sebastian asks me.

"I saved money. I had been working since I was young. I wanted to always be independent. If I wanted something I saved for it."

My phone rings. I know its Justin calling me because he has a different ring tone. I answer the phone. "Hi.."

"Hi." He says. "What are you doing?"

"I am at my mom's house."

"Piper said that. I want to see you."

"I need to go get my stuff from the condo."

Seth looks at me. "Its your condo."

I look at him.

"It seems that Larry, had been ripping you off. We are going to look into it." Sebastian says.

"I don't want anything from any of you." I say.

Justin speaks into the phone. "Sebastian?"

"Oh sorry." I say.

"Call the guard and let me in."

"Ok." I say. I pick up mom's landline and it dials right into the guard. "This is Sebastian, Justin Case is a guest of mine." I hang up the phone. "At the stop sign make a right. Go two streets. At the stop sign make a left. The house is the last one one left."

There is a knock on the door. I go to the door and open it. Justin takes me in his arms. He holds me so close. I feel so safe in his arms.

When he walks in the house, he shakes hands with Sebastian, Jacob and Seth. Astro throws himself at Justin's feet. He squats and pets Astro's belly.

The four of them sit at my mom's dining room table talking about how Larry has wronged me. While they do that, I go in the guest bedroom and change my clothes. When I am done, I make the mistake of sitting on the bed. I lay back on the bed and fall asleep.

Some time passes and Justin comes looking for me. He lays in bed with me and kisses me. I snuggle into him and he holds me while I sleep.

I drive to the condo. My friends are all at work. I am supposed to be at work, but I have taken three days off. There is only three days of work durning the week. We had off on Monday. We will have off on Friday too. I never take off work.

I sit at the counter. Astro lays on the sofa. The television is on quietly. There is a knock at the door. I roll my eyes. "I never get to just be alone." I say. I go to the door and open it. "Charlotte, please come in."

She pets Astro. She walks over to the couch and sits down. Astro jumps up on the couch with her and snuggles into her. She is dressed like she is going to walk a runway. She looks stunning.

"Get down." I tell Astro.

"He is fine." She pets him. "He is so well trained. Did you do that?"

"Not by myself. He was being trained as a service dog, but when I went to get him. All his training went out the window. I don't need him to help me get around. He was going to be given to someone else. When she came to get him, he did all his commands on cue. But when they took the harness off of him, he stayed far away from her. They called me back. Astro threw himself at me. He couldn't wait to see me. He was a puppy. He was so little. The lady who was training him, told me that I had to pay two thousand dollars for him."

"Oh my god, that's a rip off."

"I didn't pay anything for him. The guy who was training him as well told me that that's not how they run their training. He told me to leave. He snuck Astro out of the center. He lost his job. But he took Astro and he gave him to me." I smile. "We dated for a short time."

"Did he train Astro more?"

"He did. He worked with Astro and me so that I could tell him the commands I wanted."

"Show me." She says.

I click my fingers and point to my side. Astro jumps off the couch and lays down by my wheelchair. I look at Astro. "Drink." I tell him. He goes to the water bowl and drinks. "Couch." I say. He trots back over with his tail wagging to Charlotte and jumps on the couch. "I am sorry I ruined Seth's opening. I never meant for anything to be ruined."

"Sweetheart, you didn't ruin anything."

"When Larry brought his family around when my friends and I worked for him, the family wasn't all of you." I say.

Charlotte takes out her phone. She scrolls through pictures on her phone. She gets to the one and shows me the phone. "Was this the family that came with him?"

I look at the picture. "Yes." I say. "How long have you been married to him?"

"Well Seth is twenty-four years old. I married Larry twenty-six years ago. Apparently he has been divided between two women. Two families. I gave him sons, Samantha gave him daughters."

"Charlotte, you must hate me."

"I don't hate you. I am glad that my Sebastian has found you." She looks at me. "I am just curious as to how it all happened?"

"My credit cards were stolen. I was in a store buying stuff for my class. My purse dumped over. I thought that I had everything but when I got to the register, I didn't have my credit cards." I look around the room. "Can I get you anything to drink or eat?"

"No." She says.

"I get a lot of speeding tickets. So I had to go to court to pay them off. That's when I learned that there was another Sebastian and I didn't fit the profile of someone who robbed a bank."

She laughs.

"I want you to know that I am here to collect all my belongings from here."

"That's why I am here." She pets the top of Astro's head. She stands and walks over to the counter. She looks at the counter that is the height that is just perfect for me to be at. She pulls a chair over. She sits down. "Come sit with me." She says. "Larry used to run the condo."

"I know."

She holds her hands up. "The thing is, I own them. I didn't know that he sold you this unit. It has just come to my attention. I have to say that we are working on getting you back all your money that you have paid out over the years."

"NO. Its not for you to pay me back. I am not suing anyone. I am just going to get my belongings out of here and I won't bother you and your family."

"You are not bothering me and my family. My sons love you. They are all protective of you."

"Larry was right when he told me that I was causing a riff in your family."

"No. He was the riff in the family. I just found out about all his wrong doings. It was actually Ken and Diane who brought it to my attention that he was bringing another woman here and their children. Ken didn't know that Larry has two sons. They know about the daughters. But Diane knows that Larry is married to me. So she asked about his other family. The daughters are younger than my sons."

"Can you tell me about my dad. My mom can only tell me that he saved her. That he was her hero. She said she lost him before she really got to know him, but he gave her the best part of himself."

Charlotte squeezes my hand. "I would agree with that. Sebastian was a remarkable person. He was so caring. My marriage to him didn't work because he was working what seemed like a thousand hours a week. I felt like he didn't love me. When he was home, he spent endless hours with Asher. He loved being a dad. He was the kindest person."

"What happened to him?"

"He was sideswiped on a rainy night. He was killed immediately."

"Did you know about me?"

"I did. I went to the funeral. Your mom was pregnant with you. She was so nice to Sebastian. Anastasia was unconsolable. My Sebastian was only five years old."

"I didn't know that he had siblings."

"You know, they never came. They never came to the funeral. They never came to my wedding when I married him. We had a big wedding." Charlotte says. "They didn't want anything to do with him."

"Why not?"

"Like I said, your dad worked really hard. His sister and brother expected that because he was doing well they were too. They wanted him to just open his wallet. When he didn't do that they didn't come. They didn't want the car dealerships. They asked Anastasia for money and I think she gave them a bit. But she put money in a trust for you. She set up one for Sebastian."

She spends the rest of the afternoon going around to the other people that are staying or living in the condos talking to them. She buys lunch for all of the people who are at the condo. When she comes back to tell me about the lunch, I am gone.

~~~~~

I go back to my house and go through the mail. I take a book and go outside. I sit in my gazebo and read. I go back in the house and make something to eat. I sit at the table and eat lunch.

139

I put Astro's leash on him and take him for a long walk around the neighborhood. Ms. Conley comes out of her house. She walks over to us and invites us in. I go in the house. Her cat runs out of the room. Astro stays by my side.

"How are you doing? I haven't seen you and that fellow together for a while."

"He is working and I have been busy."

"How is your mom?"

"She is good. She is with Peter in New Mexico. She will be home soon."

"Is she going to marry him?"

"I don't know. He asked her to marry him."

"I hope that she doesn't feel like she can never marry because of you."

"Because of me? What does that mean? I have lived on my own since I was twenty-one."

"You live in her house."

"No. I bought the house."

She looks at me. "Oh I didn't know that."

"Ms. Conley, I mean no disrespect to you, but you did know that. You helped my mom move out. You saw the for sale sign and you knew that I bought the house from her."

"I thought that she reneged on the deal."

"No." I look at my watch. "I have to get ready for work."

"Don't be a stranger."

"I won't." I leave and go home.

When I walk up the walk to my house. Justin is there knocking on the door. "Hi." I say.

He turns to me and walks across the lawn. "Have you been avoiding me?"

"No." I unlock the door. "Want to come in?"

"Why do you look sad?"

"I am ok." I tell him.

We go in the house. He takes me in his arms and kisses me. "I want you. I need to be inside of you." He kisses me again. "Do you know how hard it is to get anything done when I only have one thing on my mind?" He deepens the kiss.

I moan into his mouth. "You. Have. Been on my. Mind. All da-. Day. Too." I say.

He lifts me and carries me to my room. He lays me on the bed. I sit up and take my clothes off. I stand up and hold onto the bed. Justin slips a condom on and stands behind me. He slips into me from behind. He makes love to me. He slips out. He picks me up and lays me on my bed again.

"Again. Do it that way again." I gasp as he touches my ever so sensitive nipples.

"I want to see you this time." He says. He puts his hand between my legs and I combust immediately. He kisses my lips. He trails down to my neck and then takes one of my nipples in his mouth. He takes the other one and squeezes the nipple between his fingers.

"Justin, please."

"Sebastian." He says as I reach my hand down and touch him.

"I need to feel you." I say.

He breathes out heavily. I scrap my nails against his skin. He straddles me before he slips back into me. We both breath heavily. I gasp as he pushes deeper into me. He pulls back and then pushes deeper and I cry out as my body quakes under him.

I get out of my bed and go in the bathroom, I shower as he sleeps. As I shower, Justin opens the door and steps into the shower with me. He takes the soap from my hand and rubs it all over me. As the water runs down my body rinsing the soap off, he runs his hands up and down my body.

I take the soap from him and rub it all over his body. When I wrap my fingers around him, he breathes heavily. He puts his head back on the wall and lets me touch him. Water rains down on both of us.

"Kiss me." I say.

Justin squats in front of me and kisses me. "Why have you been avoiding me?" He asks.

"I am not avoiding you."

"You have been acting different."

"How so?" I ask. I wrap myself up in a towel. I get in my wheelchair.

"You are avoiding everyone."

"No. Everyone has been working and busy."

"You haven't been at work in a while. Not one of your many jobs. You haven't been at the bookstore in over a week."

"Well I own it, so I don't have to be there all the time." I say.

"What? When the hell did that happen?"

"I have wanted it for a while. Its not open for anyone right now. Its being renovated. I am going to open it in a month."

"I am sure your class misses you."

"I found someone that they love to take over for me."

"Why?" Justin asks.

"I need time. I need to figure out what the fuck is going on in my life."

"Have you spoken to your mom?"

"She is still in New Mexico with Peter. I think they are married." I say kidding.

""Why wouldn't you go to the wedding?"

"Justin, I was only kidding. I don't know if they are married. My neighbor told me that I hold her back."

"That's not true." Justin says. He kisses me. "Get dressed. Do your hair. Put something nice on. We are going out tonight." He kisses me again.

"You have a big case. I don't want to keep you from your work."

"Sebastian, you are not keeping me from anything. We are dating. Unless you are seeing someone else."

"No. I am not seeing anyone else. I don't date two guys at the same time."

"Please get dressed." He says. "I will be back in twenty minutes to get you."

"I need more than twenty minutes." I tell him.

"Nope. We have reservations in an hour. I will be back for you in twenty minutes.":

"Justin, I can't." I tell him.

He leaves.

I go in my bathroom and do my hair. I pull it half up so that its not all down. I apply my makeup which only takes a few minutes. I go into my closet and pick a strappy dress. I put it on. I look at myself in the mirror and take the dress off. I go back in the closet and put on an emerald green dress that has open shoulders and a slit up my left leg. I put on black ballet shoes that strap around my ankles.

The last thing I do before leaving my room is get the matching purse. They have the same design as the shoes. I put money in my purse and my identification. I put my purse down down on the table.

I feed Astro. "Sorry my love." I say to him. "I thought that we would be alone tonight. It seems that I am going out for dinner." He wags his tail. "I love you." I tell him. He eats his food and I let him out. When he comes back in the house, he jumps on the couch. I leave the television on for him and lights. Actually, I do that so that I don't walk into a a dark house. I hate the dark.

Justin knocks on the door almost exactly twenty minutes just like he said. He looks at me.

"Am I not dressed right?" I ask him. He takes me in his arms and kisses me.

Chapter 13

Justin pulls his expensive car into the parking lot of the Marina Beach. I look at him. He pulls the car into a disabled parking spot and I hang my parking decal up on the mirror. He gets out and comes around with my wheelchair. I get out of the car and situated in my wheelchair. Justin takes my hand and we go inside.

When we go in, Joy greets us at the door. "Welcome back." She says. "Follow me, your table is right over here."

Justin walks next to me. He is still holding my hand. Joy leads us to a private room in the back corner. She shows us to the table.

We are in a room that I didn't see the first time I was here. This is a private dining room and there is only two tables in this room. Two very large tables are in there. The room is even more beautiful than the other rooms I have already seen.

"The rest of the party will be right in." Joy says. "Can I get you something to drink?" She hands Justin and me a wine list.

"I can't drink wine." I tell her.

"That's right. The last time you were here." She opens her tablet and reads something. "Vodka with raspberries."

"Thank you."

"You look beautiful." She says.

"Again thank you."

Joy looks at Justin. "House beer?"

"That's great." He says.

"I will be back."

I look at Justin, "What's going on? Why are we here?"

"Your friends and family want to celebrate you."

"Celebrate me? Why?"

"Because we have missed celebrating twenty-five of your birthdays." Sebastian says. He kisses me on the cheek. "Actually that's not true. I blew out the candles on your first birthday cake."

Mom and Peter walk in the room. They are both wearing the same colors. She is in a black and white dress that looks like it cost her a ton of money. He is wearing a suit that matches almost completely. They sit at the table next to me.

Piper walks in. She looks stunning. She is wearing my dress from the other night. She kisses me on the cheek.

Savannah walks in and she looks like a duchess. She radiates money. She hugs me. She is wearing a sapphire colored dress that falls just above her knees. She is wearing matching heals. She has it paired with silver jewelry.

Ginger walks in. She is wearing the same dress as me just in black. She looks beautiful. Her husband Brandon is with her. When I look up, I am surprised to see him. He looks at Justin. The two of them embrace. Their three girls are with them. The girls are wearing party dresses. They are all dressed in the same style dress but are in different colors. Meg is in a dark pink dress. Sara is wearing a Cinderella light blue dress. Becky is wearing a yellow dress. They all look so pretty. Their hair is French braided with matching ribbons in their hair to match the dresses.

"Long time no see." Brandon says. As Brandon and Justin talk, the three girls sit at the table and put their napkins on their laps. Sara sits closest to me.

"You two know each other?" I ask. I hug her.

"We went to law school together." Justin says.

"We were roommates in college." Brandon says. "You look beautiful." He says to me.

Ginger looks at me. "I am ok with the knowledge that he dated you." She says.

Justin looks at me. "You dated Brandon?"

"We dated for three weeks one summer a long time ago." I say.

"Why not longer?" Ginger asks.

"She worked too much." Brandon says. "She didn't like to be spoiled." He kisses Ginger when she wrinkles her nose.

"She still works really hard." Ginger says. "You know, the children miss you terribly. They are miserable without you. Sara comes home and cries for an hour before she sits and does at least three hours of homework."

"Three hours of homework?" I ask.

"The new teacher thinks that they are lacking." Ginger says. "Danny is miserable. The new teacher is mean to all the boys in the class but most of all Danny."

Piper looks at Ginger. "Jesus, Ging! You said that you wouldn't say any of that tonight. That's why we included you." She looks at Brandon. "You always wanted to change her. That's why it didn't work out with the two of you. If she wore pink you would tell her to change to blue."

"Blue matched ninety percent of the things that I wear." Brandon says.

Anastasia walks in. She sits at the head of the table. She is the most elegant woman I have ever seen. She puts a wrapped present in front of me. "This is for you."

"Thank you."

Sebastian, Jacob, Seth and Charlotte join is. Mark kisses Savannah. Edward, Justin and Mark's dad, sits at the table next to Candy. Candy is Savannah's mom. They sit next to each other.

Joy comes back with servers who are all carrying in trays of drinks. She puts the drink in front of me.

"Thank you." I say.

Everyone sits around the table. The servers give out the drinks. They hand out menus. Seth stands up. "We don't need menus."

"Sorry." One of the servers says to him. "We didn't realize that you were part of this party."

"This is my family." Seth says. "We are celebrating my sister. Its her birthday."

I look at him.

"The kitchen knows what to send over."

"Ok." The server says.

When the servers all leave, I look at Seth. "Its not my birthday."

"Well we have a sister and today we have decided that we are celebrating you." Jacob says.

Everyone raises their glasses. Seth makes a toast. "To new beginning."

The servers bring dinner for all of us. A large bowl of spaghetti. Platters of chicken parmigiana and veal parmigiana are arranged on the table in front of everyone. They also put plates on the table in front of all of us. The last plate that they add is a plate of meatballs.

Everything looks so delicious. A server comes over with individual salads. Everyone makes their own plate of food. Everyone eats.

Seth walks over to me. He sits down next to me. "Do you not like the food?"

"Everything is so good." I tell him.

"I noticed that you haven't eaten a lot."

Piper joins us. "She doesn't eat when she is sad."

I look at Piper. She knows me long enough to know that with just one look, I can shut her up.

"Why are you sad?" Seth asks.

"I feel like—" I start to say.

"Sweetheart," Grandma says. "You didn't do anything. Circumstances has brought all of you together." She gets up from where she is sitting and walks over to hug me.

Jacob sits across from me. He hands me an envelope. "Please don't read it until after this is over."

Sebastian looks at me. "There is a rumor going around that you are now the owner of the twenty-four seven bookstore."

"Its not a rumor." I say. "I am the owner of it."

"That's really great." Seth says.

"I went by to see you, but it was closed." Jacob says.

"Its being renovated." I say. I excuse myself for a moment to go to the bathroom. When I come out, Sebastian is in the hallway waiting for me. "Hi." I say.

"Hi." He says. "Why have you not been going to work? Not that I think you need to work as hard as you do, but it seems like you have stopped doing all of it."

"I am taking a break. I feel like I need to figure out who I am."

"You are Sebastian Ashley Timely. You are a teacher. You are a mentor. You are a role model."

"How do you know I am a mentor?"

"You are humble. You don't brag about the things that you do and have done. You have friends in that room that are like lionesses. They would attack for you. Your friends knew exactly where you went when we were all looking for you."

"Sebastian, I know I have said it over and over, but I don't want your money."

"I know that. I know that you keep saying that you don't want anything from us. The truth is, I want something from you."

"What could you want from me?"

"I want to get to know you. You are important to us."

"I ruined your mom's family."

"No."

In the other room, mom looks at everyone. "You know, I want to tell you about my daughter and how proud I am of her and all her accomplishments. She has always been independent. Since she found out about Sebastian and all of you, she has been hospitalized. She has been extremely sad about things that were said about her." Mom takes a long drink. "My daughter is amazing. She has always been amazing."

Jacob looks around the room. "I did say that I am really sorry I ever said that to her. I am so sorry that I assumed something about her. I don't know her well yet but I do know that I want to get to know her."

"I feel like the minute I found out about her, I was excited to know that I have a sister." Seth says.

"She feels like she has ruined your family." Savannah says.

"She did not. Us finding out about her forced us to see something that none of us wanted to admit to. But Sebastian is absolutely not destroying my family." Charlotte says.

"How do we make this right for her?" Seth asks.

"Just be there for her." Mom says.

"She is a good hider." Justin says.

"Some times she hides in her work." Piper says.

"She hasn't been going into work." Justin says.

"The kids all miss her." Ginger says. "We need to figure out how to get her back to the children." She looks at Eric. "How is Danny?" Ginger looks at her girls that are seated at the table with their heads down watching something on iPads.

"Danny is Danny. I am not going to say that he is doing well without her, but then again I am not going to say that he can only learn from her." Eric looks at the three girls. "He does learn better from her, but he has to learn what works for him."

"You have to admit he learns better with her." Ginger says.

"Ginger, leave my son out of your crusade."

Mom listens to all the conversations going on. "Do any of you tell my daughter how you all feel about her?"

Justin comes looking for me and when I see him, I rush over to him. He takes me in his arms. I kiss him. He kisses me. "Come back in the room with all of us. We all brought you here to celebrate you."

"I have gone from being nearly alone to having a big family. I don't know how to open up to them."

"Just come back in the room and be with your friends and family." Justin says. "I will be by your side the whole night."

"I would love that."

We go back in the private room. The staff clears the table of the food. One of them comes in the room with a birthday cake. It has one candle on it. The cake says 'It's a girl! Happy Birthday with love!'

I blow out the candle. The staff takes the cake and cuts it into nice sized pieces for everyone to have cake.

Someone walks over to Seth and talks quietly to him. He gets up from the table and kisses me on the cheek as he passes.

"Is everything alright?" Justin asks.

"It will be." Seth says.

"Do you need reinforcers?" Mark asks.

Seth turns to Mark. "I will let you know."

Mark looks at everyone at the table. "I was a bouncer for years." He gets up and goes with Seth.

Eric follows.

Piper looks at Justin. "Are you going to help deal with whatever is going on?"

"No."

"Why not?"

"If I don't go, I don't know what is going on. If they need a lawyer, I will be ready to take the case."

The room erupts in laughter.

Music fills the room. Savannah and Ginger jump up from the table. They start dancing. Piper and I join them. We dance like no one is watching us. Justin sits back and watches. Sebastian watches us too.

The rest of the night is a blast. Everyone laughs and shares stories that are only good stories. Before everyone leaves, we all promise that we will get together again soon. Seth finds us in the parking lot before we go. He runs over to us and hugs me.

"We host a brunch for family members of the staff. Please come. You and your friends are invited to come."

"Tomorrow?" I ask.

"Yes." Seth says.

"What time?"

"It starts at eleven."

"We will be there." Justin says.

"Thanks for tonight. It was fun." I tell Seth. "What was the interruption?"

"An unruly guest." He kisses me goodbye.

In the morning, Justin and I wake up in bed together with Astro and Bob. I spent the night at his house. Astro hears Mark and Savannah moving around in the kitchen and leaves us. Bob, moves closer to the two of us. Justin kisses me. Bob meows and paws at Justin. I reach over and pet Bob. He licks me.

"Watch out, after he licks, he usually bites." Justin says.

Bob continues to lick my fingers.

"He must like you more than us." Justin says and kisses me again.

Bob goes for the bite. He bites Justin's side.

"Ouch!" He yells.

Bob runs from the room.

"You run." He yells after the cat.

I laugh.

"Are you laughing because he bit me?"

"You knew he was going to bite."

"I thought he would bite you."

"You wanted him to bite me?" I ask.

"NO. I was giving you warning that the bite was coming."

From the kitchen we hear Savanna yell, "Why the hell would you bite me? I just put your food down for you."

"Did Bob bite you?" Mark asks.

I laugh loud enough for them to hear us.

They both come in the room and jump on the bed.

"I swear to god, if my bed breaks, you are buying me a new bed." Justin says to Mark.

Mark stands and jumps on the bed again.

We all laugh.

"That fucking cat hates me." Savannah says.

"Bob loves me." I say with a bright smile.

"Rub it in, bitch." She says.

I slap her lightly. "Are you going to go to brunch?"

"When is it?"

"At eleven."

"I have to work." Savannah says. She looks at her watch. "Let me see if Macy can fill in for me for a couple hours."

"If you don't go, I am not going." Mark says and sinks his teeth into Savannah's side.

"Why the hell am I getting bit?" She laughs. "Let me get my phone." She gets off the bed. She leaves the room.

Mark stands up on the bed and lifts me in his arms. Justin moves over and Mark drops me on the bed. I laugh as I hit the bed. Astro and Bob come in the room and pounce on the bed. Astro sits on top of me.

"Astro! Get off of me." I say. Astro licks my face. "Astro." I laugh. "Stop. It."

Savannah comes back in the room. "I have the whole day off. I am not on the schedule."

"What do you do?" Justin asks her.

"I am a nurse in the NICU."

"Oh wow, that's so great." Justin says.

"Thank you. I love my job." Savannah says. She looks at me. "I don't have anything to wear for brunch."

"We need to go to my house so I can bring Astro home. I have to get changed too." I tell her.

Savannah's phone rings. She looks at it and Piper's face smiles at her. She answers the call. "Pipes, what's going on?"

"I went home with Eric and I was calling to ask you before I call Sebastian to see if you thinks its ok if I invite Eric and Danny to come to brunch."

"I think it would be ok."

"Should I call and ask Sebastian?" Piper asks,

"Yes, but I can give her the phone. She is right here."

"I thought you went home with Mark."

"I did."

"So how are you with her?"

"She went home with Justin."

"Am I on speaker?"

"No." She says. "I am standing in the same room that she is in."

"Oh, ask her." Piper asks shyly.

"You want me to ask?"

"Yes." Piper whispers.

"Pipes, are you there?" Savannah teases her.

"Yes." She says louder.

"Yes, you are there or yes you want me to ask?" Savannah laughs.

"Savannah!" I say. "Stop teasing her. What does she want?"

"I am asking now." She says into the phone. "She is with Eric and she wants to know if she can bring him and Danny with her for brunch."

"Yes." I say.

"She said no." Savannah says laughing.

"Savannah!" I yell.

"Just so you know, I hate you." Piper says laughing.

"She told me to tell you that she hates you." Savannah says to me.

"Savannah!" Both Piper and I yell at her.

"What?" She says. "She hung up." She laughs.

"You are awful." I tell her.

Justin kisses me. "I will take you home."

"I will walk home. Its just two streets over."

"I will pick you both up in an hour." Justin says.

"That sounds great." Savannah says.

I park my car in one of the disabled parking spot. My friends pull their cars into other spaces close by. We all get out of our cars. We greet each other outside before we go inside. When Danny sees me, he runs to me and hugs me.

"I miss you so much." He says.

"I miss you too."

"Are you coming back soon?"

"Yes."

He steps back. "Good because that sub is mean to me. Mr. Ricks lets me stay in his office to do my work. Mr. Smith came in the other day and took over your class. The sub was over worked."

"She said that she was over worked?" I ask him.

"She told us that she hates all of us." Danny says. "She went to slap Addison in the face."

"Why?"

"Addie yelled at her because she was being mean to John-Paul and Luna."

Eric walks over. "Ok that's enough about the tales from school." He says to his son.

Danny hugs me again.

Twix walks over and hugs me. "Well well well! Look what the cat dragged in." She teases.

"Hi Twix." I hug her. "Its good to see you."

"Its good to see you too. The bookstore is coming along nicely."

"You go there?"

"I miss my hangout place. I have been hanging out there for years. I have felt lost without going there and seeing you almost daily."

Before we go into the Marina Beach, Sebastian walks over to me with Amanda next to him. She is holding his hand and wearing a dress

153

that matches the color of his tie. They look like a beautiful couple. They both hug me.

Seth opens the doors and we all go inside. Seth has the restaurant set up with three large tables. The food is set up in a buffet style. Seth ushers everyone inside. It looks even more regal in the day than it does at night. The restaurant is stunning.

Everyone enjoys being there. Classical music plays. There is a screen hanging on the wall and a home video is playing. When I look up at the screen, I realize its me playing the piano.

"How the hell do you have this?" I ask Seth.

"I took it from the internet. I am so proud of you. Would you like to grace us with your playing? Live?" He asks.

"You still play?" Mark asks.

"I do."

"I didn't notice a piano in your house."

"It's in the back bedroom." Piper says.

I look at her and smile. Seth takes me away from the table and takes my hand as he leads me over by the piano. I play Beethoven's Moonlight Sonata and then I play Bach's Canon in D. I return to the table.

"That is amazing." Danny say. "Is there anything you can't do?" He smiles.

"Fly." I say to him.

"No you can. There is an indoor place that you can go to and you can fly."

I look at Danny.

Ginger comes to join us with her daughters. Sara sits next to Danny and he tells her that I play the piano. Sara walks over and hugs me.

The restaurant closes at three. We all leave. Seth stays to get ready for the dinner hour. Sebastian stays with his brother. Jacob stays too. He buses all the tables and goes in the kitchen and cleans all the dishes. He sets the dishwasher so that the utensils and the glasses all get washed.

"She is amazing." Seth says. He strips off the table clothes.

"How do we really get to know her?" Jacob asks.

"She has to feel comfortable with us." Sebastian says.

I go back to the restaurant. I knock on the door. Seth opens the door. "I left my purse somewhere." I say.

"Oh, come on in. We will look for it." Seth says. He walks back into the dining room. I follow him. "Did you see Sebastian's purse anywhere?"

"Lets look for it." Jacob says.

"What are you doing?" I ask,

"Getting ready for the dinner rush." Seth says.

"You have staff that can do this." I say to him.

"I like to help out. My staff isn't here yet. They will get here in an hour. The brunch was a private event. I only had the staff that I wanted here."

"How can I help?"

"You don't have to help."

"I am here. Let me help."

Sebastian and Jacob move the tables back to where they usually go. I put fresh table clothes on them. I set the tables with the napkin sets. I make the napkins look like flowers.

Charlotte comes into the dining from the kitchen. She looks at the four of us. She walks over to me and hands me my purse. "It seems that you and I have the same purse."

"Oh thank you." I say.

"You don't have to help them set up for the dinner hour." She says.

"I want to help. I like being busy. I have been trying to find myself. I own a bookstore. Its being renovated. I stopped going to my day job."

"You haven't been teaching?" Jacob asks.

"Not lately. Two of my students were here today at brunch."

"Sara is in your class?" Charlotte asks.

"Yes. Danny too." I tell them.

"You know, if you were my teacher I would miss you a lot." Sebastian says.

"My kids will be ok." I say.

"Are you planning on going back?"

"I am. I just don't know when. I feel like I don't know who I am anymore."

"You are the sweetest person that I have ever met." Seth says. He looks at the napkins that I have placed on all the tables. "How did you learn to do that with the napkins?"

I smile. "My grandma taught me. My mom's mom."

"These are pretty. Maybe you can teach my staff."

"Sure." I say.

Jacob sits in a chair next to me. "We want to get to know you."

"What do you want to know?"

"Did you have a good childhood?" Sebastian asks.

"I really did. My mom did a great job parenting me." I sigh. "When I was old enough she dated. She brought some of them home and they would stay. They were always nice to me and always wanted me to know that I came first in my mom's life. More than one of them have asked her to marry. She never did. She was very supportive of me. I took dance classes, I took piano lessons. I played sports."

"Which ones?" Jacob asks.

"Volleyball, tennis and basketball."

"Volleyball?"

"I played with my friends not a team. But I learned how to volley and how to serve. I swim." I laugh.

"That's funny?" Charlotte asks.

"I learned how to swim by falling into a pool. My mom jumped in the pool after me. She was wearing a silk dress that she saved up for. We had gone to the cemetery to lay flowers for Sebastian and then she brought me to the park. She told me to stay away from the pool. I didn't think I was close to it. I fell in the deep end. She taught me to swim that day. It took a few hours. Then she couldn't keep me out of the pool."

"I dove into a pool when I was three from the high dive. Sebastian dove in to get me. I went to the bottom of the pool." Jacob says.

"Jacob was our dare devil." Charlotte says. "Did you do anything else?"

"I learned how to ride horses."

"That's so great."

"It was part of my therapy sessions. I walk with a walker." I say. "Working with the horses was supposed to help out with my balance. It never did, but I loved being with them."

The staff come into the dining room from the kitchen. They walk over to Seth. He walks over with them to give them directions. Charlotte and Jacob leave the room.

Sebastian sits by me. "Have you dated a lot of guys?"

"Why are you asking me that?"

"I want to know if I need to go beat up guys from your past."

The two of us laugh.

"No. Thank you, but no." I say. "Guys that I dated were really nice. When the relationship was over, there was no drama, we would just go on. The only one I was ever hurt by was Craig."

"He was the one that died?"

"Yes."

"Did you date anyone else?"

"I dated Zack Evans. He teaches science at Panther Cove Elementary School. When Craig got really sick, Zack stayed with me at the hospital with him. They were friends. When I went to college, I didn't date anyone until I was a senior in college."

"Was he nice?"

"He was nice enough. He was flashy. He liked taking me to plays. He took me to concerts. He is in a dance troupe that travels the world."

"Why did you break up?"

"His life was taking him around the world. My life was taking me back the elementary school that I went to as a child."

"Do you talk to him still?"

"I do."

"Does Justin know about him?"

"No. I haven't talked about him in a while."

"What's his name?"

"Ivan Greggory."

Sebastian looks at me. "You dated Ivan Greggory?"

"Yes,"

"That's so interesting." He drops his voice when he says it.

"Why do you say it like that?" I ask.

"What the hell was he doing in school when you were graduating? He is my age."

"He was teaching."

"You dated your teacher?"

"I didn't take his class. I was at an event and he asked me to dance with him. I said yes not knowing who he was. He never left my side for the rest of the night. I kept his secret."

"Didn't your mom wonder why an older guy was dating you?"

"My mom was caught up in her life. I lived on campus that semester. She came to visit every once in a while. I graduated and she missed it. Ivan did too. He was off in Australia dancing. He sent me the most beautiful roses."

"Justin was there."

"I wish I would have known that when I felt so alone. I graduated alone. Not one person that I know was there for me. Now three years later, I am finding out that grandma was there and so was Justin. I felt so alone." I look at my watch. "I have to go take car of Astro."

"What do you mean, you kept his secret?" Sebastian asks me.

"Ivan is gay. As long as he he was with a girl when he was seen out, no one thought differently. I knew he was. He was flashy. When we would go out, I would have to tame his look. I saw him dance once and I cried. He was so beautiful." I don't say that I cried because I wished I could dance with him. I look at my watch again. "I really have to go."

"What are you doing tomorrow?"

"Going to my bookstore to check things out."

"Can I come?"

"Of course."

"What time are you going over there?"

"I have to run an errand in the morning and then I am going to stop home and get Astro. Then I am going to head over there."

"In the afternoon?"

"Yes." I take my purse. I open it for the first time since Charlotte handed it back to me. To my surprise there is money inside of it. A lot of money. "What the hell is this?" I ask.

"What's wrong?"

"I didn't leave my house with all this money in my purse. What is this?" I take the money out and hand it to Sebastian. I run to the door and leave. I get in my car and go home.

Sebastian goes into the kitchen of the restaurant. He holds the money in his hands. Charlotte looks at him.

"I know that you think you are helping, but this is not helping. This is going to push her further away." He says to his mother.

"I just want to give her back the money that he took from her."

"Mom, what did you do?" Jacob asks. "You took her purse?"

"It was the only way I could think to give her back the money."

"This insults her." Seth says. "This isn't for you to fix it. Dad needs to fix this."

"He left. No one has heard from him." Charlotte says. "I want the three of you to know that I signed the divorce papers."

Jacob takes the money from Sebastian. "How much is here?"

"Twenty thousand. We owe her so much more." Charlotte says.

Seth looks at his family. "I hate to be rude to all of you, but my rush is going to start. Get out. My staff needs to get into action." He kisses Charlotte and hugs his brothers.

Charlotte looks at her sons with a sad face. She had commented that she signed the divorce papers and not one of them questioned her. It was like she said nothing at all. When she leaves, she goes to the condo. When she unlocks the unit that I had furnished, its completely empty.

She walks out of the condo. She knocks on Ken and Diane's door. Diane opens the door for her and invites her in.

"Do you know who removed the furniture from her unit?" Charlotte asks.

"I don't." Diane says.

"Is Ken here?"

"No." Diane puts two cups of coffee on the table. "Are you alright?"

"I am getting a divorce and my sons didn't comment when I told them."

"I am sorry. I know that you love Larry."

"I didn't know that he has another family. I wish that someone would have told me sooner."

Charlotte and Diane talk for hours.

~~~~~~~~~~

Justin and I sit at my kitchen table across from each other. Astro lays by my wheelchair and Bob Cat lays on the table. I scratch Bob Cat. The cat stretches. Justin leans over the table and kisses me.

"Tell me why you invited me for breakfast?" Justin says. He kisses me.

"I needed to see you." I tell him.

"Why?" He kisses me

I push away front the table. Bob reaches for me. Astro jumps up. "I wanted to tell you show you something in my room." I say with a devilish smile.

"Lead the way." He says.

I go into my room. Justin follows me. I remove my shirt to reveal my naked breasts. He steps closer to me and cups them. I arch my back and he kisses me.

"You invited me here to see what?" He teases.

We spend the rest of the morning in my bed. He makes love to me. When I am overcome with sleep, Justin gets out of my bed and takes a shower. He comes back and lays back in bed with me.

My phone vibrates on the nightstand. He reaches over. He sees that Sebastian is calling me. "Princess." He kisses me. "Sebastian is calling you."

I snuggle tighter into the bed.

"Can I answer it?"

I open my eyes. "What?" I ask.

"Sebastian is calling."

"I don't want to talk to any of them." I say.

"Can I talk to him?'

I put my face in the pillow. "Yes."

"I can call him from my phone." Justin says.

"No, its ok."

Justin slides to accept the call. "Hello." He says. He puts the call on speaker.

"Justin? I thought I dialed my sister's phone."

"You did. I am with her."

"Can I talk to her?"

"I have you on speaker."

"Sebastian?" He says. "Just listen. Jacob and Seth and I are together. We want you to know that we had nothing to do with our mom doing what she did."

"What did she do?" Justin asks.

"She didn't tell you?" Jacob asks.

"No. What did she do?"

"She put money in Sebastian's purse."

"How much money are we talking about?"

"Thousands." Sebastian says.

"Why?" Justin asks.

"She feels like she wants to right some of the wrongs that Larry caused." Seth says.

"How is she doing?" Jacob asks.

Justin hasn't taken his eyes off of me since he answered the phone. He wipes away the tears that fall uncontrollably.

"Justin, how is she doing?" Sebastian asks.

"She is really sad. Tell me, how did she put the money in Sebastian's purse?"

"Sebastian didn't tell you?"

"She didn't tell me. The last I spoke to her was yesterday before I left. She was going back into the restaurant to get her purse. She said that she had forgotten her purse. I kissed her goodbye. I had to do some preparation for a case that I am working." He kisses my forehead.

When he leans in to me, I wrap my arms around him. He pulls me on his lap.

"Her purse wasn't there. My mom had taken Sebastian's purse." Seth says. "Off topic, her place settings on the tables last night was a big hit."

"Ok, so your mom took Sebastian's purse. She put money in it. And?"

"And, we are calling to make sure that she is ok."

"What was the money for?" Justin asks.

"Did you know that she cleared out the condo? None of her furniture is in the condo anymore."

"I didn't know." Justin says.

"My mom is devastated." Jacob says.

"What did she do with all of that furniture?" Seth asks.

"I don't know." Justin says.

"When did she move everything out?" Sebastian asks.

Justin looks at me. "You need to talk to us." He says. "I don't have the answers."

I take my phone from Justin and end the call.

"Why did you do that?" He asks.

I cry.

"Talk to me." He kisses me. "What did you do with the furniture?"

"The bedroom set is in the garage. The couches and everything else is going in the bookstore."

"When did you move it? How did you move it?"

"I hired a moving company that works at night." I try to get off his lap. "Eric did it with Trix's dad."

"Is the bookstore ready for furniture?"

"No. The furniture is in storage." I try again to get off his lap. He puts his arms around me. "Justin let me go. I have to pee."

"I am going in the bathroom with you." He laughs.

I get in my wheelchair and go to the bathroom. I finish and go back in my room to get dressed. I have a towel wrapped around my hair. I brush out my hair.

Justin walks in my room and sits on my bed. "I thought you said you had to pee."

I smile at him. "Am I keeping you from work?"

"I do have to prepare for the trial. You can help me if you want." He kisses me. "When are you going back to work?"

"Next week. The truth is I miss my kids. They are a good distraction. They are sweet and love me."

"Distraction?" Justin asks.

"I need it. I need to get back to my life. Then I don't have to deal with my life." I take a deep breath. "First they think I am a gold digger that I somehow wanted to find out that I have a long lost older brother who happens to share my name almost exactly. Then they think that I need to be saved." I leave my room and go into the kitchen.

"Can I ask you a question?" Justin asks as he follows me to the kitchen.

"Sure."

"What did Larry say to you?"

"I told you."

"You told me what you wanted me to know. What did he say?"

"Justin, leave it alone."

He steps closer to me and kisses me. "I am not going to leave it alone. We want to fix it." He steps back. "Did he touch you?"

I look up at him. "Why do you ask that?"

"Is that a yes?"

"No. He never touched me. He told me that if I didn't get my shit out of the apartment, he would kill Astro and destroy me one way or another."

Chapter 14

I go to the bookstore and I am extremely excited at all the changes that have been made. The new sign hangs outside A Cup Of Books. I take pictures of it. Mark is doing a lot of the work. He crosses the room and kisses me on the cheek.

"This looks great." I tell him.

"The security cameras are being installed today." He says. "We are going to finish the floors and then you are ready to reopen." Mark says.

"Thanks."

He crosses the room back to where he was working. "What's going here?"

"A piano."

"You are going to have a piano in a bookstore?"

"There was a piano here before. It never bothered anyone who came in. No one is allowed to pound on it."

"Come see the new section."

I go with him. We go into the new children's section. The coffee shop bookstore will stay open twenty-four still but the children's section will be open from twelve in the afternoon until seven. We go over to where there are five steps leading up to the new section. There is a ramp but it's not yet functional or sturdy enough to use yet. There is a teen section that will stay open until ten-thirty.

"Wow this looks great." I tell him. "I can't thank you enough."

"This has been one of my favorite jobs I have done." Mark says. "Did you tell Justin that you had all your stuff moved out of the condo?"

Mark asks. When I don't answer him, he steps closer to me. "Little Mermaid, talk to me."

"I didn't tell him. Sebastian told him."

"You are referring to yourself in third person?" He teases me.

I look at him and laugh.

"Why didn't you tell him?"

"My life has been full of drama. Just when I am ready to stand up to one, another comes and is bigger than the last." I go behind the counter and make myself a cup of coffee. I make Mark coffee too. "Charlotte took my fucking purse. She knew it was my purse I don't care what she claims. She put money in my purse. A lot of fucking money." I hand him the coffee. "I don't ask anyone for anything."

"She took your purse?"

"Yes." I rub the back of my neck.

Mark walks behind me and rubs my shoulders and my neck. "Has anyone seen or heard from Larry?"

"Larry is with his other family."

"Do they live around here?"

"Close enough. They live in Lake Worth." I look up at Mark. "I just don't want them to blame me for their lives falling apart. It can't be easy for them. Charlotte always knew about me. Sebastian may or may not remember holding me when I was a baby. Jacob thinks that I am a gold digger. He thinks that I came up with some kind of scheme to get money from Sebastian. Now Charlotte puts thousands in my purse. What must they think?"

"What did you do with the money?" Mark asks.

"I left it with them. I don't need their money. I don't want their money. I don't want anything from any of them." I stay a little while longer and then leave to go grocery shopping.

I go up and down the isles at the grocery store. I take a box of tampons off the shelf and add it to my cart. Then I go to the next isle. I pick up a bag of kale chips and put them in my cart. I finish getting what I need for myself and then go over to the dog isle to get items that I need for Astro.

I take my phone out of my purse and see the envelope that Jacob gave me. I take my phone out. I call Justin. He answers right away. "Hi, I am at the grocery store. What wet food does Bob eat?"

He tells me which ones to get then tells me that I don't have to buy Bob food.

I go over to where the beer is and get the kind of beer that Justin likes. The last thing that I get is ice cream. I pay for the groceries and get in my car.

I pull into the driveway. Sebastian is there waiting for me. He runs over and hugs me once I am in my wheelchair. Ms. Conley drives down my street. She waves at me and then pulls into my driveway behind my car. I look at her and smile.

"Hi Ms. Conley." I say as she walks up my driveway.

She looks at me and then at Sebastian. She does a double take looking at him and then at me. "Is this a long lost cousin?" She asks.

"A long lost brother." I say.

"You are Sebastian's son? My good god, you look just like him."

"You knew my dad?" We both ask at the same time.

"I knew Sebastian since he was a little boy." She looks at the two of us. "I didn't know that you had a brother."

"We have different moms." He says.

"What is your name?" She asks Sebastian.

"My name is Sebastian Asher."

She gasps. "You were named after him?"

"Yes."

"Ms. Conley, its warm out here, would you like to come inside and have something to drink or eat?" I ask her. I know that when she comes by she always has a pound cake with her and strawberries.

"I have cake." She says.

"You always do." I smile at her. "Please come in. I have to get this stuff in the house before it spoils."

"You have a big brother who can carry them in for you." She says. She looks at Sebastian. "Make yourself busy."

We all go in the house. I put the groceries away. Ms. Conley sits at the table. I give her a bottle of water and a knife to cut the pound cake. She cuts the pound cake while I finish putting things away.

"Do you have a cat?" Sebastian asks.

"No. My boyfriend visits and when he comes he brings his cat. Not all the time but sometimes and I wanted to have food for him."

"He gets along with Astro?"

"Like they were born friends." I answer. "Astro? Where are you?"

He comes in the kitchen and jumps up to lick my cheek. He wags his tail. Ms. Conley digs in her bag and takes out a treat for Astro.

"Astro, sit." I tell him.

He does and wags his tail. She gives him the treat. He takes it to the kitchen rug and chews away.

"How did yo two meet?" She asks. "Do your mothers know that you know about each other?"

"We met through mutual friends." I say. Telling her the truth would be long and she doesn't need to know all my business. "Our mothers know about each other and they know that we have met."

"Is it just the two of you?" She plates the cut cake and then cuts the strawberries.

"I have two younger brothers from my mom's second marriage." Sebastian says. He looks at me. "Can I help you with anything?"

"No. I got this. Do you want coffee or beer?"

"Coffee is good. I like it with milk." He says.

I take a cup out that says my name on it. I make him coffee. I put it on the table. I make myself an iced coffee. We sit around the table with Ms. Conley.

"Tell me what you knew about my dad." He says to her.

"Your dad was the kindest man that ever walked this earth. He was one of the people that was worth knowing. I bought cars from him. When my grandchildren were learning how to drive, he let them drive in a wrecked car so that if they crashed, there was no loss." She says. "He couldn't wait to be a dad. He was so nice to kids and animals. He was friends with my son. When my son took his life, Sebastian paid for everything."

She stays for a while. She gets up from the table and goes into the guest bathroom. She opens all the cabinets. I knock on the door. "Ms. Conley, stop being a snoop." I call out to her.

She opens the door. "Why do you have condoms in the guest bathroom?"

"That's the bathroom that my boyfriends uses when he comes over."

"You need to have safe sex."

"Ok. Thank you."

"I have to go. I am late meeting the girls for cards."

"Tell your friends that I send my love."

"I will stop by later."

"Fine."

I walk her to her car. She gets in and leaves. I get the mail before I go back in the house. Sebastian is cleaning up the kitchen. I put the mail in the drawer. He looks at me.

"I thought that she would never leave."

"She is sweet. She means well."

"She is a pain in the ass." He says. We both laugh.

"She is a pain in the ass."

"She raided your bathroom." He laughs.

"I know."

He dries a dish. "Where does this go?"

"In the cabinet." I point at the one that is by his knee. "Why did you come?"

He looks at me. "I came to see that you are ok."

"Why wouldn't I be ok?" I open the drawer where I put the mail. I go over to the hook that my purse hangs on and open it. I take out the envelope that Jacob gave me.

Sebastian stands leaning against the counter. I look at him. I hold up the envelope that Jacob gave me.

"If there is money inside, I am going to scream." I tell him.

"I don't know what he did."

I open the envelope and inside a hand written letter. I take it out and just hold it. "Why don't you all just leave me alone? I am sorry that your lives are falling apart because I got a fucking speeding ticket."

"Our lives are not falling apart. I don't know what he wrote. I don't live with him. I know he has been eating his heart out about what he said to you."

"He called me a gold digger. Your mom puts twenty thousand dollars in my purse. Larry threatened to kill my dog—"

"What?"

I close my eyes. "Shit!" I yell.

"Did you say that Larry threatened to kill Astro?"

"Yes." I run my fingers through my hair. "He told me that I needed to take all my shit out of the condo or he would burn it down. He told me that he would kill Astro and record it so that the news could play it over and over and I could watch and be horrified."

He hugs me. "Why didn't you come to us and tell us?"

"Oh my god, are you really asking me that? Your mom must hate me. Is the money to pay me off to stay away? Does she want me to move? I have lived here my whole life. Was the money some sort of statement saying get out of town."

"You are being silly." He says. "My mom is devastated."

"I know. You have said that twice now."

"Not because of you. She is devastated for you. She knows that Larry wronged you and she is trying to make it better, but fucking up miserably. She really likes you." He takes the letter and he reads it.

Sebastian Ashley,

Sorry is not enough. I don't know what to do or what to say to change what I said to you. My brothers and I want to get to know you. I am the middle child and I think when I found out about you, I felt jealous. My brothers are successful, I often feel forgotten. Then we found out about you. Actually Seth found out about you first. I think that's what really pissed me off. I got caught up in the moment. I found myself in the bookstore that I have gone to a lot over the years. I have seen you there and you always look so nice. I would listen to you play the piano and sing when you thought that no one was watching or listening. I always thought to myself that you looked a lot like Sebastian. Now I know why.

We really want to get to know you. I am sorry. I am sorry that my father is an asshole who stole money from you. I am sorry that I didn't trust you from the start. What I learned about my father really makes me sick. I always thought that he was a nice guy. You are a special person. You kept his secrets and that must have been really hard. You knew that he had daughters when we didn't.

If I could ask one thing from you, it wold be to let Sebastian be in your life. I understand if you don't want me in your life, I wouldn't want me in my life either if I were you. But please give Sebastian a chance. He is a great big brother. He is devoted and always there when you need him. All you have to do is call and he drops everything to make sure he is there. You and him share a bond. You are my brother's sister, you really aren't my sister, but if you give Seth and me a chance, we would love you like you are our sister too. I know Seth fell in love with the idea of having a sister right away. I am inspired by you. Watching you at work with the children was amazing. Watching you with your friends and those children, they all love you. I think in his own way, Larry started off loving you too. I know that Sebastian feels close to you and Seth does too. I need time but I want to get to know you.

With my love,

Jacob.

Sebastian looks at the letter and rereads it. "I didn't know he felt that way."

I look at Sebastian. "What are you talking about?"

"My brother's letter to you." He hands it to me. "You should read this."

"I will." I say. "What did you do with the money?"

"I put it in the bank." He says.

"You opened an account for me?"

He doesn't answer.

"Why would you do that? I don't need money. I don't want—"

"I know all of that." He says. "Let me make dinner for you."

"What?"

"I want to make dinner for you. I also want to invite my brothers for dinner. Just the four of us."

"Ok." I say.

He opens the refrigerator. He takes his phone out of his pocket and sends text messages to Seth and Jacob. He looks at me. "I will cook for you. You just don't have enough food to make for more than one person."

I laugh. "I live alone."

Ten minutes later Jacob knocks on the door. When I open it, he hugs me with one arm. He has flowers in the other. Astro walks over wagging his tail and Jacob sits on the floor and pets him. Astro throws himself on top of Jacob.

I go into the kitchen and take a vase out for the flowers. I arrange them in the vase and then add water. "Thank you, these are beautiful."

"My friend is dancing for the Miami ballet, would you like to go?" Jacob asks.

"I would like to go. When is it?"

"Sunday." Jacob looks at Sebastian. "I have enough tickets for you and Seth to go too."

"I will be there."

Seth knocks on the door. I open it for him. He puts bags of food on the floor and hugs me. He pets Astro's head. He picks the bags of food up and goes into he kitchen. He opens the cabinets and takes out four plates. He plates the food.

"What did you bring?" Sebastian asks him.

"Chicken and veal Parmesan. I also brought stuffed mushrooms."

"I love stuffed mushrooms." I say. "What's the stuffing?"

"They are portabella mushrooms stuffed with spinach and bacon."

"Oh my god, yes." I say. "I make that. For the holidays for my friends and family." I get drinks for us. "Do you all want wine? Beer? Or something else?"

"You have wine even though you don't drink wine?" Jacob asks.

"I don't like it. My friends do. My mom does."

"Why don't you like it?" Seth asks.

"When I was in college, I drank a lot of it. I drank red and white. I dated a guy who drank a lot of wine. All different kinds. I always hated the taste of it."

Sebastian looks at me.

I look at him. "What?"

"Ivan drank wine?"

"Religiously." I say. "Good show, he drank wine. Bad show he drank more. He never got violent, he just got sloppy."

"Wait! How do you know who she dated in college?" Seth asks.

"She told me." He says.

"Your friend calls you Little Mermaid, why?" Jacob asks.

"I met Mark when I was young. His dad dated Savannah's mom. When I told him my name is Sebastian he laughed for about ten minutes. Then he called Little Mermaid and it stuck just for him."

"Why didn't you go by Ashley?"

"I love the idea that I was named after my dad. I wanted to carry on his name and honor him." I say it without even giving it a thought.

"Where do you sit at the table?" Seth asks.

"Anywhere."

"What's easiest for you?"

"Anywhere." I say again.

He puts the plates on the table. We sit around the table. Seth takes out his phone and takes a selfie of all of us at my kitchen table. He sends the picture to Charlotte. Jacob clears the table.

"You don't have to do that. I have a dishwasher. She will be excited to have dirty dishes to wash. The last time I ran the dishwasher was a month ago."

"How do you know the dishwasher is a girl?" Sebastian asks.

I laugh. "I named it."

"What did you name it?"

"Wanda." I say.

Everyone laughs.

"Want to watch a movie or something?" I ask them.

"Can we see some baby pictures?" Sebastian asks me.

"Sure. Make yourselves comfortable. I will get them."

"Will you play something for us on the piano?" Seth asks.

"Sure. The pictures are all in there too." I tell them. They follow me into the back bedroom. I hand them albums of me when I was a baby and growing up.

I sit at the piano and play Fur Elise. I then play Prelude in C Major. The last thing I play for them is Dance of the Sugar Plum Fairy. When I finish, Seth sits at the piano and plays Flight of the Bumblebee.

"You play beautifully." Sebastian says to me.

"I went to college on a music scholarship."

"What's your favorite one to play?" Jacob asked.

"My favorite is Moonlight Sonata." I smile. "When I was in college, I played Moonlight Sonata and my friend played on the violin Suite No. 1 in G Major. It was the most fun to watch the teacher contort her face because she wanted to tell us to stop but it was beautiful so she let us finish. We got into so much trouble." I look out the window at the backyard. "I was band from preforming in the last show. She called me a show off."

"Wow, I wish I was there to hear that. I bet it was beautiful." Seth says. "Did you keep in contact with your friend?"

"I do. Lindsey Gina. She travels the world playing the violin."

Jacob looks at me. "You know Lindsey Gina?"

"I do. We were roommates in college." I look at him. "Do you know her?"

"She is a client of one of my clients that rents out yachts. She plays on the yachts."

I smile. "She always loved that."

The three of them look at me.

"What?" I ask.

"She always does the Titanic scene with the violin?" Jacob asks.

I laugh. "She loves to do that."

They continue to look at pictures of me.

"You can stay in here or bring them in to the family room. I have to go take Astro out." I tell them.

"Do you want one of us to take him?" Seth asks.

"If you want to. Thank you."

Seth stands up and walks out of the room. Astro trots behind him. He sticks his head back in the room. "Is there anything that I need to know about?"

"He marks every tree he can reach from the sidewalk. He might try to take advantage because you can go further on lawns. He likes to say hello to the neighborhood cats. They are all friendly and rub against him. I only take him three streets back. Beyond that, there is a big Rottweiler that hates him."

"Ok we will be back." Seth says.

Just as he is leaving with Astro, Justin is walking up the front walk with Bob tucked under his arm. He looks at Seth. "What are you doing? Stealing her dog?"

"Hi Justin. I am taking Astro for a walk."

Bob jumps on Astro and lays flat as a pancake on his back. Justin looks at his cat. He looks at Astro. "You have destroyed my cat." Justin says petting Astro.

"Are they ok?"

"He will stay with Astro for the rest of the night." Justin smiles. He looks at Seth. "Why are you here?"

"We had a private dinner with Sebastian. She showed us pictures of her when she was little. She played the piano for us."

"That's so great." Justin says.

Astro barks and both of them look at him. Seth looks at Justin, "Did you want to walk with us?"

"Sure." He says.

The two of them walk with Astro. As they walk they talk about me.

"So Sebastian was over here when she got home. I don't know if he talked to her about what he had planned on talking to her about. But the next thing I knew, he invited me and Jacob over. We had dinner. There is left overs if you want anything. Its from my restaurant." He smiles. "She loves my stuffed mushrooms."

"Its one of her favorite things." Justin says.

"She was telling us about school and when she played the piano and her friend Lindsey played the violin."

"I showed up to see her in the concert and the teacher made an announcement that Sebastian had been withdrawn from the evening performance. I was so disappointed. She graduated the next day." Justin walks a few steps. He leans in and lifts Bob off of Astro. Astro then does all his business and Justin picks it up.

"I will take the cat." Seth says.

Justin gives him Bob. "Bob, this is Seth. Seth this is Bob Cat."

Seth holds the cat to his chest and they walk back to my house.

They come in the house. Justin stands next to Seth and they both are looking at the piano that is now in the family room. I am sitting at it playing Prelude in C. As I finish playing they all clap.

"What did I miss?" Seth asked.

"We moved the piano for her." Sebastian says.

"Thank you." I say to them.

"Did you know that Justin went to see you that night of the concert?" Seth asks.

I look at both of them. "You were there?"

"I was there. Lindsey Gina was your roommate. She is my dad's cousin's niece. She told them that the finale was going to be epic. She sent my dad a video of the two of you playing. You were playing Moonlight Sonata and she was playing something else. My dad was moved to tears. He bought me a ticket to fly to see you. He told me not to miss it." Justin walks across the room and kisses me.

"I brought dessert too." Seth says.

We go into he kitchen and Seth dishes out ice cream and donuts. We all sit at the table together. Jacob takes his phone out of his pocket and takes a selfie of all of us. Justin looks at him.

"You want me to take it of the four of you?"

"Thanks."

Justin takes my phone off the counter and takes one with my phone. He directs them to sit with me alone and then all together. When he is done taking all the pictures, he sits next to me and Seth takes my phone and takes pictures of Justin and me.

"I am eating dessert before dinner." Justin says.

"Oh my god, dinner was so good." I say.

"I am glad you liked it."

While we are sitting around the table, Jacob goes over to the piano and starts playing. He starts off by playing Chop Sticks. I join him at the piano and we play Heart and Soul together. When we finish we hug each other.

We all sit in the family room and watch a movie. They leave after the movie. Justin and I go in my room and go to bed.

"Did you have a nice day?" I ask him.

"Trial started today. It started out rough." Justin says.

"I am sorry to hear that."

"To be honest, I like when cases start out rough. They can only get better."

I kiss him. "I have to say, I had a nice evening with my brothers." I tell him about Ms. Conley's visit.

Justin settles back on the pillows and falls asleep as I am talking to him. I snuggle closer to him and close my eyes. I fall asleep with my head on his chest.

~~~~~~~~~

Sunday morning I get dressed up fancy to go to the ballet. I love watching dancing of any kind. I am excited that I am going. Tomorrow I go back to work so I am excited to be doing something different before I go back to the same old schedule as always. My bookstore will be opening up in two weeks.

I put on one of my favorite basic black dresses. I go in the closet and take out the black ballet shoes. I put them on. I sit at the vanity and apply my make up. The last thing I do before leaving my room, is grab my fancy purse. I open it to put some money in it and my identification. When I open the little zipper section to put my identification in there, I see a ring that doesn't belong to me. I take it out of the pocket and hold it up.

I call Sebastian. "Hi, I just found something in my purse that doesn't belong to me. I am not sure how it got into my purse."

"What is it?"

"I think your mom's wedding ring."

"Why would my mom's wedding ring be in your purse?"

"She put money in this purse. I only use it when I am going someplace nice."

"Bring it with you."

"I don't want to be accused of anything."

"No one is accusing you of anything at all." He tells me. "Bring the ring with you. I am getting in the shower."

"Bye." I say.

"Bye." He says.

I do put the ring back in the inner zipper pocket. I leave my room and take Astro for a quick walk. I bring him in the house and give him a treat and fill the water bowl for him. I kiss the top of his head before I leave him. "Be good my love. I will be right back." I tell him. I lock the house and get in my car.

I drive to the Marina Beach. I park my car and go into the restaurant. Sebastian and his brothers are waiting for me. I hug each of them.

"Wow you look amazing." Seth says.

"Oh thank you." I say to him. I open my purse almost immediately and get the ring. I hand it to Sebastian.

He takes it and puts it in his pocket.

"What's that?" Jacob asks.

"It's a ring." I say. "Its not mine, but somehow it found itself in my purse."

Jacob holds out his hand to Sebastian. Sebastian gives him the ring. Jacob holds it in his fingers. "Where did you find this?"

"It was in the secret pocket in my purse." I say. "I didn't ta—"

"No one is saying that you did." Jacob says. He looks at his watch. "The limo should be here in five minutes." He looks at his brothers. "I will deal with this if its ok."

Seth looks at Jacob. "I think that would be great." He looks at Sebastian. "It should be one of us."

"I agree." He says. "I think that we all need to address it together."

They all look at me.

"Why are you looking at me? I am not addressing anything."

Jacob's phone rings. He answers it. "The car is here."

We all leave the restaurant. I get in the car. They all get in the car too. The three of them chat among themselves about how they will address the ring situation. I just sit in the car watching the other cars around us. The street signs telling us the exits coming up as we drive south on I-95. I feel like I don't belong there with them.

The car exits off the highway in Downtown Miami and the driver pulls up to the performance arts center. We get out of the car.

I get in my wheelchair and follow them in. We get ushered to our seats and I am not surprised that they are not accessible to me. We are in a box. There are two steps leading to the box but Sebastian lifts me in his arms and Jacob gets my wheelchair.

"These are the best seats." Jacob says.

"Thank you." I say. I am excited now to be here.

The show starts with the ballerinas all on the stage dressed in different colors. They look beautiful. They dance all different styles. Some of them dance strictly ballet. Others dance Irish style. They dance in Spanish style as well.

I gasp when Ivan dances. I look at Jacob and Sebastian. "Did you know he was dancing?"

"I didn't know."

"Oh my god, I wish I would have known. I would have brought flowers for him."

Seth looks at me. "You know him?"

"I do."

The lights come on and the intermission starts. We all leave our seats and go to the bathroom. I meet them in the lobby when I am done.

I look at Jacob. "Do you think that the driver can get two dozen white roses?" I go in my purse and take cash out.

"I will ask him." He says.

"Why white?" Sebastian asks.

I laugh. "He always told me he was allergic to red ones." I look back at Jacob. "Actually, can you ask the driver to get twenty-one white roses. One pink, one yellow, and one lavender."

"Yes." Jacob says. He sends a text message to the driver. The driver sends an answer that he will notify Jacob when he is back with the flowers. "He wants to know long stem?"

"Yes."

The lights flicker and we go back in. This time when we go in Jacob lifts me in his arms and carries me up the steps. He sits me in the plush red chair. Sebastian and Seth move their seats closer to the one that Jacob sat me in.

Chapter 15

Ivan dances every style. As I watch him dance, I cry silently. I cry for how my body won't allow me to move. I cry for how beautiful he is in his rhinestone sparkling glory. He looks the same as he did when I last saw him.

Memories flood my mind. I had just watched him dance and I was so happy for him. He called me on stage with him and he asked me to play the piano while he danced. When I played the last note, he waltzed over and kissed me on the lips. The audience erupted into the loudest cheers I had ever heard.

Ivan asked two of his fellow dancers who were much more manly then he was to hold me and he danced with me. They knew which way to move me so that I was dancing in unison with Ivan.

I blink the tears that are stinging my eyes. When he finishes his dance he looks up in the audience and we make eye contact. He descends the steps on the side of the stage. He runs into the audience and climbs up to where we are sitting. Ivan takes me in his arms and we cry together.

"I knew you were here." He says. "I wanted you to be here. Thank you for being here."

"Oh Ivan. You are beautiful as ever."

"I know right?" He says and we both laugh. "I will find you in the lobby. You look gorgeous." He kisses me on the lips but its not passionate. He looks at Sebastian, Seth and Jacob. "Hi."

"Hi." They say.

"I have to get back for my finish." Ivan says and kisses me again on the lips. "Thank you again for being here." He climbs down and runs to get back on the stage. He slips behind he dark curtain and changes his clothes. When he comes back out, he has a single red rose.,

I close my eyes and tears run down my cheeks.

Jacob leans close to me. "Are you alright?" He asks.

Ivan finds I microphone and addresses the audience. "As many of my followers know, I am allergic to red roses."

The room erupts in laughter.

"This final dance of the night, is for the love of my life. Sebastian, I always love you. This is for you love." He looks up at me.

An usher runs over to me and hands me a single red rose. I hold it up for him. "I love you." I say to him.

He dances a tango with a beautiful female dancer. As the steamy tango ends, the whole room is on their feet screaming their praise.

As the room empties, Jacob picks me up and seats me back in my wheelchair. I hug him tight. "Thank you so much."

"I am so glad that you liked it."

"I loved this." I take my purse and the playbill. "Oh my god, that was so beautiful." I look at Jacob. "Which one was your friend?"

"The one who did the final dance with Ivan." He says.

"She is beautiful." I wipe the tears out of my eyes.

Sebastian steps behind me and pushes my wheelchair as we join the crowd of people that are exiting to the lobby.

The driver of the limo comes into the lobby with the most beautiful flowers. He hands them to me to give to Ivan. He hands long stem pink roses to Jacob. He then leaves to go wait for us to come out.

Ivan walks out into the lobby and the room goes crazy loud with cheers. People line up to take pictures with him and the other dancers. After one steps away and others wait to get their pictures taken with him, he looks at me.

We wait.

A woman dressed in tight fitting black leather that hugs her skin steps in front of me. I look at her. "Lindsey?"

"Sebastian?" She hugs me tight. "Its so good to see you."

"Its good to see you too."

"Did you like the show?"

"You know I did." I look at Sebastian, Seth and Jacob. "This is my friend, Lindsey Gina."

She hugs Seth. And shakes hands with Sebastian and Jacob. "Its nice to see you again. And its nice to meet both of you. How do you know my friend?"

"She's our sister." Seth says.

She looks at me.

"We will have to catch up." I tell her.

Ivan walks over and takes me in his arms again. He looks at Lindsey. "I get her first."

"You always did." She laughs.

He stands and shakes hands with Sebastian, Jacob and Seth. "I am Ivan."

"Ivan, this is Sebastian. Seth and Jacob." I say.

"Its nice to meet all of you. How do you know the love of my life?"

"She's our sister."

"I will tell you all about it." I tell Ivan.

"I think I read something about the four of you in the paper." He says.

Sebastian and I look at each other and then at Ivan. "What?" We both ask.

Sebastian looks at Seth. "What did you do?"

"Nothing." He says.,

Ivan looks at the flowers. I give them to him. He pulls out the red rose that he danced with and hands it to me. "I can't believe you remembered."

"I would never forget." I say. I smell the flower that smells like his cologne.

The beautiful female dancer walks over. Jacob takes her in his is massive arms. He lifts her off her feet.

"Jacob, thanks so much for coming." She says.

"Sophia, I wouldn't have missed you being here for anything." He hugs her again. "Can you go to lunch or dinner with us?"

"We have another show." She says.

I look at Ivan. "You are going to dance again tonight?"

"Yes." He kisses me on the cheek. "I will be right back." He disappears quickly. He returns. "The seats that you had earlier, were they good for you?"

"They were great." Sebastian says.

"I will be right back." He disappears again. He comes back minutes later. "You. All of you, are my personal guests for tonight." He looks at me. "My family is coming to see me dance."

I hug him. "I am so glad."

An usher walks over to us. "I am sorry folks, you have to go." She says.

"We are leaving." Seth says.

Ivan hands all of us tickets and a coupon for a free lunch at Marina Beach Miami location. Seth smiles. Jacob hugs Sophia again. We all say goodbye and then leave. Before I get in the car, I hug the driver.

"Thank you so much." I say to him.

"Did I get what you wanted?"

"Exactly."

"Oh good. Did you enjoy the show?" He asks.

"It was breathtaking." I say.

He looks at Jacob. "Did the flowers meet your standards?"

"They were just what I asked for."

As I am getting in the car, my hand slips and I almost fall. Sebastian grabs me and helps me in the car.

"Are you ok?" He asks.

I am totally embarrassed. "I am ok." I say quietly.

"What happened?"

"I miss judged the seat in transferring." I tell them. The truth is that the car is too far away from the sidewalk that we were all on. I rub my hand.

Seth takes my hand in his hand. He squeezes it lightly and makes me wiggle my fingers.

The driver sticks his head into the car. "I am so sorry. I should have moved the car."

I look at him. "Its ok."

"Did you hurt yourself?"

183

"I will be ok."

Jacob looks at Seth. "Put your paramedic skills to use." He smiles at his brother. "Impress us. Make us proud."

"Shut up." Seth says. He rubs my hand. "Squeeze my hand as hard as you can." I do. "Good. You have good grip. Does it hurt?"

"A little."

The driver opens the window between the front and the back of car. He hands Sebastian a bag of ice. "I am really sorry."

"No worries."

My middle finger is killing me. It is swelling. Seth sees that it is swelling and takes the ice from Sebastian and wraps the bag around my hand.

"Thank you. Are we dressed alright for the night show?"

"Sebastian, you look beautiful." Sebastian says.

"We have time, we can stop at the mall."

"I know where we can go." Jacob says.

He moves over to the seat closest to the window divider and tells the driver where to go. Ten minutes later the car stops in front of boutique. The driver gets my wheelchair out of the car. I get out on my own.

"I am so sorry." He says again.

"No. Its fine." I look at Sebastian after I read the store front. "Timely's Boutique?"

"Anastasia and her daughter own a chain of these." He says.

"So if we go inside, do I get the clothes for free?" I jokingly say.

"Lets see." Seth says. He pushes my wheelchair.

We enter the store. An elegant woman stands next to a rack of clothes. She looks at me and Sebastian. She looks away quickly and then looks back at the two of us. She walks over to Sebastian. She takes his face in her hands.

"Oh my god. You are his children." She looks at me. "You both look just like him." She looks at Sebastian again. ""You are the carbon copy of him." She steps back. "I am Scarlett. Sebastian was my brother."

Neither of us say anything yet. Seth steps forward. He takes Scarlett's hand and shakes it. "I am Seth and this is Jacob. We are Sebastian's brothers." He puts his hand on Sebastian's chest.

"How long have you had this store?" I ask.

"We just opened this one in Miami about a month ago." She says.

Anastasia walks over and hugs all of us. "Grandchildren, this is your Aunt Scarlett."

I look at my grandmother. I am overwhelmed with emotions. I don't know what I want to do. Cry? Scream? Turn and run out of the store? Look around for something to wear tonight?

"I can tell this is overwhelming." She says.

Scarlett looks at Sebastian and me. "What are your names?"

"Sebastian." We both say.

"Both of you are Sebastian?" She asks. "What are your middle names? Do you have middle names?"

"My middle name is Ashley." I say.

"My middle name is Asher."

"You were both named for him?" She asks.

One of her employees walks over. "Are you looking for anything special?" She asks.

"I am looking for a dress." I say.

"What's the occasion?" The young woman asks.

"I am spending the evening with old friends and family." I say.

"You look stunning right now." Anastasia says.

"We told her that." Jacob says.

"I wore this dress to the afternoon show. I can't be in the same dress tonight." I say. "It's a girl thing."

The three guys laugh.

A very handsome man walks over to Scarlett and kisses her on the lips. He steps back and looks around the room.

The young employee is my age. She takes a couple of dresses of the racks. "Come with me. Lets see if any of these will be good. I go in the fitting room with her. She puts the dresses on the hook. "If you need anything, let me know." She turns to leave and then turns back. "Just in case you don't find anything that you like, we can dress that dress up with a scarf or something. Scarlett is really good at accessorizing."

"Thanks."

She closes the door.

I put on the first dress and no matter what I decide, I am definitely getting this dress. I take it off and hang it back up. I put the Second one on and its even better than the first one. I take that one off and put the third and final one on. I don't take this one off. I leave the fitting room with the two other dresses and the one that I was wearing when I came into the store. It hangs on a Timely hanger.

Scarlett looks at me. "It seems like that dress was made just for you." She calls over her husband. "Aaron, look at your dress on my niece."

"Our niece." He says. "How did they other two dresses fit?"

"I will buy all three of them." I tell them.

"What do you do for a living?"

Sebastian and his brother's laugh. Sebastian speaks first. "What doesn't she do?"

"What does that mean?" Scarlett asks.

"I am a school teacher. I teach third grade."

Seth looks at me. Jacob does too. Jacob says, "She is also the owner of a bookstore. She plays piano like an angel. She tutors children in English and Reading. She is a mentor. She owns her own house and she has amazing friends."

I look at Jacob. "Thank you for saying that."

He takes his wallet out of his pocket and walks off with the young woman who was helping me. She rings up the dresses. He walks back over. "Do you need a purse to match?"

I laugh at him. "No. Thank you. My purse is good."

Aaron looks at my purse. "Where did you get that?"

"I have this purse for years." I tell him. "My college boyfriend bought it for me.?"

"Can I see it?"

I hand him the purse. "You have had this a long time. Three years at best."

"Yes." I say. "I have tried to find others like it because I love this purse so much but I can't find anything like it."

"You have taken really good care of it."

"I only use it when I go some place special."

Aaron looks at Scarlett. "She has one of my originals." He looks at me. "Where did you get this from?"

"My college boyfriend gave it to me for a graduation gift. It came with two dozen roses." I laugh. "I hope that he didn't steal it."

"No. He didn't steal it." Scarlett says. She looks at me and smiles brightly. "You look stunning."

"I feel very pretty." I tell them. My stomach rumbles because I am very hungry.

Seth looks at me. "We have a free lunch or dinner waiting for us at Marina Beach." He looks at his brothers and they laugh.

"That is my favorite place." Scarlett says.

"That is Seth's chains." I say.

"You have a gold mine." Aaron says.

I look at myself in the mirror. Jacob takes my phone out of my purse that he took from Aaron. He takes pictures of me. He looks at his expensive watch. "We should go so that we make it back for the show."

Anastasia looks at all of us. "Grandchildren, what show are you going to?"

"Our friends are in the ballet." Jacob says.

We exchange numbers with Scarlett and Aaron. Anastasia hugs all of us. Jacob walks out carrying the dresses. He puts them in the car. We get in the car and leave.

We go for a late lunch or early dinner at Marina Beach. This one is not as elegant as the new one but Seth definitely has a signature that is present from one location to the other. When we go inside, Seth walks into the kitchen and tells the staff what to bring out. By the time he does that, we are seated at a table. There are drinks for all of us.

The server puts wine in front of me. "I don't drink wine." I tell her.

"Oh, I am sorry. Let me get you something else."

Seth looks at his staff member. "If you look at the iPad, you will see her drink."

She looks at Seth. "I thought that only family was on the iPad list."

He smiles brightly. "She's my sister."

"Oh. I am sorry." She says. "I didn't know. I didn't know you have a sister."

"Technically I have three of them." He says.

"Can I have a chocolate vodka?" I ask.

"Of course." She says.

Seth walks off with her. "When you come back with her drink, bring over lavender roses."

She smiles. "Its good to see you again, Seth." She kisses his cheek. "I miss you."

"Come work in my new location."

"I think Trix would lose her mind."

He laughs. "You might be right." He kisses the top of her head. "Your sister is a knock out."

The staff brings out the food. They put chicken Marcella in front of each of us. We eat. Seth orders a plate to go for the driver. Before we leave, I go to the bathroom. I join them at the table.

"Oh my god, that was even better than the Parmesan." I tell Seth.

"I am glad you liked it."

"Everything is so good."

They leave the table first. I open my purse and leave a hundred dollars for the tip. I know that wasn't enough to cover the food. I write a napkin. Thank you, everything was so good.

I get in the car. They all get in the car. We go back to the theater. Before we go inside, Seth gives the driver the food.

Seth looks at his phone which has been chiming with text messages. He reads them.

The girl that was with you, left money in the bathroom for the staff member who cleans up the bathroom.

The girl that was with you, left a hundred dollar tip and a thank you note for all of us.

The girl that was with you, stuck money under her plate for the staff to pay for dinner.

Seth takes hold of my wheelchair and pushes me. We go inside. An usher meets us and takes us back to the seats that we were in earlier. This time when we get there, we are not alone. Ivan's sister, mother and father are there. On the one seat there is a giant teddy bear and roses. Jacob is holding me in his arms.

"Do you want to sit in your wheelchair or one of these chairs?" He asks.

"I will sit in my wheelchair." I tell him.

Seth brings my wheelchair up the steps and he holds it while Jacob lowers me into it.

I hug Ivan's family. I introduce everyone. The theater fills up quickly and then the lights are lowered for the start of the show.

This time when it starts there is a screen behind the dancers. One of the female dancers takes a microphone.

"Good evening ladies and gentlemen. Thank you for coming out to support us. We don't normally have a screen behind the dancers, but we wanted to share something with all of you. We don't show this often, but we—" she looks around the stage at the other dancers. "We want someone in the audience to know just how loved she is." The lights dim even more. "Enjoy the show everyone." She says.

A small lavender light projects on the screen. It grows slowly and the dancers are all curled up on the stage. As the light gets bigger, one by one they stand up. On the screen is me playing the piano and Linsey Gina playing the violin. I get chills watching it. The dancers on the stage are ballerinas. Sebastian hugs me.

"Oh my god, its even more than how you described it." He whispers to me.

Ivan's sister reaches out and takes my hand.

As we finish playing the audience all stands and applauds.

The same dancer who announced the video takes the microphone again. "Just so you all know, we show this video on our last night in a town. Tonight we are graced with the Pianist in the audience. Can I have a spot light on box A upper level?"

The light shines on us.

"Sebastian can you please wave at everyone?"

I wave and the audience roars with cheers.

"Thank you." The dancer says. "We usually end our show with that but we decided to change things a bit tonight. We are going to take a quick moment and then the show will go on."

The lights on the stage go black. A few minutes later, the Irish style dancers start. The guys do a fight scene and Ivan is the lead. When the dance ends, he is the victor. He holds the body of the other dancer above his head.

Ballerinas come out next and dance something similar to Swan Lake. Other ballerinas come on stage and dance something similar to Sleeping Beauty. When the finish, the lights come on and they take an intermission.

Ivan's dad looks at me. "Ivan couldn't be there for you that night. He wanted to be there that night. He asked me to go. I recorded it for him so that he didn't miss it entirely."

"Thank you." I say.

"Did you ever watch yourself play?" Jacob asks.

"No." I say. "My mom isn't tech savvy. My friends were in different schools." I look down at my hands. "I didn't know anyone recorded me playing."

"People have seen it all over the world. Ivan pays tribute to you in every city he dances in." His dad says.

"I didn't know that."

"Its so nice to see you." His mom says.

The lights go dark. Two spotlights light up the stage. The light show is a show in itself. As the dancers, dance a Paso Doble the lights travel around the stage. When they finish dancing, female dancers fill the stage and dance a Cha-Cha. As the show comes to an end, they end it with most of the dancers dancing a sexy Rumba.

The lights flicker and the dancers all take a bow. The audience erupts again in cheers. One of the dancers takes a microphone. "Ladies and gentlemen, friends and family, we have one more dance of the night. Please enjoy."

Ivan takes the stage dressed in all black. His long hair is slicked back. He looks so sexy in his rhinestones that make him glow under the lights. He glimmers. Sophia takes the stage dressed in a red dress. She looks sexy as well. Her long hair flows to her knees.

Lindsey Gina steps on the stage with her violin at ready. She plays La Cumparsita Tango. She looks beautiful playing. Her long hair shines as she sways with the movements of the violin. Sophia jumps in Ivan's arms at the end and then throws herself backwards. They end the dance with her upside down.

I wipe the tears out of my eyes. Jacob hugs me tight. He lifts me out of my wheelchair and carries me down the steps. Sebastian lifts my wheelchair this time. This time when we go out in the lobby, Ivan finds me immediately. He takes me in his arms. Cameras flash from all around us. Ivan kisses me on the lips again like he did earlier in the afternoon. He shakes hands with Sebastian, Seth and Jacob. "I have to go. I love you." He tells me.

"I love you too."

"Did you get the flowers and the teddy bear?" He asks.

"We brought them out to the car in the intermission." Seth says.

Ivan kisses me again. "Love of my life." He says and then he is gone.

There is a guy standing off to the side dressed in a sliver suit. He walks over to the four of us. He takes me in his arms and hugs me. I look at him when he steps back.

"Trevor?" I ask.

He puts his hand over his heart. "You remember me?"

"Of course." I look at my three brothers. "Sebastian, Seth and Jacob, this is Trevor Elliot. Trevor, these are my brothers."

"You have the most amazing sister in the world." He says. "She saved my life." After he says it he hugs me again.

"I saw the pictures of your beautiful wedding. I wish I could have been there for the two of you." I say.

"We wanted you there. We got married in India after one of his shows. It was unexpected. We both got down on one knee. We both proposed and then twenty minutes later we were getting married. It felt right."

"Congratulations." I say.

"We got your gift. It was so generous." He hugs me again. "I have always loved hugging you."

"I have always loved being hugged by you and Ivan." I look at Trevor. "You look amazing."

"Thank you. You look gorgeous. You are wearing Aaron Blake's designs. I have seen many models look elegant in his dresses, it looks like that dress was made for just you. No one wears it better." He kisses my cheek.

"He's my uncle." I say.

Trevor coughs. "Your uncle?"

"No I am serious. I just met him today for the first time."

"Aaron Blake is your fucking uncle." He says.

"He is married to my dad's sister."

"One of his suits costs more money then I make in a year. That dress most have cost a pretty penny."

I look at Jacob. "I don't know, it was a gift."

"Someone must love you a lot." Trevor says. "Ivan and I are going to be in town for a few days and we went to spend time with you. Are you available?"

"For the two of you? Always."

"Actually we are going to Jacksonville tomorrow to check on the young mom who is carrying for us. We will be back on Thursday through the weekend."

"You are going to have a baby?" I ask.

"Yes."

"Congratulations." I say. "Do you know what you are having?"

"We do. But we are going to have a reveal party on Saturday." He looks at all of us. "You are all invited." He looks at me. "Are you still friends with Ginger and Savannah?"

"Piper too." I say.

"Oh bring them and their boyfriends or husbands."

"I will let them know."

Ivan walks back over to us. "Sweetheart." He says kissing Trevor. He kissed Trevor like none of us are there. "We have to go take pictures." He gathers all of us. His family, the four of us and the two of them. "Take out your phones and give them to the men in black." Ivan says. All at once, phones are going off snapping pictures of all of us.

The director of the show walks over to me. She shakes my hand. "Sebastian, its nice to meet you. I have heard so many nice things about you. Would you mind coming with me for a moment. We want to have a picture taken of you with you playing the piano." She looks at Sebastian and Jacob. "I mean if that's alright."

"We don't make decisions for her." Sebastian says.

"I would love that. Can I watch the video again?"

"I think that would be more than alright." She says. She looks at her watch. "Am I keeping you from anything?"

"Not at all." The four of us say.

We go back into the theater and Sebastian lifts me up in his arms and brings me on the stage. There is a piano on the stage. Ivan and Trevor come in the theater. Ivan's family sits in the seats. Lindsey Gina walks out on the stage. She embraces me.

She sits on the bench with me. I face the piano keys and she turns her back from the keys. "Moonlight Sonata and Canon in D." She says.

I look at her. "Yes. Which one do you want me to start with?"

"Right on the mark like always." She says. "You start with Canon."

I play Canon in D. She starts playing Moonlight Sonata. When we reach a certain part in the pieces, we switch. We both smile at each other. We both end with the middle part of Canon in D. Its our favorite thing to play the middle section. When we finish everyone runs up on the stage to hug us both.

Trevor looks at both of us. "I need you both to do that at the baby reveal. When you finish playing, we will pop the balloon."

We leave shortly after. On the way home, I lean against the giant teddy bear and fall asleep. I have had the best day of my life in a long time. Tomorrow, I have to go back to work.

Chapter 16

Back to school. It feels like the first day of school all over again. Only its in the middle of October. The second I got to my classroom, unlocked the door and stepped inside, the skies opened up. A storm blew in and stayed most of the day. The children loved having Astro and me back.

Due to the rain, lunch was delivered by the cafeteria staff to the classrooms. After lunch was over, we were supposed to take a recess. The rain limits us on what we can do. Mr. Smith comes in with Sparky and Ms. Rowe brings her class into my room. We let them run around with the dogs and be as loud as they want.

Outside, lightning strikes close and the when the thunder claps, the kids hide under the desks. The storm really rages on.

Mr. Ricks makes announcements. "We are going to have early release as the weather is just going to get worse as the day goes on. I need all of the third and fifth graders to come to the office."

Mr. Smith looks at me. "You keep Sparky and I will take them up."

"Oh thanks." I say. "Due to the bad weather, I am giving you all a present."

My whole class stops and looks at me.

"No homework. I want you all to try to watch the discover channel. Pick two segments you like so we can all discuss tomorrow." I look at the clock. "I want all of you to stay out of the puddles no matter what."

One by one they hug me. Mr. Smith comes back a short time later. "There is a break in the rain, let me take them out." He takes the dogs and they go outside. Astro stands in the same spot for minutes.

Mr. Smith comes back in the room with the dogs.

"I have towels in the closet." I say.

He walks over to the closet and takes out two towels. He dries the dogs. "Where is your car?"

"Oh right, my car." I say.

"Where is it?"

"In Deerfield at the Marina Beach."

"What's it doing there?"

"I left it there yesterday because I went to Miami with family. That was the meeting point."

"How did you get home?" He asks. He helps me clean the room.

"I have no idea." I laugh.

"Ok." He says. "Now that the kids are gone, it stops raining." He says. "I am going to get out of here."

He goes into Ms. Rowe's room and I hear them laughing like they are kids on their first date. I roll my eyes. I gather my stuff and get ready to leave.

I go to the office to clock out. I am no longer doing after school care because the director who took over thought that I was irresponsible for taking time off. I am glad that I can just go home today. I didn't really want to be here in the first place.

The day was a nice distraction. I clock out. I take my phone out of my purse and without even thinking, I call Sebastian. I am surprised he answers on the first ring.

"Hi sweetheart." He says.

"Hi. I don't mean to bother you."

"You are not bothering me."

"My car is still at the Marina Beach. I walked to work with Astro. It has been raining all day."

"I will be right there." He says. "I am ten minutes away."

"I don't want to keep you from your day."

"Sebastian, I am coming to get you."

"Ok." I say.

What seems like three minutes later, he comes through the front doors of the front office. He takes Astro and my bags. He walks to the car and puts the bags in the back seat on the floor. Astro jumps on the backseat.

As I am leaving the office, I hear crying. I look around and at first don't see anyone. I hear a male voice yelling. The crying gets louder. I look around again and behind one of the support walls that is like four feet wide I see Danny. A guy I don't recognize is holding his hand and is yelling at him.

I go over. "Is there a problem?" I ask.

The new director of the after school program looks at me. "Mind you business."

"Excuse me, he is my business. That is one of my students."

He looks down at me. "Oh it's the unreliable Ms. Timely." He says.

"I am sorry, I don't know who you are." I say.

Danny tries to pull away and the guy lets go of his hand so Danny falls in the puddle. "Look what you did stupid." He says to Danny.

I reach my hand out. "Danny, come on." I say.

"You stay there. You pissed your pants, now you are all wet." The guy yells.

Sebastian runs over. He grabs the guy by the shoulders and pushes him back. Mr. Ricks comes out of the office. He looks at Danny in the water. "Daniel? What's going on?"

"He doesn't know how to to follow simple directions." The director yells.

Mr. Ricks goes behind Danny and lifts him out of the water. Danny is crying.

"Cry." The director says.

Mr. Smith walks over. "What the hell is going on?" He looks at Danny. "I thought you went to the bathroom."

Danny looks at Mr. Smith and cries harder. Mr. Smith gets on his knees in front of Danny. "He wouldn't let me go in the bathroom. He blocked the door. I really had to go. He made me go in my pants. Then he dragged me out of the school and went to hit me."

"What a fucking liar." The director yells.

"The whole school is under surveillance." Mr. Ricks says.

"Danny, lets go get you cleaned up." Mr. Smith says.

"What's a bastard?" Danny asks.

We all look at him.

"He called me a bastard. What is that?"

"Your mommy didn't want you." The director says.

Danny crumbles to the ground sobbing.

Eric pulls into the parking lot. He sees his son on the ground and he comes over running. "What's going on?"

The director looks at Eric who stands taller than him. "Nothing."

"Why is my son wet?"

"He fell in the puddle." The director says.

Eric squats in front of his son. "Tell me what happened."

Danny curls up on the sidewalk crying.

Eric looks at all of us. "Some one tell me what the fuck is going on."

"I heard crying, I came to investigate and saw this guy holding Danny's hand. Danny had apparently had an accident."

"I really had to go." He cries.

"When I came over to address the situation, Danny pulled to get away from him and he let Danny fall in the puddle."

"Shut up you lying bitch."

"Hey!" Sebastian yells. "Don't talk to my sister like that."

Eric picks Danny up. "Come on. Lets go home."

"He called me a bastard." Danny cries."

Eric puts Danny down. He walks over to the director and pushes him against the support wall. Mr. Ricks and Mr. Smith grab Eric.

"We will deal with this." Mr. Ricks says.

Piper runs over. She looks at Danny and Eric. She stands behind Danny. "I am sorry I am late. I got a flat tire. I know its my day to pick him up from work, honey."

Danny turns to Piper and hugs her.

"Did you get wet from the rain?"

Danny looks up at her. "No."

Piper looks at Eric. "I am so sorry I am late. I got the text message that they were releasing early from school but I was in a meeting. When I left, I had a flat tire."

"Piper, its ok." Eric says. "Can you take him home?"

"Yes." She says. She takes Danny by the hand. "Where's your backpack?"

I look at Piper. "He doesn't need it. I didn't give any homework."

The director looks at Danny. "I thought he was lying about that."

Danny looks at me. "He called you a lying bitch." He says. He looks at Eric. "Sorry for my language."

Mr. Ricks looks at all of us. "I am going to deal with everything. Danny when you come to school tomorrow, come to the office and get your backpack."

"Thank you." Danny says.

Piper hugs me. "Where is your car?"

"Its at the Marina Beach. I will tell you all about it."

"Good. I am coming over with dinner." She says. She kisses me on the cheek.

"Pipes, he needs to sit on a towel. I have towels in my room if you want me to get one."

"I have towels in my car. We went to the beach yesterday." She says. She puts her arm around Danny. "Come on. We have a lot to do."

Sebastian looks at me. "Astro is in my car."

"Oh right." I say.

We go get in the car.

"I have to stop somewhere before we go get your car. Are you in a rush?" He asks.

"No."

"What time do you expect Piper?"

"Whenever I get home." I say. "When we get together, they wind up staying and sleep in my bed with me."

"Fun." He says. He pulls the car out of the parking lot. He pulls on the the street and heads east. "Can I ask you a question?"

"Thank you for coming for me."

"No worries." He says. "Can I ask you a question?"

"Yes."

"Last night. Trevor said that you saved his life. What did he mean by that?"

"Can I ask you a question?"

"Yes."

"How did I get into my bed and in shorts and a tank top?"

"You were out cold. Justin came over and changed you. Don't worry my brothers and I didn't see your body. I carried you into your room. I took Astro for a long walk." He looks back at Astro who sleeps on the backseat. "I really wish I would have known about that third street. That Rottweiler wanted to kills us." He looks back at Astro. "Did he tell you that I carried him home?" He teases.

I look at Sebastian. "He mentioned something about that, but I thought that he was making it up because he thought he needed to make you sound good." I tease back.

We both laugh. Astro lets out a big snore and we laugh more.

"I answered your question. Please answer mine."

"Trevor exaggerates." I say.

"I don't think so." He looks at me. "Those two men although gay, absolutely love you. Ivan refers to you as the love of his life and Trevor says that you saved his life. I don't think they are exaggerating."

I look away from Sebastian. "Where are we going?"

"I have to stop at my house." He turns right at the light going south. He pulls into a driveway that is never ending. Gates close behind us.

"Holy shit. You live here?"

He looks at me. "This is my home."

"Do the royals live with you?" I ask.

"My cat Astro lives with me."

"You live here alone?"

"Yes." He says.

He pulls the car into a garage. He gets my wheelchair out of the car and we go into the house. Astro my dog trots after us. The second we are in the house, Astro the cat greets us. He is a big cat. He rubs his body along my wheelchair.

I look around. "Jesus, you can put two of my houses into this house and still have room."

"Sebastian, its just a home."

"No. This is not a just a home. This is incredibly beautiful." It occurs to me that I was able to just follow him into the house. He didn't have to help me in.

"Make yourself comfortable." He says.

"Why did you bring me here?"

"I have been to your house three times now. You haven't been to my house at all." He says. "Can I get you something to drink or eat?"

"No. Thank you."

"Let me show you around." He says.

"My god, this is the biggest thing I have ever seen." Everywhere I look there is more to see. "Its like a museum."

He goes in the kitchen and takes out food. He makes us dinner. He makes spaghetti with broccoli and chicken strips. He makes a salad.

"Tell me what Trevor meant when he said you saved his life."

"You don't give up."

"I will ask him."

"Ask him." I say.

"He said when he hugged you, he couldn't believe that you remembered him. What did he mean by that?"

"Sebastian." I say. "Can I have some water?"

"Flat or sparkling?"

"Flat is good."

He hands me a bottle of water. He puts a bowl of water down for my Astro. His cat comes and rubs against my wheelchair again. Sebastian picks up his cat and gives him to me. "He does that until you pick him up."

I hold the cat close. He rubs his head into my face and neck. Sebastian goes back in the kitchen. I hold Astro cat.

"I met Trevor by accident. I was driving Savannah to the airport. I dropped her off so she could go back to school. She came to surprise me for my birthday. When I was driving back home, I noticed a car was flipped upside down. I pulled over and called for help. They pulled him out just before the car burst into flames." I take a sip of water. "They were loading him into the ambulance and he begged for them to let me go with him. A firefighter drove my car to the hospital."

"What happened to him?"

"He had just come out to his family and they told him that he worthless. They told him that he would be better off dead. He drove off the overpass of I-95. I stayed in the hospital waiting to see him. When I was allowed into the room, I held his hand the whole night."

"Why did you do that?"

"I felt like I had to be there."

Sebastian puts the food on the table. "What can I give Astro to eat?"

"I have food for him in my bag."

"I will go get it."

"We can eat first. This looks really good."

"Its not as good as Seth's."

"I don't want it then." I tease.

"Fine! Be that way." He teases back. "Have you spoken to Justin?"

"Not in days. He is working a big case. I write him text messages and he answers when he can. I don't want to be needy."

"Sometimes guys like girls to be needy."

"He has my number. He can text me." I look at Sebastian. "Its because of you that he and I are dating. If we are dating. I see you and your brothers more than I see Justin." I take a bit of the food. "This is so good."

"You don't have to lie." He says.

"I am not lying. This is delicious."

"There has to be more to you saving Trevor's life."

"I went as close to the car that I could. I saw him moving so I knew he was alive. I called out to him and told him that help would be coming and he needed to hold on. I told him that he was loved. He cried that no one loved him." I blink tears back. "I told him that he hadn't found the right people to love him. I told him that the world would be broken if he was lost."

"Sebastian, you are amazing. Why does Ivan say that yo are the love of his life?"

I cover my face with my hands and cry.

"Tell me."

"Ivan drank a lot. Like I said the other night, he drank if the shows were good. He drank if the shows were bad. If he got a good review he drank. If he got a bad review he drank. He got sloppy." I drink water. "I found him naked in the shower. He had passed out. Somehow, I was able to get him out of the shower. He crawled his way to bed. I stayed with him until he woke up. He vowed never to drink again. It took him a week to get sober. The next time he danced, he was perfect. He left a week later." I cry. "He promised to be at my graduation. I wanted him there."

"Why did he leave?"

"He said he had to. We were never lovers. But he loved me. I loved him. I knew he was gay and it didn't matter to me. I think people were starting to notice that he was gay and then he was gone. My mom saw him dance in Europe. She told me that he was beautiful." I stroke my Astro. "In the chair that was meant for me if I needed it was a giant teddy bear and two dozen roses at my graduation." I look at Sebastian. "Similar to the ones in the theater."

Sebastian pulls his car into the Marina Beach. Seth is outside talking to Trix. They both walk over as I get out of Sebastian's car. Astro runs to Trix. She squats and takes his head in her hands.

I take my bags out of Sebastian's car and put them in the trunk of my car. I hug the three of them. I get in my car and I go home.

I take Astro for a walk. I walk on the front street first and then loop back to my street. I follow that up by going one more street so that Astro gets some exercise. I avoid Justin's street. As we are returning home, a car pulls into my driveway. Justin gets out.

"Where have you been? I have been so worried about you. I haven't heard anything from you since Friday."

"I sent you text messages." I tell him. "I assumed you were busy and ghosting me."

"No. I swear I didn't get any messages from you."

"I can show you my phone. I wrote and sent you messages."

"I ran into Eric at the store he told me what happened at the school. Are you ok?"

"Nothing happened to me." I say. "I am fine."

"Where were you?"

"Come inside." I tell him.

"I saw a picture of a guy kissing you."

"Before you get upset about it, that is my friend. We are just friends. He is married."

"You kissed a married guy?"

"He kissed me." I say. "Astro in." I say.

"Who is he?" Justin asks.

"You are going to meet him and his husband on Saturday." I put my stuff down when I go in the house. "If you want to come."

"Who is he?"

"Ivan." I say. "Jacob had tickets to go see the ballet. He asked me I wanted to go with them. I did. Ivan was a major dancer. I didn't know he was dancing. He didn't know I would be there. We haven't seen each other since before my graduation."

I go in my room and Justin follows. I take my shirt off and toss it on the floor. I go into the closet and get out a tank top. "I am sure that Sebastian or one of them told you a little bit about last night. Sebastian told me that you changed me out of my dress and in to my pajamas."

"Are you mad at me?" He asks.

I leave my room. I open the front door and go to the mailbox. I get the mail and come back in the house. I open the drawer and put the mail in the drawer.

"Are you mad at me?" He asks again. He crosses the room and kisses me.

"I am not mad. I thought that you were moving on."

"Why would you think that?"

"I sent you text messages all weekend. I heard nothing from you."

Justin takes his phone out of pocket to show me that he has no messages from me. As he opens the app for the messages his phone springs to life and he is flooded with many text messages.

He looks at his phone they are all from me. He reads a few. One catches his attention right away.

Sebastian: my mind is blown right now. I met my dad's sister. She owns a boutique in Miami. My uncle is some kind of famous designer. My aunt looks like my dad. My mind is blown.

"You met your aunt and uncle?"

"Yes."

"How did you meet them?"

I tell him about Jacob offering to take me to Miami to see dancing. I tell him about seeing Ivan and the rest of it. When he asks about Ivan and Trevor I tell him all about them. The same conservation that I just had with Sebastian.

"You are amazing." He says.

"How is your case going?"

"We have a week recess."

"Why?"

"The other lawyers lost their shit in court. The judge is giving everyone a week to pull ourselves together."

I laugh.

"What else happened today?"

"I think I got the new director of after school fired. But as I was driving home, I was thinking that I could offer a part of my bookstore for after school care."

"I think that would be a great idea." Justin says.

"Yeah, that way, I can go from one job to the next two all in one shot." I laugh but I am being serious.

"Show me pictures from your weekend." Justin says.

We go sit on the couch and I show him pictures.

Tuesday morning, I go into Mr. Ricks office and tell him about the idea that I had about offering some space in my bookstore. I work it out that I will only work half days at the school so that I can go to the bookstore and get it set up for the after school care.

"As long as I am not losing you." He says.

"You aren't losing me."

"The kids are going to be sad,"

"The ones who have to go to after school care are going to be happy. I can't stand what I saw yesterday. Danny is a sweet kid. His dad is a nice guy."

"I called the district and he got fired." He looks at the clock. "I will call the district and let them decide about the after the school care but I think it's a great idea."

Pam walks in. "What if the cafeteria needed some work done after school? What if we have to do a cleaning overhaul."

"Pam, you and I will talk." Mr. Ricks says.

I leave the office and go into my classroom. Zack Evans walks into the classroom. "So it seems I am going to run your class in the afternoons." He hugs me.

"I want to be here with my kids but I have to go get the bookstore organized."

"If you need help, my brothers are available to help set up. They are contractors. I know you have the Case contractor."

"Zack, send them over. I need all the help I can get. I just offered to host after school care in my bookstore."

"That's the greatest. Dumbest. Greatest idea." He says.

We laugh.

Mr. Smith walks in with Ms. Rowe. They walk over to where we are in the room.

"So it seems that you will only be working part time?"

"Good news travels fast." I say.

Ms. Rowe holds a magazine in her hand. "Are we going to lose you altogether now that you are famous?"

"What are you talking about?" I ask her.

She hands me the magazine. On the cover is Ivan, Trevor and all of us that were at the theater. "Open it up." She says. "It seems that you have a famous uncle who designs clothes. And you are a world renown piano player."

"When does she have time to be a pianist?" Zack asks.

"Read the article." Ms. Rowe says. "It seems like our little teacher lives many lives."

"Karen, you know me since college. You know who the people are in the pictures. You know that I went to school on a music scholarship. Same as you."

"The article mentions that you have brothers. That is something that I didn't know. We pledged as sisters in college not to keep secrets." She says.

"My private life is just that. Private."

"Your brother is rich. Your uncle is a famous designer. You don't need to teach."

"What I need is my friends around me."

"Are we friends?" She asks. "You always ran to Ginger, Savannah and Piper first."

"I have known Savannah and Piper since I went here as a student."

205

"It was always you and your mom. Where the hell did brothers come from?"

"Actually, I have one half brother. We had the same dad. My brother has two brothers who have taken me on as their sister. They just found out that they have two half sisters on their dad's side."

Zack looks at me. He had taken the magazine from me and was flipping through it while we were talking. He opens to the page where it's the big screen behind me on the stage while Lindsey and I played. "You both played again?" He says.

I look at him. "What do you mean again?"

"I was there at your graduation concert preview. You both were amazing. You were such a joy to watch. The funniest thing was watching the music teacher's reaction. She wanted to stop you both but it was too beautiful." He looks at me. "It was sad that she band you from playing the final show."

"She did more than that." I say.

The bell rings letting us know that the buses just pulled into the school. The day is going to start in twenty minutes.

Zack makes himself comfortable in the room. Mr. Smith leaves with Sparky and Ms. Rowe. Zack looks at me before the kids come into the room. "You know, Karen is just jealous because she and others didn't think to do what you and Lindsey did."

I smile at him.

"Wha else did the music teacher do?" He asks.

"There was a scout coming to see Lindsey and me play separately. She told me the wrong time and told Lindsey the wrong day. Lindsey's dad heard about what was happening and he got her another shot with the scout." I take a deep breath. "I graduated and came home."

"What did you guys play this time?" He asks with a bright grin.

"Moonlight and Canon in D."

"I am sorry I missed it."

"Ivan and Trevor are having a baby reveal. Want to come?"

"Am I taking over your class in the afternoons?" He asks.

I look at him and smile. "It's Saturday. When I know more details I will let you know."

At twelve thirty I leave to go to the bookstore. I stop home and take care of Astro. I take him for a long walk. I decide to take him with me to the bookstore. I pull my car into the first space. We go inside.

"Ma'am, you can't be here with a dog." A guy says.

"She can be here and the dog can be here too." Mark says. "She's the owner."

"I am sorry." Th guy says.

"No worries." I say. "Hey Mark is it too late to make changes?"

"For you, its never too late, Little Mermaid." He kisses me on the top of my head. "Tell me what you want." He looks at his watch. "Little Mermaid, schools not out yet. Why are you here at one?"

"That's what I want to talk to you about."

"Did you eat? I ordered food in."

"No. I am not hungry."

"I saw a magazine article that made my mouth drop."

"Which part?" I ask as I secure Astro behind the coffee counter.

"My bottom jaw dropped." He teases.

I laugh at him.

"It seemed as though you were kissing a guy who is not my brother."

"Wrong. I was being kissed by an old friend."

He looks at me.

"Mark when you kiss me sometime, you kiss me close to my mouth. The guy in the picture is Ivan. I dated him when I was in college."

Mark looks at me with a serious face. "Little Mermaid, you do know that he sparkles brighter than you do."

I laugh. "You are going to be with him and his husband on Saturday. We are all going to a baby shower." I go off with him and tell him what I want to do about the day care area.

Chapter 17

Thursday when I leave the school at noon, I get in my car and go to the Marina Beach. That is where the baby reveal is going to take place. I go there to help out with decorations. I pull into the parking lot and there is a parking spot that catches my attention. The concrete bumper is painted with frames from the Little Mermaid. I pull my car into the spot and get out of my car.

I open the trunk of my car and get out all the decorations. Seth meets me at the door and offers to take the bags but I have everything in my seatbelt.

Joy walk over. "Seth, aren't you going to help her?"

"She doesn't want my help."

"I got it." I tell them.

"We are going to set it up in the back room where we had your birthday celebration."

"Its nice of you to do this." I say to Seth.

Jacob walks in the Marina Beach and comes behind me and tips my wheelchair backwards. I scream as I didn't expect it and then laugh when he kisses me on the forehead. "Seth, are you fucking kidding, you didn't ask if you could help her."

"I did offer to help." Seth says.

Jacob pushes me the rest of the way in the room. I put the decorations on the table. Seth asks his staff to come in and help out.

"Just tell us how you want it." Joy tells me.

I show them the picture that Ivan sent me. He wanted something similar to the photo. Trix comes into the restaurant. She helps out too. We get it all done. I take a picture of it because I think it looks better than the picture Ivan sent me does. The picture that Ivan sent was only decorated for a boy. So we combined the pinks and the blues. In one corner of the room, I set up the signs that read it's a boy or it's a girl.

Jacob looks at Seth. "Where is the piano going to go?"

Seth looks around the room. "We don't have a piano."

"They want her to play the piano and when she finishes they are going to pop the balloon and reveal what the baby will be."

"I will see if I can get one here." Seth says.

I look at Seth. "Just show him already." I say.

"You can't keep a secret."

"Nope."

Seth walks over to the one wall that we didn't decorate and the wall opens up to reveal a stage area with a baby grand piano. "Does it need tuning?"

I go to the piano and play it. I play soft and gradually get louder. "No, its good. Whoever moved this piano did it vey carefully." I run my hand over the keys. "This is the most beautiful piano that I have ever seen."

Sebastian walks into the room. "This is amazing. Who did all of this?"

"We all did."

I look at my watch. "I have to go. Ivan and Trevor are coming to my house for dinner."

Seth leaves the room. He goes to the kitchen and comes back minutes later with bags of food. "Let me put this in your car. Will someone be there to help you get it out?"

"I can do it." I tell him.

"Its very heavy and very hot." Seth says.

Trix looks at Seth. She kisses him on the lips. "I will follow her home and help her get the food in the house. Then I have to go to my job."

"You are on a stakeout?" Jacob asks her.

"Not exactly. I can't talk about it now, but I will tell you all about when I can." She says.

I say goodbye to everyone. I hug Sebastian. He holds me tight in his arms.

"You are incredible."

I smile at him. I get in my car. Trix follows me to my house. When she carries the food in the house, I get the mail. Astro jumps all over Trix. She sits on the floor with him and pets him.

"Can I ask you a question?" I ask her.

She looks up at me. "I know what you are going to ask but go ahead."

"Which one of them are you with?"

She laughs. "The truth is, I have been with both of them. Separately. They know it. I love them both."

"I am not judging." I say to her.

She stands up and brushes her clothes off. "I have to go." She hugs me. "I will see you Saturday."

"No. Tomorrow. There is no school so I will be at the bookstore. You said you would be there."

"I will be there with my dad. Make a lot of coffee."

"I am watching Danny tomorrow for Eric."

"Oh nice. Your friend Piper is all over him when she thinks no one is looking."

"I think she has been with him for a while. She has been a bit distant from me. I am busy. She is busy. I know that when she has a boyfriend she stay away because she doesn't want any one to feel bad if they aren't in a relationship too."

"Well, I will rub it in your face everyday." Trix says. She flips her bright pink hair around. "I have to go." She hugs me before she walks out of the house.

I go in my room and change my clothes. I go in the kitchen and take the food out of the bags. Everything smells so delicious. I put the mail in the drawer. I feed Astro. I get ready to take him out for a walk and as I open the door, Justin is there. He has flowers for me and a little stuffed dog hugging a stuffed cat.

"Hi beautiful." He says.

"Hi."

"Let me take him for a walk. I will skip my street so that Bob doesn't get excited."

I laugh. "You can bring Bob over. They have cats." I kiss Justin as he leans in to get Astro's leash. "How did your case go?"

"We are on a recess." He says. "I have been working on other things. I was in court all day today and sat what seemed like a hundred cases. They were quick ins and outs." He walks outside with Astro.

I put the flowers in a vase. I put a table clothe on my dining table. I set the food up on the kitchen table. I put the flowers in the middle of the table. I have flameless candles and I get the remotes and set them. I put the stuffed animals on the windowsill.

Justin gets back with Astro. He walks in and kisses me. Astro trots behind him. "Bob is hanging out with Savanah and Mark."

I laugh. "Traitor."

Ivan and Trevor knock on the door. Ivan doesn't wait for me to open it for them, he comes in the house with two dozen roses. He looks around and sees that I have the roses from the weekend on the bar countertop. The oversized teddy bear sits on a chair by the piano. The single red rose is in a vase. I made it look like the bear is holding the vase.

Ivan smiles. He walks over and hugs me. He gets down on one knee and takes me in his arms. "Its so nice to see you, my love."

Trevor stands back. He takes the fresh roses and arranges them in a few vases. He cuts some of them short and arranges them in a square vase. He takes the ribbon from the wrapper and ties it on the vase.

Ivan stands up and introduces himself to Justin. The two of them shake hands.

Trevor gets down on both knees and takes me in his arms. "Its good to see you, beautiful." He kisses me on the cheek. He stands up. "Is that one of your uncle's designs?"

I laugh at him. "No. I have had this a long time."

"I am telling you, that is one of your uncle's designs."

"Ivan got this for me years ago. It doesn't have a label. Its one of my favorite things to have on."

"Everything looks beautiful." Ivan says. He walks over to the wall where I have pictures hanging. He looks at each one. "You hang this?" He asks. Its one of him dancing.

"It has been on the wall since I had it put on canvas." I say.

Trevor introduces himself to Justin. "It's nice to meet you. How did you meet our Sebastian?"

We tell them how we met. After we chat a while, we have dinner. Trevor makes coffee royals for each of us. We talk for hours. Ivan washes the dishes while we talk.

Justin, Ivan and Trevor exchange stories about me. Ivan tells Justin about the first time he saw me. He tells Justin about his bad habit. His drinking and how I saved him.

Trevor walks over to me and sits next to me. "Tell me about your amazing life."

I laugh. "My amazing life." I laugh again. "I teach third grade at the elementary school that I went to when I was young. My kids are great. I worked in a bookstore for three and half years. I saved up enough money to buy it and fire two of the managers." I laugh.

Justin looks at me. "You fired Matt?"

"First chance I got."

"What else do you do?" Trevor asks. "Have you saved any lives lately?"

"That's all I do." I say.

Justin walks over and sits next to me on the couch. I am not sitting on the couch. He looks at me. "She tutors children and adults. She is a mentor."

Ivan is looking at pictures on the wall again. He turns around and looks at me. "You still mentor?"

"I like to be busy."

"You leave poor Astro alone all day while you work?" Ivan asks. He sits on the floor and pets Astro.

"Actually, I bring him with me ninety percent of the time. When I teach, he comes with me. When I am at the bookstore, he comes with me. When I mentor, I take him with me for security reasons."

Justin snaps his head up from the magazine article he is reading. "What does that mean?"

"Its not in a great neighborhood, but that's where I was assigned from the court."

"From the court?"

"Community service for all my speeding tickets." I say.

"You are still getting speeding tickets?" Ivan asks.

"I need to get where I am going quickly."

"If you didn't have so many obligations you wouldn't have to speed to get places." Justin says smiling. "I will look into that community service thing tomorrow. You don't need to be in shady neighborhoods."

"If I wasn't speeding so much, I still would think that I was an only child."

Justin changes the subject asking Ivan about his dancing. "What kind of style do you dance?"

"I dance all styles. I was trained in classic ballet. I can do Latin dances. I do it all but Hip-hop. I don't like that. I do that for a workout when I think I need to be challenged." He says.

We all laugh.

Trevor takes his iPad and clicks on theYouTube app. He types in Ivan's name and we all watch Ivan dance. The one that Trevor clicked on is of not only Ivan dancing but of the video of me playing the piano.

When the video ends Justin grabs me in his arms and hugs me. "That's beautiful." He looks at Ivan. "That's really great." Justin kisses me. "You should sell the bookstore, give up teaching and go travel the world playing the piano while dancers preform."

"I am not a concert pianist." I say.

A knock sounds at the door and I am grateful for who ever is wanting to visit. I go to the door. Ms. Conley stands in front of me holding a magazine in her hands. "Does your lovely boyfriend know that you are kissing other men?" She almost yells at me.

"Ms. Conley, why does my life interest you so much?" I ask her.

"Are you going to invite me in?" She demands.

"I have company."

"What's one more person?" She asks. She pushes herself into my house. She looks at Justin. "Your girlfriend is cheating on you."

"I know." He says.

I look at him.

"She is not a faithful girl." Ms. Conley says.

Now I look at her. "How do you know that? I don't date a lot of guys. The guy in the picture—"

Ivan walks over to me and kisses me on the lips like he did at the theater. "Ms. Conley? Is it?" He asks looking down at her. "You have misjudged the best person I have ever known."

"Who are you?"

"I am the one that is kissing her in that picture."

I feel my cheeks burn. "Ms. Conley do you have nothing better to do in your life then mess with mine?"

"I am looking out for you. Someone has to. Lord knows your mother doesn't."

"Ms. Conley, I am an adult. I don't need anyone looking after me. My mother doesn't live here anymore." Now I don't feel so grateful for the interruption. "Ms. Conley, I have company. You have to go."

"Are you going to have sex with all three of them?" She asks.

Trevor walks over to all of us. He kisses Ivan on the lips romantically. Ms. Conley gasps. I look at her. "You have to go." I tell her.

"I will call your mother." She tells me.

"Please do. Tell her I am thinking of her and that I love her very much."

When she leaves, she slams the door behind her. She gets in her car and she hits the mail box. We all hear it fall. I roll my eyes.

"Your neighbor is rude." Trevor says.

"I know, she murdered my mailbox." I say.

Mark and Savannah come to the house. Mark carries Bob in the house. He hands me Bob. He walks back outside and looks at the mailbox. It is destroyed beyond repair. Mark cleans up the pieces. He walks in the house.

"She really did a number on your mailbox." Mark says. "Before I go to work tomorrow, I will fix it."

"Give her the bill." Ivan says.

Savannah hugs Ivan and Trevor. "Its good to see you both again. Congratulations on your marriage, I saw pictures. You both looked incredible."

"Thank you." Trevor says.

"Mark, this is Ivan and Trevor." I say. "This is Mark. He is Justin's brother."

"Its nice to meet you." Mark says. He looks at Ivan. "You are the dancer."

"Yes." Ivan says.

"I saw you dance in New York a few years ago. I was very impressed." Mark says.

Ivan smiles. "Thank you."

Mark looks at Trevor. "You are the designer."

"You follow us?" Trevor asks.

"I knew you were both very important to Little Mermaid. She's important to everyone in this room." Mark says

Justin kisses me on the lips.

Savannah sits at the table. She looks at all the flowers. "Wow, Sebastian. These are beautiful."

"They really are pretty." I say.

"And that is the biggest teddy bear I have ever seen." She says.

Piper and Eric knock on the door and just come in the house. They both hug me. Piper looks at Ivan and runs to him. She hugs him. "Ivan, its so good to see you." She steps back and looks at him. "You look fabulous."

Trevor sandwiches her when he hugs both Piper and Ivan.

"Congratulations on your marriage. I saw the pictures." She says.

"Oh thank you."

She rubs Ivan's flat stomach. "I am excited to hear about the baby coming." She teases.

"Listen, honey. I would have carried the baby if I could." Ivan says. He hugs Piper.

We all sit down together. I take pictures of all of us., we are really enjoying being together and getting caught up. At midnight, the grandfather clock that I have chimes. Everyone stands up. Trevor puts all the coffee cups in the dishwasher. Ivan and Trevor leave first. They hug everyone.

Eric sleeps on the couch. Piper sits next to him. I look at her. "Go sleep in the guest room." I tell her.

"We have to go to his place. My car is there and I have to be at work early." She says. She looks at herself. "I can't wear this to work."

We both laugh. She wakes Eric and they leave. Savannah and Mark return to his house. Justin goes in my room and waits for me to come to bed. I clean up the house. I clean the whole kitchen. I take out the vacuum cleaner and vacuum the kitchen and family room.

Justin comes into the kitchen. "What are you doing?"

"Cleaning up."

"Sebastian, come to bed."

"I will be right there."

"Sweetheart, you said that almost an hour ago."

"I am sorry if I woke you."

"You didn't wake me. Your house is spotless. A surgeon could preform surgery in here and it would be germ free." Justin says. "When we have to clean our house I am coming to get you." He walks over an takes the vacuum from me. He kisses me on the lips. "I love you."

"I love you too."

"Can you play something for me?"

"What do you want to hear?"

"Anything."

I sit at the piano and I play a medley of Phantom of the Opera, Memories from Cats, and Part of Your World from The Little Mermaid. I finish playing and take Astro outside.

Ms. Conley is sitting on my porch. When I close the door, she speaks to me. "You owe me an apology."

I scream. Justin comes out of my house wearing nothing but boxer shorts. I put my hand over my chest. "What are you doing here?" I ask Ms. Conley.

"You owe me an apology."

"I don't think I do." I say. I look at Astro. "Come on." I say to him. Justin takes his leash and walks.

"Are all your men still in the house?" She asks.

"Ms. Conley go home."

"You are a slut."

"Ms. Conley, I am not a slut." I look at her. "You owe me a mailbox. You murdered my mailbox."

"Now you are a liar too."

"Ms. Conley, I have never had any problems with you in all the years that I have lived here. My whole life. Why are you looking for trouble from me?"

"Does your mother know that you have all those men in her house?"

"It is not her house. She moved out. My mother knows about the men in my life."

"So you admit that you have more than one?"

"I have Astro and Justin. Those are the only men in my life. I was having a get together with my friends earlier and you ambushed it. Those men that you met, I went to college with them. They are my friends."

"Have you slept with them?"

I don't answer her right away. The truth is that I have slept in bed with all of them. I have only been intimate with Justin. I look at Ms. Conley. "To be honest, yes I have slept with all of the guys that were at my house today."

"I always thought that you were a nice girl. Now I think differently of you."

A police car drives down the street and I am grateful when he pulls his car into my driveway. He walks over. "We received a call that someone from this house screamed. I am here to make sure that everything is alright?"

"I screamed." I say.

"Is everything alright?" He asks.

"My neighbor refuses to leave my porch. She was here earlier tonight and insulted me and my friends so I told her to leave. She drove her car into my mailbox."

"That's not true." Ms. Conley says. "Her mother lives here. She is trespassing."

"Ms. Conley, what the hell are you saying? My mom hasn't lived here in years. I own this house."

Justin walks back over with Astro. The police officer looks at Justin and laughs. "Case what are you doing with a dog at this hour?"

"Tucker, this is my girlfriend, Sebastian."

The police officer looks at me. "Sebastian, is this your house?"

"I have lived here my whole life. I bought the house from my mom."

"Ma'am, where do you live?" Officer Jason Tucker asks Ms. Conley.

"A couple streets back." She says. She looks at Astro. "Her dog bit me."

"Ms. Conley! That is not true. Astro never bit anyone." I say.

Allison comes running up my walk. "Sebastian, are you ok? I am sorry I didn't get here sooner. When you screamed I was just putting the baby back to bed. He is having a rough night." She looks at Ms. Conley. "Ms. Conley, what are you doing here?"

"I am sitting on my porch." She says.

"Ms. Conley are feeling well?" Officer Tucker asks.

She looks around. "Oh right." She says. "I am at the slut's house."

Allison sits by Ms. Conley on the bench seat. "Ms. Conley, we have both been neighbors with Sebastian for many years, we all know that she hardly ever dates." She looks around. "Ms. Conley did you run into her mailbox?"

"No." She says. "Her dog bit me."

Officer Tucker looks at all of us. "Ok that's enough. Everyone needs to go home."

"She owes me an apology." Ms. Conley says.

"Why?" Allison asks.

"She threw me out of her house."

"Why?" Justin asks.

"She was entertaining men in her home."

"Ms. Conley, I have to work tomorrow. You have to go."

"There is no school tomorrow." She says.

"You sure do know a lot about her life." Officer Tucker says.

"She is a slut." Ms Conley says.

"You need to stop calling her names." Officer Tucker said.

"Ms Conley let me take you home." Allison says.

She looks at Allison. "You are going to leave the baby by himself?"

"No. My husband is with the baby and his big sister."

"I am not leaving until I get an apology." She shouts.

"Stand up." Officer Tucker says. He offers Ms. Conley his hand. "You have to go."

"No. I can't go. Her dog bit me. I can't move my leg." She starts kicking her legs out in front of her.

Officer Tucker walks away and calls for backup and for EMS. When they come, they remove her from my porch and bring her to the hospital. Officer Tucker stayed a bit longer. He takes pictures of the destroyed mailbox.

~~~~~~~~~~~~~~~~~~~

I get to the bookstore at seven-thirty in the morning. Eric is waiting in the parking lot. He gets out of his truck and Danny jumps down. He runs to me and hugs me. I kiss him on the top of his head.

"Thanks for keeping him for me."

"Not a problem." I say. "He is such a sweet kid."

"In his backpack, there is a sandwich for lunch. He has snack foods." Eric says.

"Eric, please, I got him."

"If you need me, here is my cell phone number."

"Eric, I got him. If I need anything, I will call Peter and get a message to you. Go to work and don't worry about him. He is good with me."

"Thank you." He says. He walks over to Danny and picks him up. He hugs him. "Be good. I will call you in a little while."

"Love you."

"Love you." Eric says.

We go inside. Danny looks all around. "Wow this place is so big."

"Ok freeze." I say. "Before we go any further, you can not go where the men are working. You have to stay within sight at all times. If you have to go the bathroom, you have to use the one up here. It says women but it's just a single toilet and sink."

"Can I sit up there?" He points to the stage.

"Yes." I look at him. "Danny, do you want some breakfast?"

"My dad said not to ask you for anything."

"Danny, you didn't ask me for anything. I am asking you. Do you want anything? I am limited, but I have bagels and donuts."

"I like a chocolate bagel."

"How did you know I have chocolate bagels?"

He grins.

"Go sit."

"Can I walk around?"

"Yes, but not where the workers are."

"I know." He says.

I go over to the kitchen area and cut the bagel. I pop it in the toaster. When it beeps, I put it on a plate for him. I bring it to him.

"Do you have kids books?"

"There are kids books." I say.

"Can I look?"

"Of course. Pick one and we will read it together."

"So then two books?"

"Yes." I say. "Eat your bagel first. Then you have to wash your hands."

"I know." He says.

"I know you know." I kiss the top of his head.

He laughs.

"What are you laughing at?"

"Piper does the same thing."

"She's the best." I say.

"You know her?"

"She is my best friend."

"She says that Savannah is your best friend."

"Danny, people can have more than one best friend."

A group of teenagers walk into the bookstore. I look at them. "Sorry guys, I am not opened yet." I tell them.

They all leave.

Jason Tucker walks in. "Hey, how is everything going?" He asks.

"Everything is good."

"I just wanted to let you know that your neighbor is undergoing a psych evaluation. When they loaded her in the ambulance, she went a little cooky and banged her head."

"I am sorry to hear that. Normally she is great. Nosy. But great."

"Those kids were pissed off that you aren't opened yet."

"I open next week." I say.

"We have school next week." Danny says.

"Danny, we go to school on Monday and then we are off for the rest of the week."

"That's stupid." He says.

"I didn't make the schedule." I tell him.

"Did one of the kids leave a little brother behind?" Officer Tucker asks.

"No. I am babysitting him today. He is one of my students in school. His dad is related to my mom's boyfriend."

"Too much information." He says. He looks at Danny. "What are you eating?"

"A chocolate bagel."

He looks at me. "You have chocolate bagels?"

"I do. Do you want coffee with that?" I ask.

"If its not too much?"

"Its not too much."

"This place is great." He walks around.

Danny looks at me and raises his hand.

"Danny, you don't have to raise your hand. What do you want?"

"Can I walk around with the police officer?"

"Yes. Just remember to stay away from the workers." I say. "Danny, let him know that you want to walk around with him."

"Can he help me pick out a book?"

"You can ask him." I say.

Mark walks over and kisses me on the cheek. "Little Mermaid, the work is done. You can tell your staff to get the bookcases. We will load them in."

I do just that. I call everyone who worked in the bookstore. I call the moving company that loaded the books and bookshelves out. They told me that they could have everything loaded on the trucks by one-thirty. Then delivered by three.

The movers got the shelves delivered by one-thirty. Everyone showed up by two to help set everything up. It was starting to look like a homey bookstore again.

Matt walked in the store. I looked at him. "What are doing here?"

"Sebastian, this has been my favorite place of work for years."

"Bullshit Matt. You were hired after me." I say to him.

"I want my job back." He says.

"Submit your resume." I tell him.

He looks at me. "Are you aware that there is a child in here?"

"Yes."

"I love this place. I love what you have done to it. I want to work here. I want the midnight shift."

"Let me think about it." I say to him.

"Can I at least help set things up?"

"Yes."

He calls his friends and about twelve people who I recognize from the poetry nights and open mic nights come in. Everyone works hard to get things set up. Matt walks over to me after about an hour.

"Can I point something out to you?" He says.

"Yes."

"The shelves don't go up as high as they used to."

"I know."

"Why?"

"I can not get books that are on the top shelves."

"Are we still going to use them?"

"Yes."

"For what?"

"The wall of fame." I tell him.

He looks at me. That was his idea months ago in a store meeting. His mother shot it down. She thought it would be too much work and too costly.

"We are going to all it Cup of Books wall of fame."

"Can I make the sign for it?"

"I would like that."

I look over at Danny who looks bored to tears. "Matt, can you do me a favor?"

"What?"

"Can you and some of your dramatic friends read to him?"

Matt looks at me. "My friends are not dramatic."

He no sooner says it when one of his friends takes a straw from the iced coffee he was drinking and makes like he is stabbing himself.

"Ok. They are dramatic." He says. "What's his name?"

"Danny."

"How old is he?"

"He is almost nine."

"My brother is almost nine. I think he is in your class."

"Who is your brother?"

"Tristian."

"I do have a Tristian in my class." I say.

Matt walks over to Danny and takes him by the hand to the new children's section. He picks a book and hands copies of the books to Danny and his three friends. I send Matt a text message. Letting him know that Danny struggles to read. He looks over at me and gives me a thumbs up.

They picked the One and only Ivan. Matt and his friends read through the book first so they know what they are reading. Then they start reading it as if it's a theatrical work of art. I look over at them and smile. Danny is even participating in it.

Eric comes by to get Danny after four. When he comes into the bookstore, it is sixty-five percent done. He walks over to Danny. "We have to go. You have soccer."

Matt looks at Eric. "My son— my brother plays soccer too."

I look at Matt. I heard his slip. He said his son. I know one thing about Matt for sure. A River Runs Through It is one of his favorite books. When he is really bored at work on slow nights he rereads that book.

Eric looks at Matt. "Who is your brother?"

"Tristian." Matt says.

Danny's eyes light up. "He is my best friend."

Matt looks at me. I nod my head. He smiles. After Eric and Danny leave, Matt walks over to me. "You heard my slip of fucking tongue?"

"How old were you?"

"She was seventeen. I was fifteen. My mom adopted him." He looks away from me. "You must think that I am an asshole."

"Not for that." I say. "Tristian is one of my best students. I didn't know that you were his family. Whatever you are teaching him, keep doing it because he is great. He is compassionate and always willing to help. He is the first one to finish his work. Nine out of ten times its all right."

Matt smiles. "I work really hard with him."

"It shows."

"Now that he is older, my mom lets me spend more time with him. Its going to be so nice to have kids in here."

"I agree."

"I heard you were trying to do after school care here."

"I was. It got shut down."

"What if we offered it unofficially? We are going to be here. We have the spaces set up for them. We can have a buddy system going. They help each other out with homework before they get to play."

"Lets open first."

The door opens and my mom, Peter, Anastasia, Scarlett and Aaron walk in. Scarlett gasps.

"This is beautiful." She says.

My mom walks over and hugs me. I hug her back. "What are you all doing here?" I ask.

The door opens again and Savannah and Piper walk in. Ivan and Trevor are with them. Ginger follows a few minutes later.

"What are you all doing here?" I ask. "We aren't ready."

"This is beautiful." Scarlett says again.

"Thank you. They just finished all the construction work today." I say. I look at my mom. "Its good to see you. Where are you getting back from now?"

"Peter and I went to Alaska."

"Wonderful."

"It was very nice. We had a great time."

Scarlett looks at my mom. "Let me get this straight, while your daughter is here working her ass off going from one job to another, you and your boyfriend are off vacationing every chance you get?"

"Don't judge me." Mom says.

Anastasia walks around the store taking it all in. She walks over to the piano. "Why a piano in a bookstore?"

"Its always been here. In the past, there were open mic nights and some of the performers played the piano while reciting poetry."

"I read that the book store is open twenty-four seven." Aaron says. "Are you still going to keep it open twenty-four seven?"

"Yes."

"Who will work the night shifts?" He asks me.

"I will work until midnight and then the graveyard shift starts." I look at everyone who looks at me. "The same people are going to work here that always did. The only difference is that I own the it now."

Sebastian walks in with Seth and Jacob. They stop when they walk inside and pause.

"This is amazing." Jacob says. He crosses the room to where I am and hugs me.

Mark takes out his phone and takes pictures of my family with me. He kisses me on the head before he kisses Savannah on the lips. I see the disappointment in her eyes for a moment. Mark didn't kiss me to make her feel bad.

Seth joins me in the kitchen area of the bookstore. He kisses me on the cheek. "We have to throw you a grand opening."

"That would be so nice." I say.

Matt walks over and hugs me. He shows me the artwork that he did for the wall of fame. It looks stunning. "Its not the final one but something like this?"

"Matt that is really amazing. I think that's it. I don't know if I would change anything."

"My mom called and Tristian needs a ride to soccer. She is the one who is there with him and I have to leave what I am doing to go get him."

"Go and come back. If I am gone, your keys still work." I open the drawer that has all the keys from before. I made everyone turn their keys in just in case we got different locks. I hand him back his key and his badge.

He hugs me again. He leaves.

The bookstore is loud with all the people that are there. I go into the bathroom and come out minutes later. Uncle Aaron is waiting for me. He gives me a hug. "Trevor sent me pictures from last night at your get together. He said that you were wearing my designs."

"It's my favorite thing to wear." I say. "Only I didn't know its one of your pieces. It was a gift from Ivan. It never had a label in it."

"You look beautiful in it." He says.

I smile. "I feel beautiful when I wear it." I look around the room at my family.

He looks across the room. "That's a beautiful piano."

"It really is." I say.

"Did you bring it in?"

"No. The bookstore has been open for years. I have worked here for three and half years. It was here when I used to come in as a reader. One night, I was the only person in the bookstore and I asked the guy working if I could play. He said I could. The next day, I noticed more and more people playing the piano."

"Play something for us." He says.

Lindsey Gina walks in the bookstore. She runs over to me and hugs me. "Is it still here?" She asks.

"Its where you left it." I tell her.

She hugs me again. She looks around. "I didn't know that you were open yet."

"I am not open until next week."

"Ginger told me that I should come."

"I am glad you did." I tell her.

"Who are all these people?"

"My family."

"Wait a minute. In college you were an only child." She says.

"I just found out that I have a brother. He has two brothers."

"And who is that?" She points at Anastasia.

"That is my dad's mother. The one next to her is her daughter."

"Where is your mom's mom?" Lindsey asks.

"I haven't seen her in years."

Aaron announces to the room. "Please everyone quiet down, my beautiful niece is going to play the piano for us."

Everyone sits at the tables that have been set up. I sit at the piano. Lindsey lifts the piano bench that is off to the side and takes out her violin. She sits with her back to me. We both play Moonlight Sonata. We finish and everyone cheers.

"Beautiful!" Aaron says.

We all stay for a bit longer. I leave the bookstore at seven that evening. I have been away from Astro all day. I pull into my driveway and go into the house quickly. I let him run out. I feed him. I put his leash on him and we go for a walk. He walks next to me. We go back to the house and I check the mailbox. My new mailbox is beautiful. Mark made me a mailbox that looks like a little house. It even has a chimney. I smile as I take the mail out of the box. Astro and I go in the house and relax for the evening.

Chapter 18

The reveal party is scheduled to start at noon. I get to the Marina Beach at ten. Trevor and Ivan pull into the he parking lot after I do. Trevor opens the trunk and takes out a big box. We go into the restaurant together. Seth greets us and takes the cake from Trevor. Trevor follows Seth into the kitchen.

"Don't look." Trevor says.

"Of course not." Seth says. "You still could have the balloon if you want."

"No. Ivan is terrified of of balloons."

They come into the room where we are having the party. It's the first time that they are seeing it. Ivan runs to me and takes me in his arms and hugs me tight. "This is just how I dreamed it would be. You always know what I want. You are truly the love of my life." He says. He pulls back and brushes the tears away. He kisses me on the lips.

Trevor hugs me. "This is amazing."

"I didn't do it all by myself. I had a lot of help from Seth and his employees." I say.

Seth walks over and shakes his head. "She was yelling at us when we hung things in the wrong spot."

I laugh. "I did not."

Seth kisses me on the forehead. "This is a very special person."

Sebastian walks in. "I agree." He looks at me. "Uncle Aaron wanted me to give this to you." He hands me a jewelry box.

Ivan looks at Sebastian. They exchange a look. I open the box and gasp. I close the box and hand it back to Sebastian.

"This is for you." He says.

"No." I turn and run out of the room.

Justin is coming in the restaurant and runs to me. He takes me in his arms. "What happened?"

I am crying so hard, I can't catch my breath.

"Sebastian, sweetheart, breath. What's happening?"

Sebastian comes running out of the room and runs to me. "What upset you so much?"

Ivan walks over. "I am sorry. I didn't think it would upset you that much. I asked him to design it for you."

I cry harder.

"What's going on?" Justin asks.

"I have to go to the bathroom." I say in a low voice. I leave them and go into the bathroom.

Sebastian and Ivan talk to Justin. Seth joins them. He looks around and doesn't see me. "Where is she?"

"She went in the bathroom."

"What was in the box?"

"Its ballerina pin." Sebastian says.

Jacob walks in to hear that and walks past all of them into the bathroom. He knocks before he comes in. I am in front of the sink crying. Jacob takes me in his arms. I cry on his shoulder.

I come out of the bathroom and go back in the room. I pull myself together. I go to the piano and play Carol the Bells. I play it so softly. All I want to do is leave. I also want to stay because my best friends are having a baby and I want to know if I will be an aunt to a boy or a girl.

Ivan stands next to me. "I am sorry. I thought that you would like it."

I look at him. "Ivan, when I thought that you were dying, that's what you held in your hand. The pin of the ballerina."

"Oh my god, I didn't know. It went missing. I never have found it."

I look at Ivan. "I have it. I will never take it out of where it is."

"Please don't be upset."

"I am fine. I was taken by surprise."

"I want you to have the angel dancer."

"No." I look at everyone in the room. "You can give it back to him. I am sure that its worth more than I make in a year."

"You are his niece."

"I don't know him. I don't want him to buy my love."

"You have worn his collection for years." Ivan says.

"I didn't know. He didn't know."

"You do now and so does he." Ivan leans in and whispers in my ear. "Trevor doesn't know it yet but we are having twins. One of each.

I turn from the piano and hug Ivan. "I wished for that for you."

"I know you did."

"I don't need anything from anyone." I say.

"We know that."

I hug Ivan again. Trevor walks over. "You told her." He says smiling. Ivan nods.

"Good I was going to bust if we didn't tell someone already." Trevor hugs me. "Can I ask you a question?"

I look at him. "Yes."

"We want you to be part of the reveal. So after you play the piano for us, we are going to bring the cake in. But we want you to hold up the sign that fits."

"Ok." I smile. I look at Ivan. "I lost something very important to me over the years."

"What was that?"

"That pin that you gave me."

"Which one?"

"The roses."

"I know the one." He says and opens his lapel to reveal the pin that resembles two dozen roses. "I never leave home without it. You are with me everyday."

An hour later the room is filled with what seems like too many people. Drinks are being served. Food is offered on plates by Seth's staff. Ivan's and Trevor's friends are there. Most of them are dancers. Savannah, Piper and Ginger are there.

Ivan tells me its time. I sit at the piano and play Ode to Joy. The cake is brought in the room. Ivan hands me the two signs for it's a boy or it's a girl.

"Ready." Ivan has. "One. Two. Three."

Trevor cuts the cake to reveal both colors. I hold up the signs. Trevor looks at Ivan. "Twins?"

"Yes." Ivan says. "We are having one of each."

The room erupts into cheers. I am happy for my friends. We stay at the Marina Beach most of the day. Seth lets everyone know that he needs the room for another event soon. Everyone leaves, I stay and help strip the room down. I throw all the decorations away. Justin helps out.

"Sweetheart, I noticed that you have been quite all day, are you alright?" Justin asks.

"I am fine."

"You don't seem like you are."

"Justin, let it go." I leave the room after throwing away the last design of the baby reveal. "I am going home. I have to go take care of my Astro."

"Can you give me a ride home, I came with Mark."

"I will think about it." I go to the bathroom.

Jacob is waiting for me when I come out. He takes me in his arms and hugs me. "Tomorrow, there is a cruise going out for the day, would you like to go?"

"Yes."

"We leave at nine in the morning. Astro can come too. I think you need a trip out on the water to help clear your mind."

"Where do I come?"

He looks at me and laughs.

I playfully slap at him. "That's not what I meant."

He laughs. "Right here." He kisses me on the top of my head. "Justin and your friends can come too."

"Thanks."

"My new girlfriend will be there."

"You have a new girlfriend?"

"Lindsey."

I smile. "She's great."

"You will see her do the Titanic thing tomorrow."

I laugh.

"You threw a very nice party for your friends."

"I didn't do anything,"

"You did. You did more than you think. They all left here thinking to themselves, that they just left the best party they have ever attended."

I smile. "Thanks for you saying that."

"I am not just saying that. You hosted a great party."

"Seth hosted a great party."

Seth walks over and hugs me. "You and Justin want to stay for a while?"

"If I hadn't left Astro all day long, I would." I look at Jacob. "What do I wear tomorrow?"

"You always look amazing." He says. "We are all going to wear white pants and navy blue shirts."

"I don't have a navy blue shirt."

Jacob kisses me on the cheek. "Wear whatever you want."

"How many people are going to be there?"

"Twenty-four guests and my crew."

"How many is in the crew?"

"Seven to ten depending on who shows up."

"Thirty-four." I say.

"What are you planning?"

"Nothing."

"Sebastian, just bring yourself and Astro. We are going to be out all day."

"I know it's stupid, but is there a bathroom that I can use?"

He hugs me. "Of course."

I leave to go home.

I pull into my driveway and there is a car that I don't recognize in front of my house. I get out of my car. I get to the front door. I hear a voice behind me,

"Are you Sebastian?" He asks.

I turn and look at man who looks just like the pictures of my dad. "I am." I say.

"My name is Oliver. Sebastian was my brother." He looks around the neighborhood. "This is really nice. Did my brother live here long?"

"As far as I know, just my mom and I lived here. My dad passed away three months before I was born."

"He never saw you?"

"No." I turn back to the door and do the code. The door unlocks. Astro runs out. "Hi baby." I say. He jumps all over me. "Astro, go run."

"Your dog's name is Astro?"

"Yes."

"That was the name of our cat when we were going up."

I laugh.

"That's funny?"

"Sebastian's son has a cat name Astro."

"You have a brother?"

"I have a half brother."

"What's his name?"

"His name is Sebastian Asher."

Oliver puts his hand to his chest.

"My mother named me after him too. My middle name is Ashley." I say. "Would you like to come in and have coffee or something?" As I talk to my uncle that I have never met, I hear a dog barking in the distance. It never occurs to me that its Astro.

"Coffee is good. Is your mother home?"

"Oliver, this is my house. I live by myself. My mother lives about fifteen minutes away from here." I look around. "Shit!"

"What's wrong?"

"My dog seems to have taken himself for a walk."

"I can help you find him." Oliver says.

"I know exactly where he went." I take my phone out of my purse and call Justin. "Hi, I think Astro is—"

"Walking back to you with Bob." Justin laughs. "He was very persistent with that endless barking."

"Are you coming with them?"

"Yes. I am carrying Bob."

"Great. I will see you when you get here."

He stands at the end of the street. "You have someone at your house?"

"Yes."

"Should I call Ms. Conley and tell her you have another man over there?"

I laugh. "She can murder my mailbox." I open the door and go in the house. I look around and notice that Astro has taken all of his toys out of the basket that they are usually in. The stuffed dog and cat are off the windowsill and among all his toys. "Sorry for the mess."

"Do you have children?"

"No. I have a dog. He wanted to go with me today like he does a lot of the times, but I had to leave him today. This—" I gesture around the room. "Is his way of telling me that he is pissed off." I release my armrest and pick up the toys. I pile them up on my feet bracket and put them all in the basket at once. "Oliver, sit and relax. My boyfriend is going to walk in the door with his cat and Astro in a minute or two. I need to go change."

"Where did you buy that dress?"

"In Miami last week."

"It looks like the ones my brother-in-law designs."

"It is."

"You met him?"

"And Scarlett last week."

"You look beautiful in it."

"Thank you."

There is a knock on my door. I look up at the ceiling thinking why would Justin knock. I open the door. Ivan takes me in his arms. "I am sorry I ruined your day."

"Come on in." I say.

Ivan looks at Oliver. "What are you doing here?"

I look at Ivan. "How is it that you know my family and I never knew these people exited?"

Ivan looks at me. "Oliver is the one that sews all the dresses that Aaron designs." He crosses the room and hugs Oliver. "Its good to see you again."

"How do you know each other?" Oliver asks.

"Fill him in, I have to change." I say. I go in my room and notice that my bed that I made before I left, is all in disarray. Astro's favorite stuffed toy is in the middle of my bed. I close the door and change my clothes putting shorts and a tank top on. I remake the bed. I put Astro's toy at the bottom of the bed.

I open the door and join them. Astro jumps up on me. I kiss the top of his head. Justin kisses me on the lips.

"Oliver, how did yo know where I live?"

"My mother gave me an address and told me to come here." He looks around the room. "That is a beautiful piano. Do you play?"

I look at all of them. "I do." I say. "I have played since I was four. My mother took me to see the Nutcracker. In the lobby of the theater there was a piano. I went to and played my own version of the Sugar Plum Fairies. A week later, my mom got me into piano lessons. I went to college on a duel major. Music was one of them." While I talk, I make coffee for Oliver. I also make one for Ivan. "How do you take your coffee?"

"Black." Oliver says.

I open the refrigerator and take out a beer for Justin.

"Before you pop it open, I will have coffee too." He says. "I will make it." Justin sees the stuffed dog and cat on the floor. "You didn't like my gift?" He smiles.

"Astro had it among all his toys. He was letting me know that he was pissed off at me for leaving him home. Tomorrow we are going on a cruise."

"You are bringing him with you?"

"Jacob said I could. He insisted that I bring him."

"Has Astro ever been on a boat before?" Oliver asks.

"Yes. When he was a puppy. I worked one summer on a cruse ship. The captain of the cruise ship bought him for me."

Justin looks at me. "Just another thing, I didn't know."

"Mark didn't tell you?"

"Why would Mark know?"

"He worked on the cruise ship." I say.

"How long ago was that?"

"Two summers ago."

"I was in London then." Justin says.

Ivan looks at Justin. "Such a snob." He teases.

Trevor walks in my house and hugs me. "Hi sweetheart." He says. "Thank you. That baby reveal was the best thing ever." He looks at Oliver. "Hi."

"Hi." Oliver hugs Trevor. "Its always good to see you. How do you and Ivan know my niece?"

Justin looks at me. "Were you expecting your uncle?"

"I wasn't expecting anyone. My plan for the rest of the day was to grade papers for my kids so I have their packets to return to them on Monday. Then bake a cake for tomorrow. I didn't expect any company."

There is a knock on the door. I go to the door and open it. My mom walks in. "Hi baby girl."

"Hi mom."

"Are you busy?"

"For you never."

She looks around the house. "Who are all these people?" She says it like I have a hundred people in my house.

"Mom, you know Justin, and Ivan." I say to her. "This is Trevor, Ivan's husband and this is Oliver."

She looks at him. "Oliver Timely. Its nice to see you again." She says. "I am going to take my daughter for a moment." She looks at me. "When did you meet Oliver?"

"He just came to my house."

"I need to talk to you."

"Lets go in my room."

She follows me in my room. She sits on my bed and acts all giddy. She jumps off the bed and then throws herself back on the bed. She sits up and squeals.

"What's going on?" I ask.

"I am engaged." She says.

"Congratulations. Peter is wonderful. I am glad you said yes."

I sit at my kitchen table hours after everyone has left and my mind is reeling. My dad's family has went from me just knowing my grandmother to now all of them showing up when I least expect them.

I have misread a recipe for a cake that I have made many times over the years. Its an easy recipe, but I can not concentrate. In the past couple months of my life, I have gone from being an only child to having a brother. I have gone from having no aunts and uncles to now being overwhelmed by them.

I throw out another batch of ruined cake batter. I throw the bowls that I have been using in the garbage. I take my phone off the counter. I send Jacob a text message telling him that I can't go on the cruise tomorrow. I feel like I need to catch my breath.

My phone rings. "Hello." I say bitting back tears.

"What's going on?" Jacob asks.

"I am not feeling well. I am going to stay home tomorrow and rest. I have a lot going on this coming week."

"You have to come tomorrow."

"Jacob, why is it such a big deal?"

"I can't tell you." He says.

"I have had too many surprises." I let the sob I am holding out.

"Are you crying?"

I can't answer.

"We are coming over."

"We who?" I ask but the line goes dead.

Fifteen minutes later Sebastian is holding me in his arms while I cry. Jacob and Seth are sitting on the couches. Justin is sitting on the floor between Astro and Bob. Sebastian pulls back a bit and my hand falls to my side.

"I think she is sleeping." Sebastian says.

Justin stands up and takes me in his arms. He carries me into my room and puts me to bed. I curl into the pillows. He brings my wheelchair in the room leaving it next to the bed. He walks out and sits with Sebastian, Seth and Jacob.

"Is she alright?" Sebastian asks.

"When she gets overwhelmed, she passes out. She is sleeping." Justin says.

Sebastian looks at Justin. "We really want her to be on the cruise with us tomorrow."

"I am sure she will be there."

"What did Oliver want?" Sebastian asks.

"He came to meet his niece. Apparently, Anastasia gave him her address. She told him to just come and meet his niece."

Seth gets up and goes into he kitchen. He sees the recipe on the counter. He looks around the kitchen and finds all the ingredients. He starts making the batter. The other three join him in the kitchen and they all work together to make cupcakes.

Jacob cleans everything and puts everything away. Sebastian takes Astro for a walk. Astro does everything quickly and then trots back to the house. Sebastian walks to the mailbox and opens it. He walks in the house after Astro.

"What did Oliver say?" Jacob asks.

"Nothing much. Because her mother interrupted."

They leave my house and kitchen spotless. Seth leaves one cupcake on the table for me. He writes a note.

Hope you have a great start to your Sunday. Please come to the Marina Beach at nine. You won't be sorry. You had all the ingredient for us to make cupcakes so we did. As you can see, I left you one. I hope you enjoy it. By the way, we are going to give you credit for all the cupcakes that we all made while you played sleeping beauty. Just teasing you. Love you, Seth

I take Astro for a long walk around the neighborhood. We leave the neighborhood and I walk to my bookstore. Its early enough. I unlock the door because we haven't officially opened. Matt meets me at the front of the store. Tristian is with him.

Tristian hugs me. I hug him. Danny runs over. He hugs me too. I look at Matt.

"I know we aren't opened officially yet but I was working on something. Come see what I have done. If you don't like it, I will take it down immediately." Matt says.

I follow him and the two boys. Matt has done the most elaborate art work to indicate each section.

I gasp. "Matt! This is exactly what I wanted. This is beautiful."

He hugs me.

The boys jump up and down.

"Are you alright?" He asks.

"Yeah."

"I know we aren't friends, but I can tell something is wrong."

"I will be ok."

Unexpectedly he takes my hand and pulls me into the café area of the bookstore. He lifts me out of my wheelchair and sits me on the counter. "Talk to me."

"Matt, my life is a mess right now." I indulge and tell him about meeting Sebastian and my dad's siblings that seem to be popping out of the woodwork. I tell him about Ivan and Trevor coming back in my life. I also tell him that I am thinking long and hard about giving up on teaching, but I love the children and want to stay.

"I am sorry to hear all that. Its nice to have family."

"I know, I just wish that they all knew about me when I was younger and always wanted a big family. Now they are just showing up and I don't know what they want from me." I look at my watch. "Shit!"

The boys laugh. "You said a bad word."

"I did. You can't." I tell them.

They laugh again.

"I have to go."

"Where are you going?" Matt asks.

"On a day cruise."

"What are you doing with Astro?"

"I was going to bring him with me."

"Leave him with us. I have Danny all day for Eric. The three of us can keep him safe. Mr. Smith is going to come here and help me hang some stuff. He is going to bring Sparky with him."

"We have no school tomorrow." Tristian says.

Matt lifts me and puts me back in my wheelchair. He hugs me tight. "Let me drive you home."

"Matt, I live three blocks away."

"He knows." Tristian says. "Matt used to follow you home to make sure you got there safely when you walked home alone in the middle of the night." Tristian looks at me with a serious face. "Don't you always tell us not to go anywhere alone?"

I grab him and kiss him on the top of the head.

"Say thank you." Danny insists.

Matt and I look at him.

"Ms. Timely, you should say thank you. Someone did something nice for you." Danny says.

I look at Matt. "Thank you. I didn't know that you did that."

"If I couldn't get out on time, I would call my cousin to make sure you got home."

"Your cousin?"

"Trixie is our cousin." Tristian says. "I call her Auntie Trixie."

"Ok, I have to go. I will come get my Astro baby when I get back."

"There is no school tomorrow." Danny now says.

I look at both of them. "What? Why do you keep saying that?"

Matt looks at me. "The principal sent everyone text messages saying he refuses to open school tomorrow. He wants everyone to have a nice week leading up to Thanksgiving."

"I didn't get a text message." I tell them. I hug them all. I kiss Astro. "I love you, be good." I tell him. I kiss his head again. "I have his food in the cabinet over—"

"Go. I got them. I can take care of two boys and a dog." Matt says.

I leave and walk home. I get home and go right into the shower. I get out minutes later and get dressed. I pull my hair back in a ponytail. I put my make up on and then grab a few things and put it in a tote. I take my wallet and some extra money. I take a phone chargers too.

I get in my car and it doesn't start. I take my phone out of my bag and call Justin. "Hi did you leave yet?"

"I am on my way out. What's up?"

"My car won't start."

"We will be right there to get you."

"Thanks."

Justin pulls his car into my driveway. "Ready?" He asks. He takes my wheelchair and puts it in the trunk. He comes back to the car and lifts me in his arms. "Where's Astro?"

"He is on a play date for the day with Matt, Tristian and Danny."

We get to the Marina Beach. Jacob comes out to meet us. "Don't get out, you can follow me to the marina." He looks in the car. "Where is Astro?"

"He is on a play date with his friend Sparky."

"Bob is going to get jealous." Justin says.

I laugh.

He kisses me. "A real laugh." He kisses me again.

"Drive to the marina. Park in bay twelve. That is my bay." Jacob says. "We will be just behind you."

"Sure." Justin says. Justin drives to the marina. He parks the car in the bay parking lot. Justin gets my wheelchair out of the trunk of the car. He brings it over and I get in it.

Everyone else pulls into the lot. We all gather together waiting for Jacob to tell us where we are going. The yacht is beautiful. There are steps leading up to the yacht. Before I can think twice about it, Sebastian takes me in his arms and carries me up the steps. Jacob gets my wheelchair.

Seth, Jacob, and Sebastian stand shoulder to shoulder and Sebastian is still holding me. A photographer takes a few pictures of us. Jacob takes me next in his arms and again the photographer takes pictures.

Justin stands next to Mark. "I feel like I am just here to watch out for her."

Mark looks at Justin. "Why do you say that?"

"She seems like she doesn't want me here."

"Little Mermaid wants you here. She loves you."

"How do you know that?"

Mark looks at his brother. "Everyone here loves her. She loves you."

"I am jealous."

"Of what?"

"Her relationships with Trevor and Ivan. Ivan refers to her as the love of his life."

"Justin, you have nothing to worry about. They love her differently then you do."

"I don't think she would pick me."

Mark turns Justin so that he is facing me. I am staring at him. I can't take my eyes off of Justin. "Go to her. Go to her now." Mark says.

241

Justin crosses the distance between us. I reach for him. He takes me in his arms.

"You look very serious." I say. "Is something wrong?"

"No." He says kissing me.

"Don't leave me."

He pulls back and looks at me. "I am not leaving you."

"No, I mean, today on the ship. Don't leave me."

"I will be by your side always."

Savannah, Piper, Ginger and Lindsey board. They all walk over to where I am and hug me. Sofia boards. She looks beautiful. She looks around and runs to Jacob. She kisses him on the lips. Trix boards. She looks around. She joins us and hugs all of us. When she sees Seth, she takes off at a full speed run and jumps in his arms.

Scarlett, Aaron, Oliver and a woman I don't know come on board with Anastasia. Peter and my mom come on with Eric. Ivan and Trevor board next.

Jacob takes me by the hand. "We are waiting for a few more." He says. "Then we are off." He squats down in front of me. "Are you alright?"

I smile trying to hide my concerns.

He hugs me. "They want to get to know you and Sebastian among your friends. Grandma thought that this would be a good way for you all to be together where someone can not leave."

"I might jump ship." I say.

He hugs me tighter. "You are going to be ok."

"This is overwhelming. I knew about Grandma, but the others. I didn't know about them. Somehow, I have been wearing Uncle Aaron's designs for years and never knew they were his and that he is my uncle."

Justin squeezes my shoulder. I put my hand on his hand.

Trix stands next to Jacob. She puts her hand on his back. She looks at me. "Where is Astro?"

"He is with your cousins."

She smiles. "Matt told you that we are related?"

"He did and so did Tristian."

Justin takes my hand. "You went to the bookstore this morning?"

"I couldn't sleep. Astro and I went for a big walk around the neighborhood and your house was very dark. So we went to the bookstore. Cup of Books looks like its ready. We open on Friday after Thanksgiving."

The ship sets sail. Everyone stays on the deck as we start our trip. We are going to sail ten miles out and then turn back. The staff walks around with trays of food that Seth and his staff had prepared. Everything is so delicious. A table is set up with a tower of cupcakes. I make my way over to the table.

There is a sign in front of them. Sebastian Ashley's recipe. Cupcakes made with love. The sign reads. Each cupcake has a little design on the top. I pick up a cupcake and look at it. The design is an open book that reads Cup of Books.

I find Seth in a crowd of people that I recognize from the Marina Beach. I hug him. He hugs me.

"I didn't know you made all of these." I tell him. "You must have been at it all night."

"We were at your house. I saw the recipe and decided to make the cake into cupcakes. I saw on the counter the flyer that you made for the opening of Cup of Books. Jacob, Sebastian, and Justin all helped decorate them.."

I look at another cupcake table and they have little pianos on them. "What's that?"

"It's a tribute to you." Seth says. "My staff did those. Jax made the pianos."

"They are beautiful." I say.

Chapter 19

Justin holds me in his arms while we sway to Lindsey playing the violin. He holds me so I am standing in his embrace. The photographer takes multiple pictures. Lindsey stops playing. I look at Justin,

"I have to sit." I tell him.

He sits me in my wheelchair. Savannah and Piper walk over. They take my hands and dance with me. Ginger joins in and Trix. When the music stops, Oliver walks over and dances with me.

"You know, I have wanted to come over all day long." He says. "Your mom visiting the other night ruined my visit."

"She tends to just drop in on me."

"Whose house is it?" He asks.

"Its my house. I bought it from her when she sold it and moved. My neighbor likes to give my mom details of my life that she catches when she drives by and my car is there and I have friends over."

"I really wish my mom would have told me about you sooner. I am sorry that I missed knowing you and Sebastian. What did you think of us?"

"I didn't know that my dad had siblings. Grandma used to come around a lot when I was very young, but then her visits got less and less. She would come for my birthday and I remember spending a couple christmases with her. When I was twelve, she stopped coming around."

"Did your mom stop her from visiting?"

"Never."

"Does your mom have siblings?"

"They live in Europe. She goes to visit them a few times a year."

"Have you seen them?"

"A few times. They have visited here."

The song ends. Oliver looks at me. "Lets go talk."

Justin walks over and kisses me on the lips. He takes me in his arms. I kiss him back.

Peter stands next to Oliver. "He loves her."

"He loves her." Oliver agrees. "She loves him. When they are not within hugging distance of each other, they are watching the other one."

Peter walks off with Oliver. Aaron joins them. The three of them sit where they can keep an eye on me.

"She seems like such a nice girl." Oliver says.

"She really is a sweetheart." Mark says walking up behind them. "I have known her a long time. She is a great person to know."

"Mark, Eric come join us." Peter says.

Eric looks over at me. "I have known her my whole life. We were in school together. I regret not being friends with her way back then. My son adores her. She is a hard worker."

"She is a teacher?" Aaron asks.

"She has many jobs. Too many jobs really." Mark says.

"She has many jobs." Peter confirms.

"Why does she work so much?"

Sebastian and Seth walk over to them. "She works hard so that she isn't home for a miserable neighbor to drop in and insult her. She works hard so that she can not be ambushed by family that she never knew she always had."

Oliver looks at Sebastian. "Explain this to me." He says.

"She just found out about me and my family a few months back."

Oliver looks around. "It seems like you and your brothers really love her."

"We are trying to get to know her better. Like I said, she works a lot so that she can't be found. The only thing is that we know where she works and when we can find her."

Jacob walks over to me. "Can we chat?"

"Yes."

He takes me into one of the cabins. He sits at the round table that is in the room. "Come sit with me."

I look around the room. "This is your personal room?"

"Yes."

"You have pictures of me in here?"

"You are our family."

I look around again. "Those were just taken yesterday at the reveal party."

"I know." He says.

"How did you get those done so quickly and manage to bake all those cupcakes?"

"I can't take credit for the cupcakes. Seth did that. He felt bad for the bowl in the garbage can." He laughs.

"I tried to bake a cake that I have made a lot throughout the years. Its one that I can make with my eyes full of tears usually."

"Sebastian, that's why I have invited you in here for a private chat. Seth, Sebastian and I have been talking and we think that you cry way too much. We don't know if this is something that you always do, or something that we have added in your life." He looks at me.

"No, I am not usually a crier. I have shed enough tears that could fill a river."

"Is that because of us?"

"No. Yes. No."

"What can we do to bring happiness back to your life?"

"I am working—"

"We know that you work really hard."

"I was saying that I am working on finding my new normal. I have always been an only child. I never had anyone to fall back on. I mean, I have my friends. Savannah and Piper have been there for me since elementary school, but when push comes to shove, they have their own lives and we are friends. We are not sisters. Having brothers now is weird to me."

"Why?"

"I feel like I want to call you all at different times of the day just to talk."

"You can do that."

"You are busy with your lives. You don't need a nagging female asking all sorts of questions."

"That's just it. We. I. Want that. Seth wants that. He is thinking of closing the restaurant."

"That's my favorite place." I say.

"He is thinking of closing it and moving it closer to your bookstore just so he can see you more."

I look out the sliding doors. "Can we go out there?"

"Sure." He says.

Seth knocks on the door. Sebastian and him walk in just as Jacob and I are going out on the balcony. Seth runs over and grabs the back of my wheelchair. I look back at him.

"Don't let him push you over the edge." He teases.

"That's not funny." Jacob says.

Sebastian looks out at the water. He looks sad. I put my hand in his hand and squeeze it. "Are you alright?"

He looks at me. "I feel overwhelmed right now. Dad has siblings that never wanted to know me in all my thirty-one years. Now all of a sudden they want to know me."

"I feel the same way." I say. "I have felt so alone over the years. When my mom was away with her work or her boyfriends, I dreamed of having an aunt to call. My mom's sisters are in Europe. I talk to them through email. They told me how proud they were of me when I graduated in the top twenty of my college class."

Charlotte knocks on the door. "Jacob, the natives are getting restless. They want to turn back." She says.

I laugh. "Are you referring to my mother?"

She looks at me. "Actually no. Your mother has been a doll. She seems extremely happy."

"I am sure she is." I say. I smile. I am happy for her, but I am sad too. Peter is wonderful but he has enabled my mom to miss events in my life.

"Anastasia is actually feeling ill." Charlotte says.

"We are turning back now. I just sent a text message to the captain. He will turn us around so smoothly, she will start to feel better soon." Jacob says.

Charlotte looks at me. "Those cupcakes are the most amazing thing I have ever eaten."

"Seth made them." I say.

"They are your recipe." He says.

Charlotte looks at the pictures on the wall. "Wow that looks like it was one hell of a party."

"It didn't go as I hoped it would." I say.

"Why not?"

Sebastian looks at me. He looks at Charlotte. "I will tell you later."

Charlotte looks at me and sees sadness in my eyes. She crosses the room to where I am and hugs me. "What are your plans for Thanksgiving?"

"I usually have Thanksgiving alone. I don't eat turkey."

"What about your mom?"

"I don't know what she and Peter have planned. Last year they were with his children."

"You didn't go?" Seth asks.

"I was invited to go. I was sick with a cold. I stayed home. Savannah and Piper came over in the evening with so much food. They stayed throughout the weekend. I worked at the bookstore last year. We hosted an open mic night. After listening to the sixth person talk about how horrible their holiday was, I shut down the open mic event."

Charlotte hugs me. "I host a very large Thanksgiving. There is a lot of food with a lot of options. You don't have to eat turkey. I — we will not take no for an answer."

"What can I bring?"

"Nothing. There will be plenty of food." She says. She kisses each of us on our heads. "Remember, you have a ship full of guests out there. Don't be rude to them."

"We will be out there again in a bit." Sebastian says.

I leave the three of them and go out to find my friends. Sofia walks over to me. "Hi."

"Hi." I say.

"When Jacob found out that our troupe was going to be in Miami, he showed up personally to get the tickets. He had to see where the best seats in the house were. He watched the rehearsal and moved from section to section until he sat in the box seats. He bought out the entire section for the day show." She looks around. "Where is he?"

"Talking to his brothers."

"He told me what he said to you. He told me how sorry he was after the words came out of his mouth. He wanted so badly to redo that day that Sebastian—" she laughs.

"I know its weird."

She smiles. "The day that Sebastian brought his brothers to your bookstore. Sebastian didn't want to go alone. Jacob was devastated about things that they learned about Larry. Jacob was jealous that Sebastian went to Seth for research on you."

She tells me things that I already know. She looks over at Lindsey and sees her in Jacobs arms. She turns her back so she doesn't have to see them. I take my phone out and send him a text message.

Me: you are making her crazy. Sophia loves you.

Jacob: I am setting Lindsey up with my friend. We are talking about him.

Me: Sophia can't stand to watch you. OMG tears.

Jacob comes running over and takes Sophia in his arms. He kisses her like she is his last dying breath. She jumps in his arms and wraps her legs around him.

Savannah, Piper and Ginger are standing off on their own. Eric can't take his eyes off of Piper. She glances his way and than back at the horizon. I put my hand out as I get close to Piper.

"You are making him crazy." I tell her.

"I don't want your family to think poorly of me." She says seriously.

I look at her. "What are you talking about? My mom is all over Peter."

"You have more than your mom on this vessel."

"Pipes, my mom is the only one who matters. The others never wanted to know me before, now they want to get to know me and Sebastian and they are doing a really shitty job at it right now. Go kiss him."

"You know I don't like to—"

"Piper, we are all in relationships currently. Go to him."

"I will go to him if you play something on the piano." She says.

"What do you want?" I ask her.

"Hallelujah." She says.

"Piper, I haven't played that in a long time."

"Eric's happiness depends on it." She teases.

I go over to the piano and I play Hallelujah. Lindsey gets her violin and she plays with me. Savannah gets her violin and she plays too. Mark and Justin sit at a table beaming.

Savannah taps me into the shoulder. "Phantom. Lets play Phantom."

"Start us off." I tell her.

Piper runs to Eric and kisses him on the lips. She hugs him tight. He kisses her. "Go play with your friends. You always feel left out. Don't get left out." He tells her.

"I didn't bring my violin with me." She says.

"Its on the piano waiting for you." He says and kisses her again.

"How did you know?"

"You are all best friends. You have been playing together the three of you since elementary school. Play like you used to."

She looks at him.

"Sit at her back. Like you used to."

"I didn't know that anyone knew we did that."

"I have been watching you since we were kids. Go play with your friends."

She runs over and takes her violin off the piano. She leans in and kisses me. She stands behind me so we are back to back. I sit taller in my wheelchair. She starts playing Think of Me from Phantom. We all join in. All three violins sound different from each other.

We finish and everyone cheers.

Oliver looks at the photographer. "Did you take pictures of them?"

"Yes." He says.

Scarlett walks over. "The four of you play like you have been doing that all your lives."

"Savannah, Piper and I have been playing since elementary school together. Lindsay and I met in college and—" I look at her and laugh. "And we got into a lot of trouble playing together. We were band from playing in our final show at graduation because of our shenanigans."

We laugh.

Lindsey kisses me on the cheek. "We had a lot of shenanigans."

"Show us." Justin says. "Play for us."

Lindsey and Piper start playing Cannon in D. Savannah and I start playing Moonlight Sonata. At the bridge, we switch playing the pieces. We end with Heart and Soul. Jacob sits with me at the piano a and plays with me as a duet.

Again everyone cheers.

"That is really amazing." Mom says.

Ivan looks at her. "You have missed her playing a lot."

Mom looks at him. "You are judging me."

"I am making a statement. You were in Europe when she had the concert of her life. You missed it. You missed her graduation."

"If I remember correctly," mom starts. "You missed her graduation too." She leans in to him. "Does she know that you were going to be arrested for being with her?"

I read my mom's lips from across the deck. I push away from the piano. "Leave him alone." I tell her. "You don't know what you are talking about."

"If he's with Trevor, what was he doing with you?" She asks.

"Mother, drinking doesn't do you well." I say to her.

Before I can back away from her, she slaps me in the face. Peter runs to her and takes her away. Justin, Ivan and Trevor run to me. I hold my cheek and fight the tears.

Trix walks over. "I can arrest her for abuse of a disabled person." She says.

I look at her and laugh. She hugs me.

"The truth hurts." She says. "You play like an angel." She hugs me.

Mom and Peter walk over. Mom is crying. "I have never hit my daughter a day of her life. I am so sorry." She says.

I stay quiet. My friends surround me. Sebastian, Jacob and Seth all gather close to me as well. Jacob hugs me. "We are going to dock in like fifteen minutes."

Scarlett walks over with the cupcakes. "What's the significance of all of these cupcakes?"

Seth looks at me. "Sebastian made them for everyone last night."

"You threw that great party for your friends and still found time to make cupcakes?" She asks.

"I find time to do a lot of things." I look at my mom. "Linda has always instilled in me to stay busy."

Mom looks hurt that I referred to her by her name and not mom. Too bad. My cheek is throbbing. She has never hit me before. Now in front of my dad's whole family she decides that its time for a slap across the face.

Charlotte walks over and kisses me on the forehead. Mom looks at her. "I am her mother."

"I know who you are." Charlotte says.

"She never asked me to be at any of her concerts."

"I didn't know I had to ask." I say.

The ship docks. Justin carries me off. Mark gets my wheelchair for me. Because everyone got there after Justin and I did, we can't leave right away. I go wait by the car. Mom walks over.

"I have decided that Peter and I will be spending Christmas in Europe."

"Wonderful." I say. "Please tell all of your family that I send my love."

"I just figured you don't want to be with me."

Peter walks over. "Do you have plans for Thanksgiving?"

"No." I say.

Seth walks over and hugs me. "Please come back to the restaurant."

"I have to go get Astro." I say.

"She loves that dog more than she loves anyone." Mom says.

I look at her. "Lets go chat." I almost yell at her. "Excuse us, we will be right back." We walk into the he bathroom and I look at her. "What is your problem?"

"You are surrounded by your new family. You don't need me."

"Have you lost your mind? They are not my new family. And you have no right to be jealous when you knew about Sebastian. You know, it would have been nice to know that I had a half brother out there so that I was not alone, I could have called family and not felt so alone."

"You have always been good with being by yourself."

252

"Mom."

Peter knocks on the door. "Ladies? Are you alright?"

"We are fine." Mom says. "We will be right out."

"You slapped me in front of everyone I know. Why?"

"Were you mean to me Ms. Conley?"

"Your spy came into my house and called me a slut in front of my guests."

"She did what?"

"She came over and wanted an apology because I asked her to leave. I had friends over."

"What friends?"

"Does it matter? Its my home."

"You are right."

"So she came over and called me a slut in front of Justin and my friends. Then I asked her to leave. She drove her car into the mailbox."

Mom looks at me. "She destroyed the mailbox?" She burst into tears. "Sebastian built that mailbox."

I cry too. "I have loved that mailbox my whole life. I promised to take care of it when you left. I begged you to leave it. If you would have taken it, we would still have a piece of him." We hold each other and cry.

"Ms. Conley's son called me to tell me that she was hospitalized."

"She was. They came and got her from my front porch. She refused to leave, she wasn't leaving until I apologized to her."

"For what?"

"Removing her from my home." I say. "She scared the shit out of me. She said that Astro bit her."

"I will talk to her."

"She thinks that—"

"What?"

"She thinks that you abandoned me and she has to watch out for me because no one else does."

"I will talk to her." Mom hugs me. "What are your plans for Thanksgiving?"

"Charlotte has asked me if I want to come to her house for the holiday."

Mom looks at me. "You know, I can't cook."

"You can open a can of tuna." We laugh.

We leave the bathroom.

Seth walks over to us. "We are asking everyone to come back to the restaurant for dinner."

"I do have to get Astro."

Justin looks at me. "Matt is going to bring him to the Marina Beach. He is going to join us for dinner with the boys." He takes me in his arms and hugs me. "Were you in there crying?"

"Yes."

"Why?"

"The mailbox that Ms. Conley destroyed was one that my dad made for my mom before he passed away."

Justin kisses me. "I am so sorry to hear that."

"Me too because I never knew. My mom wanted to take it with her when she moved and I insisted that she leave it. Now I wish that I would have agreed for her to take it. We would still have it."

Oliver hears me tell Justin about the mailbox. He walks over to say goodbye to us. "Hi." He says. "I don't think you ever met my wife." She steps out from behind him.

"Grace? You are Oliver's wife?" I ask.

"Yes." She says. "We have been married for twenty-one years."

"Did you know you were my aunt?" I ask her.

"How do you know my Grace?" Oliver asks.

I look at her. "Did you know you were my aunt?"

"Yes. That's why I had you back at the farm all the time. You were a pleasure to know."

Oliver looks at her, "you knew about Sebastian all these years and never said anything?"

"You didn't want to know about my work. You were busy with Aaron and the designs."

Justin squeezes my hand. "You worked on a farm?"

I laugh. "No."

"The farm is next to a butterfly sanctuary and Sebastian would go there a lot. I met her on a rainy day when the sanctuary closed due to the bad weather. Sebastian was telling a friend that she needed a ride because her mom wasn't going to come get her until after work. She had one more house to show for her interior designs. I invited her to come to the farm with me. She did."

"That's where my Astro came from isn't it?"

"He is the puppy that you held when he was just hours old." She says.

I hug her. "I wanted him."

"You got him."

Oliver looks at the two of us. "Ok, we have to go. Will we see you on Thanksgiving?"

Sebastian walks over. "Normally my mom hosts Thanksgiving as it is one of her favorite holidays. Her house, although its large, will not fit all of us. So I will be hosting Thanksgiving at my house." He kisses me on the cheek. "No steps remember."

I hug him.

Seth is getting in his car but just before he does, he walks over to us. "Sebastian do you want to ride with me?" He asks me.

"No, she is going to ride with me." Jacob says.

I take Justin's hand. "I am going to ride back with Justin."

"We will see you all at the Marina Beach." Seth says.

The second that we are in the parking lot and I open the car door, Astro comes running. He jumps on me.

"Hi love." I say to him. "Did you have a nice day while I was busy?"

Matt walks over. "He is so good."

"Thanks for keeping him for me."

"Any time." Matt takes Astro's leash and pulls him back so I can get in my wheelchair. "Just so you know, Trix's dad went to your house and fixed your car. He changed the battery for you."

"Thanks."

Astro never leaves me side for the rest of the day. We go into the restaurant which is open for dinner. As we go in, a lady sitting at one of the front tables looks at me coming in with Astro and she rolls her eyes.

Seth walks over.

"Sir!" The lady at the table says. "Sir, that woman has a dog in the restaurant."

"I know." Seth says.

"You allow dogs here?"

"I will go tell the owner your complaints about his sister being her with her dog." Seth says. He turns around quickly and grabs Jax. "Get that bitch whatever she wants and get her out of here quickly."

"Will do." Jax says. "When you tell the owner about the dog, tell him that his pants are split open."

Seth turns to see that his pants are split open. He laughs on way into the kitchen.

We go into the back room which seems to be the only area of the restaurant that we ever go in. Everyone comes into the room. Astro lays right next to me. We enjoy dinner. There are conversations going on all around me. I am not really paying attention to any one conversation. Usually I can keep up with may conversations going on at the same time.

Savannah reaches over and takes my hand. "Are you alright?"

"I am fine." I say.

Ginger sits next to me. "Are you doing ok?"

"I am fine." I tell her.

Piper joins us. "What's going on? Normally you are involved with all different conversations. You seems like you are ten thousand miles away from us. Did we leave you on the water?"

"I am fine."

"Sebastian, what's your favorite thing about Thanksgiving?" Anastasia asks.

Sebastian looks at her. "Are you asking me or Sebastian?"

She smiles. "Either one of you. Both of you."

"I like the parade." I say. "Astro and I sit on the couch and enjoy the parade."

"Have you ever been to the parade?"

"I went one year with Piper and Ginger." I say. I stayed out watching the parade while they slept off hangovers in the hotel room that I paid for.

Savannah looks at me. "I was there too." She is right. She was there too. She had her head in a trash can the whole time the parade was going on. She had food poisoning on top of a hangover.

"Did you enjoy it?" Grace asks.

"More than anyone else." I say smiling. "The parade was wonderful."

"What year did you do that?" Oliver asks.

"Two years ago when we graduated. It was a our gift to each other." I paid for the whole thing by myself. The tickets for the flights, the hotel, and the meals that we ate.

"Ginger, are you the same age as my niece?" Grace asks. Grace knows about the trip to New York. I told her about it when I got back.

"I am three years older."

"How old are your children?" Grace asks with ice in her tone.

"Ten, eight and five."

"So you were—"

Jack, looks at Grace. "Meg is my daughter from another relationship. Ginger adopted her when we got married nine years ago. We were young when we started having children. We didn't plan on it, it just happened while we were in college."

"Jack, you played baseball in college?" Ivan asks.

"Yes."

"Shortstop?"

"Yes." Jack says.

"Ginger, if you went to school with my granddaughter, do you play an instrument too?"Anastasia asks.

Lindsey and I make eye contact from across the table and she bursts out laughing. I try hard not to laugh. I take a drink of water and choke on it.

Justin jumps up and rushes to my side. I put my head on his shoulder and try harder not to laugh. Seth, Sebastian and Jacob join us along with Mark and Savannah.

"I don't anymore." She says. "I did a long time ago." She looks at me. "Are you alright?"

I look up. "I am good." I say.

Jack looks at me. "When are you opening your bookstore?"

"Cup of Books officially opens on Wednesday."

"I can't wait to come in and see it."

"Come anytime you want. I am going to be there all week."

"You are going to be at your bookstore all week?" Aaron asks.

"Yes. We are getting ready to open. I own the bookstore now so I will be there a lot of the time."

"Its not just you?" Anastasia asks.

"I have a staff full of great people. I should say that we are reopening." I tell them.

Astro sits up and puts his paws on my lap. I pet him.

Justin looks at me. "Does he have to go out?"

"Yes." I say. I take Astro's leash and slip it on the collar. "Can I take him out the back?"

Seth takes the leash. "Let me take him." He walks out the main room to the door. The lady is still there. Astro trots right next to Seth. The lady looks at Seth. She watches him walk out with Astro. She flags down Jax.

"I would like to speak with the manager." The lady says.

"Is there a problem?" Jax asks.

"I would like to report that guy to the manager."

"Did he do something to you?"

"He offended me."

"In what way?" Jax asks.

"I need to speak with the manager."

"I am the manager on staff tonight."

"That man, how can he even afford eating in a place like this?" The lady asks.

Jax looks around the the room. "Ma'am, people are all dressed differently, how do you know that he can't afford to eat here?"

"He just seems like he came in off the street."

Jax throws her head back. "Oh that's rich."

"I am sorry." The lady insists.

Sebastian walks over. "Jax, is there a problem?"

"This lady has a complaint." She says.

Sebastian looks at the lady. "What seems to be the problem?"

"I am not sure that this is the place where people can just come in off the street."

"That's how we get business." Sebastian says.

"I am offended by that man and his dog."

"The dog belongs to a woman." Jax says. "You watched her come in with the dog."

"I have been here a while now and I have heard that dog barking nonstop."

Trix walks over. She is now dressed in full uniform. She looks very official as a police officer with the exception of her pink hair. "Ma'am, what seems to be the problem?"

"You called the police?" She asks.

"I just don't know what you want us to do. We have tried to make you as comfortable as possible. The dog never made a peep. He has been as quiet as that baby sleeping over there." Jax says and points to a woman holding a baby in her arms.

"Dogs don't belong in a four star restaurant." The lady carries on.

"The dog is a service dog for a woman who is disabled." Trix says. "I don't know why her dog and that man is any concern of yours."

"I want him removed."

"Ma'am, I advise you finish your meal and go." Jax says.

Amanda walks in. She walks over to Jax. "Excuse me, is my table available yet?"

Jax looks at her. "It will be ready for you in about ten minutes."

"No. I made a reservation and I want my table."

The lady looks at Amanda. "Wait your turn to complain."

"I have been waiting for you to get your ass up. You are sitting at my table. I reserved this table for my dinner tonight." Amanda says.

Sebastian rubs the small of her back.

"I am waiting for the bill." The lady says.

"Ma'am, your bill has been paid for." Jax says. "Your dinner is on us."

The main doors to the restaurant opens and Seth walks in wearing a suit. He has Astro with him. He walks past the table and drops something on it. Jax tries to intercept the paper but misses it because the lady snatches it up immediately.

"He wants me." She says.

Trix is still standing there. "In your dreams." She says.

Sebastian looks at Trix and smiles.

"What does it say?" Trix asks.

Seth put a flyer on the table. The flyer had a picture of him opening the restaurant. On the back of it the flyer he wrote. Per the owner! Please leave!

She gathers her belongings and stands abruptly. She pushes the uneaten food on the floor. Dishes shatter. "I have never been treated like this ever." She runs to the door. When she steps out, there are police waiting for her.

The staff cleans up the mess.

Everyone returns back to the room and we stay for a long time. Justin takes my hand. "Come talk to me."

I let him pull me away from everyone. He stops and talks to Seth for a moment. Seth nods. He leads me to the elevator and we go upstairs. When we get up there he takes me in his arms and kisses me. He cups my face where my mom hit me.

"Are you doing ok?" He asks.

"I am tired. I am ready to go home."

"You seem sad to me."

"I am fine." I tell him and kiss him. "What are you doing for Thanksgiving?"

"Sebastian invited me to come spend the holidays with all of you."

"You aren't going to see your dad or mom?"

"Sebastian, I want to spend the holiday with you."

"Lets go to your family."

"What do you normally do for Thanksgiving?" He asks.

"I spend a quiet day at home with Astro." I look at him. "My mom doesn't cook. She would find ways to disappear on Thanksgiving and come back home hours later tipsy." I start to cry. "She has never hit me." I put my hand on my cheek. "Then when she does, she does it in front of everyone I know."

He kisses my cheek. "I am sorry that she hit you." He hugs me. "Let me take you home."

Chapter 20

Wednesday morning the staff of the bookstore meets in the café. Sebastian, Seth and Jacob come. Justin and Mark are here too. The ribbon cutting which I didn't want to do, will be done at eight in the morning and that will be the official start to the bookstore being reopen.

Aaron and Oliver get there with Grace, Charlotte, and Anastasia. The same photographer that was on the ship with us is there for this event.

Oliver walks over to me with a big box. "This is for you."

"Should I open it now?"

"No. It might take away from the event. It might make you cry but I hope that it will bring you happiness."

"Oliver, how come you stayed away from my dad?"

"We were on different career paths. He wanted us to go into business with him. I didn't want to sell cars. I am not a good people person." He looks around. "Can I put this in your car."

"Oh, you want me to take it home?"

"Yes." He kisses the top of my head. "My daughters want to come on Friday."

"Bring them. We will be open and I will be here."

Matt waits for me outside of the bookstore. He hands me the big scissors. I cut the robin. Everyone cheers. "Welcome to Cup of Books we are officially open." I say.

We have a catered party. Everyone is happy that the bookstore opened again. There are reporters from the local news stations. One reporter follows me into the café.

"Tell me, Ms. Timely, how is it being related to a multi-millionaire?" She asks.

"I am sorry."

"You are sorry to be related to Oliver Timely?"

"No, I am sorry that this day is not about my family. Its about this bookstore and its grand re-opening." I look at her. "Enjoy your visit." I say and push my wheelchair away. I go in the new back room that we never had before. I run my fingers through my hair.

Grace walks into the back room. She hugs me. "This is a beautiful store."

"Thank you."

"How are you doing?"

"I am excited to be open. I love this place. I have always loved it. The whole idea of it being open twenty-four hours seven days a week. I enjoy it. I love that in addition to Wal-mart if I am up at three in the morning, I have some place to go. I am really excited."

She looks at me.

"Can I ask you a question?"

"Of course."

"Why didn't you ever tell me that you are my aunt?"

"I didn't want to scare you off. I wanted you to keep coming back."

"Why didn't you tell Oliver about me?"

"I didn't want him coming to you and scaring you."

"He did know that Sebastian had children?"

"He knew that Sebastian was married and had a son. Oliver was out of the country when Sebastian was hit by a car. He was on the motorcycle. He went to go pick up his suit for his wedding. Aaron made it for him. Oliver sewed it. He never made it to get the suit. He was killed instantly."

I look away. "Did you know him?"

"I knew him. He was a wonderful person. He wanted so much for people to be happy. He loved have dealerships. He had a lot of them. They were very successful."

"Did they all close?"

"No. Other dealers bought them. They were divided."

Matt walks in. He takes my hand. "You are needed on the floor." He says.

I go with him. When we are out on the floor, the bookstore is full of people. Most I recognize. They all stand in a semicircle and clap.

"This is beautiful." A woman with bright blue hair says. I know her from when we do open mic nights. "Sebastian, this is truly nice."

"I am glad that you all like it."

"I can't wait to being my kids here. What a nice thing. I can bring them and they will be in their own section. Its going to be exciting."

Matt looks at everyone. "The children sections close down though."

"Well they should." Someone says. "The adults need their time to be adults in this place."

I go home in the early afternoon. I park my car in the driveway and go to the mailbox. I go in the house and Astro again has littered the house with his toys. I let him out in the backyard while I go change my clothes and pick up his toys. I feed Astro.

Tomorrow is Thanksgiving and all I want to do is stay home and hide. Mom and Peter are going to dinner together just the two of them. Justin is going to be with his dad, Mark and Savannah. Piper is going to be with Eric and Danny. I know that Sebastian wants me to come to his house for the holiday but I just feel like that's something I am not sure I want to do. I don't want to be alone but I don't want to be ambushed by family that I never knew I always had.

Justin comes over. Astro wags his tail in greeting. He jumps on Justin. Justin takes Astro and leads him outside. Bob jumps up on the chair next to where I am sitting. I pick him up and hug him. He rubs his head against my chin. Justin walks in the house with Astro.

"What smells so good?" He asks.

"I am baking pumpkin pies."

"You have them in the oven already?"

I laugh. "No. I am preheating the oven. I am going to bake pies for your family. I thought I would bring two of them with me to Sebastian's."

"Are you going?"

"I don't know. If I bake the pies then I have to go."

"You can't really like spending the day by yourself." He says kissing me.

"Its not that bad. The day goes by quickly and then I work in the bookstore. I don't eat turkey."

"What do you have?"

"Don't laugh."

"I wouldn't laugh." He says.

"I stuff a chicken breast. I like the stuffing. I just don't like turkey. I never did. I remember my mom forced me to eat it one year and she was so mad at me for getting sick in her boyfriend's dining room."

"Awe, I am sorry to hear that."

"Yeah well. Anastasia used to come for Thanksgiving until I was twelve. Then she stopped coming. We would go out for dinner. My mom never cooked. She could burn water."

"Let me help you make the pies." He looks around. "What's with the flour?"

"I make the crust."

"Really?"

"It's the best."

"I like pumpkin pie but I don't like the crust."

"I will make you a crust less pie."

"That's too much work."

"It's the same amount of work." I laugh. My phone rings. The tone lets me know its Piper. "Hi Pipes."

"Are you baking the pies?"

"I am just getting started."

"I am coming over. Its my favorite thing we do together."

"The door is open."

"Hey, what did Oliver give you?" She asks.

"Oh its still in my car."

Justin looks at me. "Want me to get it?"

"Is someone there with you?" Piper asks.

"Justin is here." I say. My phone beeps. "Pipes come over whenever you want."

"I am on my way. Eric is coming too."

"Great." I say. We hang up. I click to phone. "Hi Seth."

"What are you doing?"

"Baking pumpkin pies."

"I was just calling to invite you to come over to Sebastian's. We do that every year. The three of us bake pies."

"Pumpkin pie wars." I say joking.

"Oh you are on." Seth says.

I laugh. "I was just joking."

"We will bring all of our own stuff with us." Seth speaks to Jacob and Sebastian. "What can we bring for dinner?"

"Nothing." I say.

"We are not bringing nothing." He says. "We will be there in twenty minutes."

I put the phone on the counter. My phone rings. "Hi Savannah."

She sniffs.

"Are you crying?" I ask her.

"I can't believe that we aren't going to be together for Thanksgiving. Are we going to bake pies at least?"

"I am preheating the oven."

"I am on my way." She says.

Justin sends Mark a text message.

I clean the kitchen and put my iPad on the counter. I go to my playlist and put the River Dance soundtrack on. Justin looks at me.

"What?"

"I like it." He says.

"This is what we do. The girls come here and we bake pies while River Dance plays in the background. When we are done, we watch a movie and crash on the couch."

Mark comes in the house with a bag full of groceries. Justin looks at him. "What did you do?"

"I brought cookies to bake."

"How are we going to bake so much when she only has one oven?" Justin asks.

"Justin, I have two ovens and my toaster is an oven."

Savannah walks in. "I brought pie pans." She says.

I smile. "You know, I always forget them."

She hugs me. "But your heart is always in the right place." She teases.

We laugh. She hugs Mark.

Piper comes in with Eric. They both hug me. Piper puts pie pans of all sizes on the counter.

There is a knock at the door. Seth, Jacob and Sebastian walk in. They bring bags of stuff with them. Seth hugs me. He sees the bag of flour. "You make your own crust?"

"Yes. Always." I say.

"Us too."

Everyone hugs each other. Jacob takes my iPad off the counter. "I like the music."

"That's our baking soundtrack." Piper says.

Jacob looks at me. "Is it ok if Sophia comes? She will be leaving on Friday?"

"Yes." I tell him. "Will she be with us tomorrow?"

"No. She will be doing her last dance here. They leave on Friday for a new city."

"Of course she can come." I look at Seth. "If you want to invite Trix, she can come over too."

He hugs me. "Thanks."

"Its amazing how spacious your kitchen is." Sebastian says.

"When I had it renovated I wanted the kitchen larger because whenever I have anyone over, we stay mostly in the kitchen." I say. I hug Sebastian. "If you want to invite Amanda over to join us that would be—"

"Are you sure?"

"Of course."

"Someone call Ms. Conley." Piper says.

"No Ms. Conley jokes tonight." I say. "She is still in the hospital." Justin kisses me on the lips.

"We have to start baking." I say.

Seth starts making the dough. He puts balls of dough in the refrigerator. "They need like a half hour."

"While we wait, lets make cookies." Jacob says.

"I think that's good." Piper says.

"We have different ones." He says. He takes them out of the bags that they brought.

Savannah smiles. "This is cheating."

"Sav!" I say.

There is a knock on the door. I open the door and its Amanda. She hugs me. "I live really close to you."

"Welcome."

"Thank you for having me." She says. "I stopped by the bookstore, people are lined up around the block to get in it."

"Wonderful." I say.

"I brought cookies." She looks around the kitchen. "The ones I brought, we can eat right now." She says with a shy smile.

We spend the next couple of hours baking pies and cookies. Its nonstop laughter. The cookies come out in many shapes and sizes. The pies all turn out looking really beautiful. Everyone helps clean up the mess. When we finish completely, we sit on the couch and watch Love Actually.

Moments after I sit on the couch between Justin and Mark, I fall asleep. Justin lets me sleep on him. They watch the movie until the end. Everyone leaves taking pies and cookies with them. Justin stays with me. We sleep on the couch together with Bob sleeping next to me and Astro sleeping on his loveseat.

I wake up in the morning to Justin's hand on my stomach. I stretch and he pulls me into him. He kisses me.

"I am the worst person ever." I laugh.

"Why do you say that?"

"I can't sit and watch movies like ever. I fall asleep."

"You worked really hard yesterday."

"Everyone did." I say. "Last night was the most fun I have had in a long time."

"I think that is true. You seemed very happy."

"It seemed stress free. It was just fun." I kiss him. "It's a moment that I have dreamed of having my whole life."

We spend the morning together. We watch the Macy's Parade together. Justin makes breakfast for the two of us and he feeds Astro and Bob. We pause the parade and take Astro out together.

A car slows at the end of the street. A teenaged girl gets out of the car. "Ms. Timely?"

"Yes." I say.

"Hi. Happy Thanksgiving!"

"Happy Thanksgiving." I say to her.

"You don't recognize me?"

Justin intercepts the conversation. He reaches his hand out. "Hi, Happy Thanksgiving. I am Justin."

"Tina. Christina Menno." She looks at me. "You still don't remember me?"

"Refresh my memory."

"You mentored me three and half years ago. I was being bullied in school and you told me that all I needed was to believe in myself and not listen to what they say."

"I am glad you are doing well." I say to her. I have no idea who she is. For a moment I think that she is lying to me.

"I am here to stay with my grandma Conley. She is going to be coming home today."

"Oh that's wonderful to hear." I say.

"Can I pet your dog?" She asks.

"Yes."

"What's his name?"

"Bob." Justin says. I look at him and smile. He kisses me on the lips. "We have to go." He tells her. "Tell your grandma Happy Thanksgiving from Justin and Sebastian."

"I will." She says. She gets back in the car.

I look at Justin. "I would never tell someone to just believe in herself of himself. I have no idea who that girl is. I do know like ninety percent of the people I mentor. She was not one of them."

Justin takes his phone out of his pocket. He punishes in a phone number. "Hey, its Justin. You know which Justin, asshole. I need you to run something for me. Christina Menno. Staying at 777 NW 28th Street. Yes. Ms. Conley's address. Claims she's the granddaughter. I know what fucking day it is. This just happened. The girl approached my fiancé."

I look at Justin. He kisses me on the lips.

"Yes. I am here." He says. "I will. All day. No we are going to her brother's house for the day. And you will have— great. I appreciate it. The bookstore too. Oh wonderful. I will check-in in a couple hours." He sticks his phone in his pocket.

I look at Justin. "You are my fiancé?" I smile.

He looks at me. "I have a ring."

"Justin be serious."

"I am."

We go back to my house. As we pass my car, I open the door. "Can you bring that in the house for me?"

Justin gets the box that Oliver put in the car yesterday. He carries it in the house. "Where do you want this?"

"You can put it on the piano bench." I tell him. "I am going to get showered."

"Want some help?" He smiles.

"No." I go in the bathroom and shower. I come out and do my hair. I sit at the variety and put my makeup on. I go in the closet and pick one of the dresses from Miami. I come out of my room all dressed. "Justin?"

He walks in the back door with Astro and Bob. "We were playing in the backyard while you got ready."

"What time are you going to your dad's?"

"I am not going to my dad's for dinner. I am going with you."

"Justin, I don't want to keep you from what you normally do."

"Sebastian, you are not keeping me from anything. I want to be with you. My friend is looking into details for me and told me to stay with you until he has answers."

"While I was in the shower, I was thinking. I never use my last name when I mentor. I go by Ash."

"We are going to get to the bottom of what just happened." He says. He looks at the box on the piano bench. "You have to open it. I am dying to know whats inside."

I laugh. "Fine." I say. I take the box on my lap and open it. I gasp. Oliver gave me a mailbox that is almost identical to the one that Ms.

Conley broke. "Oh my god, its beautiful." I look at it and on the bottom of it its signed by Sebastian Timely.

Justin takes me in his arms.

"I thought I lost the one thing that I never knew was what he left us." I cry.

"Its ok." He says. "He is always with you. He lives within you. He would be so proud of you."

"I wish I knew."

"Get to know him through Scarlett and Oliver. Aaron's dress looks beautiful on you."

"I feel beautiful when I wear his dresses." I say. "They feel so comfortable."

He looks at his watch. "I have to go home and get changed." He kisses me on the lips.

An hour later, we load up the pies in my car. I drive over to A Cup of Books. Matt comes out. The parking lot is packed. Matt hugs me. I give him two pumpkin pies and a big tray of cookies.

"Go enjoy your day." He says. "I don't want to see you until tomorrow."

"Thanks Matt."

"This pie looks great."

"It is really good." I tell him.

"Happy Thanksgiving." Matt says. "Oh, the three guys who were doing security before, they showed up again."

"They are going to be here a lot." Justin tells him.

"Good." Matt says. "You guys go. I got this."

I put the car in reverse and drive to Sebastian's house. I drive up to the gate. The gate opens. Justin opens his mouth. "Does he live in a museum?" Justin asks.

"The inside is very inviting." I tell him. I drive up the long driveway. Sebastian is outside with Seth and Jacob. Astro jumps up in the backseat and wags his tail. "Where do you want me to park?"

"Sebastian, you can park anywhere you want."

"I don't want to be in the way." I tell them.

"If your car is in the way, we will move it. Its not a problem. The driveway is ten miles long." Seth says.

Sebastian punches him in the arm.

I park the car and get out. Astro runs around everyone and finds a spot to do his business. Before I close the door, I reach in and go in the glove box. I take out bags. Justin takes them from me.

"Its fine." Sebastian says. "My lawn man will get it." He hugs me. "You look beautiful."

I hug Seth and then Jacob. "Thank you for the dress." It's the first time that I notice the steps that lead up to the house. "This is so beautiful." I say.

"Come on, we will go inside. Its warm out here." Sebastian says.

"I didn't remember steps." I say.

"We went through the garage. I drove into the secret entrance."

"Oh." I say.

"Nothing is off limits to you." Jacob says. He takes my hand and leads me to an elevator. I look at all of them. "You have an elevator?"

"It came with the house." Sebastian says.

Justin takes Astro in his arms. We all get in the elevator. It opens right into the house. Justin puts Astro down. Astro the cat rubs up against my Astro. They sniff each other.

We go into the kitchen. There are Brussels spouts on the counter. I take a knife and cut them in half. We all get busy doing something.

Charlotte comes in the house through the front door. She follows the laughter coming from the kitchen. She smiles when sees all of us. She hugs all of us.

"There is a lot going on right now." Charlotte says. "What time is dinner?"

"Well the turkey is in the oven. That takes a while. I am going to put a chicken breast in the oven." Seth says. "We have a ham too. And then all the extras."

Charlotte looks at the pies. "These look great. Who made these?"

"All of us." Jacob says.

"The house looks very clean if you made all of these." Charlotte says.

"We made them all and cookies too. We went to Sebastian's house. Her friends showed up. We had a pie war." Seth says. He hugs me.

"Who won?"

"Its up to you and everyone else when you taste them." I tell her.

"This is so wonderful that you all get along." Charlotte says. "What time is Oliver and Grace coming?"

"They are coming in two hours." Sebastian says.

"Nice." Charlotte looks around. "Where is Astro? He normally greets me when I come in."

"He is with my Astro." I say. I mix the Brussels sprouts with olive oil. "Do you have a glass baking dish?"

Seth puts one in front of me. I put the veggies in the baking dish. I sprinkle them with garlic powder and salt.

"Those are ready to go in the oven. What's next?"

"We got it all." Seth says.

"What about the stuffing?" I ask.

"Oh shit. I forgot the stuffing." Jacob says. "I was supposed to make that."

"We can make it now." Justin says. He takes the bag of stuffing off the counter and reads how to do it. "Where's a pot?"

Sebastian gets a pot for Justin. Justin puts the dry ingredients in the pot.

"You are doing it wrong." I says. "We have to cook the celery and onions first."

"We don't have that cut yet." Sebastian says.

"Do you have them?" I ask.

"I like doing a lot of things in the kitchen but cutting vegetables."

"I will do it." I say. "I like doing it."

"Onions make me cry." Jacob says.

"Wimps." Charlotte says. "I will help out." She looks at me. "You look too pretty to prepare food."

I look at Sebastian, "Do you have a shirt I can borrow?"

"Of c course." He says. He pushes me into his room. He takes out a shirt. I look at the one underneath the one he hands me. "Harvard? You went to Harvard?"

"I did." He says.

"Can I wear that one?"

He laughs. "You can wear whatever you want." He opens another drawer and takes out a pair of boxer shorts. "I think these will fit you. They are new."

"Thanks." I say.

He leaves the room and I change. I lay my dress across his bed. I put his shorts and shirt on. When I join them back in the kitchen, Charlotte looks at all of us and has tears in her eyes. Jacob is closest to her. He takes her in his arms.

"What's the matter?" He asks.

"I just wish that Larry would have let us know he knew Sebastian sooner. It would have been so nice having you here all those years ago." She says.

I burst into tears. "Thank you."

Seth and Justin hug me.

"When you salt the vegetables use the sea salt and not tears." Sebastian says.

I rush to him and hug him. "I love you all very much."

It's the first time that I have said it. They all run over and hug me.

"We love you too." They all say.

I cut the vegetables. Justin puts them in the pot with olive oil. Once they are all browned up, he adds the dry stuffing ingredients.

"When its done, we will put it in the casserole dish and stick that in the oven." Seth says.

We all set the table. Sebastian stands back. He looks around the room. "This is my first formal dinner here."

"The first of many." Seth says.

I fold the napkins.

"Everyone will be coming soon. You need to change back into your dress." Charlotte says. She kisses my cheek. "You know, if I was blessed with a daughter, I would want you." She hugs me tight. "I am glad you are part of this family."

"Me too." I say. I go in Sebastian's room. I put my dress back on. I join everyone out on the balcony.

Everyone comes for dinner. Sebastian has invited Anastasia, Oliver, Grace and their children. He also invites Scarlett, Aaron and their children. Aaron's sisters also come with their children. Amanda comes with two children, a little boy and girl. She walks over to Sebastian with the children.

"This is my nephew Liam and my niece Sammie. Thank you for letting me bring them with me. My brother is on shift today and my sister-in-law is with the new baby. It was sweet of Seth to send over all that food. The pies must have cost a fortune on their own."

"We made the pies." He says. "It's a pleasure to have you all with us today."

She kisses him on the lips.

There is a knock at the door. Sebastian opens it and Ivan, Trevor and Sophia walk in. Jacob hugs Sophia the second she is in the house.

"I thought that you had a show."

"The theater is dark. All of Miami is in a blackout." Sophia says. "Sebastian sent a car for all of us."

"I am so glad you are here." He tells her.

"Me too." She says.

Ivan walks over and takes me in his arms like he always does. "Happy Thanksgiving."

"Happy Thanksgiving."

"You look beautiful." He says.

"Thank you. You look very nice too."

He stands and hugs Justin.

"Its good to see you again."

"You too." Ivan says.

Some of the kitchen staff from the Marina Beach come. They take over getting the dinner on plates for everyone there. We all sit down at the table.

"Everything looks so great." Anastasia says. "Seth, did you have the food brought in?" She beams at him.

"No. Actually we all did it. My two brothers, Sebastian and Justin we all prepared the meal together. We also baked pies and cookies." He looks around the room. "Happy Thanksgiving everyone."

After dinner, everyone sits around Sebastian's very large den. The children all sit on the floor playing games.

I approach Uncle Oliver. "I want to thank you so much for the beautiful gift."

"Oh I am so glad you liked it."

"I love it."

"I was told that your boyfriend's brother made you a replacement mailbox."

"He did."

"You keep the one I gave you. Your dad did made it. He would make mailboxes for everyone he knew. He loved doing it."

"It's beautiful." I hug him. "I always thought that you lived out of state."

"I do. Grace—" he looks at her from across the room. "Grace and I also own a farm with rescued animals. She loves being here." He looks around. "Where is your mom?"

"She is with Peter."

"She didn't want to come?"

"We don't see each other on Thanksgiving. She doesn't cook at all. I don't eat turkey. I will see her tomorrow."

"Are you close to your mom?"

"I was close to her. She has missed a lot of events in my life over the years."

"I am sorry to hear that."

"Thank you."

He looks at me. "You look beautiful in that dress."

"I love this dress."

He looks over at Justin. "Your boyfriend seems really nice. He seems to really love you. That phone call must be very important."

"Before we came here, a strange thing happened." I tell him all about it. Sebastian joins us and hears what I tell Oliver. Jacob also joins us.

"Do you know who she is?" Jacob asks.

"No. When I mentor, I don't go use my name. I have always gone by Ash."

"Is someone doing something about it?" Sebastian asks.

"Justin called a friend of his right away and told him the details. She told us that she is Ms. Conley's granddaughter."

"How is Ms. Conley?"

"She apparently is getting out of the hospital today."

"I don't want you to go home to your neighborhood." Sebastian says.

"I have to."

"Why?"

"I am working later tonight at the bookstore."

"Sebastian, come on. Its Thanksgiving."

"Sebastian, tomorrow is a big deal for retail. I own a bookstore that is open twenty-four hours."

For the first time all day, I hear my phone ringing. I retrieve it from my purse and look at it. I have missed twenty calls from Matt. I look at the text messages and there are many. I call him.

"Ok, just so you know, everyone is safe." He blurts out.

"What does that mean?"

"The girl who set the fire in the bathroom has been arrested."

"Fire." I say.

"Fire?" Sebastian, Justin, Seth and Jacob all repeat.

"There was a massive fire. We are all alright but the bookstore is—gone." He says.

I squeeze my eyes shut. Justin grabs me before I fall out of my wheelchair. Sebastian takes my phone and talks to Matt.

"The bookstore is destroyed." Matt tells him.

"What happened?"

"A teenager went into the bathroom and set books on fire. It spread quickly. They think that she put an accelerate in the bathroom."

"Oh my god." Sebastian says. "What about the piano?"

"Everything is gone." Matt says.

"Was anyone hurt?"

"No." Matt's voice catches. "I tried to put it out. The guards that are here tried to put it out."

"Do you know who the girl is?"

"I don't know her name. She has been hanging around all morning. She was flicking a lighter. One of the guards told her to put it away. We thought she left but apparently she went in the bathroom and started a fire in a garbage can."

"Matt, let us call you back. Sebastian has fainted."

"She does that."

"She what?"

"When she gets overwhelmed, she faints."

Justin holds me in his arms. Charlotte, Scarlett, Anastasia and Grace gather around Justin. Sebastian gives the phone to Jacob. "Call one of the guards and find out what happened. I want all details."

"I am on it."

Sebastian leads Justin into a guest room. "What do we do for her?"

"Just wait for her to open her eyes. The first time I met her, she passed out. It took her a few days to wake up." Justin says.

Grace comes in the room. "What happened?"

"There was a fire. Her bookstore burned and everything was destroyed."

"Do you have a shirt and shorts I can change her into?" Grace asks.

"I will go get something." Sebastian says.

Amanda looks at Sebastian. "My brother is a firefighter EMT, I called him when she passed out. He is on his way before he goes home to be with his family."

"Thank you." He says and kisses her.

"I am just going to stay long enough for him to come and then I have to take these two home. This has been the best Thanksgiving I have had in a long time. I am sorry that Sebastian's store burned. I heard how beautiful it was."

"Amanda, I am scared for her." Sebastian says. "She is overworked and doesn't allow anyone to help her. My heart is broken to know that she lost the bookstore. She was going to give up teaching to be there full time."

Sebastian's phone rings. Amanda looks at the number calling. "Your brother?" He asks her.

She nods her head.

Amanda greets her brother Vinny at the door. Sebastian brings him into the guest bedroom. Vinny looks at me. "Its Sebastian." He says.

Sebastian looks at him. "You know my sister?"

"When did she get a brother?"

"We recently found out about each other. How do you know her?"

"She works in that twenty-four hour bookstore. She plays the piano when she thinks that no one is in there. I used to go there a lot when I was studying to be a fire fighter. She tutored me." He walks to the side of the bed. "When did she pass out?"

"Its like a half hour now." Justin says.

"Was she drinking?"

"No. She can't drink wine. I forgot to get her what she likes to drink." Sebastian says.

"What happened before she passed out?"

"She found out bad news."

"What?" He asks. He goes in his bag and takes out a saline drip. He puts the needle in my arm.

"The bookstore burned down." Jacob says.

Vinny looks up. "What? When? It just opened yesterday."

"Someone went into a bathroom and set books on fire. The bookstore burned."

"Oh wow." He says.

I try to move my arm. He holds it steady with his hand. I open my eyes in a panic. Justin sits on the bed next to me. "You are ok."

"I need to move." I say.

"Just lay back and relax for a bit." Vinny says.

I turn my head and look at him.

Seth walks in the room. He has my phone. "Your mom keeps calling."

"Answer it. Tell her that her dream came true." I say and cover my face with my free hand.

Justin leans in and kisses me.

"I really need to sit up." I say. "It bothers me to lay flat on my back."

Jacob climbs on the bed and goes behind me. He gently sits me up. He makes me rest my arm on his leg. "Why would the bookstore burning down be a good thing?"

"My mom was pissed off when I took a job there. She said that all the education I had was going to be wasted in the bookstore." I put my hand over my face and cry. "That really hurts." I say looking at the needle in my arm.

"Just a few more minutes." Vinny says.

I look at Justin. "I passed out again on you?"

"You did." He says. He kisses me.

"You passing out, is that a common thing?" Vinny asks.

"I have been tested for everything, doctors can't find a reason why it happens." I say.

"Ok, the saline is done. If I were you, I would just rest for the rest of evening. Take it easy tomorrow. If you need anything, Amanda can get in contact with me." He hugs me.

"Thanks, Vinny." I say. I look at my dress hanging on the oversized chair in the room. "How did I get changed?"

Grace looks at me. "I did it."

"Thank you."

"Why don't you come join us. We are going to watch a movie." Sebastian says. "You have napped so I am guessing you will stay awake this time." He teases. He hugs me tight.

"When can I go see the damages?"

Seth looks at me. "Trix just texted me that its not safe for anyone to be there right now."

"Was the piano—"

"Everything is gone." Seth says.

"I don't know why anyone wants to hurt me. I am a nice person. I do nice things for people. Ms. Conley has always been nice to me my whole life, now that I have a boyfriend and my friends have come to visit, she has problem with me. She destroyed my mailbox. I don't get it. Just because I asked her to leave my house after she called me a slut." I look at Justin. "I have only slept with three guys before you." I say.

"Sweetheart, I am not asking you. I trust you. We are going to figure out whats going on."

"Will it be safe for me to go home?"

"Not tonight."

"I haven't seen my Astro." I say.

"He is with the children." Grace says.

Everyone leaves shortly after they make sure that I am alright. Oliver wants to stay to make sure I am fine. Grace convinces him to leave. He says that he will be back to check on all of us tomorrow.

We go back into the den and watch a movie. "What do you want to watch?" Sebastian asks.

"I know its silly but I watch the Twilight movies. We. Savannah, Piper and I watch a marathon of them." I say.

"Twilight it is." Sebastian says.

"We can watch something else." I say.

"No. We want to be apart of your traditions." Seth says.

We go from one movie right to the next one. After the third movie I look at all of them. "If you want to watch football or something—"

"No. We have two movies left to go." Sebastian says.

I look over at Jacob sleeping on the one couch. On the couch next to him, Justin is sleeping too. Astro comes and puts his head on my leg.

"Do you have to go outside?" I ask him. He wags his tail.

Seth looks at me. "I will take him."

I look at Sebastian. "Is all the food put away?"

"Are you hungry?"

"I am."

"Me too." Sebastian says.

I get in my wheelchair and when I pass the couch that Justin is sleeping on, I lean over and kiss his head. "I love you." I whisper.

Sebastian, Seth and I go into the kitchen. Seth goes outside with Astro. He comes back moments later. He comes back in the house. "Do you have a toy for him to play with?"

I point at a bag. "The toys are in the bag."

"Does he have a favorite one?"

"Everything in there are his favorite."

Astro the cat comes in the kitchen and rubs against my wheelchair. He sits next to me and puts his front paws on my leg. Sebastian picks him up and kisses the top of his head. He hands Astro to me. The cat rubs his head against my chin and cheek.

"He really likes you." Sebastian says. "What do you want me to take out for you?"

"I want the sweet potato pie. That's the best thing I have eaten."

Seth walks in. He puts a bowl of water on the floor for Astro.

"Astro drink." I say. He stands and laps up the water.

"Can I give him treats?"

"Of course." I say. I look at my cell phone. I open the app from the bookstore.

"What's that?" Sebastian asks.

"I can see inside the bookstore."

"Lets have a look." He says and sits next to me.

Justin walks in the kitchen. "Did we finish all those movies?"

I smile. "No we have two left."

"Good god, really?"

"We are hungry so we took a break."

"Sweet potato pie? I want some of that."

Jacob walks in the kitchen he walks over to me and hugs me tight. "How are you feeling?"

"I am doing ok."

He looks down at my phone. "What are you looking at?"

"I have an app so I can access the inside of the bookstore."

"Are the cameras still working?"

"Yes." I say.

"Lets look." They all sit with me and we look at the damage to my beautiful store. Its true, everything looks like it is ruined. I access the one camera that overlooks the piano. The piano stands there looking shiny as always. "It looks like the piano is safe." I smile.

Justin takes my phone. He clicks on another camera. "What's this?" He asks.

"The children's section." I say.

"It looks like this is not ruined."

I look away. They all look at me.

"What's wrong?" Sebastian asks.

"I don't have money to rebuild it." I close my eyes. Again they all watch me.

"What's going on?" Jacob asks.

"The bookstore was the one place that I would go and feel safe."

"You are safe." Justin says. "We are all going to keep you safe."

281

My phone pings with an alert. I look at it. We all watch Paul Dun-in show up at the bookstore. He smiles when he sees that its all dark.

"Who is that?" Seth asks.

"The old principal at my school. He got reassigned."

We eat again. We sit around the kitchen table.

My phone rings. Piper's ring tone. "Hi, Sav and I are together. Are you alright?"

"I am fine." I tell them.

"The bookstore." Savannah says.

"I know. Matt called me to tell me about it."

"Do they know who did it?"

"They arrested a girl who set fire in the bathroom."

"Oh my god, Sebastian we are so sorry." They say.

"Thanks. I am sorry too."

"We are at your house. Where are you?"

"I am still at Sebastian's."

"Oh good." Piper says. "Someone vandalized your mailbox."

"Why?" I cry.

"Whats going on?" Jacob asks.

"Someone destroyed my mailbox again."

"Sebastian, the police are here. They say that someone tried to break in to your house."

I put my phone on speaker and access my surveillance cameras for my house. I send the footage over to the police immediately.

Shortly after I hang up the phone with my friends. We go back in the den and finish watching the movies. When the last credits roll for the last movie, I am the only one still awake. I turn the movie off and leave the television on at a low volume. I go into the guest bedroom. I get in bed. Astro and Astro come in the room. They both jump on the bed with me.

I snuggle in the most comfortable bed I have ever laid in and fall asleep almost immediately. Some time in the middle of the night, Justin climbs in bed with me. When he gets in the bed, I snuggle close to him. I whimper in my sleep.

"I will keep you safe." He says and kisses my forehead. "I love you."

Chapter 21

Saturday morning, my phone rings and the police and firefighters want me to come and see the wreckage. When I get there, I can not park in the lot of the bookstore. The parking lot is gone. I park at the grocery store across the street. I can only get as far as the sidewalk that leads up to the bookstore parking lot.

A police officer walks over to me. "Ma'am you can't be here. Its dangerous."

"I am Sebastian Timely. I am the owner of the bookstore."

"Can I see some ID?"

I open my purse and get my wallet. I show him my ID. Trix runs over. She hugs me. "Sebastian!"

"Hi." I say. "What happen to the parking lot?"

"It caught fire too." She looks at me. "I am so glad you weren't here."

"Thanks."

The officer gives me back my ID.

Seth and Jacob run over. They hug me. I am glad that they are with me. Justin needed to do some work. Sebastian was needed at the bank. Savannah and Piper run over with Eric.

"How are we going to get inside?" Piper asks.

One of the firefighters walks over. "We put down boards for safety. I am not sure that its wide enough for a wheelchair."

Jacob picks me up. Eric takes my wheelchair. They follow the firefighter into the bookstore. When we get inside, the wood floors are gone. Jacob sits me on the counter. The firefighter stands next to me.

"I think that's a safe spot for her."

I put my head on Seth's shoulder and cry. "Everything I picked out and designed is gone. I put so much money into this and now its all done."

He hugs me.

"Do you know why she did it?" I ask.

"She? It was a boy who did this." The officer says.

"I was told that a girl did this."

"There was a girl arrested but she only set a small fire in the bathroom. A boy did this."

"Why?' I ask. "Did they say why?"

"No."

I look around and cry.

We are only allowed to stay a bit longer before they tell us that we need to go for our own safety. Eric lifts me into his arms and carries me outside. When he sits me in my wheelchair I hug him.

"Does Peter and my mom know about this?" Seth asks.

"They are in Kentucky." Eric says.

"His family always gets them." I say.

"His mother is in the hospital. She broke her pelvis." Eric says. "Your mom didn't call you?"

"I haven't spoken to her since the ship. We did make up but I haven't heard from her. She didn't call me on Thanksgiving of anything."

"Did you call her?" Savannah asks.

"Right after I called you and Piper. I called her and left her a message wishing her a Happy Thanksgiving."

We all walk over to the grocery parking lot and I look at my car. The windows are smashed in and the tires are all slashed.

"What? What the fuck did I ever do to piss someone off so badly?" I yell.

The police officer walks over. "Is this your car?"

"Yes."

"Do you have any enemies?" He asks.

"I didn't think so, but now I am thinking I do. I just don't know what I did to get enemies."

"You know, Trix was telling us that your house was almost broken into. I advise that you don't go home."

"I won't." I say.

"Do you have a dog?"

"I do. I left him at my brother's house. I have been staying there since Thursday."

Ms. Conley comes out fo the grocery store. She walks past me. "Slut."

I look at Savannah and Piper. "She's charming." I say.

"Do you know her?"

"She's someone from my neighborhood."

"She doesn't like you?"

"Normally she has but she was recently hospitalized because she wouldn't leave my front porch and she wouldn't stop calling me a slut."

"Why the sudden change of events?" The officer asks.

"I had a dinner party with friends of mine. She dropped in like she often does. I asked her to leave. She did. She drove into my mailbox. She left and then came back saying that she wasn't leaving until I apologized to her."

Ms. Conley walks by again. "Deserves you right." She says.

The officer walks over to her. "Ma'am, can I ask what you are referring to?"

"Her little cup of books burned down. All that beautiful wood on the floor."

No one other than my family was there for the opening. She wasn't released from the hospital until Thursday afternoon. I look at her. "How did you know about the wood on the floor?"

"The bookstore always had wooden floors." She says.

"No." I say. "The bookstore was carpeted before."

"The wood burned so much faster than we all thought it would." She says.

The officer looks at her. "What do you know about the fire?"

She looks at him. She gets a confused look on her face. "There was a fire?" She asks.

Seth looks at me. "Lets go."

Ms. Conley looks at him. "Another one of your men?"

Eric walks over to Trix. "If you don't remove this woman, I am going to need you to arrest me."

"Eric, I am not going to arrest you." Trix says.

"Are you?" Ms. Conley asks Seth. "Are you her new man?"

Justin runs over. He looks at me, he steps in front of Ms. Conley and takes my hand in his hands. He slips a ring on my left hand. "Your wedding ring just came in the mail all sized for you." He kisses me on the lips. He looks around and sees my car.

Eric walks over. "I called my buddy with a tow truck. He is on his way."

"Thanks." I say.

"You married her?" Ms. Conley asks.

Justin looks at me. He kisses me on the lips. " Why wouldn't I? I love her."

"She was supposed to marry Paul."

"Paul? Paul Dun-in?" I ask.

"Yes. My nephew loves you." She says.

"Am I living in a delusion?" I ask.

The police officer looks at me. "Excuse me?"

"The nephew that she is referring to has broken the windows in my car and slashed my tires in the past. I can't say that he did it today but he did show up the night of the fire. He stood in the parking lot laughing."

"You saw him?" Ms. Conley asks.

"The surveillance cameras got it all." Justin says. He looks at the police officer and hands him his business card.

"Case? Are you Mark's brother?" The police officer asks.

Mark parks his truck next to my car. He runs over and hugs me.

I burst into tears. "All your hard work. I am so sorry." I cry.

"You didn't do this." He says.

Matt walks over with Tristin. Tristin waits for Mark to step back before he hugs me. "Those boys came back." He says.

"What boys?"

"The ones that came in and you told them that the bookstore wasn't opened yet. Those boys. They came back into the bookstore. The girls too."

I feel lightheaded. I look at everyone. "I need to go."

Seth and Jacob talk to Justin for a moment. Jacob walks back over by me. "I am going to take you to my house." He says. "Justin needs to get back to work and Seth has a dinner party. We will stop at Sebastian's and get Astro."

I look at my car. "What about my car?"

Eric kisses me on the top of my head. "I will take care of it. Is anything missing?"

"I don't travel with anything in it any more." I say.

Savannah and Piper hug me. "Tomorrow we are all getting together for brunch."

I hug them. "I love you both."

"We love you too."

Piper takes my left hand in her hand. "That is some ring."

I look at my hand for the first time. The ring really is stunning. I say goodbye to all my friends. Jacob pushes me to where his car is parked. He unlocks his car and I get in the car. He puts my wheelchair in the trunk. I look down at my hand again.

"Did you know he had a ring?" Jacob asks.

"He told me on Thanksgiving that he had a ring. I didn't know he was serious."

Jacob pulls up to Sebastian's house. "I will go get Astro."

"Thanks."

He comes out minutes later with Astro. When Astro sees me, he pulls Jacob across the driveway. Jacob opens the door for Astro. He jumps in the car and licks my face.

"Hi love. I missed you too. I know you wanted to go with me, but you couldn't."

Jacob gets in the car.

"Can we go to my house so I can get some clothes?" I look at what I am wearing. "I love this shirt. He is never getting it back."

"That's his favorite shirt."

"He shouldn't have let me wear it." I say and smile.

Jacob takes his phone out. "Hi, can you meet us at her house? She wants to get some clothes." He puts the phone in the cup holder.

"What was that?"

"I called Trix. She is going to meet us at your house."

"Great."

He pulls into my driveway. I open the front door. Jacob goes in with me. Trix walks in and hugs me.

I look around. When I go in my bedroom, I see where someone tried to break in. The impact window is shattered but it didn't break. Spray painted on the window is the words Move Bitch! Slut!

"What the fuck did I do to make someone dislike me so much?"

I go into the bathroom and that window is smashed too. On the window reads Gold Digging Bitch

I go over to the vanity and put my head down and cry. Astro trots in and licks my face. Jacob hugs me. He takes his phone out and calls Sebastian and Seth. He tells them to come to my house. He also sends text messages to Justin and Mark.

Mark runs in the house. "Sebastian!" He runs into the bathroom. He takes me in his arms. "What the fuck? Who the fuck did this?" He looks at Jacob. "Thank you for texting me." Mark holds me tight in his arms. "We are going to put a stop to this. We will find out who is doing this and Justin will prosecute."

Seth and Sebastian run in. Trix comes running in. She has a crime scene investigator with her.

"Don't touch anything." He tells me. "Did you touch anything?"

"No." I say.

Mom and Peter come running in. "Sebastian!"

"I am in my bedroom."

Mom comes running in."who did this?" She asks.

"No one got in." I say.

Savannah, Piper and Ginger come running into my room with Eric. He looks at me. He looks at Peter. "Can I talk to you?"

Peter walks into the kitchen with Eric.

"Her car is being impounded. When it was on the tow truck, it caught fire."

"Wow. This is getting really out of hand."

Mark walks into the kitchen where they are. "The first time it happened that her car was vandalized should have been the last time."

"Does she have surveillance cameras?" Eric asks.

"She does."

There is a knock on the front door. My driveway is full of cars. Ms. Conley stands at the front door with a christmas bag in her hands. Peter opens the door.

"Oh my god, she has moved on to older men." She says.

"Excuse me."

"I came to see my neighbor. I heard all about her bookstore and wanted to extend my condolences."

"My step-daughter is not taking any visitors at this time." Peter says.

"You married Linda?" She jumps up and down.

"We are just as good as married." He says.

"Can you answer me one thing?"

"I will try."

"How did she get the boyfriend to get a ring that fast?"

Justin stands next to Peter. "Ms. Conley, you have three minutes to get out of here or we are calling the police and the boyfriend will prosecute."

"I am just wondering how the little slut is doing?"

Mom steps from behind the two of them. Ms. Conley steps back. Mom walks right over to her. She points her finger in Ms. Conley's face. "Rita, I am telling you for the first and last time. Leave my daughter alone. Do not come here and offer her pound cake. Don't drive past this house again. Don't go near her bookstore. If you see her in the grocery store, walk the other way. Rita, I don't need you keeping tabs on my daughter. She is a great girl. She is strong and independent."

"She has a lot of men in her house."

"What concern is it of yours?" Mom asks.

"Linda, you travel a lot, she is a lone and needs someone to guide her."

"She is twenty-five years old. She doesn't need to be guided."

A police car pulls up in the street. The officer gets out of the car. He walks over to mom and Ms. Conley.

"Hello officer." Ms. Conley says.

"Ma'am, I got a call about a disturbance." He says.

I scream from inside the house. The officer and mom come running. The officer looks around. He walks over to me. "Are you alright?" He asks.

I play back the surveillance video. Ms. Conley and her granddaughter are walking around my house. Ms. Conley looks in the windows. We see her take out the spray paint and shake it up. She sprays an outline of a dog by my pool. She takes another color and puts Astro's name in the outline. We watch her spray paint the words on the windows. Her granddaughter takes the broken mailbox pieces and throws them at the doors.

The police officer calls for backup. He takes my laptop. "I need this and the access codes."

"The codes are the same. Eight-eight-two-two-one." I say.

The photographer who came in with Trix walks over to the police officer. He gives him a sheet of paper. "Its worst than this."

"Can I ask you some questions?" The officer asks me.

"Of course."

"Have you eve had any trouble with her before?"

I tell him about when it started. I tell him about Paul Dun-in. I tell him about my car getting smashed up. He writes it all down. I tell him about the encounter with the granddaughter.

The police make four arrests. They tell me that I can take some clothes but other than that, I have to go. I can not stay in my house. The police officer looks at the wall where all the pictures are hanging. He smiles.

"You are his Sebastian." He says

I look at the police officer. "What?"

"You are the one who stayed with Trevor." He looks at me. "You saved my brother's life." He steps close to me. "I told him that if I ever had a chance to meet you, I would hug you. Can I hug you?"

"Yes." I say.

"Not everyone felt the same way my parents did about him. My dad has come around to just loving his son no matter the lifestyle. My mom, well she—"

"Is missing out on knowing him and how amazing he is. Ivan and him are married. They are expecting twins." I tell him.

"I know. Trevor told me."

"I didn't know he has a brother. I would have invited you to the reveal."

"He told me about it. He told our sister too. She told my dad. We are going to surprise them both and see Ivan dance in New York just before Christmas." He hugs me again before he leaves. On his way out he walks over to Justin. "She is great."

"I know."

"She can't stay here. There is an officer who is going to stay outside. All of you have twenty minutes and then you have to go." He walks down by his car. "Hey Justin—"

Justin walks over. "What?"

"Let me know when you all leave. Remember don't go outside in the backyard and disturb anything."

"We will be leaving in a few minutes." Justin says.

"I know you live in the neighborhood, I don't think that there will be any more problems. But I would feel better knowing that she isn't going to stay here."

"She is going to stay with her brother."

"Oh good." He gets in the car and leaves.

I put clothes in two suit cases. I sit in my room and just cry. Sebastian walks in the room. "This is going to end. You are going to be back here. You are going to be fine."

"I have to be at work on Monday. I don't have a car."

"You have a lot of people who absolutely love you. We will get you to work and picked up. Let us take care of you."

I hug him.

I leave with Jacob. He puts my stuff in his car. Astro jumps in the back seat like he owns it. He rubs all over the backseat.

"I am so sorry about that."

He laughs at me. "I take it that Astro approves of this arrangement."

"Yeah, I guess." I say.

"Do you go to church?"

291

I look at Jacob. "I do. I don't have to go tomorrow."

"We go too. We will be going with you."

He pulls into a small parking lot. He gets my wheelchair out of the car. "In my neighborhood, we can't park in our driveways. I am not sure why I fell in love with this place, but welcome."

We go inside. I look around. "Holy shit!"

"What?"

"I know why you fell in love with this place. This is beautiful."

"Come see the guest room."

I follow him into a beautiful room. It's a master bedroom. I look at him. "I won't take your room."

"This is the guest room. My room is down the hall." He puts the suit cases on the loveseat that is in the room.

Astro jumps up on the loveseat. "Astro down!" I say.

"No. He is fine." He kisses the top of my head. "I have two cats."

"I didn't see cats."

"They sleep on my bed. They love other animals. I know that Astro is good with cats." He looks around. "Before I forget, one of the cats likes to sleep on the bedpost in here. I am not sure why she does it but if it bothers you, I will keep her out of here."

"I love cats." I say.

"Are you hungry?" He walks out of the room. "Seth sent over a lot of food. He is going to stop by after his dinner party that he is hosting."

"Thank you."

"Just so you know, I told Justin to come over when he wants." He goes into the kitchen. "Make yourself at home."

Jacob sits on the couch and puts the television on. College football is on. When I join him by the couch, he sits up. "I can change this."

"Its fine." I say.

"Want to sit on the couch?"

"Yes."

"Can you do it or do you need help?"

"I got it." I open the feet plates and put my feet on the floor. The carpet under my feet is the softest I have ever felt. It is so thick. I transfer on the couch. I get myself comfortable.

Astro jumps up on the couch next to me.

"He is fine." Jacob says.

Within a few minutes of just sitting and relaxing on the couch, I fall asleep. Jacob stands and gets a blanket, he covers me. He sits back on the couch and watches the next game that plays.

I open my eyes when I hear a lot of voices. I stretch and slip off the couch. I sit on the floor and laugh. Justin walks over. He sits on the floor with me. He hugs me. I get on my knees and hug him.

"Sleeping beauty woke up." Jacob says.

"You made a grave mistake." Justin teases.

"What's that?"

"You invited her to watch television with you."

I laugh. I am still on my knees in front of Justin. He slips his arms around me and stands up taking me with him.

We sit around the table having dinner. Seth has prepared another fabulous dinner for us. An eggplant dish that is my favorite. We all clean up the kitchen together which is not as easy as it is in my house or Sebastian's house. Jacob's kitchen is smaller but we all make it work somehow.

Sebastian's phone rings. Charlotte is calling to check on all of us. "Ok you are on speaker." He sys.

"We never revealed who won the pie wars the other night."

"Oh that's right." Seth says. "I am sure that you loved ours the best." He refers to Sebastian, Jacob and his pies."

"Yes your pie was delicious but I have to say that the one that tops the cake is Sebastian's."

He smiles,

"Don't gloat I was referring to the girls' pies. That was the best pumpkin pie I have ever had." She says.

I smile.

"Oh boy, now we won't be able to live with her. She is gloating. She is smiling as big as a Macy's float." Seth teases.

"And those pumpkin cookies were so good too."

"I am glad you enjoyed them." I say.

"I put some in the freezer so I can eat one whenever I want." She says.

I smile. "Charlotte, I can make more for you. Its one of my favorite things to make. Its easy."

"I would love that." She says. She sends Sebastian a text message to take her off speaker. He does and walks away from all of us. "I am going to take Astro out for a walk."

I look at him. "If you pass by cats, just say 'not our friend'."

"Will do." He says and kisses my forehead. He walks outside with Astro. "Hi." He says into the phone.

"How bad is it?"

"They didn't break in to the house but they tried to. The window is smashed and two French doors. But she has the impact windows and doors so they couldn't get through. They spray painted stuff on the window and doors. They did an outline of Astro by the pool. Its just creepy. I can't help but think, wasn't the bookstore enough. Her car is destroyed. When they loaded it on the flatbed, it caught fire."

"Sebastian, that's awful. I know one thing for sure, you and your brothers have to keep her calm. When she stresses out, she faints."

He laughs.

"Why is that funny?"

"Sit her on a couch and put football on, she passes out too." He laughs.

"I hope that your brother is being considerate."

"Mom, Jacob is on cloud nine. He is protecting her. This means the world to him."

"What are you all doing tomorrow?"

"She wants to go to church. We are going with her."

"Text me where and when. I want to come." Charlotte says.

"I will." Sebastian says.

"I love you, baby."

"I love you too." He says.

Chapter 22

Monday morning, Seth drops me off in front the elementary school. He gets my wheelchair out of the car and watches me enter the school. I go into the main office and clock in. Mr. Smith is waiting for me. Astro and Sparky sniff each other.

Mr. Ricks hugs me. I hug him. "How was your Thanksgiving?" I ask.

"It was great." He hugs me again. "I am so sorry about the bookstore."

I burst into tears. "I feel like I lost my best friend." I say.

"We called in a substitute teacher for you. We didn't think that you would be here. You can help with the pretesting. I didn't want to bring someone else in."

"That's fine." I say. "I need to be here. My family is making sure that I have a babysitter at all times. So at least here, I get to be the babysitter."

Mr. Smith looks around. "Don't be mad, I am the hired babysitter." He hugs me.

Karen Rowe walks in the front door. She drops her bags and runs over to me. "Hi." When she hugs me, we both cry. "I am so sorry."

I wipe my tears. "This is my distraction." I say to them.

A grief counselor walks in the front doors of the main office. He walks over to Mr. Smith. The two of them walk into his office and close the door.

"Whats that about?" I ask.

"Its been on the news all that has been going on with the bookstore. Some of the parents expressed a concern that the children were upset for you and were scared for themselves." Karen says.

"Should I leave?" I ask.

"No. That will make it worst. The children need to see you. They need to know that you are ok."

Eric walks in the front door with Danny. Danny comes running over to me. He hugs me tight. Matt comes in with Tristian. He runs over to me too.

Tristian cries. "It was so scary." He says.

I hug him. "It was scary."

"If you were there, you wouldn't have been able to get out." He cries.

"Tristian, I am fine. I wasn't there."

The grief counselor comes out of Mr. Ricks' office. He sits in a chair.

Danny looks at him. "Who are you?"

"Mr. Kevin."

"Are you our substitute teacher?"

Mr. Kevin looks at Mr. Ricks. "No."

The front office doors open. I look at the door. I go rushing over to Edward Case. Justin's dad takes me in his arms. He brings me outside. "Sweetheart, I am so sorry."

"I feel like I lost a family member." I cry.

"Go get your stuff. I am taking you for the day. You can't be here. I got a call from— oh my god, my phone kept ringing. I would hang up with one and the phone would ring. Justin called me. Mark called me. Savannah called next. I got a call from a Sebastian Timely. Then his brother called me. I got a call from a Mr. Ricks who said that he would keep you here at work, but he doesn't think that its good for you to be here."

"Edward, I need to be here. They have a grief counselor here to help the kids who are struggling with the idea that my bookstore burned down and I could have been there. You can stay."

"I will stay until lunch time." Edward says.

"I have a lot of babysitters in there." I smile. I look at Edward. "You know what makes me sadder?"

"Whats that?"

"Mark worked so hard to renovate it the way I wanted it. The wood floors alone were stunning." I look at the school bus pulling into the lot. "I can't afford to rebuild it. I worked so hard for three years never going anywhere never doing anything extra so I could afford to buy the bookstore." I look at Edward. "I need a new car, I didn't count on that expense."

"Sweetheart, its all going to work out the way it should." He kisses my forehead.

"I work so hard."

"No one thinks otherwise." He says.

I look at him. "You know, I always wanted to have a dad like you."

He hugs me.

By the end of the day, the whole school has come to tell me how sorry they are that the bookstore burned down. Edward stayed until lunch time. When the final bell rings for the day, I am grateful that the day is over. I get Astro and my stuff and go outside of the front office. Jacob is parked in my spot. He walks over and takes my stuff from me. Astro follows him. I get in the car.

"Did you have a nice day?" He asks.

"It was a day. Overwhelming with concern for me."

"I have to go to the marina, do you want me to take you to the restaurant? Do you want to go to the bank? Do you want to go—"

"I will go with you to the marina." I say.

"I thought that I would be done with the job, but I need a few more hours."

"Jacob, its fine." I look at the ring on my finger.

"Did anyone ask about the ring?" He asks.

"No. Everyone was too concerned about the bookstore."

"They were concerned about you." He says.

"Yeah." I put my head back on the headrest and within seconds, I fall asleep.

Sebastian calls Jacob. "How is she doing?"

"I guess she finds peace with me." Jacob says.

"What does that mean?"

"I picked her up from work. She got in the car. She spoke to me for a few minutes. I tuned on to the main road and she sleeping."

"That's so sweet. Are you going home with her?"

"No. I have to go to the Marina. I have to finish my job."

"Swing by the bank. I can let her sleep in my office."

"Yeah, I think I will do that. I will be there in a few minutes."

"Come to the side door."

"Ok." Jacob says and merges into the turning lane. He pulls into the shopping center where the bank is located. He parks the car. He takes Astro into the bank through the side entrance.

Sebastian comes outside. He opens the passenger door. He unbuckles my seatbelt. He lifts me into his arms. I don't even stir. Jacob holds the door for Sebastian. Jacob gets my wheelchair.

Sebastian lays me on the couch. Jacob kisses me on the forehead before he leaves. Astro lays on the floor next to me. I sleep the rest of the day. When the bank closes, he finishes his work for the day. Sebastian checks on me. I am still sleeping. He kisses my forehead.

Amanda comes into his office. She looks at me. "She is so pretty."

Sebastian looks at me. "She looks like our dad."

"She is exhausted." Amanda sits on the floor and pets Astro. "Make sure she drinks water. She needs to stay hydrated."

"I will."

"Which one of you is going to take her?"

"She seems most relaxed with Jacob."

"That's odd."

"I know. She is my sister. She's not their sister."

"Sebastian, don't be a baby."

"I want to get to know her."

"Well then spend time with her."

"I want to."

"Sebastian, what do you worry about?"

"What if she doesn't like me."

"She loves you." Amanda looks up and catches sight of the ring on my finger. "What's that?"

"What?"

"She's wearing an engagement ring."

"Justin put it on her finger Saturday. He didn't ask her to marry him yet."

"Do you approve of him?"

"Amanda, its not like I have any say on what she does." He looks at me. "Justin is the one who brought us together. I am grateful."

Amanda gets my wheelchair on the way out. Sebastian lifts me in his arms and carries me to his car. "Take her back to your house." She tells Sebastian.

He puts me in the front seat and buckles the seatbelt. He puts my wheelchair in the trunk. Amanda walks Astro over. She opens the back door for him and he jumps in the car.

Sebastian drives to his house. He pulls in garage. He brings Astro outside and lets him sniff around. He trots next to Sebastian. Sebastian pets his head. He opens the passenger door and scoops me up in his arms. He carries me into the guest room and lays me in bed.

Seth arrives and gets my wheelchair. He brings it in the house with my purse and the bag that I have all Astro's stuff in. "Is she alright?"

"She's been sleeping since Jacob picked her up from work. I have lifted her three times now and she didn't move."

"How did her day go?"

"I don't know. She has been sleeping the whole time."

"How can we find out?" He asks.

"We will ask her when she wakes up."

"Did you have dinner?"

"I just got home. Dinner? No. I didn't think of anything for dinner? Are you staying at mom's?"

"She has a date."

"Mom?"

"Yes."

"Good for her."

"I guess, but I can't be there."

"Stay in your room." Sebastian tells him.

Seth opens the refrigerator. He takes out the leftovers from Thanksgiving. He puts it in the oven to warm it all up. "Should we wake her up?"

"No."

Jacob walks in the house. "Hey how is she?"

"Still sleeping. I have literally picked her up three or four times now and she didn't move."

"She feels safe with us." Jacob says.

They both look at Jacob.

"Why do you say that?" Seth asks.

I open my eyes and I know where I am. I have no idea how I got to Sebastian's house. I sit up. Astro the cat is on the bed. I pet him. He meows.

"Ok, ok. I am awake." I get in my wheelchair. Astro steps on my legs. I go into the kitchen. Sebastian hugs me first. Seth hugs me next and last, Jacob hugs me. "I am sorry I fell asleep."

"No. Its ok." Jacob says.

"I really wanted to go with you to the marina."

He smiles. "You fell asleep almost immediately."

I look around the kitchen. "It smells so good in here."

"I have dinner in the oven." Seth says.

"I can't wait."

"Did you have a nice day?" Sebastian asks.

I smile. "It was overwhelming. I went to work but I didn't work at all. They had a substitute teacher for me. My class found ways to be more in the office than where they needed to be. It was nice to be there but it was sad too. Edward Case, Justin's dad stayed with me until noon. Then he had a meeting to get to." I look at all the of them. "The day was overwhelming. I cried because I told one of my friends at work that I feel like I lost a family member. I wanted one of you to come get me."

Sebastian hugs me. "You should have called me."

"I didn't want to take any of you from your work."

"Sebastian, we are here for you."

I start to cry. "I don't know that I can go back to work tomorrow. I don't think I want to."

"Ok well, I have the day off. I have errands to run but you can come with me." Sebastian says.

"I have the day off too." Seth says.

"I have to work." Jacob says. "I am taking a yacht out tomorrow. Come out with me."

"I would love that." I say.

"I would love that too." Seth says.

I call Mr. Ricks and leave a message that I need some time. I tell him that if he needs me to come to work, I will but I can not stop crying and I don't want to scare the children.

I climb into bed. I sit with my phone in my hand. I send text messages to mom. I also send them to Piper and Savannah. I tell them about my day and how hard it was for me. I tell them that I feel like I lost a family member.

Mom calls my phone. "Hi sweetheart."

"Hi mom."

"How are you?"

"I am sad. I feel like I am lost. I went to work today and there was a grief counselor there. He talked to the children. I felt like I needed to talk to him myself. I feel like I lost a family member."

"Where are you now?"

"I am at Sebastian's house."

"Why not with Justin?'

"The police and everyone else don't want me in the neighborhood." I start to cry. "I love that house."

"I know you do."

"Are you going to work tomorrow?"

"No. I can't concentrate when I am there. I am going to take some time off."

"What are you going to do tomorrow?"

"Everyone is working. I don't know what I am going to do tomorrow."

"Will you see Justin?"

"Maybe. He is on a case. I can't keep him from his work."

"He put a ring on your finger." She says.

I look down at my hand. "That he did."

"Did he ask you to marry him?"

"No. No he didn't."

"What would you say if he did?"

"What do you think I would say? I would say yes. I feel safe when I am with him." I look at the ring again. "How are you doing?"

"Peter and I are scheduled to leave tomorrow."

"I know."

"Do you want me to cancel my trip?"

Yes. My mind screams yes. "No. You have had this planned for a while. I am sure that your sisters and grandma want to meet your fiancé."

"They have met Peter."

"They have not met Peter the fiancé."

"We could go after the new year."

"Mom go."

Peter takes the phone. "Hi honey."

"Hi Peter."

"I just want you to know that your car is destroyed."

"I know." I yawn.

"Get some rest. We love you."

"I love you both very much."

I turn on my side and lay back in the most comfort bed I have been in. I sleep so well. I feel safe. I feel relaxed.

When I wake up in the morning, I am startled by someone being in bed with me. I sit up immediately. Justin sits up and takes me in his arms.

"I spoke to Sebastian when I got off work last night. I turned the case over to my partner for the day. I am going to spend time with you."

"I don't—"

"Sebastian, let us all love you. You have been through a lot this year."

I look at him. "What aren't you saying?" I put my face in his neck so I don't have to hear bad news. I know its bad news coming.

"Ms. Conley and her granddaughter were involved in a fatal accident last night. They were being transported back to jail. The car that they were in was struck by a gas truck."

I pull back. "Wow, I am sorry to hear that." I cover my face with my hands and scream.

Sebastian, Jacob and Seth come running in the room. They all sit on the bed with me. They all hold me while I cry.

My phone rings. Seth reaches over to the night stand and gets the phone. He answers it. "Hello."

"Sebastian?" Mom says.

"Its Seth."

"Oh, I thought that she said that she was staying at Sebastian's."

"We are all here with her. She just heard some bad news."

"What happened now?" Mom asks with announce in her voice. "If she doesn't want me to go to Europe all she had to do was say."

"Linda. Ms. Conley was tragically killed in an accident and her granddaughter was with her."

"I am sorry to hear that. I am guessing that my Sebastian is taking this hard."

Seth takes the phone away from his ear and looks at it.

"Seth? Are you there?"

"Yes."

"Please tell her that she shouldn't feel bad. I have to board now. Tell her that I love her."

"I will." He puts the phone back on the night stand.

Charlotte comes running into the house. She comes running into the guest room and takes me in her arms "Oh sweetheart." She stays with all of us. She looks at her three sons and Justin.

"She was so nice to me when I was young. I don't know why she changed so dramatically."

My phone rings. Oliver's face springs up on my phone.

"Its Oliver." Seth says.

"Answer it." I say.

"Hello." Seth says.

"Seth?" Oliver asks. "I thought that I called Sebastian's phone."

"You did."

"How is she? I just heard the news about her her neighbor." He takes in an audible breath. "How is our girl?"

"She's upset."

"Is she going into work?"

"No. She has taken a few days off." He gets up from the bed. He leans in and kisses me on the cheek. He leaves he room. "I am going to take Astro out." He announces. He has my phone with him. He puts Astro's leash on and steps outside. "Her mom went to Europe."

"Well we will have to make sure that she is never alone until things start to get back to normal."

"What is that?"

"Seth—"

"I just want to see her happy. I mean, when I went into her bookstore before we knew her, she was always smiling and seemed so happy. Even when she thought that no ones was around, she would smile and sing along with the radio. She was fucking happy."

"She will be happy again." Oliver says.

"My dad was the first person that ruined her. Then this principal stalked her. Broke into her car. The neighbor, seemed like a nice person was a wacko. She tried to break into her house."

"What?"

"The neighbor's granddaughter turns up and sets the bookstore on fire. What else? What else is she going to have to live through?"

"What about her house?"

"The neighbor destroyed the mailbox. Two mailboxes actually. The granddaughter and her tried to break into Sebastian's house. Oliver, I think that she has lost weight too and she is so thin to begin with."

"What are you going to do today?"

"Our plan was to take her out on the water. Now that she has found out about the neighbor, I don't know. We are all with her. My mom is here too."

"If you all need anything, don't hesitate to call me or Aaron."

"Thanks."

"Hug her for me."

"I will." Seth takes Astro for a long walk. My phone rings in his pocket none-stop. He never looks at it. He runs Astro the last mile home.

Astro runs into the room where I am and he jumps on the bed. Jacob is sitting on the loveseat with his laptop on his legs. He is doing work. I am sleeping. Jacob watches me. Seth walks into the room and sits on the loveseat with Jacob.

"Where is everyone?"

"Justin and Sebastian went to her house to see when she can return."

"Isn't it creepy that you are in here watching her sleep?"

Jacob looks at me. "She wanted someone to stay."

"Where is mom?"

"She was called away. Larry needed her."

"She is still running when he calls."

"Mom needs help from him signing papers for the building."

"How long has she been out?"

Jacob looks at his watch. "About a half hour."

Seth looks at me. "Does she seem peaceful?"

"She cried out a few times."

Seth lowers his voice. "Is it wrong that I am glad that the neighbor can't bother her anymore?"

"No." Jacob says.

~~~~~

I pull my new car into the parking lot of the courthouse. I have to testify against Paul Dun-in. He will be in the courtroom. I park my car and get out. He walks by me.

"Can I talk to you?" He asks.

Sebastian and Jacob run over. Justin walks over and takes my hand. When they have established that I am unharmed, they surround me and we go inside.

Paul follows us. He walks over to Sebastian. "Can I talk to her?"

"Why are you asking me?"

"I just want to talk to her."

Justin steps up. "Talk to her in the courtroom."

"I just want her to know that I will leave her alone."

"Save it." Justin says.

"Listen, I never meant for any of this to get out of hand."

A woman walks over to him. She takes him by the arm and pulls him away from all of us. She hisses at him. "Don't talk to them."

He looks at his lawyer. "I don't want to do a trial."

305

"You don't get a choice."

"Why not?" Paul asks.

What seems like four hours later we are in the courtroom. The judge is reading all the documents that pertain to our case. "Mr. Dun-in please stand up." She waits until he does. "Did you follow Miss Timely from school to the bookstore?"

"Did I do it?"

"That's what I am asking you."

"Did I follow her once or more than that?"

"Mr. Dun-in answer the questions." The judge says.

He looks at me. "I just want to talk to her."

"Well talk to her."

"Privately."

"Not happening."

"Sebastian is a tease. She always flirted with me. She was nice to me one minute and then she would turn. I wanted to make sure that she got from one job to another safely."

"Why did you break into her car?"

"She was hiding something." He says.

"What was she hiding?"

"She was hiding her love from me." Paul looks at me. "You flirted with me, you bitch. All I wanted to do was make sure that you got what you asked for."

"What did she ask for?"

He jumps up and puts his hand on the wood in front of him while he stands in the witness box. He digs his fingers into the wood. "She wanted me." He bellows.

"Sit down." The judge says. She looks at me. "Can you come forward?"

I do.

"Tell me, Miss Timely, did you flirt with Mr. Dun-in?"

"Never." I say.

"Go on." She says. "Talk freely."

"When I was hired to teach, Paul— Mr. Dun-in never liked me. He told me from day one that I was hired to fill a quota. I am nice to everyone that I work with. I was there for the children. I didn't want to date anyone. I haven't dated anyone since I was in college."

"How many jobs do you have?"

"I am currently not working."

"How many jobs did you have?"

"I worked three jobs. I taught third grade. I worked in a bookstore and I mentored."

"Why aren't you working now?"

"I took over ownership of the bookstore and unfortunately it was burned down."

"Oh, I am sorry to hear that."

"Thank you. His niece is the one who set fire to my bookstore. He was seen in the parking lot laughing as flames shot from the bookstore." Tears choke me. "I have taken time off of my other responsibilities because I feel like I lost a family member when the bookstore was destroyed. Mr. Dun-in, continued to follow me. Every time he would show up, my car would be vandalized."

"What did you do?"

"I would show up to work every day and never give into the fear that I felt on a daily basis. He didn't like me. Told me flat out that he hated that I was teaching in his school. Now he claims that he did it because he loved me. This is different from a little boy pulling the pigtails of a little girl at the playground. He stalked me. He showed up everywhere I went. Then he had his aunt turn on me." I start to cry. "I loved my neighbor. I am sad that she is no longer here. I am sad that she was made to think the worst of me. I just want to go home."

"Excuse me."

"I haven't been able to go home since he helped his niece burn down my bookstore. His aunt and niece broke my windows. They spray painted the worst things on my windows and doors." I put my head down and cry harder. I feel dizzy. I sit up and hold my head.

"Miss Timely are you alright?"

Justin jumps over the table he is sitting at and catches me before I fall out of my wheelchair.

"Is she alright?"

"She faints when she is overstressed." Justin says.

Paul jumps up. "She wants me."

The police officers in the room tackle him as he runs towards me.

"Mr. Dun-in, I sentence you to six months in jail. Please take him into custody." The judge says. "Mr. Case, bring her into my chambers and stay with her until she wakes up."

Justin lifts me into his arms. He kisses me on the lips. "You are safe. I am going to take care of you." He kisses me on the lips again. "You are safe, princess. I love you."

Sebastian, Seth and Jacob stand in unison. Jacob gets my wheelchair. The judge looks at them. "Can I ask the three of you a question?"

Sebastian looks up at her.

"Are you related to her?"

"We are her brothers." Jacob says.

"Come talk to me. Tell me about her." She says. She leads them into a conference room. They sit and talk for a while. "After everything you all have told me about her, I think that you should spend every holiday with her. It seems that she has been alone a long time. It seems that she could use some much needed fun in her life."

Justin kisses me deeply. He holds me in his arms. He runs his hands up and down my body. He kisses my neck and covers my body with his. I open my eyes.

"You are awake." He says. "How are you feeling?"

I blush profusely.

"Are you cheeks burning?" He asks with a laugh. "Look how red you are getting."

I look away from him. "It felt so real."

"What did?"

"Where am I?"

"Don't change the subject." Justin says.

"Really, where am I?"

"You are in the courthouse. You fainted."

I sit up and cover my face. I cry.

"Why are you crying?"

"How long have I been out?"

He looks at his watch. "Twenty minutes."

"What happened?"

"He's in jail for at least six months." He walks over and kisses me on the lips. "Is that what you felt?" He kisses me again and again.

I wrap my arms around his neck and I kiss him.

"What seemed real?"

"I felt. NO. I feel safe when I am with you. I feel loved."

"Sebastian." He hisses my name. "You are not alone. You are loved. I love you."

"I love you. Can you take me home? I want you to make love to me."

He holds me close.

"I never flirted with him."

"I know that."

"Justin, I love you."

"I love you too."

Chapter 23

I sit in the airport surrounded by my new found family and my friends. We are waiting to board a plane for New York City. Justin is sitting with Astro between his feet. He is going with us to New York City. Sophia had sent Jacob tickets for the ballet for an early Christmas present. She sent tickets for me, Sebastian, and Seth. When Jacob got them, he got on a plane and flew to New York to see about the seats like he had done in Miami. When he returned home, he had tickets for a group of us.

Mark takes Astro from Justin. He walks over to me where Savannah and I are sitting with our heads together. We are looking at my phone. "Little Mermaid, we are going to board soon. I am going to take Astro out before we board."

I look at Mark. "I can take him."

"I will. We fear that if you take him, you won't go with us to New York." Mark says.

Savannah looks at him. "Mark."

"What?"

"Don't give her any ideas."

He kisses Savannah on the lips. He kisses me on the forehead.

"We aren't boarding—" I start to say.

"Now boarding SouthWest Air to New York City at gate eight. Now boarding those passengers that need assistances." A woman announcers. "Passengers boarding with service animals need to board first."

A man walks over to where are sitting. "What flight are you on?" He asks.

"The nine-zero-five.'"

"Come with me." He says. "You can have one person board with you at this time. And from the manifesto, I see that you are flying with a service dog."

"Yes."

"Can you verify your name and the dog's name?"

"My name is Sebastian Ashley Timely and the dog's name is Astro." I say.

He reads the iPad. "Follow me." He says. "Will someone be boarding with you?"

"Yes." Justin says. "Case, Justin." He says.

The guy looks at Justin. He smiles. "Right the way Mr. Case."

We go down the jetway. Astro walks right next to me. When we enter the plane, the guy tells us that we are ten rows back.

Justin looks at him. "She paid extra money to have the front seat. Her dog is staying with her in the front of the plane."

He looks at the iPad he is carrying. "Oh I apologize for that. Do you need help getting into the chair?"

"No." I say. "Thank you."

I get in the chair and they take my wheelchair. "Remember first one on, last one off."

"Thank you."

Justin sits next to me.

I look at him. "You know, Sebastian wanted to sit next to me."

"Too bad." He says and kisses me on the lips.

A half hour later, the plane is taxiing the runway. I am in the front of the plane. Justin sits next to me and holds my hand the whole flight. They moved Astro to the row behind us. He is sitting in a seat next to Savannah. Mark is across the isle from her.

The female pilots get us to John F. Kennedy International Airport two and half hours later. Everyone disembarks the plane. I wait with excitement for someone to let me get off. One of the employees brings my wheelchair and I get in it. I thank the staff and the pilots before leaving the plane.

Justin takes my hand and Astro's leash. We enter the airport and go to the carousel to get our luggage. We all gather our belongings. We leave the airport and get in two limos that are waiting for us.

The driver shows us all the places that we should go see. He pulls up to the entrance of the hotel that we are staying in. He jumps out of the car and gets my wheelchair out for me. He holds it while I get in it. I take Astro's leach. We go into the resort.

I am waiting for something to go wrong as it hasn't up until now. I see the clerk's face when she watches me with Astro. I smile at her and she looks away. I approach the front desk.

"Checking in." I say. Its not the first time that I have stayed at this resort. I know that there are great accommodations.

"We have a no pet policy." She says.

"He's a service dog." I say.

"We are very strict on those accommodations. No dogs."

"He is more than a pet. He is a service dog." I say.

She gets louder. "Ma'am, you can not have an animal in this establishment."

A man walks over to her. "What seems to be the problem?"

"The problem is that I just flew in with my family and friends from Florida. We are staying here through Christmas and when I made the reservations I made sure that I booked a resort that I could bring my service dog to. Now that I am here, she is telling me that I can not stay here with my dog."

She looks at her boss. "I never said that she couldn't stay here, but the dog can not stay here."

"Well if he can't stay, then I can't stay."

Justin walks over. He kisses me on the lips. "Sweetheart, let me deal with this."

"Justin, I stayed here before with Astro. That's why we booked this place." I say.

He opens his wallet and takes out one of his business cards. One falls out of his wallet and onto my lap. I look at it as he hands one to the manager. American With Disabilities Act Lawyer.

The manager looks at him. "We will have your rooms ready within the hour."

I turn around and leave the resort. Savannah comes running after me.

"Hey! Hey! Slow down." She says as she runs after me. "What's wrong?"

"Did you know he is an ADA lawyer?"

"Yes. How did you not know that?" She stands in front of me. "Does it matter?"

"Why can't I just get into the resort on my own? Why is that I turned twenty-five fucking years old and my life has changed so much. I used to do everything alone. I mean independently."

"You don't have to do it on your own anymore."

I get up in the morning and put warm clothes on. I brush my hair and put make up on. Its very early in the morning and everyone is still sleeping. I quietly get Astro and we leave the room. We get in the elevator and go downstairs. The clerk looks at me as I pass her. She tries to stop me, but I leave through the front doors with Astro.

We walk down the sidewalk and Astro sniffs every inch of the ground. I enter Central Park. I walk until I find a spot that catches my attention. Astro sits next to me. I open my purse to get my phone out and I don't have it with me.

Justin wakes up and reaches for me. He sits up and looks around the room. "Sebastian!"

"What?" Sebastian answers from the other bedroom.

"Um, not the one I am looking for."

"Maybe she went to get a cup of coffee. Yesterday she was craving Starbucks." Sebastian says from the doorway.

Justin looks where Astro's leash was. Its gone. My purse is gone but my phone is there on the table charging. "She could be anywhere." He jumps out of bed. "Damn! I knew she was upset about me not telling her that I am an ADA lawyer. I don't usually tell people that. Its just something that I do as one aspect of the law."

"Why didn't you tell her?"

"I don't get a lot of time to just sit and talk to her about my life when we are always dealing with her life." Justin says. "I love her. I want to marry her."

"You put that ring on her finger. Did you ever pop the question?"

Justin looks at him. "You know I didn't."

"When are you going to do it? She's not going to take that ring off her finger. She looks at it all the time."

"I just want to make it special for her."

"Justin, anything you do will be special. She loves you. She feels safe with you. She is always looking for you."

Justin gets dressed quickly.

My phone rings. Sebastian looks at it. Its Savannah calling. He answers it. "Hi."

"Wow, Seb you sound so different." She jokes.

He laughs. "She forgot her phone. She's not here and Astro is gone."

"She took Astro for a walk. They probably went to Central Park."

"Did she tell you that she was upset?"

"Of course she was upset. We stayed her the last time we came. She had Astro with us. There was no problems then. I am not sure why there was such an issue yesterday."

I come into the lobby with Astro. All my friends are standing in the lobby waiting for me. Justin grabs me and hugs me. I hug him.

"I am sorry." I say. "You were sleeping. Astro was crying to go out. I had to take him. I thought that I would only be gone a few minutes. I opened my purse to call you all and realized I didn't have my phone. Then I got a little lost."

"We are glad you are alright." Trix says.

Justin takes my hand. "Can I talk to you?"

"Of course."

Piper reaches over and takes Astro's leash. Savannah stands shoulder to shoulder with Piper. Piper looks at Savannah and takes her hand squeezing it. "The last time we were here, I thought I our friendship was over."

Savannah laughs. "We know too much." She laughs.

Piper looks away in the direction that Justin is leading me. There is a lounge area that is quiet because its eight-thirty in the morning. She looks back at Savannah. "Are we all going to stand here and watch the show?"

The front doors open as Ivan and Trevor walk in. They great everyone. Ivan looks around the lobby. "Where is she?"

"Justin and her are talking." Seth says. "He woke up and she wasn't in the room. She took Astro for walk and didn't have her phone."

Trevor looks around the lobby. "Why don't we all go have something to eat. Let them have a moment."

"What if he is breaking up with her?" Trix asks.

Seth takes Trix's hand. "He loves her too much for that."

Piper, Savannah, Seth, Jacob, Trix, Mark, Eric and Danny all go to the café. They all sit at half booth tables. Matt and Tristian come out of the elevator and join them. Matt looks at everyone.

"What's going on?" Matt says.

"We are having breakfast." Eric says.

"Where are the Sebastians?" Matt asks.

Everyone laughs. It's the first time that everyone is relaxed since they have all been in the lobby. They all order breakfast and discuss what everyone wants to do on the trip.

Justin sits in a chair with his legs spread around my wheelchair so that we are facing each other. He holds my hands in his hands and runs his fingers over the ring on my finger. He bounces his legs.

"I am sorry I didn't wake you up." I say. I put my right hand on his left leg.

"I don't care that you didn't wake up me. I was nervous when I looked around the room and saw your phone was on the table."

"Justin, I am ok."

"I would have went with you." He says.

"I was wide awake. Astro was getting loud and you were sleeping."

Justin rubs his fingers over the ring again. "Tell me something about you that no one knows."

"When I was young, I would wish on every star I saw in the sky that I could meet my dad."

Justin hugs me.

"Tell me something about you." I say.

"You know a lot about me. What do you want to know?"

"What do you want to tell me?"

"I want to tell you that I love you unconditionally."

"I love you too."

He rubs the ring again.

I look down at my hand. "Do you want me to take it off?"

"No. Never."

I cover his hand with my hand.

"I am going to ask."

"I will wait."

He looks at me. "Really?"

"Yes. I will wait. I don't want you to rush into anything." I look at my hand. "I have the ring on my finger. I love it. I will wait for you to ask." I look at him. "Why didn't you tell me that you are an ADA lawyer?"

"I don't know."

"Justin, I already think that you are a superhero."

"I am not a superhero."

"You are in my eyes."

"What do you want to do today?"

"Sightsee. I think I would like to see as much as possible."

"We will do it." He says. He kisses me. "I am so hungry."

I laugh. "Me too."

"Before we go join our friends and family, I want you to know something." He stands and then squats in front of me. "I want you to know that I intend to make this the best vacation of your life." He takes me in his arms and kisses me.

"How do you plan on doing that?" I ask smiling against his lips.

"I will show you."

Ivan laughs at something that was said in the café. It interrupts our romantic moment. Justin looks at me. "What the hell is that?"

"Someone must have complemented his dancing. That's his fake laugh." I say. "He does the hyena laugh when he shows off."

"Doesn't he always show off?"

"No. He has moments of clarity."

"What does that mean?"

"He is fake for his public fan, but when he is with his friends and family he is great and very giving."

"Lets go be with everyone." He says.

"Just a few more minutes."

He kisses me. "Anything you want."

"What I want—" I kiss him. I slide my hand down his chest. He takes my hand in his and brings up to his lips and kisses my fingers. He kisses the ring on my finger.

"Listen, if anyone asks you, we are engaged."

I look at him. "Why?"

"I am just asking you to do this."

"Those people over there are my chosen family. I don't lie to them. They are the people that would build bridges for me or move mountains."

He kisses my hand once again and slips the ring off my finger. I push away from him. He stands and takes my hand. I try to pull away from him but he holds it firmly. We walk over to join our friends and family.

Tristian stands up and runs to me. He hugs me. I hug him. "This is my first time here. We are going to see Santa Claus."

"I am sure that Santa Claus will bring you all that you want for Christmas. You have been a very good boy this year."

Tristian looks at Matt. He looks back at me. I know what he is thinking without him saying a word. Because the bookstore burned down, Matt hasn't been working. Unlike me, he doesn't have a fall back career. He relied on his mom letting him work the graveyard shift so that he got paid extra money. With one look at Tristian, I know that they don't have money for Christmas and being here with us must have set Matt back a lot. I hug Tristian.

"Make your Christmas list." I tell him. I kiss him on the top of his head. "Be good."

He laughs. "You always say that, Ms. Timely."

"While we are here, you can call me by my name. Sebastian."

He smiles.

I pick a spot at the table across the table from Justin. He watches me the whole time we are having breakfast. I don't make eye contact with him at all. Savannah looks at me. Before she can make her way over to sit next to me, Trevor sits next to me.

He hugs me. I hug him. "How are you?"

"I am so excited to see him dance again. Thank you for telling Jacob about it. I am glad to be here."

"You know, we never intended to stay away from you as long as we have."

"I know. Everyone got busy with their lives. Its what happens."

He looks at me. "What's going on?"

I smile. "I am excited to get this day started." I look at Astro. "I need to go feed him."

I excuse myself from the table. I take Astro's leash and leave the café. I get in the elevator and when the doors close, I let out my breath that I feel I have been holding forever. I unlock the door to the room and go inside.

Justin is sitting on the loveseat in the room. I look at him. I go into the room and get Astro's food. I stay with him while he eats. Justin waits for me. I get in the shower. I get out and wrap myself in the towel. Justin walks in the bathroom. "How long are you going to ignore me?"

I look at him. "Is that what I am doing? Justin, what do you want from me?" I push past him and go into the bedroom. I take clothes out and get dressed.

"I want you." He says.

I look at him. I push past him again and head back into the bathroom. I brush my hair.

"Sebastian, did you hear what I said?"

"My hearing is a hundred percent, my balance is a hundred percent not in my favor. Hearing you I did. I just don't understand what you mean." I look at him through the mirror. "I am in one of my favorite places. I am with all the people that I love in this world."

"Let me explain."

"You don't have to. I don't want you to."

"Let me explain."

"You feel threatened by Ivan."

"He refers to you as the love of his life."

I turn and face Justin. "He loves me like I love your brother. It's innocent love."

"There is no such thing."

"Justin, he is not a threat to you. I was never intimate with him."

"You still gave him your heart."

"Its big enough for everyone to have a piece." I tell him. I pull him to me and kiss him.

Savannah, Piper, Trix, Amanda and I sit together in Starbucks. We decided that we needed girls' time. The guys went in one direction and we went in the other. We sit enjoying our coffee drinks.

Trix looks at me. "I want to follow my instinct and arrest your ass for drinking an iced coffee when we are all freezing our nipples off."

We all laugh.

A barista looks at us. "Which one of you has a phone?"

We all turn and look at her.

"Give me one, you are the best group of girls that I have had in here in a long time." She looks at Trix. "How is that you fit it into this mix?"

Trix looks at all of us. "She thinks that I don't fit into the mix of all you bitches."

We laugh again. I hand the barista my phone. She takes multiple shots of us. She smiles. "I don't know what has gotten into all of you, there is no alcohol in those coffees."

Piper looks at her name tag. "Megs, take a picture with us."

She sits on Trix's lap. We do a selfie of all of us. She kisses us all as she takes the empty cups off the table. "Enjoy your stay here. Come back and visit before you go."

Mark pulls Justin aside. They are walking around the city. "What is going on with you?"

Justin takes the ring out of his pocket.

"She gave it back?"

"No. I took it off her finger."

"Why?"

"I asked her to tell anyone who asked that we are engaged. She said she wouldn't do it."

"Justin, if you love her like we all know you do, ask her."

"I want to make it special." He looks at Ivan and Trevor. "I am jealous."

"Why?"

Justin rakes his fingers through his hair. "She said that they—" he gestures to Ivan and Trevor. "She said that they have built bridges for her and would move mountains."

"You don't think you have done that for her?"

Justin leans against a street sign. "I just don't think I am an enough for her."

"Then you don't know her."

"What do you mean?"

"She doesn't have a high standard, she just wants someone to love her."

"I do love her."

"Then that should be enough."

He looks over at Ivan again. "She still has all of the flowers that he gave her. As far as I know, she let my flowers die."

Mark laughs. "Flowers die."

"You should see the ones he gave her. They are still thriving."

"Ask her about them." He punches Justin in the arm. "Put that ring back on her finger."

"I will."

Ivan walks over to them. "Do you want to watch us rehearse? I have to go dance for a couple hours."

Mark looks at Ivan. "I think we are going to try to catch up with the girls. I feel like they need supervision." He laughs.

"I think that's wise." He hugs Justin and Mark. "Please know that you are welcome to come watch us all day." He flutters around. "I am off." He says.

They watch him dance down the sidewalk. They smile and both of them take out their phones. Mark sends text messages to Savannah and me. We answer telling him where we are. I don't answer Justin's text messages.

Savannah looks at me. "You do know that Mark is with Justin."

"Yeah well if he comes along fine. I am not telling him where I am. He doesn't care. All he wants is—"

"For you, my best friend in this whole world, to be happy. He loves you."

"Conditionally." I say. I push alway from the table. "I have to pee."

Piper jumps up. "I will go with you. I was waiting for someone to have to pee for a while."

We all laugh.

"You should have said something." Trix says.

"I didn't want to miss out on the fun."

Eric walks in the door with Danny. He runs to Piper. She hugs him tight in her arms. "Did you have fun?"

"We didn't see Santa."

"Well we have an appointment to go see him in one hour."

Eric looks at her. "What did you do?"

"We are going to see the Rockettes Christmas show." She says.

"That's very expensive." Eric says.

"Its on me." She says.

"We are all going?" Tristian asks.

"We wouldn't dream of leaving you out." She says.

The two boys smile brightly.

Savannah step into Mark's arms. She kisses him. "I hope you won't mind watching thirty-six smoking hot girls dance on stage?"

"I think I can suffer through it."

She stands on tip-toes and whispers in Mark's ear. "They are going to call the boys up on stage and give them presents."

"How the hell did you pull that off?"

"I didn't. Sebastian did it."

"That was very nice of him."

"No. Our Sebastian did it."

"Oh wow. That's fabulous."

Savannah looks at Justin. He is sitting off by himself. "Why doesn't he just tell her that he lost his big case?"

"He doesn't want to ruin her Christmas."

She steps away from him and looks at him. "Are you joking? He took the ring off her finger. I think that ruined her holidays. She thinks that he loves her conditionally."

"He doesn't think that he is enough for her. He is jealous of Ivan and Trevor. They both refer to her as the love of their lives."

I take the time to go to the bathroom. All of my friends are busy talking with each other. When I come out, everyone is engaged in conversations. No one seems to notice that I am outside looking in the windows at them. We are going to see the Rockettes show in a little while. I want to see Radio City and walk around. I set a timer so that I know to meet back with my friends and family in a half hour.

Justin looks around the Starbucks. He realizes that I am gone. He gets up and checks the bathrooms. He knows that I am not there. Seth and Jacob look at Justin.

"Whats going on?" Jacob asks.

"She's gone."

"She needed to get some air."

"So we are letting her go around on her own?"

"She knows how to navigate on her own. She's been on her own for a long time." Seth says.

"Why isn't she talking to you?" Jacob asks.

Justin takes the ring out of his pocket.

"You don't want to marry her now?"

"I want o marry her. I asked her to say that we are engaged."

"Why?" Seth asks.

"Because."

"That's not an answer counselor." Jacob says.

"I don't know. I wanted to make Ivan jealous." Justin says.

"You are aware that he is withTrevor, right?" Seth says.

"Yes I know that. I just don't think that I am enough for her."

"When you fell asleep on the plane, she never stopped talking about you." Jacob says. "She never stops looking at that ring." Jacob slaps his hand hard on Justin's shoulder. "You are enough. She never stops talking about you." He says it again.

Justin's phone pings with a text message. He fishes it out of his pocket. He smiles. The text says I am outside of Starbucks.

"What was that?" Seth asks.

"She wrote me a text."

"What did she say?"

He turns around and runs out of Starbucks. He walks down the sidewalk and takes me into his arms. He takes the ring out of his pocket and he gets down on one knee. "Will you marry me?"

"In a heartbeat." I say.

He puts the ring back on my finger. He lifts me out of my wheelchair and spins around. "I love you."

"I love you." I look at my watch. "We have to go."

"What?"

"We are going to see the Rockettes' Christmas show."

"How did you pull that off?"

I smile. "The boys want to see Santa Claus."

"Let's go see Santa." Justin says.

We enter Starbucks and everyone hugs me. We all leave and walk to Rockefeller Center. We go see the Christmas show. At the end of it, Santa Claus rides on a sleigh across the stage and they announce the children in the audience. The boys go on stage with eight other children. Santa gives them presents that I bought for them.

"Did you do that?" Justin asks.

"No. Santa's elf did that."

"How did you know what they wanted?"

"That's between the elf and Santa."

"With all that you have been through—"

"They needed this more than I need a new purse or a new dress. Eric and Matt struggle to make ends meet." I whisper. I kiss Justin.

We leave there and go to a fancy restaurant for dinner. Seth set it all up. We stand in front of La Marina La Spiaggia Italiano Ristorante translation Mariana Beach Italian Restaurant. I hug him. He puts his finger to his lips.

"Congratulations." I say. "Wait! Does this mean that we are going to lose you to New York City?"

"No. I have to come here at least once a month."

"When you come back, can I come with you?"

"Every time." He says. "Don't tell anyone. No one noticed yet."

"Your secret is safe with me." I tell him.

Trevor and Ivan join us. They both look at my hand and the gleaming ring on my finger. Ivan says nothing but takes me in his arms and hugs me. Trevor kisses me on the forehead. We wait to be seated. Justin sits on one side of me and Sebastian sits on the other. It's the first time that he has joined us all day.

"You were missed today." I tell him.

"I had meetings." He says.

"We are on vacation."

"It's a working vacation for me. I have a bank here that needed my attention. I did hear that I missed a lot of drama." He kisses me on the forehead. "I am glad that its been resolved." He looks down at the menu. He looks across the table at Seth. Seth looks at him and looks away.

Trix kisses Seth.

Jacob looks at them. "Get a room."

"We will later tonight." Seth jokes.

Sebastian takes his phone out and sends Jacob a text message. Sebastian: check out the menu

Jacob: you didn't know?

Sebastian: No

Jacob: Does anyone else know?

I look at Jacob and smile.

Jacob: She knows

Sebastian stands and takes his wine glass in his a hand. He clinks his fork against the glass. "I would like to make a toast." He waits for everyone to stop talking. Every eye is on him. "To family, friends, and successes. Merry Christmas." He nods his head at Seth.

Everyone murmurs Merry Christmas.

Seth stands and squats between Eric and Matt. "What do the boys like?"

Eric looks at the prices.

"Don't do that." Seth says. "Dinner is on me. This is my place." He looks at the two boys who appear to be intoxicated with excitement from the day.

Matt looks at Seth. "Tristian eats just about anything."

Eric says the same about Danny.

Seth stands and disappears into the kitchen. By now he knows what we all like and dislike. He sets up the order for the whole table. Family style food. Baked ziti with meatballs and sausages.

Drinks come out to the table without anyone coming to take our orders. Everyone's drink is exactly what we would order at the Marina Beach. Seth puts my drink in front of me. An iced coffee.

"We have baked ziti and meatballs coming for the table. If anyone wants anything else, please let me know." Seth says.

Danny looks sad.

"Danny, whats the matter?"

"I don't like ziti."

"I know. You and Tristian are getting ravioli."

Danny smiles.

"See, I remembered."

Their food comes first. Ravioli and meatballs. The two boys eat everything in front of them. Then they both fall asleep at the table.

Eric looks at Danny and then at Piper. "I think the excitement finally claimed the two of them."

Sebastian looks at everyone at the table. "After dinner, I am inviting all of you to come to the roof top of the bank for a party my staff is having."

"That sounds like a lot of fun." I say.

Eric looks at Sebastian. "Thanks for the invite, but I am going to take my little guy back to the hotel."

"Actually, there is a babysitting service that is complementary for my staff and family." He looks at Eric and Matt. "They come highly recommended. They are twin daughters of my manager who runs the bank for me."

"Thank you." Matt says.

We stay in the restaurant for a while more. Seth has a tray of desserts brought out. There is a little cake brought out that reads Congratulations! The staff puts the cake in front of Justin and me. Justin slips the ring off my finger again and stands up. The whole table looks at him. Pipe and Savannah take out their phones.

Justin gets down on one knee. "Sebastian, you make the happiest person in the world. Will you marry me?" He slips the ring back on my finger for the third time.

"Yes. I can't wait to be your wife."

He kisses me and the whole restaurant erupts in cheers. I hug him tight and he lifts me in his arms. He holds me tight.

"Don't take that ring off my finger again." I tease him.

"Its on there for life." He says. He kisses me again.

"I love you."

"I love you too."

Everyone has dessert and then we leave. Pictures are taken. Many hugs are exchanged.

We all go to the bank that Sebastian owns. He directs everyone how to get up to the roof. It occurs to me then that there are only steps leading up to the roof.

"We are going to get you on the roof." Sebastian says.

"I could stay down here with the boys." I tell him.

"This party that we are having is for you." He says. "We are celebrating having a sister. We are celebrating your engagement. We are celebrating Christmases gone by that we have missed having with you."

"I have your presents back at the hotel." I say.

"This isn't about presents. This is about you." He hugs me.

A security guard walks over to us. He asks Sebastian to step aside. "Sir, there is an elevator that goes to the roof entrance. For whatever reason when the elevator doors open, you have to walk up twelve steps."

"That's it?" Sebastian asks. "When they said there were many steps, I was thinking fifty to a hundred."

The guard laughs. "No. Not that many. Twelve. I have climbed them. They are big steps. Its like each one is a landing."

"That makes no sense but it does somehow make sense."

"I know." The guard says. "When yo are ready to go up, I will go up with you."

"Thanks." Sebastian says.

"I heard a rumor that the girl and you have the same name." The guard says.

"Not a rumor. You heard correctly. The differences is our middle names."

"I read that your middle name is Asher. What's her middle name?"

"Ashley."

The guard puts his hand to his chest and laughs. "What a world of difference." He teases.

"Marcus, you are lucky I like you."

The guard laughs harder. He hugs Sebastian.

Oliver and Aaron get off the elevator on the floor we are on. Aaron runs over to me and takes my hand in his hand. He studies the ring.

"Give me ten minutes to finish something before you go upstairs." He says. He kisses me on the cheek. "Hello my darling niece. That boy of yours did good. That is one of the best rings I have ever seen. It sort of looks like your aunt's ring." He kisses me again on the top of my head this time and then he runs off with Oliver.

Ten true minutes goes by and they walk over. They have a black garment bag with them. Oliver kisses me on one cheek, Aaron kisses me on the other.

"This is for you." Oliver says.

Piper and Savannah run over with Trix. Piper looks at Sebastian. "Point us to the lady's room."

"She can change in the lounge." Sebastian says.,

I look at my clothes. "I kind of like what I am wearing."

Aaron opens the garment bag. He hold up a dress that is by far the most beautiful dress I have ever seen in my life.

"Uncle Aaron—"

"This is for you. Both Oliver and I have worked on this. You make our clothes beautiful."

Savannah takes the dress. We find a bathroom and we all go in it. I change my clothes. The dress that my uncles made for me makes me feel beautiful. I look at myself in the mirror. Piper gets out her makeup and touches up mine. She hugs me.

"I am so happy for you." She says.

I hug her back.

Savannah hugs me. "You look beautiful." She says. "We need to do something with your hair." She leaves that bathroom and comes back with a chair. She sits down and French braids my hair. We leave the bathroom.

The photographer who seems to be around whenever Aaron is around steps around a pillar and snaps pictures of me and my friends.

Oliver walks over to us. He hands a garment bag to Trix, Amanda, Savannah and Piper. "These are for you." He says.

Trix opens the garment bag to reveal a black dress with lots of sparkling rhinestones. She looks at Oliver. "This is the dress from the window." She says. She squeals with excitement. She runs in the bathroom and changes her clothes almost immediately. "Thank you so much." She spins around. "Every time I have to go somewhere fancy, this is my new go-to dress."

"The truth is, you will be a niece soon enough." Oliver says.

Sebastian beams from where he stands across the room. He joins Aaron where he is standing. "What's going on?"

"I have many models who are stunning. No one." He looks at Sebastian. "No one wears my gowns like Sebastian and that pink haired girl."

Sebastian laughs. "That's Trix."

"Her name is Trix? Did her mother not like her?"

"Her mother adores her." Sebastian says. "Her dad named her."

They watch when the bathroom door swings opened and Amanda walks out. She is wearing an emerald green dress that falls just above her knees. When she sees Sebastian she runs to him. She hugs him.

"Are you crying?" He asks her smiling against her ear.

"I have never worn a dress like this. This is the most beautiful dress I have put on." She says. She hugs Aaron. "I feel like I am wearing noting more than a slip."

"You look stunning." He says.,

Piper and Savannah both come out wearing different shades of red dresses. They both look gorgeous. The both hug Oliver first and then Aaron.

They look at me. Savannah smiles. "Silver and gold looks good on her." She says.

Piper smiles. "Remember when she wore that dress? The one that looked like it was blue and then when we looked at it again it was silver."

"The dress she wore when she played the concert of her life here in New York." Savannah says.

Aaron looks at her. "The girl that wore that dress wasn't in a wheelchair."

"When she plays, she sits on the piano benches." Piper says.

"I was at that concert." Aaron says. "I wondered how one of my dresses was being worn before it went to the catwalk."

Ivan walks over. "I bought it for her. As far as she ever knew, the dress was something that the concert hall had for her. She never knew whose dress it was or where it came from."

"Where is the dress now?" Oliver asks.

"Hanging in my apartment." He laughs. "Don't worry, I never wore it."

Everyone laughs. I look over at my friends and family and smile. I join them. "There seems to be a lot of fun being had over here."

"You look stunning." Aaron says.

"I always feel extremely pretty when I am wearing one of your dresses."

Seth and Jacob walk over. They hug everyone. Seth kisses Trix. She stands on tip toes to kiss him.

"We are ready to join the others." Jacob says. He looks around for Sophia. She isn't there.

They all go up to the roof top. I wait with Sebastian. Justin, Mark, Eric and Matt are no where in sight.

I look at Sebastian. "Is it many steps?"

"No." He says. "Its all going to be fine."

We get in the elevator and go all the way up to the rooftop entrance. The doors open to steps. Marcus the guard is with us. He goes behind me and Sebastian steps in front of me. In one quick movment, they left my wheelchair up and walk up the stairs carrying me.

I can't help but smile. When we reach the roof top, I hug Sebastian. "Thank you."

"Any time." He says.

I look behind me. "Thank you."

"Anything for my boss's sister." Marcus says. He looks at Sebastian. "If you need me, I programmed my cell into your phone."

Sebastian hugs Marcus. "Thank you so much. For everything."

Lindsey Gina walks over. She hugs me. "I am in love." She says.

"When are you not?" I tease her.

She pulls my hair.

Savannah walks over. "Hey, I worked very hard braiding her hair." She teases.

Lindsey looks at Jacob. "I know that he loves that dancer, but I love him."

"His dancer is married." I say.

"Does he know that?"

"I don't think so."

"He gives me butterflies." Lindsey says. She starts laughing. "Did he tell you what happened?"

We all look at her.

"If I had to guess, you fell off the ship when you did your Titanic moment." I say.

We all laugh.

She turns as pink as Trix's hair.

Trix hugs Lindsey. "I have it on good authority that Jacob thinks you are adorable."

"He probably laughed when he told all his friends and family."

"Actually no. He was very concerned. Said that you hit the water really hard. Said that he thought that you sprained your ankle."

She laughs. "I did. He knew I did. He took me to the hospital and he stayed with me. He held my hand the whole time." Lindsey says. "Then he took me to the store and he bought me a brand new violin." She leans against me. "I feel the way you described how you feel about Justin."

I smile at her.

Sebastian takes the microphone. "Welcome all. Its nice to see all of you. We are going to warm up in just a few minutes. The heaters are working. I want to take the time to thank you all for being here. For my employees, your bonus cheeks are on your desks. For my friends and family, you all mean the world to me. Merry Christmas and enjoy your evening."

Jacob stands off in the corner. He watches everyone having a good time. Linsey walks over to him. She holds up mistletoe above his head. He doesn't hesitate, he kisses her like there is no one on that roof with them.

She steps back. "I never thanked you for plucking me out of the water, taking me to the hospital and for buying me a brand new violin."

"You did thank me."

"I am sorry to hear about your dancer."

"Thanks." He kisses her again.

Justin watches me from where he stands. Seth walks over to him. "Can I ask you a question?" Seth says.

Justin looks at him."Sure."

"Why are you not with her?"

"I love to watch her."

"She really is pretty."

I look at the two of them and wave.

Justin waves back. Jacob punishes Justin in the shoulder. "Go to her."

"She's with her friends."

"She wants you to go rescue her."

"How do you know that?"

"She just texted me." Jacob shows Justin his phone. "She said that she's been texting you the whole night."

"My phone is in my coat, downstairs." Justin hugs Jacob. He runs over to me.

"Dance with me." I say.

"Absolutely."

We dance to Let it Snow. From that point on, Justin doesn't leave my side because I never let go of his hand.

Sebastian and Amanda come over. "Just so that you know, we are going to shut this party down in a half hour." He looks around. "This has been the best holiday party."

"Thank you for having us." I say.

"From here on out you are always invited to whatever we are doing." He says.

"I need some assistance getting to the elevator. I have to go the bathroom." I say.

Justin and Eric carry me down the steps to the elevator. We get in the elevator and go down stairs. The elevator doors open. Eric kisses me on the head.

"I will see you back at the hotel. I will take Astro for a walk when I get back with Danny."

"Thanks Eric."

I go into the bathroom. Before I come out, I change back into my clothes. Justin smiles when I open the bathroom door.

"Why are you smiling?"

"Cinderella turned back." He teases.

I laugh. I put my coat on and we gather our stuff. My friends come downstairs and they change too into their clothes. We leave the building and get in the cars that are waiting to take us back to the hotel.

Tristian sits on one side of me and Danny is on the other side. They both close their eyes and fall asleep almost immediately. I run my fingers through both of their hair.

We get back to the hotel. Justin takes the elevator to the floor we are staying on and gets Astro. He brings him down in the elevator. Justin and Eric take Astro outside. Danny sits on my lap sleeping. Piper is holding Tristian.

They come back into the lobby and we all go to the bank of elevators. Eric takes Danny. I take Astro's leash. We all get into two elevators. We go into our rooms. I get on the bed with my clothes on and fall asleep the second my head touches the pillows.

Justin sits on the floor with Astro. Mark sits on the floor with him. "Today was nice."

"Today was nice." Justin agrees.

"That photographer never stopped taking pictures of you and Sebastian."

Justin yawns.

"Don't forget, its against the law to undress her if she is unconscious."

"Shut up." Justin says.

Mark grabs Justin. "Listen, love her. Little Mermaid is worth it."

Justin gets into bed with me and I snuggle into him. He takes me in his arms. "Sweetheart, sit up." He says. He helps me sit up. He takes my sweater off. Then he takes off the turtle neck shirt. He laughs. "You are like a Russian nesting doll. So many layers." He says. He takes the tank top off. I am now only in my bra and pants. He lays me back and unzips my pants. He slides them downs. "Where are your pajamas?"

I roll over, pull the blanket over myself and fall back to sleep. "Justin." I say in my sleep.

"What"

"Justin, I love you. I can't wait to be your wife."

He kisses me on the cheek. "Sleep princess."

Astro jumps on the bottom of the bend with us.

Chapter 24

I sit among my friends and family members in the most beautiful auditorium I have ever been in. The stage is dark as we wait for the lights to dim to start the show. Ivan is going to dance. Trevor sits on the end of the row.

Sophia takes the stage dancing from one side to the other. She takes the microphone from the orchestra pit. She turns on her toe shoes. "Ladies and gentlemen, I want to take a moment to thank you for coming. We will be getting our show started in just about fifteen minutes. We had a slight medical emergency with two of our dancers. Two or our dancers are being transported to the hospital. Please be patient. The show will go on. In your programs you will see that we take two breaks. We are going to take only one. Thank you and enjoy the show."

The lights flicker to indicate that the show will be starting soon. The auditorium goes dark. A little girl with a flashlight dances across the stage. She spins on one leg and then shines the light towards the back of the stage before her light goes out. Then all anyone sees is the flashlight high up and it flickers once then goes out and candles light the stage and the girl is standing on Ivan's shoulders. She jumps straight up and Ivan catches her with ease. He sets her down on her toes and she dances off the stage. The whole auditorium erupts in cheers.

The show is full of all sorts of dance styles. Children dance hip-hop numbers to Christmas songs. The adults and children do RiverDance style together. Ivan comes out on stage wearing more sparkles anyone has ever seen. He looks amazing. I know that Oliver made his outfit. The sparkles make him glow like Edward does in the Twilight series under the lights.

The lights come on for a quick break. Sophia comes back on the stage. "Ladies and gentlemen, just a quick reminder. This will be only one break. A quick update on our injured dancers, they have returned and they will be dancing in the final dance. The dancers are Maggie Davis and Glenn Baker." She looks at her watch and laughs. "Ok, you have twenty minutes."

"Glenn Baker?" Sebastian says. "I went to school with him. I didn't know he was still dancing."

"He just married Sophia." Seth says.

Jacob looks at all of us. Lindsey puts her hand in his hand. They stand up together. "Does anyone need anything? Want anything? I am going to get a drink."

I look at him. "Can I talk to you before you go?"

"Yes." He kisses Lindsey. "I will catch up with you."

"I will wait." She says.

I look at both of them, "I will wait."

Justin walks over to sit next me. He sits down and takes mistletoe out of his pocket. I laugh against his lips. He does too.

"Where did you get mistletoe? I have been looking for it everywhere."

He laughs. "Do you know how hard it has been for me going everywhere you mentioned and asked them to move their mistletoe?"

I laugh. "You did this for me?"

"I would do anything for you." He says.

Everyone of our friends and family leaves to get drinks or check out the souvenirs. Savannah comes back. She taps me on the shoulder. I look up at her. "I just wanted to know, do you want me to buy the Ivan Teddybear if I see it?"

"Oh, let me give you the money."

"Stop." She looks at Justin. "Hold her hands." She looks back and me. "If I see it, I am getting it."

"Thank you." I say. "I love you."

"I love you too." She kisses me on the cheek. She smiles deviously at the two of us. "I love what you are doing. Just remember that there are others around you and children."

"Shut up." I laugh.

"The old mans over there is going to—"

"Savannah!" I laugh.

She leans in close to both of us so that no one can over hear what she says. "He is going to have an erection."

"Savannah!" I laugh. Justin puts his head on my shoulder and laughs.

"Ok, I am going. Make good choices." She says. She kisses me again on the cheek. "I love you."

"I love you too."

When she leaves, Justin stands up and lifts me into his arms. He sits back in the chair with me on his lap. He holds me.

"Is she always like that?"

"Ask Mark. She hasn't always been like that. I feel like Mark rubbed off on her. Your dad too."

"Oh sure, blame my family." He laughs.

"I am saying that they brought her out of her shell. She was always so shy."

"How did you meet?"

"God, I have known her since elementary school. We were seat partners because our names both start with S. There was another girl who was assigned to sit with us but she refused because she didn't want to sit next to someone who she could get cooties from."

"I hope you beat her up."

I laugh.

"Its not funny."

"Stephanie and I are still friends too. She was referring to getting cooties from Savannah. She was homely and wore the ugliest glasses. People made fun of her. Our teacher asked me — she didn't ask anyone else, but she asked me if I would be friendly to Savannah because she had no friends and her dad left them. Because I didn't have a dad, she thought that we could relate. I tend to think she knew what she was doing." I laugh. "Our teacher encouraged me to make Savannah act up in class. She would yell if anyone talked during her lessons. She would clap her hands when Savannah and I were engrossed in children's conversations. Our teacher would give me extra stickers on my work."

"Stephanie and you are still friends?" Justin asks.

"I always told them that a girl could have more than one best friend. They are friends too. Stephanie and I went college together."

"I haven't met her yet."

"You will meet her. She knows all about you."

"Should I be scared?" He asks kissing me.

"Should you be scared of what?" Piper asks as she sits in my wheelchair.

"About Stephanie."

"Scared? No not at all. You should be terrified." She says.

She and I laugh.

"Now I am getting worried." Justin says. "Did you live with her in college?"

"I lived with Lindsey Gina and Stephanie. It always felt like I lived with only Lindsey because Stephanie did night classes. She worked while going to school in her dad's diner. He made her work the morning and day shifts."

"She told me that she only got through school because of you." Piper says.

"What did you do?" Justin asks.

"She took all the same classes that I did, but she did the night classes. I gave her my notes when she needed them."

"That's cheating." Justin says.

"I didn't give her test questions. I could have but never did. She took night classes and went to everyone of them, but she would fall asleep because her dad made her work really hard."

"Where is she now?"

"She lives in Colorado now. She is married and has two girls. I am their godmother."

"That's so sweet. Have you been to Colorado?"

"No never." I say.

"We will have to go to Colorado."

"It would be nice to see my nieces." I say.

Sebastian and everyone come back. He looks at me. "How does an only child have nieces?"

"I have a friend Stephanie. She made me the godmother to her daughters and an honorary aunt." I say.

"That's so great." Seth says. "Do you see them often?"

"No. They live in Colorado. Stephanie and her husband got married in Florida so I could be there. They had their daughters in Florida so I could be there. They had the girls christened in Florida so I could be there."

The lights flicker so that everyone knows to take their seats. Piper stands up and hugs Eric. She kisses him on the lips. She sits next to Danny. Justin stands and sits me back in my wheelchair.

Tristian walks over and hugs me. I hug him. "Are you having a good time?" I ask him.

"Thank you so much. This is the first time I have ever been out of Florida. This has been the best trip of my life."

"I am glad you are having such a great time."

He looks at me. "You are the best."

"Why do you say that?"

"I know that you bought our tickets for all this." He gestures with his hand. "You don't even like my dad."

"Tristian, I like your dad. Why do you think I don't?"

"He told my grandma and Pops how mean he was to you all the time."

"I like your dad."

"When we go home, are you going to teach us again?"

"I don't know. I don't know if I am going back to work yet."

"Is it because we are bad?" Danny asks.

I hug him. "You guys are not bad. None of you are bad. I love being with all of you. I don't know if I an ready to come back to work, but that has nothing— nothing to do with all of you." I tell them.

The lights go dark and I am grateful. The show starts again. Glenn Baker walks out on the stage carrying Sophia draped in his arms. Her hair hangs almost to the stage floor. He dances around the stage with her. Then he goes down on one knee and kisses her. She wraps her arms around his neck and they dance off the stage together.

The children come out dancing. This time they do a tango. A young boy and girl stay on the stage, the other children dance off. The two that stay on stage are joined by older children dancers. They all dance a paso doble. The younger children dance just as well as the older children. When the dance ends, all the boys walk off the stage pulling the girls who are all seated on the stage. The audience cheers loudly.

Another young boy and girl run out on the stage. They are dressed like Irish dancers. The Celtic music starts and all the dancers of all ages are on the stage. Ivan runs out and leads them all. They all leave the stage. Two of the older children come out on stage. She looks like Cinderella. He looks like Prince Charming. They dance a waltz. All the dancers come out and dance the waltz.

The stage lights go off. A screen emerges from the orchestra pit. The conductor turns and looks at the audience. The spot light is on him. He points his wand out into the audience and finds me, the spotlight shines on me and then I appear on the screen playing Caroling the Bells. The dancers all take the stage and dance one last dance. As I hit the last note, they all point up to where I am sitting in the audience and they all clap. The whole audience erupts in cheers.

The couple sitting next to us stand up and clap. This causes everyone in the audience to stand. The couple face me for what seems like a lifetime, then they turn and face the stage.

Ivan takes the microphone. "I want to thank all of you for coming and supporting us during the holidays. It means the world to all of us. As many of you know, I have been dancing for many years. This is my last dance. The woman playing Caroling the Bells on the screen is one of my friends I have been blessed to have in my life. She is truly the love of my life. Sebastian Timely I love you always. Merry Christmas everyone. Best wishes to a happy new year as well. Thank you."

Glenn takes the microphone from Ivan. "Thank you all for coming. All of the dancers will be out in the lobby in about eight minutes. Happy holidays everyone."

The couple near us gather their belongings. The woman looks at me. "You have been kissing this guy the whole night, and yet that dancer just claimed that you are the love of his life."

Trevor walks over to all of us. "My husband loves her deeply."

The husband takes his wife's hand and they leave.

Trevor looks at all of us. "I am going to show you out a private way. The company wants to meet all of you." He looks at Justin. "The way we need to go out is steps."

"I got her." Justin says.

"Is it a lot of steps?" Mark asks.

"Its four flights down." Trevor says.

"Theres not an elevator?" I ask.

"There is, but they will be in use for a while. No one is taking the stairs where we are going."

All the guys that are with me say at the same time. "We will get her there."

Eric looks at Trevor. "Just lead the way."

Justin picks me up in his arms. Danny pushes my wheelchair down the hallway that leads to the stairwell. Eric folds my wheelchair and carries it down the stairs. We go down two flights. Trevor looks at everyone. "The next two levels are shorter."

"Continue leading the way." Tristian says.

Matt squats down in front of Tristian. "Get on my back."

Seth Squats down in front of Danny. "Get on my back. We will race."

Savannah stands against the wall. Mark steps next to her. "Whats going on?"

"Stairwells scare me. I can't keep going down." She says. She puts her hand to her chest. "I feel like I can't breath."

I look at Justin. "Can you go over by her. I need to be there for my friend." He does. He stands next to Mark. "Hey, Sav, its alright we are all together. If you can't go down, we don't have to go. We can all walk out into the lobby."

"They want to meet you. Ivan planned something special for you." She takes her coat off and stands with her shoulders against the cold wall.

Eric looks at Piper. "Whats that about?"

"She was attacked at college in a stairwell. The guys chased her down six flights of stairs." She steps closer to him. "They took her clothes off of her and attempted to—"

"Did they rape her?"

"No." She says.

Eric hugs Piper. "Did she tell anyone?"

"She told everyone. She has been in counseling for this for years."

Savannah closes her eyes. Mark takes her hand. He talks softly to her. "You are among people who love you. No one is going to hurt you. You are safe."

"I can't." Her knees buckle.

Mark picks her up. "Close your eyes. When you open them, we will be on ground level. You are safe. I've got you. I am not going to let anything bad is going to happen to you." He kisses her lips.

Piper walks over and takes Savannah's hand. "I won't let go." She says.

We continue down the stairs. I feel sad for a moment because I can't be there for my friend who has always been there for me. We all go down what seems like the never ending stairs. When we finally come to a door, Trevor turns the knob and we go through the door to the most elaborate stage. It looked beautiful from where we sat but up close its even more beautiful. There are pictures of Ivan throughout his career all set up.

Eric unfolds my wheelchair. Justin sits me in it. I pull him in for a kiss.

"Thank you." I say.

"You don't have to thank me."

"I love you."

He kisses me. "Go hug Savannah. I know you felt bad when Piper took her hand."

I kiss him. I make my way to Savannah and she gets down on her knees and hugs me. She cries on my shoulder. "I know." I tell her rubbing her back. "You were with us all of us. You were safe. We are surrounded by all these buff guys, no one would let anyone hurt you." I kiss her head.

She wraps her arms around me. Piper joins us.

Trix looks at the three of us. She looks away. Seth takes her hand. She squeezes his. He kisses her on the lips. "Go join them."

She looks up at him. "I am not one of them."

341

"If that were true, you wouldn't be on this trip." He reasons with her. "Go join them. The more support Savannah has right now the better."

Lindsey takes Trix's hand and they walk over to join us. I reach my hand out to them both. Lindsey goes down on her knees next to Savannah. "Honey, you are ok. We were all with you."

"I am so embarrassed." She says.

"No. You have nothing to be embarrassed about." Lindsey says. "What you went through was really scary. Just take a breath."

The whole dance company comes back to the stage. Ivan is not with them. They all gather around. Some of them step out of their shoes and slip their feet into sneakers. Most of them step behind screens and change into warmer clothes. Its like the don't even notice a big group of strangers standing around.

One of the little girls walks over to me. "You're Sebastian?"

"I am." I say.

"Mr. Ivan never stops talking about you." She says hugging me.

"Thank you. You are a beautiful dancer." I tell her. "Your tango was the best dance I have ever seen."

She smiles brightly. "Thank you. Its my first professional dance."

"I am going to remember your name. I am sure I am going to see you on stages more often."

Her smile gets even bigger.

A boy walks over to us with more children. They include Danny and Tristian. One of the boys look at both Danny and Tristian. "Do you dance?"

"I can do the floss." Danny says.

This starts all of the children doing the floss. Piper takes out her phone and records them. They all dance a bit more.

The lights dim and Ivan runs out to join everyone. Everyone claps for him. He stands there excited to see all of us there for him.

One of the stagehands hands me twenty-three white roses and one pink one. "This is for you to give to him." He tells me. He walks away and comes back moments later with a giant stuffed dog.

"How did you know?" I ask him.

"We know everything about you and Ivan." He says. "Thanks for being here for his last performance. It means to the world to him."

"Why is it his last one?"

"He has been dancing on a broken foot for almost two years. The doctors just told him in Florida that if he continues to dance on it for much longer, he is going to cause too much damage."

"I didn't know." I say and look around to find where Ivan is.

He is no where to be seen. When he does reappear is wearing a boot on his leg that goes from his toes to his knee. He runs to me and takes me in his arms. We both burst into tears. "Thank you so much for being here. I know that my family is all here too but you being here means so much more."

"I am so glad that I could have been here." I tell him. "I wouldn't have missed it for the world. I am sorry about your foot."

"We are going to have a big party tomorrow for the whole company at the Four Seasons by the World Trade Center. We want all of you to join us. It's a private party." Ivan says.

I give him the flowers and the stuffed dog. He hugs me again. He kisses me on the lips. People snap pictures of our interactions.

A dancer walks over to Ivan. "They cancelled our reservation at the Four Seasons."

"What? That's the second time that they said they would host us and dropped us." Glenn says. He walks over to Sebastian and hugs him. "Old man! Its good to see you."

"I am younger than you are, prick." Sebastian says.

Glenn laughs. "Three days."

"So you married Sophia?" Sebastian says.

"We have been together for a long time." He looks at Jacob who is standing off to the side with Lindsey Gina. They are hugging each other. "She told me about her relationship with your brother. The thing is, she's pregnant."

Sophia stops dead in her tracks. "Glenn! Are you fucking kidding me?" She yells. She looks at Jacob. He looks away from her. He turns his back on everyone. She falls to the floor Jacob who wasn't watching her catches her before she hits hard. "I am sorry." She cries. "I should have told you."

Lindsey looks around. She walks over to Glenn and slaps in his face. "You bastard."

"Lindsey, mind your own business." Glenn says.

"When you hurt my sister, you hurt me. Asshole."

Jacob looks at both of them. "Sisters?"

"At heart." Sophia says. "We have known each other a long time. She has traveled with the company for years playing her violin." She goes to stand up and her knees buckle. Jacob grabs her so she doesn't fall again. "I am so sorry." She says.

Jacob embraces her. Lindsey watches them. I take Lindsey's hand. She looks at me and smiles. He reaches out for Lindsey. She takes his hand.

Glenn looks around the room. "Ok everyone, I am out." He says. He turns to leave and trips on a pair of shoes. Everyone hears his ankle break. He winces in pain immediately. Jacob springs into action just as quickly.

"Get the children out of here." He says. He looks at Glenn. "You are not my favorite person in this room, but I have training as a medic so I can help you." Jacob gets on his knees in front of Glenn. "I need something to wrap around his ankle."

Glenn is in so much pain. Sophia sits behind him. She kisses him. He takes her hand and holds it. "I am so sorry." He says.

A teenaged boy walks over and gives Jacob an air cast. "Will this work?"

Jacob looks at him. "How many of you dance with injuries?" He takes it from the boy. "This will do." Jacob puts the air cast around Glenn's ankle. He tightens it.

A girl taps Jacob on the shoulder. "The dispatcher wants to talk to you." She says just above a whisper.

He takes the phone. Glenn tries to get up. "No. Don't move." Jacob says. He looks up. "They want to know the address. I don't know it. I don't live here."

The teenaged boy takes the phone and tells the dispatcher where to come. He puts his hand on Glenn's shoulder. "Uncle Glenn, you are going to be ok."

The paramedics get there within minutes. Jacob tells them what happened. He goes with the paramedics to take Glenn to the hospital. Lindsey takes Sophia. They got a taxi and follow the ambulance to the hospital.

Sebastian tells Ivan that they can host their party at his bank. That they can use the rooftop. Everyone leaves shortly after. With Glenn getting hurt, we all decide to go to the hospital to wait to see what happens.

As we sit in the lobby of the hospital, Seth finds me. He hugs me. "That was nasty." He says.

"It was bad."

"You wanted to talk to Jacob earlier. What were you going to tell him?"

"It wasn't important."

"What was it?"

"I wanted to thank him for this. I wanted to thank him for Miami."

"You have done that."

"I am grateful to have all of you in my life." I tell him.

Sebastian walks over. "Whats going on?"

"We were just talking." Seth says.

"About what?"

"I just wanted to thank Jacob for Miami again. And for this trip. I am grateful to have all of you in my life."

Sebastian hugs me. "We are the grateful ones."

"We always wanted a sister." Jacob says as he joins us. "We were hoping that when mom was pregnant with Seth that she was giving us a sister. No such luck." He says smiling. "What did you want to tell me at the show? I should have let you talk to me."

"Thank you." I say.

"For what?"

"This. For Miami. For being fabulous."

He hugs me. "I feel like I have a lot to make up for."

"Stop. You don't have anything to make up for." I tell him.

A doctor comes out to give everyone an update. Glenn is having emergency surgery. He tells us that it will be a while so if we want to go we should and come back tomorrow. It is late. We all decide to leave and go back to the hotel. Ivan and Trevor stay at the hospital.

~~~~~~~~~

My cell phone rings in the morning. I sit up in bed and reach over to get it. "Good morning mom. Merry Christmas!"

"Merry Christmas, sweetheart. How are you doing?"

"I am well. How are you and Peter doing?"

"We are good. Where are you?"

"I am in New York City. Last night was Ivan's last dance."

"You didn't tell me that you were doing that."

"I did tell you and Peter."

"What are you doing for Christmas? Are you all by yourself in the city?"

"I am going to Uncle Aaron's for dinner. No I am not alone in the city. I am here with Justin, Sebastian, Jacob and Seth. Savannah and Piper and my friends."

"Aaron has a house in New York?"

"He has houses all over the world." I hear the sadness in her tone. "Where are you spending Christmas?"

"We are home in Florida. We were calling to see if you wanted to come for the day to be with us."

"I will be back home next week. We can plan something then."

"I know there has been so much going on this year and I haven't seen you a lot. Will you be home for New Years?"

"I will be home the day after New Year's Day."

"I am not going to see you until next year?" She asks.

I put my hand over my mouth to stifle my laugh. "I will be home in a week and half." I tell her."

"If I would have known that your were going to be in New York for Christmas, I would have made plans to be there too."

"Stop saying that because I did tell you and Peter. You put it on your calendar when I told you." I tell her. "I needed to be out of Florida for Christmas. I can't go to my house yet."

"When can you return there?"

"January tenth."

"Oh that long? Where will you stay until you can go home?"

"With anyone who will have me and Astro."

"Tell me about your trip so far."

I tell her all that we have done so far. I leave out the part that Justin proposed to me twice now.

"Well it sounds like you are having a great time."

"We are all having a great time." I tell her.

"I saw on Facebook that you were on a rooftop."

"I was at Sebastian's Christmas work party."

"He has a bank in New York." She makes a statement. It is not a question. She realizes what she says. "Does he?"

I let it go for now. One day I will address how long she knew about him and never let me know him. Today is Christmas and I am not for one minute going to let her ruin it for me. "Are you making your duck for dinner?" I ask her changing the subject all together.

She and I laugh. "Darling, you know its pigeon that I make."

We laugh again. "Oh right." I say. "Is Peter going to cook dinner?"

"We are going to his sister's house for dinner." She says. "He just told me. She lives in Lake Worth."

"Will you bring your pudding?"

"No." She says. "Stop teasing me about my cooking."

"Merry Christmas."

"Merry Christmas sweetheart. Please tell everyone that I send my love."

"I will."

"Hug Astro for me."

"He is licking me right now." I smile. "Astro stop." I tell him. He lays on top of the covers between my legs.

"Call me later."

"I will." I tell her. "I love you, mom."

"I love you too."

I put my phone back on the night stand. Justin pulls me on his lap. Astro jumps up on the bed and starts barking. Sebastian walks in the room. He comes and sits on the bed.

"What did your mom say?" Justin asks. "It sounded like she was giving you a hard time."

"She was." I say. "She was saying that I didn't tell her that I was coming to New York."

"You did too. I was with you and Peter." Justin says.

"I know. " I say.

"Ok so I didn't want to tell you but I will tell you, my mom is on her way over to get your mom and Peter. Also your dad." He looks at Justin. "They are going to take a private plane and be at Uncle Aaron's tonight for dinner."

"Oh thank you." I say and hug him tight.

"We have time and I want all of us to open presents before we go out. I have arranged for all of us to have breakfast in the banquet hall downstairs in an hour." Sebastian says. He looks at Justin. "Your mom will be here too."

"Oh man, thank you so much."

"She said that she can't stay long because she has to be with your grandparents."

"Yeah. I normally don't spend Christmas with my mom. She spends time up here with her parents. I spend New Years with her."

"She is actually on her way here."

I pull the covers over my face.

Justin and Sebastian both look at me. "What's going on here?" They both ask.

"What if she doesn't like me?"

"What?" Justin asks.

"I have known your dad since I was young. I never met your mom. What is she doesn't like me. What if I am not what she expects." I pull the cover tighter.

"Do you think I don't talk about you to my mom? I told her about you the day that I met you."

"Oh god!"

"What?"

"She must think I am a flake. I pass out when I get stressed out."

"Can you come out and talk to us?" Sebastian says.

"Mark and I talk about you and Savannah all the time to our mom." Justin says. He takes the cover away. He hugs me. "You are going to meet my mom, Jayne and my step-dad Joe."

I scoot to the edge of the bed and get in my wheelchair. I put Astro's leash on him. Sebastian takes his leash. "I will take him. You get yourself ready." He kisses me on the head. "I will feed Astro in the banquet room."

"He can spend the morning with us?"

"The whole day. Uncle Aaron told me that we are to bring him with us."

I smile.

Justin gets out of bed and goes into the other room. He comes back with a box for Sebastian and me. He hands them to us.

"I don't know what happened to all the presents that I had for all of you." I say.

"Open the present before you take Astro." Justin says.

We open the boxes. Inside there are sweaters. Mine is pink and reads 'The Best Little... Big Sister!'. Sebastian has a sweater that is baby blue. His reads 'The Best Big Brother in the World!'. We both hug Justin.

"You don't have to wear them all day. As a matter of fact, Oliver has something in store for all of us for a family picture later. But Mark and I bought these for you both and Jacob and Seth too." He leaves the room and come back with another present. They are Christmas ornaments that are little sweaters that read the same thing. Its dated 2019. On the bottom it reads 'First Christmas together'.

"Justin, this is great. Thank you so much." I say.

"Justin, this is really nice of you." Sebastian says.

In a half hour we are all downstairs. We go into the banquet room and there are Christmas trees all around the room. Its so pretty. I take my phone out and take pictures. Danny and Tristian run over. Danny stands behind me and pushes my wheelchair to one tree.

"This one is for me and my dad." He says. He points to the tree next to it. "That one is for Matt and Tristian." He looks around the room. "Santa didn't forget me this year."

Piper and Eric join us. We all hug each other. Piper looks at me and smiles. I hug her again.

"I like the sweater."

"Justin and Mark bought them for Sebastian, Jacob, Seth and me."

349

"It's the first Christmas in a long time that we are all together too." She says. She hugs me again.

"Whats the plan for the rest of the day?" Eric asks. "I am going to take Danny sight seeing."

"You are all invited to join me and my brothers at my Aunt and Uncle's house."

"We wouldn't want to intrude on you and your family."

"Eric, as far as I am concerned you are my family too." I say. "You are going to be my honorary brother when you marry my best friend. My sister at heart. And Danny is one of my favorite children I have even been blessed to know."

Danny hugs me.

"As long as it won't be too much."

The doors open and Justin's mom, Jayne, walks into the room with Joe. They are joined by Matt's mom. Tristian runs to her and jumps in her arms. Trix's dad walks in the room behind Matt's mom. She runs to him.

We all sit around the trees. The boys open their presents first. Everyone of us bought them presents. Matt gets up from where he is sitting and walks over to me. He hugs me tight.

"You didn't need to do this."

"I did." I told him.

"And you flew my mom in to be with us."

"I can't take credit for that. My brothers did that."

Mark sits with Jayne. Justin is with them too. Joe sits amongst the rest of us. He enjoys watching the boys open their presents.

"I have never seen my sons so happy." Jayne says. She hugs both of them. "I have met Savannah over the years, but look at her now. She is stunning." She looks at me. "And I look forward to meeting Sebastian."

Justin gets up and walks over to me. "Come meet my mom." He says. He takes my hand and pulls me across the room.

I look up at Justin. "Wait."

"Whats the matter?"

"I can't meet her without a gift for her."

He kisses me. "You don't need anything."

"I have to make a good first impression. I can't do that empty handed."

Mark walks over and hands me a present. "Give her this." He kisses the top of my head. "Come on Little Mermaid."

I look at him. "I don't feel well." I say.

He gets down on his knees in front of me. "Little Mermaid, she already loves you."

"How could she?"

"She knows all about you. She has always known all about you. When I would go stay with her, I would tell her about you." He taps my forehead with his knuckle. "Now that you are engaged to her favorite son, she truly loves you."

Justin holds my hand. The three of us go over. Mark stands behind me. Jayne stands up and hugs me.

"Its so nice to finally meet you. You are everything I dreamed you would be." She tells me.

"Its nice to meet you too." I tell her.

"Come chat with me. Let me introduce you to my Joey." She says.

Justin comes with us. We go off in the corner where Joe sits in front of a computer screen. He looks up at Jayne. She kisses him on the lips. He pulls her on his lap.

"Mom!" Justin says.

"My mom and Peter do the same thing." I laugh.

Justin puts his hand on Joe's shoulder. "This is why Mark is distant."

Joe looks up at Justin. He looks over t me. "All the pictures we saw of your girl, never showed her in a wheelchair." He says.

I try to move away but Justin is holding tight to my wheelchair.

"I am Sebastian." I say.

"A girl with a boy's name? Is there a reason for that?"

"I was named for my dad. He passed away three months before I was born." I say. "I would say that its nice to meet you but I am not sure that it is in fact nice to meet you."

"A girl with fight." He says. "I like her."

Tristian runs over. "Come see what Santa brought." He says with such joy in his voice.

Matt walks over. "I need to talk to you." He says.

"I am coming."

I go out in the hallway with Matt. Eric joins us. Eric takes me in his arms and hugs me tight. He kisses me on the cheek over and over again.

Matt looks down at his feet. "I can't repay you and your family." He says.

I look at him. "I am not asking you to."

"Sebastian, I don't have a job. I can't repay you."

"Matt, you can repay me."

"How?"

"When we reopen Cup of Books, I need you to work full time with weekends off unless you want to work them. Three weeks paid vacation and paid sick days. Plus, I need you to run the young mentoring program."

"This all sounds wonderful but we don't have a bookstore anymore."

"Its being rebuilt as we speak." I say.

"How did you pull that off?"

"My aunts and uncles put up the money for the rebuild."

"Are you going to have pay them back?" Eric asks. "They stayed away all this time."

We hear one of the boys crying so we all go back into the room quickly. Tristian is sitting in the middle of the room holding a broken robot. It was the one the one toy that Matt bought for him. He holds it cradled in his arms.

Matt runs to him. "What happened?"

"I went to put the batteries in it and it broke."

"I will get you another one."

"You can't." He says and jumps into Matt's arms. "I didn't do it on purpose."

"Tristian, I never thought that you did."

"Should I go up to the room?" He asks.

"Tristian, when have I ever punished you?" Matt asks.

"Grandma looks upset."

"Grandma is not upset."

"She gets mad when I break my toys." He says. "I didn't mean to break the robot. It's the one that I wanted." He jumps out of Matt's arms and takes off running out of the room.

We all here a loud thud and go running from the room. Jacob gets to him first. His head is bleeding. Matt goes to pick him up but Jacob stops him.

A woman stands next to them. "He came out of nowhere. I didn't see him when I was twirling around."

"What can we do?" Seth asks.

A woman runs over with a towel. Jacob takes it. Tristian is screaming crying. He rolls on his side and vomits. Matt goes to pick him up again. Jacob again stops him.

"Head wounds bleed harder." Jacob says. He holds the towel to Tristian's head.

Paramedics come running in the door immediately. They take over caring for Tristian. They take him into an ambulance. They don't leave right away.

Danny finds Matt. "I fixed it." He says handing the robot to Matt. "Will he be ok?"

"He will be ok." Matt says.

Matt's mom joins them. "What happened?" She asks.

Matt looks at her.

Trix comes running out of the room. "Aunt Barb!"

Barb looks at Matt. "Why are you looking at me like that?"

"My son freaked out over a broken toy. He was scared to death that you were going to be mad. Do you get mad at him for broken toys?"

"Money doesn't grow on trees." She says.

"When we get home, my son and I are out of your house for good." Matt says between clenched teeth. "I need to find a way to get to my son."

The lady who was twirling taps Matt on the shoulder. "Please let me go with you the hospital. Its because of me that the little boy got hurt." She says. She laces her fingers with Matt's. "I am Britt." She says.

"I am Matt." He says. "I have to go to my son." He says.

When the doors of the resort open, we can all hear Tristian screaming for Matt.

I take Justin's hand. He squeezes my hand. Danny runs to me and hugs me.

Eric looks at us. "Matt is my best friend. I need to go with him."

"I will keep Danny for you." Piper says.

"I want to go." Danny says.

The staff from the resort come and clean the floor where Tristian vomited. They also clean up the blood. They direct us to go back into the banquet room. We all decided to go back up the rooms and get ready for the rest of the day.

Barb, Matt's mom knocks on the door to the room that I am staying in. I open the door. She looks at me. "You must think that I am awful."

"I don't think that you are anything. Tristian is a great young boy because of all your hard work. Barb, I know how hard you all work to give him a happy home."

"I just wanted to tell you so that you can tell all of them, I am on my way to the airport. I am going home. My son is very upset with me."

"Barb, not for nothing, Matt is a great dad. He is a great guy. He truly loves Tristian."

"I don't think that Matt is ever going to talk to me again." She says.

"Barb, you have to stay to see that your grandson is going to be ok. Matt loves you. Tristian thinks the world of you. He talks about you all the time. You are the most important people in his life. Children break toys. That kid—" I choke on my words. "That kid is the best one in my class. Always the first to help out or the first one to protect someone. He is always the first one who wants to be with Astro. He learned that from both Matt and you."

Trix comes out of her room. She runs over. "They are on their way back. Tristian is ok. He did bang his head but the blood was not blood it was a dye pack that exploded."

"A dye pack?" I ask. "You mean like when someone robs a bank?"

"Exactly." She says.

"The woman robbed a bank?"

"They are looking into it." Trix says. She looks at her aunt. "Matt is a great dad. If you can't see that, you need new glasses." She says.

"Don't talk to me like that."

"Matt is a great dad. He adores Tristian."

Justin steps out into the hallway. "We have to get ready to go." He says kissing me on the lips. He looks at Trix. "Are you going to wait for them?"

"Seth and I are going to wait." She looks back at the door. She looks back at me.

"Trix, what's the matter?"

"He didn't want me to say anything."

"About what?"

"He doesn't think that he should go to Aaron's Christmas party."

"Why?"

"He's not family." She says.

"The hell he isn't." I say.

Chapter 25

I go back in the banquet room to clean up. We didn't get a chance to open all the presents. The adults didn't open presents at all. When I go in there, Sebastian is in there with Jacob and Seth. At first they don't know that I am in the room.

"I just want to make this Christmas one that no one will forget. I feel like now having her in our lives we are forever changed for the better. I wish that she was more happy. She seems like she is always concerned with how everyone is doing. I notice a lot of the time that she sits off to the side and smiles when she sees that others are happy." Sebastian says. "Maybe its overwhelming. I feel overwhelmed a little by all this family just popping out of the woodwork."

I sneeze. The three of them look around the room. I look at all of them. "I didn't mean to interrupt." I say. "I was just waiting for Justin to say goodbye to his mom."

"Why aren't you with them?"

"I wanted to find a place to hide."

"This is a good spot." Seth says.

"I heard that you don't want to go to the family Christmas party. If you don't go, I am not going."

"They are not my family." Seth says.

"They are your family because you are my family." Sebastian says. "We are all going. They have planned a lovely day for all of us. But first we are going to make a stop with Justin somewhere. Mark and Savannah are going as well." Sebastian says.

"Did they ever find that woman Britt?" I ask.

"Wait a minute, you know her name?" Jacob asks. He hugs me.

"She told Matt her name is Britt." I say.

"They didn't find her. Yet." Sebastian says. "She robbed my bank this morning. Merry Christmas."

"I took a picture of her." Danny says.

We all nearly jump out of our skins. He runs over and hugs me. Sebastian picks him jump and spins him around. "Can I see the picture of her?"

"Sure." Danny says. He shows them. "I showed Aunt Trix already. She has been working with the policeman and lady in the lobby."

Sebastian kisses Danny's cheek over and over. Danny squeals with laughter. Eric walks in the room. He runs over and joins in on tickling Danny. Danny laughs more."Ms. Timely save me!" He says.

Piper comes in the room. She walks over. She tickles Danny too. She takes him from Sebastian and kisses him on the cheek. She looks at Sebastian. "Britt Daily has been arrested. The money has all been accounted for with the exception of a thousand dollars."

I look at her and notice that she is not dressed for the party but is dressed like a professional woman. She has her hair in a tight ponytail. She is just short of having her briefcase with her and all her file folders. She looks at me. I smile at her. She steps closer and hugs me.

"Are you working?" I ask her.

"No. Not really. Sort of." She says.

"Its good to see you in action." I tell her.

"They don't know what I do." She says. "I didn't want to tell them and make anyone feel like he is not enough." She says.

"I am sure if they knew, they would be as proud as I am of you." I say.

She hugs me again. "I love them too much to hurt them." She tells me in a whisper. "As far as I am concerned, they come first."

"I totally agree." I say.

Danny walks over and hugs both of us. "Sebastian."

"What?" I ask.

"Did you know that Piper is a superhero?"

"Since the day I met her." I tell him.

"That's a long time." He says.

"It is a long time." I agree with Danny. He looks around the room. "No one opened their presents."

"Christmas is all day." Eric says. He looks at Piper. "I know what you do for a living. I googled you. If you need to work, we will wait for you."

She kisses him. "It's Christmas and I am not working on Christmas. If we were home, I still wouldn't be working on Christmas Day. I am on vacation through the new year." She kisses him. "Does Danny know?"

"He thinks you are a superhero."

"I like that he thinks that."

"We love you." Eric says. "You know he was looking around the room and is concerned for all of us that we didn't get to open presents yet. He was looking for the ones that he got for you and me."

"I put them in our room."

"Oh maybe we can tell him."

Tristian walks into the room holding tightly to Matt's hand. His eyes are dilated. I see it across the room. His usually blue eyes are just black circles in his face. Matt sits with him on his lap.

"This is the first time I have sat down in hours." Matt says. "We are going to stay here so I can keep an eye on him."

"Matt, we want to all be together." Sebastian says. "We came here as a family and we are going to do things as a family." He cross the room and lifts Tristian up holding him against his chest. "You are a hero. I know you have a concussion but you are a hero. You know what we do with heroes that catch bank robbers?"

"I don't know." Tristian says. He puts his head on Sebastian's shoulder.

"Don't let him fall asleep." Matt says.

"I have had many concussions growing up. I know the game plan." He walks around the room with Tristian. "Close your eyes and rest for a little while. I won't put you down."

Matt looks at all of us. "Can I go upstairs and get a shower? Did my mom leave?"

"Go get yourself ready. I have him." Sebastian walks over to Matt. He hands him a check for ten thousand dollars. "Put this away for him."

"I don't need — want this."

Amanda walks in the room. "Don't let him sleep." She says about Tristian.

"I know how concussions work. I have had them growing up. He is just resting."

She walks over to Matt. "The money that he is giving you is the reward money that is issued from the bank to the person who helped catch a bank robber. She walks across the room and hands Eric a check for ten thousand dollars. "This is for Danny. Without his Christmas present camera that takes the best pictures I have ever seen, he helped us get her. I don't know how he did it but he got her ID shot too. There was no denying who she was."

We all go outside and get into the cars that are waiting for us. They all take us to Justin's grandparents' house. It's a big house. The cars stop in the driveway. Justin and Mark get out of the car first. They walk up the steps to the house and wait for some one to open the door.

Everyone gets out of the car. Tristian is sitting next to me. He is wide awake but seems like he is far away.

"Where are we?" He asks.

"We are going to meet Justin and Mark's grandparents." I tell him.

"Did they all forget about you?"

"I hope so." I say. I look at Tristian. "No, I don't think so."

He smiles at me. "I heard you."

"Don't tell anyone." I say kissing his head.

"Ouch."

"Oh, I forgot." I tell him.

The door to the limo opens. Justin gets in. "You ready to meet them?"

"What if they don't—"

"I don't care what they do or don't do. We are here. You are going to meet them. That's it. My dad is here too. You are going to meet his dad."

"Grandpa is here?" I ask.

"Oh right, you met him."

"I love him."

"He loves you too. He is so excited to meet my fiancé." Justin says.

Astro barks. He wags his tail. Justin scratches him under his chin. Astro licks me in the face.

"We can't bring him in my grandparents' house." Justin says.

Matt sits in the car. "I am going to let him nap for a couple minutes. I will keep Astro with us. He is like a safety blanket." He looks at me. "I have to tell you, I always felt safer at work when you came with him."

Astro curls up on the seat next to Tristian. Tristian uses him as a pillow. Before we even get out of the car, he is sleeping.

"We won't be long." Justin says.

We go into the house. Justin carries me in. Edward hugs us both while Justin is still holding me. Jayne walks over and also hugs us when Edward steps away. Grandpa Eddie comes over. He hugs us next.

"My sweet girl, its good to see you again." Grandpa Eddie says. He looks at Justin. "When you put her down, come find me." He leans into both of us. "These stuffy people make me itch."

We all laugh. He takes our hands and holds them. He takes my left hand in his hand and looks at the ring.

"Do you still have the earrings I gave you for graduation?" He asks me.

I push my hair away from my ear. "I never take them off." I say.

Justin looks at his grandfather. He knows that his cousins have asked what happened to their grandmother's earrings. Justin knows too that Grandpa Eddie always told them that he had no idea what she did with them. He told his granddaughters that they must have been lost over the years.

"Like I said, come find me when you put her down." He kisses me on the cheek. "Or bring her with you and we will all chat."

Rosetta walks over. She is the most elegant elder woman I have ever seen in my life next to my own grandmother. She holds out her hand for Justin.

Jacob walks over with my wheelchair. "Astro jumped in it when we took it out of the car. He wouldn't get out of it."

I laugh. "That sounds like my Astro."

Justin sits me in my wheelchair and kisses me on the lips. I wrap my arms around him and hug him.

Rosetta sees the ring on my finger. "Justin that is a beautiful ring that you got her." She looks at me. "Did you pick it out?"

"No." Justin and I say together.

"I didn't know anything about it." I say.

"Have you known each other long?" Rosetta asks.

"We have known each other a few months."

"Robert asked me to marry him after ten days." She says.

Mark walks over. "She is not a stranger. Justin and her met this year, but I have known her since I was young." He says kissing his grandma on the head. "This is Sebastian. The one I refer to as Little Mermaid."

"This is Savannah's friend?" She asks.

"Yes." We all say together.

"I have heard about you for a long time." She says. "Wait! Is this one that you kissed at the party?" She asks Justin.

"How is it that everyone remembers that but us?" Justin asks.

"It wasn't a big deal." Edward says.

"That's not what Little Mermaid told me." Grandpa Eddie says.

I look at him and feel my cheeks burn with embarrassment. I feel really hot. I take my jacket off.

He doesn't seem to notice my embarrassment. He continues. "She told me that—"

"Excuse me. I have to use the bathroom." I say.

"Let me show you where to go." Rosetta says. She looks at me. "Are you feeling alright?"

"I am just hot." I say.

Justin runs over to me. "Are you ok?"

"I am just hot."

"Let me get you some water." Rosetta says.

Jayne walks over with a glass of water. "Here sweetheart." She says.

I drink the whole cup. I reach my hand out for Justin's. "I have to go to the bathroom." I say.

Justin looks at Rosetta. She points down the hallway. He lifts me up and carries me to the bathroom.

"If I faint from embarrassment, just bring me back to the hotel and leave me there." I say. He stands in front of me holding me. When I finish using the bathroom, he sits me on the counter.

"Why are you going to pass out from embarrassment?"

I start sweating.

"Talk to me." He says. "Whats going on?"

"I remember the kiss." I say. "I never forgot you. I looked for you everywhere I went. I hoped I would see you again. I never did see you again. I told your grandpa about that kiss. I didn't know he was your grandpa until years later. That kiss made me feel like boys saw me like they saw Savannah and Piper. It made me feel like I was just a regular girl."

"Sebastian, why did you say you didn't remember the kiss?"

"Because Savannah teased me about it. She said that she had a picture of us but she never showed it to me. I didn't know that my mom had a picture of our kiss either."

"You talked to my grandpa about me?"

I cover my face with my hands.

"Sebastian, what's going on?"

"My mom left me with Candy for days and your grandpa was there visiting your dad. He saw my notebook."

"Your notebook?"

"I wrote our names on it with hearts. I was sad that I never saw you anywhere."

"We were meant to be together." He says and kisses me. He lifts me into his arms and we leave the bathroom.

Mark walks over to us. "I hope you behaved yourselves."

"Shut up." Justin says.

"We need to go." I say.

"We are going to stay a bit more." Mark says.

"Matt is in the car with Tristian and Astro." I say.

"We will be leaving in about twenty minutes." Mark says.

"Justin, I can't take the smells." I say.

"Alright, lets say goodbye." Justin says.

"Can we do it outside? I am not feeling well."

There are too many smells. Different scented candles are burning. Its warm because the fireplace is burning too. Its too hot in the house and there is a lot of people. The heat I am feeling is radiating from the inside out. I am trying everything I can think of not to hyperventilate. I don't want to embarrass Justin, Mark and myself.

We go outside. Robert, Justin's grandfather is outside smoking a pipe. The smell of the pipe chokes me. I feel Justin take me in his arms.

Matt gets out of the limo and comes running. "Look how flushed she is. What happened?"

"We were trying to get to the car. She said there where too many—"

"Smells?" Matt asks. "She is very sensitive to scents. They bother her. She can't take too many different ones at the same time. She never goes into candle stores."

"I didn't know." Justin says. He carries me to the car.

"When she passes out, she sometimes she comes out of it angry." Matt says.

"Does that happen a lot to her?" Robert asks.

"When she gets overwhelmed." Justin says.

"Is it part of her problem?" Robert asks.

"Her problem?" Mark asks. "Her problem is that old man in there embarrassed the hell out of her. There was no where for her to go and no way for her to get out on her own." Mark looks at Justin. "She nearly had to beg you to take her outside."

"I was trying." Justin says.

"He was trying." Edward says. "I will talk to my dad."

"Dad, do something." Justin says.

"Put her in the empty car and get inside."

Justin gets in the other limo with me. He holds me closer to him. He rocks me in his arms.

Edward gets in the car. He has a glass of water.

"Are you going to throw that in her face?" Justin asks.

"No." Edward says. He puts peppermint oil in it. He holds it under my nose.

I open my eyes. I look around and cover my face. I scream before I burst into tears.

"No. None of that." Edward says. "No one knows that you passed out but us."

Robert knocks on the window before he opens the door. "How is the girl?"

I bury my face in Justin's chest. "I am such an embarrassment to you." I say.

He looks at me. "Never!"

Edward kisses us both on our heads and gets out of the car. "If the windows steam up, we will know what you are doing." He teases us.

"Dad!" Justin laughs.

"I will tell everyone that you had to go. Go enjoy the rest of your Christmas. I will see you all later tonight at the hotel. I love you both."

Sebastian comes out with Jacob and Seth. They are coughing. Edward runs to them. "Whats going on?" He asks.

"Too many different smells." Sebastian says. "I can't catch my breath." He bends over and puts his hands on his knees.

"There is a haze in the air in that house." Jacob says. "We should get everyone out of there. I think the fireplace is causing it."

"Its like the more wood they burn, the worst it gets in there." Seth says.

Piper comes out with Savannah. Piper is holding her up. She is struggling to catch her breath.

"What the fuck?" Edward says.

"Mark is passed out in there."

Edward goes running in with Jacob. They carry him out. Jacob gets everyone else out on the back porch. He calls the fire department. He gives the address and tells them whats going on.

Jacob comes back out and joins all of us. They get in the car with Justin and me. Sebastian hugs me. "You doing ok?" He looks at me. "Have you been crying?"

"I just feel like I embarrass everyone every time I pass out. I do it a lot."

"No. You don't." They all say to me.

"You don't embarrass anyone."

Mark gets in the car. "Holy shit, I couldn't breath in there." He says.

Savannah slides in the car. She hugs me. "How are you doing?"

"I am ok." I say. "How are you doing?"

"Mark. Justin. I mean no disrespect to your mom and her parents but they think that you are dating me because I am pregnant. I have to say, I have never been so insulted in my life."

"I am sorry." Mark says. "I want to be supportive right now, but my head is swimming."

Jacob hands Mark a bottle of water. "Drink it up."

Mark leans his head back on the seat. He closes his eyes and takes Savannah's hand.

The limo pulls out onto the highway and drives back towards the city. Twenty minutes later, the limo stops at a gate and waits for them to let us in. When the limo pulls up into the driveway, Aaron and Scarlett are waiting for us on the driveway. When the limos stop, they wait for all of us to get out of the cars.

She hugs Sebastian first. Aaron waits for me. When I get in my wheelchair, he takes me in his arms and hugs me tighter than I have had anyone hug me ever in my life.

"Uncle Aaron." I say. "Merry Christmas."

"Merry Christmas." He says. "Come in the house and meet my family."

A beautiful woman stands at the entrance of the house. She waves from where she stands. A younger teenaged girl stands next to her. They are dressed almost the same. They look beautiful. The younger girl walks down the steps and into Aaron's extended arms.

"This is my daughter, Bianca."

She smiles at all of us.

"These are your cousins." Scarlett says.

She looks around the driveway at all of us standing around. "All of them?"

Scarlett taps her nose. "Don't be rude."

She walks behind Aaron.

He steps aside and takes her in his arms again. "Bianca, this is Sebastian."

"I have googled both of them." She says. "Its nice to meet you." She says shaking hands with Piper.

"I am Piper." She says. "This is Sebastian." She says putting her hand on my shoulder.

She looks around and then takes off running back to the house.

Sebastian looks at me. He pulls me aside. "This is going to be—"

365

"A long fucking day." I say.

We both laugh.

"The one in the door that hasn't taken her eagle eyes off of us all, I feel like I know her." I say.

"Well lets go find out." He says.

Justin and Sebastian carry me up the steps in my wheelchair. When we go in the house Oliver greets us with a round of hugs.

"You alright?" He asks all of us.

"Its been a day." Sebastian says.

"Good I hope."

"Good. Bad. Happy. Long. And here we are." I say. For a moment I didn't realize I said it out loud.

They all look at me.

"I am sorry." I say. "Merry Christmas."

Tristian and Danny run up the steps and run over to me. I hug them both. I rub Tristian's head.

"It doesn't hurt as much." He says.

"The more the day goes on, the better you will feel." I tell him.

"Sebastian, you look sad." Danny says.

"I am fine." I tell him. "I am with everyone that I love."

Astro trots over and puts his front paws on my legs. He stands on his haunches and licks me in the face. He can sense that I am sad too. I kiss his muzzle.

We are all led into the kitchen that is as big as my whole house. Everyone stands around doing something.

Anastasia walks in the room. "Darlings, lets do presents before we have dinner. Come gather around the tree."

We all follow everyone into the oversized family room where a ten foot Christmas tree stands. There are presents piled high around the tree. It looks like a scene from a store window.

Anastasia clicks her fingers together, "I am glad and beyond blessed to have my whole family together for Christmas. This means the world to me." She says.

Everyone opens presents. I don't. Sebastian doesn't open any either. Jacob and Seth sit with Astro between them.

Anastasia walks over to all of us. "I see that you aren't opening presents."

I haven't opened presents other than the sweater that Justin gave me.

"Why aren't you opening presents?"

"I want to wait for my mom." Sebastian says.

"We haven't opened any presents." Jacob says.

"This year, the best present is being with all of you." I say.

"You still have to open presents." Anastasia says.

Justin stands next to me. "Why aren't you opening presents?"

"I usually spend the day by myself with Astro. He doesn't get me presents that I can open."

"Your mom doesn't get you presents?"

"No. I mean she gives me gift cards so I can go buy whatever I want for myself."

"What do you ever buy for yourself?"

"I do."

"What was the last thing that you got for yourself?"

"A boyfriend." I say.

"I am being serious. You don't open presents?"

"I do."

"Why aren't you?"

"There are so many people here."

"So what?"

"I don't expect anything from anyone."

"That's why it should be so special."

"It is special. I just don't want to be disappointed."

He kisses me. "Why would you be disappointed?"

"Its hard to put my finger on what I am feeling. I am happy to be here with everyone. I am sad too."

"Why?"

I kiss him.

"Don't change the subject." He says.

"I want to."

Savannah and Piper join me. They bring over presents. They both hug me.

"Open mine." Savannah says. She hands me a big box.

I open it. Inside the box is a photo album. "Oh my goodness. This is beautiful."

Piper gives me her present next. I open it. It's a pair of earrings that I was looking at in the store. I hug her. "Thank you." I say. "I have your presents back at the hotel."

"We have more for you at the hotel too." Savannah says. "I am sorry that you got sick at Rosetta's."

Justin and Mark's phones ring at the same time. They both answer it. Jayne and Joey call them to tell them that because of me, they were able to catch a gas leak. Rosetta and Robert want all of us to come back back and join them for dinner tomorrow.

"Let us see how the day goes and we will call you tomorrow morning and tell you what we are going to do." Mark tells Jayne. "You know, I can't talk right now."

They both hang up the phone.

This time I find Justin. He is standing in the kitchen. I go to him and hug him. He holds me tight in his arms.

"I love you so much." I tell him.

"I love you." He smiles "What did Savannah give you?"

"A photo album. Its of us. Our first kiss. She has pictures of you holding my hand in the hospital. I will have to show it to you."

"Where did your cousins go?"

"I haven't seen them since we got here."

"Bianca seems like she wants to know all about you and Sebastian. The other one didn't even introduce herself to any of us."

"They only knew that they had cousins from Uncle Oliver and Aunt Grace."

"Where is Aunt Grace?" Justin asks.

She walks in the kitchen. "I thought I might find my favorite girl hiding out in here." She says.

"I am not hiding." I say.

"We just heard how your day went. I would be hiding." She smiles. "I am glad that everyone is ok." She looks at Justin. "Your grandparents are ok?"

"They are doing well. Thank you."

She takes my hand in her hand and looks at the ring on my finger. "Congratulations!" She says. "Come find me later, I have something for you that I have had for many years."

"Thanks Aunt Grace."

Scarlett comes into the he kitchen. She and Grace hug each other as Grace leaves and she comes in the kitchen. "Are you two doing ok?"

"We are fine." Justin says.

She hands me a box. "Open this later. I wanted to give this to you since I found out about you. It has traveled back and forth with me from Miami to here. I gave one to Sebastian too. Maybe you can open them together. But don't open it here." She kisses me on forehead.

"Bianca seems really sweet."

"My girls are great. You didn't meet Francesca?"

"No." I say.

"Don't hold it against them. They are nervous that you won't like them."

"I feel the same way." Sebastian says as he walks into the kitchen with Jacob and Seth.

"Jacob, I heard that you were a hero today." She says. "You must be very proud of yourself."

"I was just there." He says.

I take his hand. "You were there and the people that you helped think you are a hero."

We are all gathered around the table. Seth makes sure that the food is perfectly plated. He smiles at Aaron. "Sorry it's a sickness." Seth laughs.

"You are doing a great job." Aaron says.

"Thanks for having Jacob and me. I know we aren't—"

"You are family, son. I heard that when you found about Sebastian, you were so excited to have a sister."

"I had been at that bookstore so many times and she was always so nice and friendly to everyone."

Francesca finally makes an appearance. "Daddy." She says.

He turns to face her.

"Where do you want us to sit?"

He looks at her. "Sit wherever you feel comfortable."

"I can eat in my room?" She asks.

"Its Christmas. Your mother and I would appreciate your sister and you joining the family."

"Grandma loves them more."

Seth stands off to the side. "Has your grandma been to every event in your life?"

She looks at Seth. "Who the hell are you?"

"Answer my question first." He says.

"She has been to every major event in my life."

"Go ask my brother how many she was there for him. Then go ask our sister the same question." He looks at Aaron. "I am sorry."

Jacob isn't far away and when Seth walks past him, Jacob grabs Seth and hugs him. "Wow little brother."

Two girls stand by the piano singing. They sing in a round with each other. Everyone stops what they are doing to listen to them. They stop singing. They both look at me.

The younger runs over to me. "I am Lilliana." She says.

I hug her. "I remember you from the farm." I tell her.

"I told you we could have been cousins." She says. She hugs me tighter. "You always look so pretty." She says.

"You do too." I tell her.

Julianna walks over and hugs me. "You remember us?"

"I do." I say. "Its nice to see both of you again."

"Will you sing with us?" Lilliana asks.

"I think that you both are doing such a great job. I will sing with you both later." I say.

Julianna hugs me. "Do you remember in the barn when we all sang together?"

"Yes."

"Can we sing like that again?"

"We will." I tell her.

Scarlett comes in the room looking like she just left a runway red carpet event. "Please everyone, dinner is ready." She says.

Sebastian sits with his brothers, Amanda, Trix and Lindsey. There are two seats left open. I want to sit with them, but then I want to sit with my friends too. I am at a total loss.

Justin kisses me. "Go sit with your family."

"That's just it. Savannah and Piper have been my family longer." I say.

Aaron hears me. "Not a problem. You can all sit at the larger table. You are right. Your friends have been your family longer."

I look at him. "I am sorry."

"None of that." He says. He kisses me on the cheek. "I am sorry that my daughters are being so rude."

"They are fine." I say. "Its not like Sebastian and I came alone to meet them. We brought a hundred people with us."

"Not a hundred people." Aaron says. "The boys are so happy to be playing video games. There is a big play room."

"Thank you for allowing us all to be together."

Ivan and Trevor walk in the front door. Justin goes to walk away. I grab his hand and I don't let go. He looks at me.

We all sit together and have dinner. The room is so large with tables full of people. My mom and Peter sit with Eric and Danny. Piper sits at their table half the time then she sits with me and Savannah.

After dinner, they usher everyone outside by the pool. The pool is covered for the winter. There is a bridge over it that everyone goes on. I stay off to the side. Lindsey stands with me.

"Thank you for having me with all your family." She says.

"Lindsey, you are my family too."

Oliver joins us. "After dinner, my girls want to sing with you. They want Lindsey to play the violin."

"I think we will enjoy that." I say. "I always enjoyed singing with the two of them."

I find a bathroom that is as big as my kitchen. I go in side it and look at myself in the mirror. There is a knock on the door. Before I can say that I am in there, the door bursts open.

"You want my mom's money!" Francesca accuses me.

"What?"

"Poor little orphan."

"I have a mother." I tell her.

"Where is she now?"

"On her way here."

"Bullshit." Francesca says.

There is a knock on the door. Before either of us can say anything, Amanda walks in the bathroom. "What's going on in here?" Amanda asks.

"I just want to know what this imposter wants from my parents. Their money?" Francesca says.

"I don't want anything. I have lived twenty-five years without knowing any of you. I don't want anything from any of you other than to get know you all. You are the only connection to my dad."

"From what I know of him, he was a—" Francesca squints her eyes.

Amanda puts her hands up. "If you are going to say something mean, please hold your tongue."

I go to leave the bathroom.

"Your dad didn't even want to marry your mom. He never wanted you. She was a bloodsucker who wanted his money and now you want our money."

"You bitch!" I yell as loud as I can.

Sebastian runs in the bathroom with Jacob and Seth behind him. Justin takes me in his arms.

"What's going on in here?" Aaron asks.

Scarlett comes in the bathroom. She looks at her daughter. "What did you say?" She knows it had to have been something awful because Amanda is sitting on the counter crying.

Sebastian hugs her. "What happened?"

"She was snooping around." Francesca says.

"In the bathroom?" Scarlett asks. "What was she going to take, the toilet paper?"

"I survived my whole life without knowing all of you. Thank you for having me. It was a pleasure being with my dad's family." I put my hand in Justin's hand. "Let's go."

"No." Scarlett says.

Jacob and Seth stand next to me.

"This day has been overwhelming. Merry Christmas." I say. I leave the bathroom. Justin, Seth and Jacob come with me. I let Savannah, Piper, Mark and Eric know that we are leaving.

We all leave after saying goodbye to everyone. Anastasia tries to make us stay. Sebastian and Amanda do not leave with us.

We all go back to the hotel. Astro sits next to me in the car. He puts his head on my lap.

Savannah looks at me. "What happened?"

"It was just time to leave." I say.

Matt takes my hand. "This has been a crazy day."

"True."

The driver takes the long way back to the resort. I just want to get out of my warm clothes. I want to be back in Florida. I want this day to be over. I put my head back on the headrest. I close my eyes after taking Justin and Jacob's hands. A tear slips out.

"What was said?" Piper asks. We are laying in bed together.

"She called me a gold digger." I say.

Savannah hugs me. "She doesn't know what a hard worker you are."

"I don't want to talk about it. Christmas is always such an adventure." I close my eyes so I don't cry.

There is a big commotion going on just outside the bedroom. The suite fills with voices. My mom bursts through the door. She gets in bed with the three of us. She takes me in her arms. We cry together. Piper and Savannah cry with us.

"Sebastian told us what Francesca said. Amanda wouldn't stop crying." Mom says.

I don't say anything.

"Listen to me. Your dad—" She chokes. "Your dad couldn't wait to be your dad. He loved you the second he found out that we were having you." She says. "They thought that I was a gold digger too. I showed them that I wasn't when I didn't take a penny from any of them."

"I didn't go looking for them. I didn't know that any of them existed. Grandma stopped coming when I was twelve. I guess that the other grandchildren meant more to her."

"I know that when Scarlett got pregnant with Bianca she had a hard pregnancy. She was bed ridden for months."

"I just want to go home. Actually, I want to go somewhere that no one knows me."

Piper hugs me. "We would ruin that for you. We would come and visit you all the time. We would have loud parties and sing karaoke totally off key."

I laugh for the first time in a while. "Why? We went to school for music and vocals."

"Well you want to be unrecognizable. If you sing like an angel and play the piano like you do, people would know who you are in a hot second." Savannah says.

"We would miss you terribly." Mom says.

"I just want to know why every one thinks that I am a gold digger. Jacob called me that when he first met me." I sit up. "The thing is, I know I have seen Francesca before. I don't know where I know her from but I definitely know her from somewhere."

"I have been trying to put my finger on it too." Savannah says. "I think she is our age or close to it."

"Liliana and Julianna were happy to see you." Piper says.

"They are really sweet." I say. I scoot to the edge of the bed.

"Where are you going?"

"I have to go to the bathroom." I leave the room and go to use the other bathroom. I go in there and close the door. I run the sink and cry my eyes out.

Jacob knocks on the door. I wash my face before I open the door. When I do he gets on his knees and hugs me. "I am so sorry." He says.

I cry on his shoulder. "You didn't do anything. I am glad that I have all of you."

"I am sorry for what she said to you."

Sebastian comes into the room because he is staying in the room with Justin and me. He takes me in his arms and we cry together.

"I can tell you from what I remember of our dad, that he was looking forward to having a little girl. He couldn't wait to marry your mom. He couldn't wait to have both of us together playing. He was thrilled to pieces to have you. I don't know why she would say that to you." He holds me closer. "You should have seen Amanda." He pulls back. "She acted so fast no one could stop her. She smacked Francesca in the face once and then back handed her."

"Why would she do that?"

"In your honor. She lost her shit with all of them. Once she got started, she didn't stop for a while."

"Where is she now?"

"She's in our bedroom. She is washing the day off." He says.

"What did everyone do?"

He laughs. "Nothing. Everyone was stunned." He hugs me. "I know we only know each other a short time, but I feel like I know you my whole life and I love having you in our lives." He squeezes tighter. "We are all so glad to have you."

"I am overjoyed to have brothers." I say.

Seth joins us and Jacob too. Justin watches us from where he is sitting on the couch with Astro. Mark is sitting next to him. They both jump off the couch and come hug all of us. Astro jumps up on us and joins in the hug. Savannah and Piper come out the room that Justin and I are sharing. They join us too.

Mom takes out her phone and takes pictures of all of us together. I look up and smile at her. She smiles back. "I love you." She mouths.

Chapter 26

I sit in the lobby with my Astro and my iPad having a cup of coffee. It is really early in the morning. I am enjoying a Starbucks coffee. Uncle Oliver comes and sits at the table with me. He takes my hand. I look at him.

"What are you and your friends going to do today?" He asks.

"I am not sure."

"Lili and Julie want to know if they can spend time with you." Uncle Oliver says.

"I am sure I can make that happen. I think my friends are going to explore the city."

"You aren't going with them?"

"Not today. I think Astro and I are going to take it easy around here."

"Is that what you want to do?"

"I feel like I am keeping my friends from doing what they want to do while they are here on their vacations."

"What do they think?"

"They all want me to go with them."

"What do you want?"

"Uncle Oliver, I am in one of the most romantic cities in the world. I want to go with my fiancé and hold hands. I want to go site seeing with him. Since we have been here, all we seem to do is sleep in bed with each other."

"Sweetheart, T.M.I."

I laugh. "No I mean we literally sleep in bed together."

"Sweetheart, tell him what you want."

"I feel like he doesn't want to be with me. He swears that he loves me and he wants to be with me, but he seems like he is distant." I look around the café. "I love him. I have dated other guys before, but I never felt the way I do since I met him. I get all flustered. I think of him when I should be busy doing something else. I want to be with him all the time. Then when I am with him, I feel nervous and yet somehow safe."

Edward and Mark are in the café too. They hear what I tell my uncle. Mark sends Justin a text message. Letting him know some of what I told my uncle. They talk quietly among themselves. Mark's phone rings and he answers it. He excuses himself from the table. He walks outside and talks to Justin.

"Sebastian is in the café talking to Oliver. She wants to spend the day with you. You alone. She wants to go see the sites of the city with you holding her hand and kissing her whenever you feel the need." He laughs. "I added the last part." He gets serious. "Just, you make her feel safe."

"Mark, someone gave her a journal. She wrote all about me. She just didn't know that it was me. She never knew my name. She has pictures of me in this journal. She has loved me since she was twelve years old. She wrote that no one ever measured up to the boy who gave her first kiss. That was me."

"Why are you reading her journal?"

"Grace told me to find it and read it." He says.

"Hey, dad is leaving soon. Come to the café and join us."

"I am drinking your coffee." Justin says.

"You are always such a child." Mark says.

When he walks back into the hotel, Astro jerks away from me and runs to Mark. That's when I see Edward sitting with Justin. I go to him and hug him. He kisses me like we are the only two people in the room.

Oliver joins us at the table. We have breakfast together. Matt comes down with Tristian. When he sees us he hugs us all. He hugs me last.

"We are going to see the Statue of Liberty." He says.

"I know. We are all going." Justin says.

"We are going to take a boat."

"A ferry." Edward says.

"What time are you leaving?" Justin asks.

"I am not sure." Edward says.

"Do you want to go with us to the Statue of Liberty?"

"We need a parent with us to make sure that we all behave ourselves." Mark says.

"Mark!" I say.

"Little Mermaid!" Mark says. "You are the reason we need supervision."

I feel the blush rising on my cheeks.

Justin stands up and lifts me into his arms. He walks over to one of the fancy chairs in the lobby and sits with me on his lap. He kisses me.

Within an hour, we are waiting to get on a ferry to take us to the Statue of Liberty. When we get there, we start the tour. I can only go so far. The boys want to go as far up as possible. Piper takes Danny's hand and Eric's hand as they go up the stairs. Matt and Tristian go up with them.

Savannah and Mark disappear next. Little by little I find myself completely alone. I am limited on where I can go and what I can see. I wander into the gift shop. I look around a bit and then leave.

I sit outside in the cool winter air waiting for my friends and family to come find me. Its been hours since I have heard from any of them. I am used to being on my own but right now I feel so alone.

Grace walks over with Liliana and Julianna. The girls run over and hug me. Grace hugs me.

"Where is everyone?"

"They went to see the different levels." I tell her.

"Where is Justin?" She asks.

"I haven't seen him in hours."

"Did you call him?"

"No."

"We are going inside."

"Go ahead." I tell her.

"Want to come with us?" Julianna asks.

"I don't think so." I say.

When they walk away, I wander off to the ferry. I decide to leave. I board the ferry. I take it to Elise Island. I pay for the entrance fee and go inside. I look at everything. When I am done with the tour, I go to get back on the ferry.

My phone rings. I take it out of purse. Justin's face fills my phone. "Hello."

"Where are you?" He asks.

"I am at Elise Island."

"We are on the ferry coming there."

"I am on the ferry going back to mainland."

"Sebastian, where did you disappear to?"

"You were all gone. I can only see so much. I am limited on where I can go. Everyone was gone."

"I got a phone call. When I came back I couldn't find anyone."

There is an announcement that they are boarding the ferry.

"Sebastian, wait for us." He says.

"Everyone left me. I am going back to the hotel. I am going to get my shit and I am going back to my life."

"Sebastian!" He yells.

I hang up.

Justin runs to me and hugs me. "I am sorry. When I took the call, you were with everyone."

"Its ok." I say. "I am going back to the hotel. I am ready for this trip to be over."

"My mom called. My grandparents want us to come have dinner with them. They want just us there. Savannah and Mark. You and me."

"Justin, this trip has been a little more than I planned for."

"Please just stick it out today. If you want to go tomorrow, I will go home with you."

I agree. Everyone walks around the museum. I go with them. When we get on the ferry, Justin doesn't let go of my hand.

We get in a waiting car that takes the four of us and Astro back to Rosetta's house. The car pulls into the driveway. Everyone gets out of the car. Justin holds my hand.

"Wait!" I say.

"What's wrong?"

"What if they don't like me?"

Savannah hugs me. "They will love you."

Mark hugs me. "Little Mermaid, they already met you. They already love you."

"Grandpa Eddie is not going to be here. Grandpa Robert and Grandma love you." Justin says. "My mom thinks you are adorable." He kisses me.

Rosetta walks out. She hugs everyone. She hugs me tight. "Sebastian come in." She looks around. "Where are your sweet brothers."

"They went to my grandma's for the day." I tell her.

"It was a pleasure meeting all of you."

"Thank you."

"Come in. We have a lot of good stuff."

We go in the house. Jayne and Joe are there. Everyone exchanges hugs.

"Its good to see you again." Joe says. "Did you have a great Christmas?"

"It was nice." Savannah and I say together.

"I don't believe that for a second."

"It was a roller coaster Christmas." I say. "It had a lot of ups and downs. Its one for the books. One to remember forever." I smile.

Justin takes me in his arms. He kisses me on the lips.

Mark hugs me too.

We spend the whole day there. Everyone really enjoys the day and also enjoys Astro. He enjoys being with me. He ventures out to everyone. Robert is the one that he goes to the most. He sits with his head on Roberts lap.

We all go into the kitchen to help make dinner for Rosetta and Robert. The four of us all do something different. I prepare the chicken. I put it in the pan with olive oil and garlic powder. I add soy sauce. Mark puts it in the oven for me.

Savannah makes salad.

"What kinds of vegetables goes with this?" Mark asks.

"Broccoli or green beans. Brussels sprouts if I had more time." I say.

"Did you think that you would be cooking for my family?" Justin asks kissing me.

"This is great. This is one of my best dinners that I make."

Savannah smiles. "Are you going to double cook it like you always do?"

"Yes." I say.

"You cook it twice?" Justins asks.

"You will see." I tell him.

WE join everyone outside on the patio. Robert is showing old videos of the family. He is telling everyone stories from the olden days. He talks about how he met Rosetta. Everyone sits around laughing and listening to his stories.

Rosetta pulls both her grandsons away from all of us. She takes them into her room. She opens her jewelry box and takes out two rings. One is a sapphire and the other is garnet. She sits on the bed between Justin and Mark.

"When the time is right, I want you to give these to your fiancés. I want them to have something from me."

"Grandma. You don't have to do this." Justin says.

"I want to do it. I know that your cousins have been eyeing these rings since they were young. I don't want them to have them. I want you to have them. I want to pass them down to the women I want wearing them."

"I know that Jenny will be crushed." Justin says.

"I have another ring for Jenny and she will get my earrings. I mean, your mom and her sisters will get them."

"Grandma, this means the world to me." Mark says.

"Me too." Justin says.

Rosetta looks from one to the other one. "Did her cousin really call her a gold digger?"

"Yes." Justin says. "Jacob did too when he met her."

"Don't they see how special she is? Don't they see how wonderful she is." Rosetta looks at Justin. "Don't they notice how much love she radiates? She radiates love. I feel like when I hugged her, I hugged an angel."

"Awe grandma, that is so sweet." Mark says.

"I mean it." She gets up and walks back over to another jewelry box. This one is bigger. She opens it up and shuffles through the gems in there. She finds what she is looking for. She turns with a smile on her face. She hands Justin a little gold shovel pin. "Do you think I could give this to her without hurting her feelings?"

"Why do you have this?"

"Robert bought it for me. His family thought that I was a gold digger too. They were never nice to me. Until one day that they had no choice. His dad got deathly ill. I was there and my nursing skills took over. Much like that boy, Jacob, who I want to see again before you all leave. I saved his life. Then and only then did things change. Little did Robert's family know that every time he asked me out, I paid my own way. If I asked him out on a date, I paid for both of us. Robert's sister saw us out one night and she watched me go in my wallet and pay for us to go to a movie. When we left there we went to a fair. I paid. She watched me again pay. She confronted her brother about it and he told her that I always did that. She asked him what was wrong with him. Things changed. I made them one of my famous dinners and that did it. They stopped calling me a gold digger. Robert bought it for me one Christmas and I wore it every time we were together with his family."

They all laugh.

Outside, I pull Savannah off to the side., I open up a little box. She looks at it and we laugh until our sides hurt.

"Where did you get that?" She asks.

"I saw it in a store yesterday. I couldn't resist. Everyone thinks that I am one. I thought I needed this." I say.

She hugs me. "Not everyone thinks that you are a gold digger."

Jacob, Seth and Sebastian walk up. Jacob looks at what we are looking at. He tries to take it away from me.

"Stop." I tell him.

"Where did you get that?"

"I bought it in a store yesterday."

"Please take it back. I should never have said that to you. I will always feel guilty for saying that."

I put my hand on his chest. "Stop. I didn't buy it because of you. I got it as a joke. I saw it and I burst into laughter. I think Oliver designed it. It says O-D on it."

Sebastian takes it from me. He looks at it. "Oh my god, where did you find a golden shovel?"

"It was in a store. There were all different kinds of pins in there. That is just one of them that I bought."

"Do you have the others with you?"

"They are back at the hotel."

Rosetta walks back outside. "My grandsons are in the kitchen. Can they be trusted in there?"

Savannah and I laugh.

"We will go check on them." I say.

Seth runs in ahead of us. When we walks in the kitchen he smiles. "It smells so good in here. What are you making?"

"Sebastian is making a chicken dinner for everyone." Justin says.

"Little Mermaid makes this as her go to meal. When she wants to impress people she makes this." Mark says.

"Does she double cook the chicken to make a stir fry?" Seth asks.

"Yes." Mark says.

"I got this." Seth says. "Are there mushrooms?"

"In the refrigerator." Justin says.

"Get them out."

Savannah and I come in the kitchen. I look around and see that Seth has taken over. He looks at me. "Did Anastasia teach you how to do this?"

"Actually no. She told me that she used to make this all time for me when I was little but I did it when I was college. We had baked chicken the night before and then we didn't eat it. The next day it was a little dried out so I cut up the chicken and put it in the sauce and added broccoli and mushrooms. I served it over rice and everyone loved it. Then it became my go to meal. Its easy. I don't always cook the chicken twice but I find its always better when I do."

Seth hugs me. "That's amazing." He says sticking a piece of chicken in his mouth. "Do you make it with butter?"

"No. Olive oil." I tell him.

"Its so good." Seth says. "You will have to make this for the restaurant."

I smile.

Jacob sits outside with Rosetta. She sits next to him at the picnic table. She takes his hand. "It means the world to us that you saved us on Christmas."

"It's actually because of Sebastian. She complained about not feeling well. When I saw that she looked like she was going to faint, I thought there had to be a problem."

"Isn't fainting her thing?" Robert asks.

"It was different signs this time." Jacob says.

"You are close to her?" He asks.

"We are trying to get close to her. It seems like we take three steps forward and then there is a major set backs." Jacob says.

"Have you seen your dad since she came into your lives?" Robert asks.

Sebastian walks over. He puts his hand on Jacob's shoulder.

"No but that's not her fault. My dad has a second family. Since he screwed her out of her condo that she paid double for, he stopped coming around."

"Do you miss him?"

"My dad did a lot of horrible things to people. He did a lot of horrible things to Sebastian. When I was running a cruise out one night some of the business men were talking freely about my dad. They didn't know that I run the cruises. They didn't know that I was on the ship. What I overheard, was unforgivable."

"How did you know that it was face value?" Jayne asks.

"I researched what they were saying. Everything was exact."

"Who has the condo now?" Joe asks.

"An investor came in. Everyone who was living there had to find somewhere else to live until they can settle everything." Sebastian says. "She moved everything out of her condo that she had for five years. I think it was that long."

"It was sad to hear about her bookstore burning down." Jayne says.

"Mark worked so hard on the floors and getting the shelves not only to code, but so that she can reach everything on them."

"My Mark?" Jayne asks.

"Your Mark." Jacob says. "He is extremely over protective of his Little Mermaid."

"Its nice to know that someone looks out for her." Rosetta says. "Wasn't the little mermaid's name Ariel?"

"Yes it is." Jayne says. "Mark would always say that it wasn't everyday that you would meet a girl named Sebastian." She looks around. "He always adored her."

"Did they ever date?" Jacob asks.

"No. He has always had a thing for Savannah. He has always looked out for Sebastian. He took her under his wing like she was his little sister. He always made it a point to make sure he knew where she was." Jayne says.

"How do you know that?" Sebastian asks.

"Edward and I didn't make it as a married couple but we always kept in touch about our boys. Justin lived with me more. Mark was pissed off about the divorce and he went to live with Edward. We arranged it that we would swap them every six months. Neither of them wanted that. Justin would go visit Edward and Mark but he would always come back to me for school."

"How is it that they don't remember meeting each other?" Rosetta asks.

"It was a Halloween party. They were both in costumes."

"He didn't notice her wheelchair?"

"She used a walker more back in those days. She was sitting on the floor with everyone else. She was an equal."

I look outside the window. I reach for Justin's hand. He steps closer to me. He kisses me on the lips when I look up at him.

"Do you think they are talking about us?" He asks.

"Its always possible. They are so proud of you and Mark." I say.

"No. I meant us. You and me."

"I don't know."

"Sebastian!" Seth says excitedly. "This is the best thing I have ever eaten." He takes another bite.

"We are going to have kick you out of the kitchen." Savannah says.

"You don't add salt to this?" He asks.

"No. The soy sauce is enough."

"You put onion powder in this too?" He asks.

"Shut up. You are giving out all my secrets."

"And did you use ginger?" Seth asks,

"You need to stop."

"No. I want to make this in the restaurant. I want you to make this. As a matter of fact lets make this in the New York one in a few days. Lets see how it goes over."

"I would love that." I tell him.

We sit down to a formally set table. Seth plates the food for everyone. He makes it look so pretty. Once everyone has a plate in front of them, there isn't a word spoken until the plates are empty.

Robert is the first one to say something. "That was the best dinner I have had in a long time." He looks at Seth. "No wonder why you have a five-star restaurant."

"I plated the food. I can't take the credit for making it. Sebastian made this. This is her recipe."

Robert looks at me. "My grandson will never go hungry."

Everyone laughs.

"What else do you make?" Jayne asks.

"Eggplant Parmesan." I say.

"Oh my god yes. It's the best." Savannah says.

"You will have to make that for us next time." Rosetta says.

"I made dessert too." I say.

"What did you make?"

"Chocolate peanut butter brownies. With peanut butter chips on top."

Robert smiles. "That's my favorite thing. Brownies." He says. He stands and leaves the the table. Then he comes back to the table holding mistletoe. He stands behind Rosetta and taps her on the shoulder. She looks up at him and he kisses her passionately.

"Dad." Jayne says laughing.

"No matter how old you are, you have to let the one you love know that she is the one and only." Robert says.

"That's so sweet." Savannah and I say together.

"Always be there for the one that you love." Robert says. "Seth do you have a significant other?"

"The little one with the pink hair that was here on Christmas. She is my girl friend."

"You should have invited her." Robert says.

"She is site seating with her nephew." Seth says.

"Jacob do you have a girlfriend?" Rosetta asks.

"Yes. She is actually one of Sebastian's friends. They went to school together. I met her on one of my cruises. She plays violin."

"Lindsey Gina?" Joe asks.

"Yes." Jacob says.

Joe looks at me. "You went to school with my niece?"

"Lindsey Gina is your niece?" I ask. "Yes we went to school together. She and I were band from playing in our final show at school. Our teacher thought that we were showboating." I laugh.

"Wait a second. You are the one that played the piano with her. I heard you. I saw the video she sent her dad." Joe says. "You are the concert pianist?"

"I am not a concert pianist." I say.

"You are really good. Do you still play?" Joe asks.

"Yes." Everyone says. I say nothing.

"Play something for us." Rosetta says. "No one plays my Baby Grand any more."

Savannah smiles. "You have a Baby Grand?"

"Do you play too?" Robert asks her.

"I play the violin and piano." She says.

"Did you go to college on a music scholarship too?" Joe asks.

"I did." She says.

"Did you two go to the same college?" He asks.

"No." We both say with a bit of sadness in our tones.

"Why not?" Rosetta asks.

"I stayed in state." I say. "My scholarship didn't include out of state schools."

"You must play for us." Rosetta says.

I sit at the piano and play Moon Light Sonata. When I finish that, I play the top part of Heart and Soul. I wait for anyone to jump in and play with me. Jacob joins me at the piano. When we finish. He kisses me on the head. He tells me in my ear that he loves me.

Savannah sits with me at the piano. "Do you remember our duet?"

"Always." I say.

"Play it with me." She says.

"We have to switch sides."

"Oh right." She says. She stands up. I scoot over to play the lower side of the duet. Savannah starts it off. We play it and when we finish, we hug each other.

"Does your friend Piper play too?" Jayne asks.

"Piper plays the violin." We sat together.

We sit and have brownies and cookies for dessert. We talk for a while. We go in the kitchen and we clean up everything. We leave the kitchen spotless. We leave it better than we found it.

I leave a card for them on the counter next to the coffee pot.

Thank you so much for having us. Astro and I will never forget your kindness. It was the best day that we have had in New York since we got here. I have loved your grandson, Mark since I met him when I was young. And I am blessed to have found Justin. He makes me a better person. He makes me feel happy and safe. Merry Christmas and best wishes for the happiest New Year.

All our love always,

Sebastian and Astro

~~~~~~~~~~

We all go into the resort. The clerk that greeted us on the first day we arrived approaches us. She looks at Sebastian. "Sir, we are going to need to use our banquet room for a wedding in two days."

"Why are you telling me?" He asks.

"There are still presents under Christmas trees in there."

"Oh that's right. We didn't open presents." He says. "We will move them immediately."

"Thank you." She says. She sticks her hand out and pets Astro under his chin. She looks at me. "I am so sorry for how you started this trip. I heard from some of the guest that this hasn't been a stellar trip for you."

"I have enjoyed my stay." I say with a smile. "I will be glad to go home."

"I wanted to apologize again for the way you started your trip."

"Thank you." I say.

She turns on her heal and walks away.

Matt, Tristian, Eric, Danny, Piper and Trix walk in the lobby from outside. Tristian and Danny run over to me first. They hug me.

Piper walks over and hugs all of us. "Did you have a nice day?' She asks sincerely.

"We had a great time. You were missed." I tell her.

"You all were missed too. We went to LEGO Land." She says.

I look at Danny and Tristian. "You went without me?"

They both hug me.

"It was so much fun." Danny says.

"I am glad you had fun."

"Piper made a lego guitar."

"Not a guitar. It's a violin." She says kissing him on the head.

Sebastian looks at everyone. "We still have presents left to open. Apparently we forgot about our Christmas."

"Lets get everyone else." Seth says.

"Amanda is the only one missing. She went back to Fort Lauderdale today. Her friend is having a baby tomorrow and wanted Amanda to be there for her."

"Awe, That's so sweet."

"We could ship all the presents home and open them together." I say.

He looks at me. "You would wait."

"Of course. We need to find a way to recreate this room, but yes I would wait so we can all be together. Maybe we can do Christmas at The Marina Beach."

Everyone agrees.

Justin and I sit on the couch in our room. We are snuggled into each other. He holds me while we watch a movie. A cheesy holiday movie is on the television. Astro is on the couch with us.

"Did you have a nice day?" Justin asks.

"I did." I say. "Your family is great."

"They really are."

"I hope that they didn't think I took you away from them."

"What?"

"You were in the kitchen with me when you should have been with your grandparents."

"I spent time with my grandparents too. We had private time together. My grandfather wanted to know all about you."

"He was really nice. And Joe was so much nicer once he found out that Lindsey and I are friends." I laugh. "It's a small world."

"It really is." Justin says. "I noticed that Jacob seemed upset when he first saw you. What happened?"

"Always the lawyer." I say.

"What happened?"

"I found something in a store and I bought it."

"Why would it upset him?"

"I will show you." I say. I get off the couch. I go into the bedroom and get the pin. I put it on my sweater. I go back by the couch.

"I can't believe you bought that." He says laughing.

"I think Oliver designed it."

"I can't believe you bought a golden shovel."

"Why?"

"My grandma has one and she was going to give it to you as a joke."

"I bought it as a joke."

He hugs me. "My grandma gave me something to give you."

"She gave you something to give me?" I smile. "Will I like it?"

"I hope that you will love it." He says. "It's a family heirloom." He stands and walks into the bedroom. Astro follows him. "Do you think he has to go out?" Justin asks.

There is a knock on the door. I go to the door and open it. Eric and Danny stand there.

"We are going to get ice cream. Can we take Astro with us?" Danny asks.

"I am sure that he would love that." I say with a smile. I look at Eric. "How did you know he had to go out?"

"I would say that he sent me a text message, but really its just a coincidence. Piper and I are going to take Danny and Tristian for ice cream and Danny asked if we can take Astro with us."

"Thank you." I say to Danny.

"I know." Danny says. "Only vanilla yogurt for him."

I hug Danny. "I love you."

"I love you too."

Eric notices the pin. "Owning it." He teases as he points at my pin.

I laugh. "I think my uncle designed it."

"You got that in the store down the street." Danny says.

"I did."

He looks up at Eric. "It was very expensive." He looks down at his feet.

"Danny, I can assure you that it wasn't that expensive." I tell him. "Let me get Astro ready." I say. "Come on in."

Danny looks at the television. "We were watching the same movie. Piper ruined it for us." He laughs.

"She told you the end so you could go get ice cream?" I ask.

"How did you know?"

"She used to do the same thing when we were your age. If she wanted to do something, she would tell us how the the movie ended just so we could go."

Eric smiles. "I love that about her." He looks at me. "Sometimes she tells the wrong ending."

I laugh. "I know." I put Astro's leash on him.

They take him with them. Danny runs back to give me another hug. "You know, we really missed you today."

"I missed you too." I tell him. "Tomorrow we are all going to be together."

"When do we go home?"

"In a few days."

"I wish we could all be together always." He says.,

Eric stands by the elevators. "Danny come on."

"Do you want us to bring you an ice cream?" Danny asks.

"That is so nice of you. If you do, Piper knows what I like." I hug him again. "Danny, thanks for being so great." I close the door after watching him walk to the elevators, take Astro's leash in one hand and Eric's hand in the other.

Justin comes back to the couch. He sits down. He is all showered and smells like aftershave and soap. When I hug him, I can't help but breath him in.

"Your dinner was the best chicken I have ever eaten. I usually don't like chicken." He kisses me. "But whenever you make that, I will eat it every time."

"I am glad that you liked it."

He takes a little box out of his pocket. He opens the box and takes my right hand. He slips the ring on my middle finger. "My Rosetta wants you to have this."

I look at the garnet ring on my finger. "Oh my god, this is beautiful." I look at Justin. "Why?"

"She adores you and Savannah."

"She just met us."

"My mom and dad divorced. My grandparents always kept in touch with my dad. He is forever the son that they always wanted. They were sad to see the marriage break apart."

"Why did it?" I ask.

"Its hard to really tell what happened. If you ask my mom, she tells one story. If you ask my dad he tells a different story. If you ask my grandparents they tell one that is half his and half hers. They stood by both of them. When my dad was dating Candy they thought that my mom would run back to him. She didn't."

"So your dad told them about me."

"My dad did. Mark did too. I didn't because I wanted to keep you as my secret."

"Can I call her to thank her for the ring?" I ask.

His phone rings. She is calling him. He answers the phone. "Hi Grandma."

"Sweetheart, she left me a note. She wrote me a thank you note for having her over." She gushes. "You know how much I love that."

"I know." He tells her. "I gave her the ring."

"Which one?"

"The garnet one."

"Oh perfect. That's one I wanted her to have."

"You know the pin you showed me?"

"Yes."

"She has one. She bought herself the exact pin that you showed me."

"When are you leaving?"

"In two days."

"Grandpa and I want to see all of you. The whole group of you before you go. And your aunts are coming in with your cousins."

"Should we hide the ring?"

"No. Justin, I don't ever want you to hide anything that I give you. I can give my stuff to anyone I fucking want to give it to."

He laughs.

"Don't laugh at me when I am upset." She says. "Listen, your grandpa and I are going on a date. I will call you in the morning."

"You are going on a date?"

"We go on dates every three or four days." She says.

"Enjoy yourselves."

"We won't be able to. Your mom and Joe are going with us."

Justin laughs again. "Grandma, I love you."

"I love you too."

"Kiss that girl for me."

Justin kisses me hard on the lips.

"Sloppy kisses." She says. "Love you baby."

"Love you too." We say together.

Our phones ping with text messages. They are from Piper and Eric. It says come join us. We put our jackets on and go down to the lobby.

Sebastian, Seth, and Jacob join us. Savannah and Mark step out of the elevator with Lindsey and Trix.

"What's going on?" Trix asks.

Matt comes running into the lobby. "Why did I get a nine-one-one text from my son? They were going for ice cream."

"Lets not freak out on until we know we need to." I say.

We leave and go down the street to the ice cream shop. When we get there there is a snowman contest going on. Piper runs over. She hugs me. She hugs Matt.

"Sorry we scared you. I didn't know he texted a nine-one-one alert until after he sent it. We wanted to have fun. We haven't had a lot of fun all together. Lets build a snowman." She says.

Savannah and I look at her. We start singing from Frozen. "Do you want to build a snowman? Doesn't have to be a snowman. Ok. Bye."

We all start laughing.

Piper starts singing Deck the Halls and everyone of us sing with her. We all have a lot of fun building snowmen. Astro even has fun eating the snow.

"Snow angels!" Danny says. "Can we all make snow angels?"

"I think that would be great." Eric says.

Danny throws himself back on the snow and starts making his snow angel. He jumps up and runs to Eric in tears.

"What's wrong?" Eric asks lifting Danny up.

"I didn't think about something."

"What?"

"Sebastian can't make a snow angel."

When the words are out of his mouth, Justin picks me up and puts me in the snow. I flail my arms while he moves my legs to make the dress.

"Look." Eric says. "She's making a snow angel."

Danny hugs Eric. "I didn't mean to be insensitive."

"Danny, you weren't."

With the help of Justin, I sit up. I roll a snowball in my hands and throw it at Danny. When it hits his jacket it explodes. Danny jumps down and this starts a snowball fight. We have so much fun.

We all return back to he hotel. I go to the front desk. "Hi is it possible to get a towel?"

"Right away." The clerk says. He retrieves a towel and hands it to me.

"Thank you." I say taking it. I go outside and dry Astro. "Foot." I say and he sits and gives me his front paw. "Good boy. Other one." He gives me the other paw. "Wow, you need a bath."

The clerk comes outside. "There is a pet store about two blocks up the road. I called and they are open. If you want to take him so that he doesn't catch a cold. It looked like you all had a lot of fun." He takes the towel and helps dry Astro. He reads Astro's name. "No shit." He says looking at me. "Your dog's name is Astro?"

"Yes."

"That's my dog's name." He says. "If you want, I will take him for you. They should have him washed and dried in an hour. I can bring him back."

"Thank you." I say. "My fiancé and I will take him. Thank you so much."

Chapter 27

The elevator doors open and we all get out in the lobby. There are two beautiful women standing at the counter asking for Mark and Justin Case. They hear them asking for them, so they walk ahead of us. The two young women jump into each one's arms.

We all go over by the café to wait for them. We don't want to invade. Savannah takes my hand and sits next to me. Piper sits next to us too.

"Do you think those are the cousins?" She asks.

"I hope that one of them is not a girlfriend from Christmases past." I say.

Eric sits with us too. "You doing ok?" He asks Savannah because she looks like she is ready to cry.

She blinks a few times. "I am ok."

We watch them look at us and then turn away to talk to Justin and Mark. Savannah grabs my hand and squeezes it. We hear the one laugh. Savannah lets my hand drop and runs out of the resort.

Mark watches her and takes off after her. He takes her in his arms and kisses her. She tries to pull away. He holds her tighter. "Stop. What's wrong?"

"I have been waiting for someone to show up and ruin what we have." Savannah says.

"Those two are my cousins. Jessica and Jennifer. Come inside and meet them."

She looks down at her finger. Not her ring finger but her middle finger on her right hand. She has the sapphire ring from Rosetta.

"My grandma wanted you to have this. No one is going to say a word. Looks might be exchanged but they will be very nice to you."

"And what about to Sebastian?"

"They will be equally as sweet to her." Mark kisses her. "Savannah, I have to go inside, I am freezing out here."

She laughs. "You don't like the cold?"

"We live in Florida sweetheart. This is too cold for me."

They come back in the lobby.

Jessica and Jennifer are still talking to Justin. He looks over at me a few times but then turns back to them.

Matt sits next to me with Tristian. I hug both of them. Matt hugs me tighter. "Who are those two?"

"I don't know. When he tells me he tells me." I say.

"You aren't jealous?"

"I don't have a reason to be jealous. There are always going to be women who greet him like that." I look at Savannah who is standing with them now.

"Shouldn't you be there with them?"

"If he wants me over there, he will ask me to join them."

"Are you sticking to that?" Matt teases.

"He is a big time lawyer. I am not going to get jealous."

Matt looks over. "Savannah sure as hell got jealous."

"Matt, I am not like that." I say. I hug Tristian. "You feeling ok?" I kiss him on the top of his head.

"I am doing ok." He says. He looks up at me. "We went into that big room and all the presents are gone."

I look at Matt and smile. "Santa swooped in and took them with him."

"Why?" Tristian asks.

"Because they weren't opened."

"Really?" He asks.

"No. We sent them home so we can all be together when we open them." I tell him.

"Where did Sebastian, Jacob and Seth go? They left early." Matt asks.

"Sebastian said he had something to take care of. Jacob and Seth went with him."

"What do you think that is all about?"

"Matt, they said they had to go, they went. I didn't ask. I don't have the right to ask."

"When they were customers in our bookstore a year ago, you didn't have the right to ask. Now, you are their sister. They should have told you." Matt looks over at Justin who is still standing with his cousins, Savannah and Mark.

I look over at them. "Ok, lets go." I say.

"What are we doing today?" Tristian asks.

"Just walking around the city." Matt says.

I want to be brave as I said I was but the longer Justin stands there with his family and my friend, I feel my heart breaking. I look over at where they are one more time before I take Astro outside. Matt and Tristian go with me. Piper, Eric and Danny come too.

We go into Central Park. We stick to the dog trail. I let Astro pull me along.

"She needs to tell him how she is feeling." Eric says.

"It amazes me how strong she is." Piper says.

"She acts strong." Eric says.

"Eric maybe you can answer a question that I am just dying to ask." He holds her hands.

"Why won't he tell her how he feels? Does he love her? Because if he is just stringing her along, I am going to ruin his life."

"Wow! Down kitty." He teases.

She laughs. "I am serious. Does he love her?"

"He does love her."

"Since we have been here its like watching a ping pong tournament. He is on. He is off. He is on."

"I know. I see it too."

Danny comes running over. "She needs help!" He yells. He takes off running. They run after him.

I am laying on my back with my feet up in the air because my wheelchair flipped over. Astro is sitting next to me whimpering.

Piper looks at me. "Are you hurt?"

I laugh. "No. I just need help."

Eric steps behind my head and lifts my wheelchair in the upright position. "You ok?"

"I am fine." I say. "I mean it. I am great." Astro jumps up on me. He puts his paws on my shoulders. "I am ok, buddy." I tell him. I pet his head.

Justin comes running over to us and takes me in his arms. He takes my face in his hands and looks at me. He runs his hands over my head.

"Justin! What are you doing?" I ask.

"I couldn't get to you. Are you alright?"

"I am fine. I didn't bang my head. I just flipped backwards. Astro jerked to go after an animal and I pulled back on the wheels."

He kisses me over and over on the lips.

I put my hands on his chest. I don't push him away. I just rest them on his chest.

"I am sorry." He says.

I put my finger on his lips. He kisses it. "I love you."

"Come meet my cousins."

"Sure."

"What's wrong?"

"Nothing."

"I sense something."

"Its nothing." I say.

"Would you tell me if there was?"

"Lets go meet your cousins." I say.

"Changing the subject."

I push away from him.

"Sebastian!" He yells after me.

Piper walks over to him. "You really don't know?" She says so matter-of-factly. "Are you sure you are a lawyer who can read people?"

"What?" He snaps.

"You stood there in the lobby with your back to her. To us. Savannah was there with all of you and your fiancé was left out of it. Left out of the family circle. She is too kind to ever say anything." Piper says. "Justin, I swear if you hurt her, I will ruin you."

"Piper!" He snaps. "Sometimes, I am at a loss."

"What are you talking about?"

"I don't know how to make her feel comfortable."

"Just treat her like you want her to be around."

"She likes to hide away."

"When you hide, no one can tell if you are hurt or not." Piper says. "She loves you."

"I know."

"She's not going to chase you."

"Maybe I want her to. Not all the time, but sometimes I feel like she doesn't want me."

There is a commotion that gets all of their attention. They all look around to see where I am. A guy dressed as a snowman is dancing with me. He takes my hands and dances with me. He tips me back like he is dipping me.

Everyone stands and watches. When he finishes the dance, he hugs me. "Sweetheart, give him a chance. He loves you. I know that look. I used to look at you like that when we were together. I love you."

I pull back and look at Trevor.

"Go to him. Start the dance with him. Don't let it stop." He says.

Justin walks over and the snowman reaches out his hand to him. Justin takes the snowman's hands. He dances with Justin. "Love her. She loves you. She is worth it. You are worth it."

Justin pulls back and dips Trevor. He kisses him on the snowman's cheek.

"Go to her." He laughs. "I have to be the fairy godfather."

They both laugh.

Jessica and Jennifer stand off to the side watching us. They look at each other. "I wish someone looked at me the way Justin looks at her." Jessica says.

"I know." Jennifer says.

"I hope that she will like us."

"I hope that we will like her."

"Why wouldn't we like her? She means a lot to Justin. He means a lot to her. We love him like he is our brother and we always want whats best for him." Jessica says.

"Lets go meet her." Jennifer says.

They run over to Justin and hug him. He hugs them. He holds my hand so that I can't leave. They both hug me. They both notice the ring that previously was their grandmother's. Jennifer takes my hand in her hand and raises it so she can see it.

"Grams gave you the ruby? It looks great on you." She says. She looks at Jessica. "I didn't have the heart to tell grams how much I hated this ring." She looks at me. "Did you get the sapphire one too?"

"No." I say.

She looks at Justin. "I am so happy to see the ring will stay in the family. She always wondered how she would give it to you."

Jessica looks at my left hand. "Oh my god! That is the most beautiful ring I have ever seen. Congratulations! Did you two set a date?"

"No." Justin says.

"I look forward to hearing when you do." She says. "Its so nice to meet you. We have heard a lot about you over the years. Mark would tell us all about you. We thought that your name was Ariel because he always referred to you as Little Mermaid. When he told us that your name is Sebastian, we knew that you were someone extremely special."

I look at them and smile. "Wait! You are Jess and Jenn?"

"Yes." They both say together.

"You were at my birthday party years ago."

"You remember us?" Jessica asks.

"Yes. You both were the sweetest people. You got me the best gift that year. You gave me a journal and the best colored pens. I used that journal religiously and those pens were my favorite ones. I looked in every store looking for them."

Justin looks at me and smiles. I smile at him. He leans forward and kisses me. "The journal that you wrote all about me in?" He whispers in my ear.

I feel the burn climbing up my cheeks. I pull him closer and kiss him. Jessica looks at us. "We are going for lunch. Do you want to join us?"

"Yes. I would love that." I say.

Justin puts his hand on my shoulder.

Savannah and Mark walk over with Piper and Eric. Everyone exchanges hugs. Jessica looks at Savannah's hand and notices the sapphire ring. Savannah pushes her hand into her pocket.

"Wear it and enjoy it." Jennifer says.

"If Gram gave that to Mark to give to you, she knows how much you mean to him." Jessica says.

"It really is one of the prettiest things I have ever worn." Savannah says.

"Just think, it goes with everything." Jessica says.

We all laugh.

"It matches your eyes." Jennifer says. "We are going to lunch. You want to go with us?"

"Yes."

Astro barks. "I should take him back to the hotel for a nap." I say.

"You are going to nap?"

"No. He needs one."

"He can nap where we are going. Bring him with us." Jessica says. "I remember this dog from the farm."

"Oh my god, the puppy that we were helping to train." Jennifer says.

"Small world." I say. "Its funny how small it is at times."

"Did you ever open that bookstore?" Jessica asks.

"It burned down." I say.

The two of them look at each other. They look at Justin. Jennifer takes her phone out of her pocket. She excuses herself from the group. "I will be right back." She says. She turns on her heal and then turns again almost like a ballerina would. She kisses me on the cheek. She turns again on her heal and walks away from us quickly.

"I hope she's ok." I say.

"Its her job. She has to check in while we are off gallivanting."

My phone rings. Seth calls me. He tells me that he wants us to come to his restaurant for lunch. He tells me to bring everyone who is with me and anyone else I want to grab. I laugh before hanging up the phone.

"Seth wants us to go to his restaurant for lunch. Would that be ok?"

"Sure." Jessica says.

"Can we bring Astro there?" Jennifer asks.

"Seth is my brother. Astro goes everywhere I go. They love him."

"They?"

"You will meet everyone when we get to the restaurant." Justin says.

My phone rings again. This time its Sebastian calling me. "Where are you?" He asks.

"Central Park." I tell him.

"I am coming to get you." He says.

"Ok."

The limo pulls up and we all get in the car. Astro lays on the seat next to me.

Sebastian sits next to me and hugs me tight. I hug him back. "Did you have a great time?"

"Yes." I say. "Where's Jacob?"

"He has something to take care of. He will meet back up with us at the hotel."

"Can I ask you a question?"

"Of course."

"Do you know Francesca? I mean, did you know her before we met her up here?"

"I don't know."

'I don't know where I know her from, but I know that I have met her before. The only thing was that she gave another name."

"You are sure?"

"Positive." I tell him.

Savannah looks at the two of us. "She does seem very familiar. I know that our paths have crossed a time or two."

"We will look into it."

"Is Jacob mad at me?" I ask.

"No. Of course not. Why would he be mad?"

"Its just the last couple of days, he has been avoiding me."

"Not intentionally." Sebastian says.

"Your lives got a shit load of drama when you met me. I bet you think—"

"NO." Sebastian says. "We don't think that at all. We wish that we could bring more happiness to your life."

"I know I cry a lot, but I swear I am happy to have found all of you." I tell him.

He takes me in his arms and hugs me tight.

We get to the restaurant. I get out of the car and into my wheelchair. I take Astro off to the side so he can do his business. I turn to go into the restaurant when he finishes. Francesca is blocking the door. She looks at me.

"I want to talk to you." She says.

"About what?"

"My mom won't talk to me. She told me that I am wrong about you."

I just look at her. I am grateful when the doors open and Seth walks outside. "What's taking so long? Did Astro get cold feet?" He asks.

Astro is wearing dog shoes. He hates them but they protect his feet when we do big walking.

Seth looks at Francesca. "What are you doing here?"

"I wanted to talk to all of you."

"Not today. Today is about celebrations. So if you don't mind, you need to go." He says. He steps behind me and pushes my wheelchair into the restaurant.

She comes inside. She looks around. "Oh my god, this is beautiful."

Seth walks over to his day manager. "Get rid of her." He says.

She looks at Seth. "I am on it." She looks at Francesca and then looks at Seth. "Do you know her?"

"She is my brother's cousin."

"Not your cousin?"

"No." He says.

"What does she want?"

"To upset my sister. Its not happening again." Seth says.

"Like I said, I am on it." She walks over to Francesca. "Hi, I heard from the owner that you are a VIP guest. Please come with me." She says.

Francesca walks with her. The manager walks her to a side door that looks very elegant. She opens the door and when Francesca walks through the opened doors, the manager slams the door behind her. She walks back over to Seth and notifies him that the issue has been taken care of.

We sit around a large table and everyone is involved with conversations. Danny sits next to me. He puts his head on my shoulder and within minutes of him reading a book he falls asleep.

"Does he do that in school?" Eric asks.

"Sometimes. Not always. It depends on the day that we have. If we are super busy with education stuff in the morning, then they are all tired. I let them read just to keep them quiet. If they fall asleep, better for me." I laugh.

"Are you going back to teaching when we go home?"

"I think I will."

"Danny and Tristian are concerned that whomever takes over for you, will be mean to Danny."

"I don't know if I will be there full time, but I will be there. I will make sure that nothing happens to them. I love them."

"They love you." Piper says. "Mr. Chatterbox never stops talking about how great he thinks you are." She leans in and kisses my cheek. "I know the truth."

"Pipes!" I say.

"Have you seen Lindsey lately?"

"Not in a few days."

"I know she is planning to tour again." Piper says.

"She told me that too."

"Did you ever tell her that you went to see her preform in like seven cities?"

"She knows about four cities." I say.

"Whats wrong?" Piper asks.

"I am just thinking that we are going to go home soon and I can't return to my house until January tenth. I am ready to go home. I am ready to just relax. I want to find out whats happening on the rebuild of the bookstore." I look around the room. Again Jennifer and Jessica are standing off to the side talking to Justin. They have their heads together. I look back at Piper.

"I know you a long time, girly. I know what you are thinking."

"I am not thinking anything." I tell her.

"Go to him. Grab him. Kiss him. Sometimes you have to make the effort too."

"He's with his family." I say.

"You are going to be the best part of his family." Eric says. "Go to him. Just take his hand. Take his hand, squeeze it, let it go and run out of the restaurant."

I look at him and smile. "I like the way you think."

"I am your step-brother." He says and kisses me on the cheek.

I take a drink of beer. Its Eric's drink.

He smiles. "Liquid courage always helps." He says.

"Just in case I don't say it later, I love you all very much." I tell them.

"We love you too." Piper says. "Go make us proud."

I push away from the table and make my way to Justin. I take his hand in my hand. He looks at me.

"I have been waiting for you." He says.

"I didn't want to interrupt." I tell them.

"You can always interrupt." Justin says.

"We were just telling Justin that we have two extra tickets for a Broadway show if you would like to go with us." Jessica says.

"Which one?" Justin asks.

"Come on, we told you already." Jennifer says.

"I haven't heard of that one." I tease.

We all laugh.

I look over at Savannah who is sitting on Mark's lap. She normally doesn't do that in public. Justin looks at me and takes my hand. I look at him.

"Have you spoken to her?"

"Not recently. I don't want to." I say. "I love her too much to fight with her here."

"That's one fight I would pay to watch." Piper says.

I turn and she hugs me.

Seth clinks a fork on a glass. "Hi can I get everyone's attention please?" Everyone looks at him. "I would like to take this time to raise our glasses to family and friends who are family too."

"Cheers!" Trix yells. "I love you, boo."

"I love you too." He says.

We all raise our glasses and say cheers.

"The lunch we are having today is my sister's recipe. I would like all of you to write on the postcards how you liked or disliked the meal. Be honest." Seth says.

The room is quiet as everyone eats every morsel of food. Everyone writes on the postcards what they think. Then the murmurs start. Everyone brags about how good the food was.

Trix walks over and hugs me. "The double cooked chicken stir fry. You gave your recipe away?"

"Not exactly." I say.

"This tastes almost exactly to what you make back home." She hugs me. "When you made that for my dad when he got sick, he ate the whole thing and loved every bite of it."

I laugh. "Your dad just likes me."

"You know that he loves you. But you also know how picky he is about what he eats."

Justin takes my hand. "This is delicious."

"I know. Its very good. It was inspired by what I made, but I didn't make this."

He kisses me. "I love you." He says against my lips.

Jacob walks into the restaurant. He hugs Sebastian first. They talk for a few minutes. He finds Seth and hugs him. They also talk for a few minutes. Then he comes to find me. He takes me in his arms and hugs me.

"I am not mad at you." He says. "I have been busy. I needed to take care of stuff while we are here in New York." He hugs me again. "We are not going to fly home, we are going to take a boat home."

"Tell me you didn't sell your fleet." I say.

He looks at me. He looks away at Sebastian.

"You sold them so that you could give me the money that Larry owes me?"

He hugs me. "We will talk about this later."

"I love you." I tell him.

We stay in the restaurant for a while more. There isn't a harsh word between any of us there. Justin takes my cell phone off the table and stands next to me. He kisses me on the lips and snaps a selfie of us. Trix walks over and takes my phone from him and she snaps a bunch of pictures.

We look at her and her normally hot pink hair is now the most beautiful dirty blonde shade. She looks beautiful. I take her hand and she takes selfies with me. Piper and Savannah jump in the pictures with us. Justin takes the phone and snaps pictures of us.

Lindsey walks over. "Are you all doing this without me?" She asks. She hugs me tight.

"Where the hell have you been?" I ask her playfully.

"You know, someone has bills to pay." She laughs. "When we get back to Florida, I have to find a place to live. My sister has to move."

"I have a bedroom with your name on it always." I tell her.

"I couldn't impose."

"You never do. You are always welcome in my house. We have been friends for so long."

"Thanks. Can I tell my brother that he can pack up my stuff?"

"Yes. And you are welcome anytime for as long as you want."

Jacob walks over and grabs her from behind. He spins her around and kisses her on the lips. "Did you hear anything about the new job?"

She kisses him. "They picked another violinist." She says.

"I am sorry to hear that."

"She and I compete a lot of times for the same jobs. They usually try to alternate between the two of us. They picked her this time." She says it with a smile on her face. "Now I can spend time with all of you. I will play local jobs. I have a long standing job with the Miami symphony. I will just sit in with them when they need me."

Seth walks over and takes Trix in his arms. He kisses her. Then he gets down on one knee and takes her hands in his. She looks at him. Her knees buckle and he jumps up to support her. He stands with her leaning against him. He opens the ring box. "Trix, will you marry me?"

She turns in his arms and jumps up. "Yes." She says.

He slips the ring on her finger. "I love you."

"I love you." She tells him.

Savannah walks out of the main room. She looks around for Mark but doesn't see him anywhere.

Mark sits next to me. "Can I talk to you?"

"Of course." I tell him.

"I love her. I have for years. I am not ready to propose to her."

"Then don't."

"I feel like she is pressuring me. I want to marry her. I see my life with her, but I don't have a ring."

"Mark, you are one of the best people I know in my life. You have always been wonderful. When you are ready it will happen. Until then, she has to wait."

Piper sits next to Mark. "I agree with what Sebastian just told you. If you aren't ready, you aren't ready. She loves you. She can wait."

Mark looks at Piper. "Just do me a favor, don't get engaged for New Years."

She laughs. "I can't promise anything. If it happens, I won't flaunt it."

"Flaunt it." Lindsey says. "Sing it on the mountaintops." She looks around and sees Savannah off in a distance crying. "Can I go slap her?"

Piper and I look at Lindsey. "No." We both laugh.

"You two are no fun." She says. She looks at me. "She cried like that when you got that scholarship and she didn't."

I look at her. We weren't friends then. I didn't know that anyone noticed Savannah's flair of jealousy.

"I saw it." Lindsey says.

"We got it into the biggest fight over that." Piper says. "I didn't talk to her for months."

I look at Piper. "I am speechless."

We laugh.

Justin walks over to us. "Whats going on?"

"Girl moment." Piper says.

"And you allowed Mark to be apart of it?" Justin asks.

"Well at heart, he has a girly spirit." Piper says.

We all laugh.

Trix walks over and shows us the ring. It is amazing. It fills her thin finger like it was made just for her. It sparkles and catches the light as she moves her hand.

"Congratulations!" I say.

"I always wanted to have a sister." Trix says. "Now I get you as mine."

We hug.

"My dad called and told me that when I get home, my apartment is going to be redone. I need to find a place to stay for a week or more." Trix says.

"I have a guest room." I say.

"You will be able to go home when we get home?" She asks.

"I am going home when we get home." I tell her.

"I may take you up on the room." She says. "You are closer to work than Seth."

"Oh thank you." I say.

"No. I didn't mean it like that." She says.

I take her hand in my hand. "I know." I tell her.

She hugs me. She looks over and sees that Savannah is still off by herself crying. "Can I go over and punch her in the face?"

"They wouldn't let me do it." Lindsey says.

We all laugh.

Savannah turns and looks at us. She walks over slowly. "Are you making fun of me?"

"Savannah, why would we be making fun of you?" I ask.

She walks away from us again.

Piper takes my hand. "Hold me back." She says. "I want to deck her right now."

"Just leave her alone. She needs to dwell on the situation." I say.

"And here we thought it was going to be a drama-free day." Trix says.

We all hug each other. Music plays from the speakers and we start dancing. We take our glasses off the table and clink them together.

Mark finds me later that day in the library of the resort. He sits next to me and then stands up and hugs me. I hug him. We hold each other tight for a few long moments.

He sits down. "I love Savannah."

"I know you do." I tell him.

"The way she acted today, I was embarrassed."

"We were too."

"Listen, I know she is your best friend, but has she always been like that?"

"Actually, yes. That's why Piper keeps things from me. Whenever one of us or two of us had boyfriends and Savannah didn't she would act like that. Cry and carry on until her mom would go find one of the neighborhood boys. She would pay them to take her to a movie and out for ice cream."

"She isn't happy for you?"

"She is as long as she has someone too. And she is a step ahead."

"I won't marry her like this." Mark says.

I don't say anything.

"How do you deal with her?"

"When I need her, she comes through for me. She always has. She loves you. She doesn't want to rush you into anything. She is happy for Piper and me. When Seth proposed to Trix, that threw her."

"Whats going on with you and Justin?"

"We take one step forward and three steps back." I say. "Sometimes I feel like he doesn't think he's made the right choice."

"Oh, don't say that. He loves you."

"I love him." I rub my fingers over the ring. "I just feel like maybe he is rushing into things and might not think that he is, but maybe he is."

"He just wants to go home and be back to normal. He wants to be able to go to your house and spend time with you without anyone hovering."

I look at Mark. "My house is going to be full. Trix is going to move in with me for a while and so is Lindsey."

"But you have your own room." He says.

"Of course."

"And you have that private living room."

"True." I laugh. "We can always sneak off to the bookstore."

"We will rebuild it." We hug each other.

Savannah gasps loudly. "I knew it."

I look at her. "You knew what?"

"That you would go after Mark."

Piper walks into the library. "Savannah, what the fuck are you talking about? Sebastian is not going after Mark. She is head over heals in love with her fiancé. You know that." She stands with her hands on her hips. "If anyone is ruining your relationship with Mark, its you. You are acting so jealous. Your best friend got engaged. Deal with it."

Candy walks into the library with my mom. The two of them put their hands on Piper's shoulders and Savannah's shoulders and push them into the room and close the door. Candy looks at Savannah. "I am stunned at how you are acting."

"Mom!" She says and hugs her.

"Come talk to me." Candy says. She looks at all of us. "Excuse us."

When they walk out of the room, Piper puts her hands up. "Go cry to mommy." She says.

Mom hugs Piper. She hugs my mom back. Mom looks at me. "I have some news."

I look at her.

"Peter and I are going to live in London for a year. We leave right after the new year."

I feel like my stomach twists. Somehow I don't let my feelings show. I go to her and hug her. "I am sure that your family would love to have you and Peter with them for a whole year. That's great." In my heart I am crying like a child who just got her finger slammed in a door.

"We can spend New Years together." She says.

"You are going to be here?" I ask.

"No. We are going to be with his children."

Again I feel like I have been punched in the stomach. I feel myself getting lightheaded. Its like Justin knows that I need him. He comes running into the library and takes me in his arms. He lifts me out o my wheelchair and leaves the library carrying me. I hug him. He walks over to the bar and sits me on a pub seat. He stands in front of me.

"She's going to London for a year."

"I know. Peter was telling Eric that he is signing over executive power to Eric for a year. I knew I had to find you."

"She never thinks of me. She's the only parent I have and she never thinks of me." I tell him.

He takes me in his arms and holds me.

Peter sits at a table in the corner of the bar watching the two of us. He sees Justin wiping tears from my eyes. Peter watches Justin kiss me. He watches us talking to each other and can not hear what we are saying, but he watches Justin talk and me smile happily.

He gets up and leaves money on the table. He walks over to us. He puts his hand on Justin's shoulder. "What's going on over here?"

"Justin, Astro and I are flying home tonight." I say.

"Oh it was my understanding that you were going to sail home."

"I want to go home immediately. I am ready for this holiday to be over. Its had a lot of ups and downs." I look at him. "I hope that you and my mom will have a happy new year spent with your children and then in London."

"She told you that we are spending New Years with my children?"

"Yes." I say.

"Excuse me." He says kissing me on the cheek. He leaves us. He comes back quickly. "Don't go until I see you." He walks away quickly.

I look at Justin. "Can you get my wheelchair so I can take Astro out and then go upstairs and pack."

We go to the elevator. Jacob is coming out of it. He walks over to us. "I heard that you are leaving. I really want you to go home with us. Sail home with me. Please don't leave without us."

"Jacob, I am ready to go now. I want to be done with this trip." I tell him.

"We can leave tomorrow. We all want to do one more thing together with all of us. Something very special. Something that I know. I hope that you will like. Please just give me until tomorrow."

"Tomorrow either way, I am going home." I say.

"Ok." He says. He hugs me.

"My mom is going to London for a year." I say. "She doesn't even care that I want her to stay here. I need her." Jacob holds me tighter and Justin holds me too while I cry.

Sebastian walks over. He rushes over with Trix. "Are you alright?"

"My mom is going to London for a year." I say. I swat at the tears that run down my cheeks. "I want to go home."

Jacob looks at Sebastian. "We are set to leave tomorrow. If everyone is ready to leave tonight, we can get clearance and leave tonight.

"Lets stick to the plan and leave tomorrow." Sebastian looks at me. "There is still one more thing I want to share with you before we all leave here."

I look at him. I try to smile but the tears that are brimming win the battle and pour down my face.

"We can share our mom with you. She loves you. You are still going to be able to be in touch with your mom." Jacob says.

"She is just so selfish." I say.

She walks over and and taps me on the shoulder. "Let me tell you how selfish I am. My father is in the hospital. He may not live to see the new year. That is why we are going."

"Your father is climbing the mountains in the Alps. Grandpa text messages me every other day about his trip."

"My father text messages you daily?" She asks. "When did that start?"

"When he came into my bookstore."

"He was here visiting?"

"He was with his beautiful girl friend."

"Why didn't you tell me that you saw my dad?"

"My bookstore burned down the next day. I was a little preoccupied." I tell her. "Its not like you care."

Mom looks at me. "I do care? Don't tell me I don't care."

"I found out that I have a brother. You left town. My bookstore burned down. You left town. I can't go home to my house until January. You are going to London for a year." I say on choked sobs.

Sebastian puts his hand on my shoulder. "You and your friends can stay with me in my house until your house is ready." He looks at me. "You know I have the room."

Justin takes my hand in his hand and squeezes it. He kisses me on the head. "I love you." He whispers in my ear. "You have a wealth of people who will take care of you. We want to."

"I love you too." I tell him and kiss him passionately.

Mom gasps. "I didn't raise you to kiss publicly."

I bury my face in Justin's chest. He puts his head next to mine. "Hug me." I tell him. He does and I laugh quietly until I can't contain it anymore. I laugh until my sides hurt. Justin laughs with me.

"Are you laughing at me?" Mom demands.

I can't stop laughing.

Sebastian laughs too. He looks at me. "What are we laughing at?"

Justin just holds me tighter to him.

Mark walks over. "What's going on?"

"Kissing shaming." I say laughing.

"Young lady! Stop this." Mom says.

This pisses me off. I finally gain my composure. "You always kissed men in public places. My piano recitals. My winter concert. Any time you got a chance to kiss a guy you did it in front of me anywhere we were." I leave the area. I go upstairs and pack my stuff.

Chapter 28

I open my eyes and feel sick to my stomach. We have been on the ship for days. The ship rocks as I get in my wheelchair. I get dressed quickly and rush out of the room in need for fresh air. When I get out of the room, Piper holds the back of my wheelchair. She looks as green as I feel. Savannah comes out of her room. She takes Piper's arm.

"This is the worst ship that I have ever been on. If we don't get off soon, I am going to-" Piper starts. The three of us vomit.

Jacob comes running over to us. "We have been met with a freak storm. Its best if you stay in your rooms."

"I can't breath in my room." I say.

"I have to get off." Savannah says. She vomits again causing Piper, Jacob and me to follow her and throw up as well.

Seth walks over. "Lets get you back in your room." He says to me.

"I can't breath in there." I say.

Justin walks over. He takes me out of my wheelchair and carries me to the side of the boat that is not being overwhelmed by high speed winds. "Just close your eyes and breath in the fresh air. You are safe. I have you."

"I can't find Astro."

"He is with Mark."

"Justin, I have to get off of the ship. I feel like I am going to die."

"You are not going to die."

Jacob walks over to us. Sebastian is with him. "We have been talking and we are going to airlift you ladies off the ship. We have to move fast because Piper is pregnant." Sebastian says it and I jerk my head up. The movement makes me dizzy. I feel the bile rise in my throat. I swallow hard. Sebastian looks at me. "You are really green." He says.

"I can't take another moment of this."

"I thought you worked on boats." Sebastian says.

"I did. I did it for a year. It was wonderful. I need to get off of this ship immediately." I say. "Why won't he dock?"

Jacob walks over. "We will be docking soon. In about an hour and a half." He says.

"I can't take it. I haven't been on my feet in days. When I try to stand up, I feel the sway of the ship." I say.

Justin is still holding me in his arms. Sebastian gets on his knees in front of Justin. Justin puts me on my feet and holds me so that I am supported completely. Sebastian holds me too. I hold on to the railing too. The wind blows my hair over Justin's shoulder.

The ship rocks with the high waves. Justin loses his balance. Sebastian grabs the two of us before we all fall over. Justin steadies himself and lifts me in his arms Sebastian supports the two of us as we make our way back into confines of the ship.

The second we are back in the confines of the ship, I feel my stomach roll and I heave. I feel my cheeks heat and I start to sweat. My head rolls on Justin's shoulder and I pass out.

"Oh shit!" Justin says and sits on the floor with me in his arms.

"Come on, we will take her to her room." Sebastian says.

"She said she could've breath in there." Justin says.

Sebastian goes to the cabin that I am staying in. When he opens the door, he smells a chemical oder. He closes the door and runs to find Jacob. "She passed out." He says.

"Sebastian, something is so wrong. I can't steer the fucking ship." Jacob says. He grabs the radio and calls for help.

Coast guard boats surround the ship that we are on. Tug boats surround us too. They have tires on them and they take the hit from the ship that stops it dead. The coast guard takes command of the ship and get all of us off. They medically treat Savannah, Piper, and me.

Justin never lets me go. He sits with blankets over him which makes him sweat, but I am shivering cold.

Danny sits next to Justin and Eric. "She looks really bad." Danny says.

"She's going to be ok." Eric tells his son.

Piper walks over. "We have never been that sick on a boat. None of us. We worked on boats for a full year. I mean we worked on two ships during hurricane season. There were ten to twelve foot waves and we didn't get sick." She says.

Eric puts his hand on her stomach. "That can't help any." He says.

She puts her hand on top of his hand. She smiles brightly. "Well I was never in this condition."

Danny looks at both of them. "What's going on?" He asks.

Piper looks at Eric. They both look at Danny and then back at each other. Eric takes Danny in his arms. "Piper and I are going to have a baby." He says softly.

Danny turns in Eric's arms and hugs his dad. Then he launches himself at Piper. "Is it a sister? I want a sister."

Piper hugs Danny. "We don't know yet. We won't know for a while."

"I want a sister." Danny says again. He looks at both of them again seriously. "Are you going to marry us?" He asks Piper.

"I am going to marry you." She says to Eric and Danny. "But your dad has to ask me first."

Danny looks at Eric. He is still in Piper's embrace. "You didn't give her the Christmas present?"

Piper looks at Eric.

Eric looks at Piper and smiles. "I have a ring."

She looks at him. "Whenever you ask, I am ready." She says. The ship rocks and she turns green. She stands quickly and rushes to the side of the boat and vomits. Eric jumps up and runs to her.

Danny sits next to Justin and me and puts his head on Justin's shoulder as he covers his ears with his hands. He looks at me. "Is she going to wake up soon?"

Justin looks at Danny. "She is just sleeping."

"She passed out."

"She woke up, but the medics gave her something to sleep. She's ok."

"She's shivering."

Justin looks at me and then at Danny. "I know."

An hour later, we are back on dry land. I sit in my wheelchair and I take Astro's leash. I buckle it into my seatbelt and then I take off as fast as I can so that Astro is running next to me. He trots with such beauty to him. He sits and puts his head on my lap. I pet him and he jumps up to put his paws on my shoulders. I bury my face in his chest.

Justin walks over and Astro side steps on his back legs and puts his paws on Justin's shoulders. He licks Justin's face. I take Justin's hand in mine.

"I am so glad to be off that boat."

There are police officers surrounding the area. "We need everyone to vacate the area. We think the vessel is going to bl—" he never finishes what he is saying. The ship blows up.

We all huddle with each other. Jacob looks at it and crumbles to the ground. I put my hand on his shoulder. He goes on his knees and hugs me. Astro flips himself over on Jacob.

"Oh my god, I could have killed all of you." He says.

"This is not your fault." Sebastian says to him.

A police officer walks over. "Who owns the ship?"

"The owner is in Miami, we are just bringing it to him." Jacob says.

"Son, you didn't do anything wrong." Another officer says. "You saved everyone because you called the coast guard for help. You got everyone off."

"We only got off because my sister and her friends were so sick."

"Well then, thank them. But you saved their lives." The officer says. He walks away and then turns back. "The woman in the wheelchair, is she single?"

We all look at him.

"I am engaged." I say.

"What a shame. I would sweep you off your feet in a heartbeat." He says.

I take Justin's hand in my hand. "Thank you."

Savannah walks over. She looks at all of us. She looks at me. "Can I talk to you?"

"Of course." I say.

Piper walks over with Danny. "Sebastian, can we talk to you?" She asks.

"Yes." I say.

Piper looks at Savannah. "Do you mind if I take her first?"

Savannah looks wounded. "Are you mad at me?" She asks Piper.

"If you know what is good for you, don't talk to me until we are home and after I have consumed a few bottles of wine." Piper says. "By the way, I am pregnant."

I look at Savannah and then at Piper. Savannah looks at the two of us. She looks at me. "You knew?"

"She found out before we were pulled off the boat." Piper says. "Savannah, I am ashamed of you."

Savannah walks away with her head held high.

I go with Piper.

"You think I am wrong?" Piper asks me.

"No. I didn't say that."

"We are going to fly home." Piper says. "I have to get back to work. Eric has to go over stuff at work too and Danny wants to enjoy his presents that he really never got a chance to play with."

"Justin and I are going to fly home too." I say.

Justin comes over. "We are in North Carolina. We are going to rent a van and drive home."

"Ok. But can we get home tonight or tomorrow?" I ask.

"Tomorrow." Justin says.

Piper looks at us. "Peter has supplied us with a private plane. We can all fly home and be there in two hours."

"I am flying home." I say.

Justin looks at me. "Flying it is." He agrees. "I will go tell everyone." He looks at Piper. "Will we all be able to go together?"

"It seats thirty people." Eric says. "There will be plenty of room."

Jacob walks over. He hugs me. "I am so sorry." He says.

I wrap my arms around him and hold him tight. "It wasn't your fault."

"I should have had it inspected before we all got on it." He says hoarsely.

"Its not your fault." I say again.

"They are going to investigate." He says.

"They need to. Its standard. They don't suspect you of anything wrong."

Eric looks at everyone. "I am going to check on the plane." He puts his hand on Jacob's shoulder. "It is a big expense."

Jacob looks up and there is no hiding the tears in his eyes. Eric pulls him to his feet and hugs him. Seth and Sebastian join them. Seth takes my hand and doesn't let go. Jacob sobs at what could have happened. Sebastian takes him in his arms and holds his younger brother.

"I am sorry." Jacob says.

Peter comes running over he takes Jacob and hugs him. "We have been trying to track you all down. Someone set up a death trap in the ship that if the boat went too fast in speed or hit high waves it would explode."

"How do you know this?" Sebastian and I ask together.

"Someone? Was it Larry?" Seth asks.

"What are you doing here?" Eric and I ask Peter.

"Where is my mom?" I ask.

"She went to London for a year. I will be joining her, but I wanted to make sure that my children all made it home safely."

I look at him. "Your children live—"

"You and Eric." Peter says. "Eric is like my son. Danny is my grandson." He looks at me. "You are my daughter. I do have my own children, but you are my children too."

I look at him and feel the tears stinging my eyes. Peter takes me in his arms.

"I am not your dad, but I have adored you for years and I am going to marry your mother. I will be there for you always." He hugs me tighter. "Sebastian, I know that your mom has missed a lot of things in your life. I was at your graduation from college." He kisses the top of my head.

I look up at him. "I know." I cry. "Thank you for loving me and my mom."

"Sweet girl, I have always loved you."

"I love you too." I cry.

421

"Let me get you home and make sure that all of you are safe. Then I will leave to go be with your mom in a few weeks." He kisses the top of my head. "I want you to know that if you need me at any time, I will fly home immediately."

"You would do that?"

"Always." He says.

We all go to the executive air port and board the plane to go home. The plane touches down in Boca Raton. A few cars wait for us. Peter gets in one car. He gets out and walks over to me.

"Princess, your house is ready for you to return to."

I hug him.

"And if you want to go check out your bookstore, I recommend that you do it tomorrow or once you are settled in."

I hug him again. "Thank you so much for everything."

He kisses me on the head. "I will be here for a few weeks. Lets have dinner tomorrow."

"The Marina Beach will be opened for dinner tomorrow." Seth says. "Please come join us."

"I will be there." Peter says. He hugs all of us before he gets back in the car that was waiting for him. "I love you all." He says from the rolled down window.

"Love you too." I yell as the car pulls away.

We all stand at the executive airport with each other. It's the first time in weeks that are separating to go back to our own lives. Savannah walks away first. She turns back and runs to me. She hugs me.

"I will call you in a few days." She says.

"No matter what, I love you." I tell her.

"I love you too." She tells me. She looks at Piper.

"Give her a few days." I tell Savannah.

Piper takes Savannah in her arms and hugs her. "I love you. I am mad at you but I always love you."

Mark takes Savannah's hand and they get in a car.

Justin kisses me on the lips. "You coming?"

"Yes." I say. "Come Astro."

A half hour later, I unlock the front door to my house. Astro runs ahead of me and gets his favorite toys. I go in the house followed by Justin. He carries my stuff in my room. Lindsey and Trix stand in the kitchen.

I look at both of them. "There is a room over there." I point to the left. "And there is a second room over there." I point to the right. "Make yourselves at home."

They both walk off together. Lindsey picks the room on the left. She walks out of the room and finds me. She kisses me on the cheek. "Thank you for letting me stay here."

"As long as you need." I tell her.

Trix comes out of the other room. She is dressed for work. Her uniform makes her look so official. "I have to go to work for a few hours." She says. "When I get back, I will be quiet."

"Not for my sake." I tell her. "Besides Astro will alert us that you are home." I tell her. "When you get back, the food in the refrigerator is there for all of us. Feel free to eat anything. It seems that Peter has stocked it for all of us."

Trix leaves for work. Lindsey goes into her room. I go into the kitchen and go through the mail. I pay the bills that need to be paid.

I feed Astro. I take him for a long walk around the neighborhood. When we go past Justin's house, we hear Bob Cat screaming his loud meows. Justin walks out the front door and Bob shoots out the door. He jumps on my lap and rubs his face in my face. He flattens himself on my lap. I pet him.

Justin walks down the steps of the house. He kisses me. "How are your roommates?"

"Trix had to go to work for a few hours. Lindsey was so tired. She went in her room and she was sleeping before I left."

"Its nice of you to open your home to two women who are going to be related to you soon enough."

"I am glad that I have roommates. I love my house, but I am just glad I don't have to live there alone. At least for a while." I say.

"Have you spoken to Savannah?"

"Not since I have been home."

"Mark and her broke up."

I look down at Bob who is curled up on my lap. Then I look at Justin. "I am sorry to hear that."

"He is furious."

"I don't blame him." I whisper.

"Savannah went to go stay with her mom."

"I think she sent me text messages but I didn't read them." I look at Justin. "Are you going to go back to work?"

"In a few days. I will go back on Monday." He says. He sits on the grass and takes Astro in his arms. "Are you going back to work?"

I look at him. "Not teaching." I say. "I will miss the children and the people that I work with but I am going to get my bookstore back up and running."

"Its nice to be home."

"Its nice to be home." I agree.

"When do you want to get married?" He asks.

I look at him. "Is tomorrow an option?"

"I am being serious." He says.

"So am I. I would marry you tomorrow."

He looks up at me again. "What about children?"

I look at Astro and then at Bob Cat who is sleeping on my lap. "I can have children." I say softly.

"Do you want any?"

"At least two." I tell him.

"Why so quiet?" Justin asks.

Mark walks out of the house and runs down the driveway and hugs me. I welcome the hug. I bury my face in his chest. He whispers in my ear. "I will tell him." I shake my head and he just holds me tighter. "I love you always."

"Me too." I tell him. "Always."

Justin watches us. "Secrets." He says under his breath but loud enough for us to hear him.

Mark looks at Justin. He takes Bob off my lap. He kisses me on the lips but not romantically. "I always love her. I always will love my Little Mermaid."

"I will always love you too." I tell Mark.

Justin stands up. "Will you tell me about your relationship?"

We go back to my house. Astro runs into Lindsey's room and jumps on the bed with her. She is sleeping across the bed. Her bare feet hang off the edge. Astro curls up on the bed with her and puts his head on the spare pillow. Classical music fills the room. She taps her fingers on Astro like she is playing the piano.

Justin and I go into the private den. He looks around the room because he has never been in here before. He looks around the room and sees pictures hanging on the walls. He walks around and looks close. He looks at me.

"How do you have pictures from our trip hanging on the walls? We just got back."

"I didn't take these." I tell him. "It's the first I am seeing them too."

"How are they here?" He looks at one. He is holding me in his arms. It appears that I am standing in front of him. We are kissing. It was at Sebastian's Christmas party.

"So you want to know about Mark and my relationship?" I ask not looking at him. "Like Ivan and Trevor, Mark will always be in my life. I have loved them and I always will." I still don't look at Justin. I take a pillow off the couch and hold it to my chest. "Your brother has always been wonderful to me. He has always — always loved Savannah." My words catch in my throat and that was not my intentions.

"Are you sad that he is with her?" He asks.

I turn to face him. "I am so excited to have you." I say honestly.

"Are you sad that he is with her?"

"They have been my family for so long, if they are meant to be together, I am happy for them. But I have to say— I wish they were with other people. When it didn't work out with her mom and your dad, they found comfort in each other. Mark deserves someone who is going to love him unconditionally. I am not sure that Savannah is capable of that kind of love." I look back at the pictures hanging on the walls. "I don't want to come between them. I love them both. But if the time ever comes that I have to pick which one I would love forever over the other—" my words catch in my throat. "Your brother hands down."

He kisses me with such force. "Lets go to your room. I want to make love to you." We go in my room and he picks me up and places me on the bed. He undresses me slowly and runs his fingers up and down my naked body. He leans in and kisses my breasts one at a time. He cups one breast in his hand and takes the other in his mouth and sucks at my nipple.

I gasp and arch my back to get closer to him. He slips his other hand down between my legs and pushes his thin fingers inside me. I gasp again. I put my hands on his shoulders. Within seconds we are one being and I have never felt so deeply loved. He lifts my hips and pushes deeper.

"I love you!" I tell him.

When we part, I feel cold. I want to be connected to him. He pushes his finger inside me and I combust with an earth shattering orgasm. He holds me in his other arm as he pushes me even more over the edge. I cry out and he covers my mouth with his mouth and kisses me so deeply. All my nerves are on the brink of exploding. He pushes his finger a bit deeper and my body jolts and he holds me while my world goes to a complete fog. I hear nothing but a violin playing softly a lullaby that I wrote with Lindsey Gina years ago.

Justin holds me in his arms as he carries me into the shower. He gets in with me and he holds me agains the wall. I wrap my arms around his neck.

"Justin, don't let me go." I whisper because I can't find my voice.

"Never. I will never let you go." He says.

We are wrapped in each other in bed. Justin sleeps flat on his back, I sleep with my head on his chest. I hear Astro crying at the closed door. I never close the door. Since I have had him, he has always been allowed anywhere that I go.

Justin stretches and kisses me on the cheek. He slips out of the bed and opens the door for Astro. Astro jumps on the bed and licks me. Justin gets back on the bed and Astro lays right on top of him.

I sit up and Astro circles on the bed and lays on my lap. I pet him. I bury my face in his fur.

Justin's phone rings. He reaches to the nightstand, lifts it and looks at the call list. "My dad." He says.

"Oh, tell him I send my love." I say.

He kisses me and gets out of bed for a second time. He walks in the double closet and answers. "Hi dad."

"Hi."

"Whats going on?"

"I wanted to invite you and your brother to dinner. I already called Mark and he is coming."

"Ok. I will come."

"Oh good."

"When?"

"Tomorrow night. I know that you are all going to the Marina Beach for dinner tonight. I wouldn't want to take you away from your created family."

"Join us."

"Mark said the same thing."

"Well then you should come. I know that Sebastian would love to see you." Justin says.

"Alright I will come."

"Did you hear about Savannah?"

"She is with Candy." He says.

"Are you with Candy?"

"We are still friends."

"Dad, I know you love Savannah, but stay out of it. Mark is devastated at how she reacted to Sebastian."

"I know. You know that they will make up."

"Are you referring to Sebastian and Savannah or Savannah and Mark?"

"The girls will make up. Mark told me that he is done with the drama."

"Dad, just don't get stuck in the middle. I know Savannah goes to you and tells you deep secrets that she has. Just remember, Mark needs you to be there for him too."

"Justin, does Mark know what a great younger brother he has?"

"I don't know." Justin says.

"Where are you now?"

Justin laughs hysterically for a moment. "I am in Sebastian's closet."

"Go enjoy your sweet girl." He takes a deep breath. "Justin, when you get a chance, come over. I want to show you and Sebastian something that I found."

"We will stop by in a little while."

Justin returns to the bedroom. Astro and I aren't in there. He checks the bathroom. He puts jeans on and walks into the family room. We aren't in there. Lindsey sits at the table having breakfast with Trix.

"She went for a run." Trix says.

"Why?"

"She always does." She looks at her watch. "She will be back in about twenty minutes."

"Do you know her route?"

"The neighborhood." Trix says. She puts a spoonful of cereal in her mouth.

"Should I go after her?" Justin asks.

Lindsey runs her fingers through her hair and looks at him with a smirk. "You went in her closet to have a phone call?"

He looks at both of them. "I did."

Lindsey gets up and goes to get more coffee. "What were you thinking?"

Justin looks at both of them. "I needed to talk privately to my dad."

"She heard most of what you told him." Trix says.

I come in the front door. Astro pants and trots to his water bowl. He laps up a lot of water. I go in the kitchen and get his food ready. I put the food on the floor for Astro. I go in the cabinet and take out my favorite cup for iced coffee. I make a cup of coffee. I join my friends at the table.

I look at Justin. I look away as I take a long sip of my coffee. I hold the cup to my lips. Lindsey walks over and puts her hand on my shoulder. I close my eyes. Justin sits next to me and takes me in his arms.

"I am sorry if I upset you. My dad wants us to come to his house."

"So he can tell you in front of me that I am the wrong person for you?" I ask.

"No one ever said that. He said just the opposite." He kisses me.

I put my hands on his chest to push him away. He pulls me closer to him. "Always one step forward and then two major steps back."

"No." He says. "We aren't going backwards." He kisses me again.

I leave the table and go in the shower. While I am in the shower, Justin goes home and gets showered and dressed. He comes back to the house with his car.

He knocks on the door. I open it. He looks at me like there is no other woman in the world. He looks me over from head to toe. He puts his hand on his chest.

"Hi." I say.

"Hi." He looks at me and smiles. He kisses me again.

"You are smudging my makeup."

"You look beautiful." He takes Astro's leash and puts his collar on him. "You ready?"

"We have to be at the Marina Beach at four."

"I know. We will be there."

~~~~~~~~~~~

Savannah sits at a coffee shop with her laptop in front of her. She is busy at work. She can work anywhere she wants. She sits there and types a mile a minute. She is so focused on what she is doing, she doesn't notice others around her.

A guy grabs her from behind. She freezes. He takes her in his arms and pulls her against him with such force that it knocks the breath out of her. He shoves her agains the wall. "Give me your car keys, bitch."

"I don't have a car with me." She says shaking.

"Bullshit! Bitch! Give me the fucking keys."

"I don't have a car with me." She says louder.

"Give me your money."

"I don't have any money."

"What the fuck?" He yells. He grabs her laptop and closes it. He slams it on the table and then smacks her in the head with it.

She slumps to the ground. She takes her phone out of her pocket and dials Mark's number. She puts the phone down.

Mark hears the commotion. He listens. "Savannah!" He yells into the phone.

"Help me." Savannah says in a low voice.

"Tell me where you are?"

"The Coffee Inn." She says.

"Savannah, I am coming."

"Help me." She says.

"Keep me on the line." He tell her. "I am coming."

She says nothing more. She puts her hands to her head and holds her head. She sits under the table with her broken computer next to her.

People run over to help. She crawls further under the table. A girl reaches out to her. "We are here to help you."

Not five minutes passes, and Mark bursts into the door. He looks around and doesn't see Savannah right away. He sees a group of people sitting on the floor so he walks over. He looks at them. He sees Savannah under the table all wrapped up in herself. He sees her shattered computer and the blood on her head.

"Savannah." He says softly.

"Mister, you know her?"

"I am her boyfriend." Mark says. He sits on the floor and pushes a few chairs out of the way. "Sweetheart, open your eyes." He says softly. "I am here. Come on, baby."

"I can't open my eyes. My head hurts too much."

"You have to come out from under the table."

"I can't move." She says.

"I am going to move you." He moves further under the table.

"Sir? Do you want us to pick the table up and move it?" A young guy asks him. He gets his friends together. They lift the table up.

Mark picks up Savannah. She cries out. "I know baby." He holds her closer to him.

The young girl who first approached her picked up the smashed computer. "Sir, my dad owns this place. Let me go get him."

"Leave the laptop."

She looks at him with reddened cheeks. "Oh I was going to let my brother fix it."

"That's great and we will let him see if he can, but the police have to see it first."

"Oh right." She says.

Trix walks in the coffee shop. She looks around and then sees Mark holding Savannah in his arms. Before she can walk over to him, she overhears a conversation.

"That guy walked in and took that lady's laptop, smashed it to the table and then cracked her in the head with it."

"He wanted car keys."

"She didn't even have a purse. She just had that laptop."

"That guy that has her now, hasn't let her go since he got here. I wish I had a guy like that in my life." The girl says.

Trix smiles briefly. She then springs to her job. She starts asking questions about the guy who did this.

A young girl who works there walks over to Trix. "We have cameras and the police are tapping into now."

"What police?" Trix asks. She runs over to the manager. "Don't give anyone access to your cameras. Its not the police." She says.

"What?"

"Do not let the police access anything remotely. That's my job. That's why I am here."

Savannah hugs Mark. "Can you take me home?"

"I will take you home but I am sure that they want to ask you questions about what happened." Mark says.

"I didn't see the guy. He was behind me." She puts her hand to the side of her head. "Can you call Sebastian? I need her."

"Yes." Mark says. He takes his phone out to his pocket and calls me. "I need you to come the coffee shop." He tells me.

I get to the coffee shop with Justin. When we go inside, Savannah runs to me. I hug her. She cries harder than she has through the whole ordeal. Piper walks in and the three of us hug. Trix clears everything so Savannah leaves with Mark.

Justin holds my hand while we find out what all occurred. I hold her laptop against my chest. I sit it on the counter and access it through my code. I have a code on her laptop because I use it too at times. I access the camera recognition and I am able to access what happened. I show it to Trix. She hugs me.

"You are a fucking genius." She says. "I am going to take the laptop."

I hug her. "I will see you at dinner."

"I will be there in a short time." Trix says. She hugs me.

Justin and I finally make it to Edward's house. Candy is sitting on the couch. We all exchange hugs. Candy hugs me tighter the second time she hugs me. Mark and Savannah show up shortly after.

I look at Edward. "You always try to hard to smooth things over."

"That's not what happened here." He says.

"Bullshit." I say softly. "You always make what Savannah does right. She was wrong. I love her more than I do anyone, but she is never happy for her friends. If she would have been the one engaged before me, I would have been thrilled for her." I say.

Candy looks at me. "You were always jealous of her."

"That makes no sense at all after what I just said."

"Candy? Do you honestly think that Sebastian would ever want anything but the best for her friends who have become her family?" Justin asks.

The lawyer in him makes me smile. I take his hand. "Lets go. My brothers expect us."

"Brothers?" Candy asks. "You only have one brother."

I look at her. "Candy, I have loved you my whole life. Don't make me think that I was wrong to do that. You have been there for me more than my own—" I choke on my words. I look at Justin. "We need to go." I say. I feel like the room is spinning. I feel like I am at the most magical place on earth, Walt Disney World on the tea cups. I put my hands over my eyes.

Justin takes me in his arms. "Sweetheart, just breath. You are ok."

Candy looks at me. "What the hell is happening here?"

Savannah and Mark walk in the house. Savannah runs over to me. She gets down on her knees and hugs me. "Sebastian— close your eyes." She takes my hand in her hands. "Lets count to ten." She puts her hands on my knees. "One. Two. Three." She kisses my cheek. "Count with me." She says. "Four. Five."

"What's going on?" Candy asks with a bark of anger.

"The room is spinning." I say.

Edward looks at Justin. "How often does this happen to her?"

Savannah puts her hands on my shoulders. "The room is not spinning. Close your eyes and breath. Lets count again. Ten. Nine."

"Eight. Seven. Six." I put my hand over my mouth because the bile is in my throat. I gag on the bile.

Savannah jumps up and goes running into the kitchen. She gets the garbage can and brings it to me. I vomit. I feel like I am still on the tea cups and now I am spinning more and more out of control. I vomit again.

Mark stands behind me and rubs my temples. "Listen to my voice. You are ok. You haven't done anything wrong. Just take a deep breath. You are surrounded by everyone who loves you. We all love you." He says. He voice is soothing as it always was.

Justin stands next to Mark and rubs my shoulder. He squats down. "Sweetheart, I love you. We all love you."

I put my hand on his hand over my shoulder. "I have to go to the bathroom." I say. I excuse myself and go in the bathroom and lose even more of the contents of my stomach. Justin walks in the bathroom. He hands me a bottle of water.

"Are you alright?"

I take a sip of water and then turn the sink on. I wash my hands and splash water on my face. I look at Justin. "I am so embarrassed." I say with tears in my eyes.

Savannah walks in the bathroom with Mark. Savannah sits on the counter. "I am sorry." She says.

"I know." I tell her.

"My mom thinks that she is doing what's best for everyone."

Mark puts his hands on the side of her face. She winces with pain when his thumbs touch where she was cracked in the head.

I look at all of my friends. "I am going to leave. I need to leave." I say.

Edward knocks on the door. "I need to talk to all four of my loves." He says. "When you are ready, please come in the family room."

I look at my friends again. "Justin, I have to go. Please. I came with you. Please take me home so I can get my car. I have to go." I was becoming hysterical. I didn't like the way I felt like I was forced to beg for what I wanted.

Justin kisses the top of my head. "You want to leave— lets go." He takes my hand and we leave the bathroom. He hugs Edward. "I will call you later. Sebastian has to be at the Marina Beach."

"I needed to tell all of you something very important." Edward says.

"Tell Mark. He will tell me when we catch up later." Justin says in is lawyer tone.

"No!" Edward yells. "I need to tell you all something right now!"

"What is it?" Mark asks in a low voice.

Edward looks at all four of us. "I have recently come into money. A lot of money. I am going to divide the money up so that all four of you can live better." He looks at me. "I am giving you money so that you can rebuild your store. So you can hire a manager and you can live like a Princess."

Candy looks at Edward. "Tell them the best part." She says.

Savannah looks at her mother. Candy has snaked herself around Edward. He looks at Candy and then back at the rest of us.

"What's the best part?" Savannah and I ask together.

He looks again at Candy.

"Whats the best part?" Mark and Justin now ask.

"I am going to pay for your weddings."

None of say anything. Its like we are stunned into shock.

"I am not saying that you have to get married right now. But the money will be there for you." He looks at me. "I want to pay for your dream wedding. I want to give you away. I know that I am not your dad but I have loved you like a daughter for as long as I know you."

"I don't know what to say." I say. "Thank you."

He looks at Savannah. "Sweetheart, I know the last couple of weeks have been really hard for you. I think once you work through all of it, you are going to find your happily ever after." He looks at Candy. "I have spent the very last penny I am going to spend on you. I got you an apartment. Its fully furnished and paid for for the next two years." He looks at all of us. "Thank you for coming here." He steps closer to his sons. "We will meet with a lawyer next week to finalize all of the plans that I have set up. My lawyers will be in touch with all of you."

Edward hugs his sons. He then hugs Savannah. He hugs me last. "I didn't know your dad, but I am sure he is smiling down at you and the wonderful woman you have become. I am sure that he is proud of you. I am so proud of you."

I hug him. "I love you, Edward."

"I love you too." He says.

We all walk into the Marina Beach. Eric is there with Danny and Piper. We all hug each other. Matt and Tristian are there too. We hug them. Seth comes out of the kitchen and greets us all with hugs.

"Please go upstairs. Christmas awaits us." He watches everyone go upstairs. They walk up the steps. He looks at me waiting for the elevator. He walks over to Justin and me. He hugs me again. "Are you alright?"

"I am good." I say.

"Trix told me what happened with Savannah. I am so sorry to hear that."

"Thanks. She seems to be doing ok." I say.

"Are you?"

I look at him. I feel like he can tell that I was sick. I put my hand on his shoulder when he leans closer to me. "I am ok." I tell him.

"I wanted to thank you for letting Trix stay with you." Seth says.

"She is really doing me a favor more than me doing one for her. I don't live alone anymore. I know that its short terms for both Trix and Lindsey, but as long as they need a place to stay, my house is their house."

Trix walks in the door and runs over like she heard me talking about her. She hugs Justin, me and Seth. Then she stands on her tiptoes and kisses Seth. She is wearing a short dress. Her hair is bright pink again. She puts her hands on Seth's shoulders and jumps into his arms and out of her shoes. She kisses him like they are the only two living souls in the room. She slides down and back into her heals. She runs her hands down the front of her dress. She turns to us and giggles. "I haven't seen my boyfriend in a while." She says. She takes my hand and pulls me into the bathroom with her. Once we are alone she steps out of her shoes again and sits on my lap. "I hope I didn't get carried away."

I look at her and laugh. "You did. You really did."

She looks at me. "I had to do it."

"I know." I told her.

"You know, Justin is going to have a big case coming up. You don't have anywhere to be. You should go watch him in action." She steps back into her shoes. She stands and fixes her lipstick.

"I will." I look at her. "Can anyone go into a court room?"

"Yes."

"I will go."

She looks at me first from the mirror then she turns and looks at me. "Were you sick?"

"I am alright." I say.

"That's not what I asked."

"Don't always be a cop." I tell her.

She looks at me. "I am always a cop." She turns back to the mirror and fixes her hair. "I look forward to hearing about your day and why you look like you are surviving the dawn of the dead."

"Trix!" I yell at her.

"You look like you were sick."

"I was."

"Ok."

"Ok." I repeat.

"Are you pregnant?"

I gawk at her. "You can't say anything."

"Does Justin know?"

"No one knows."

"How far along?"

"Maybe a month."

"Don't you have protected sex?" She asks.

"How is it that my best friends didn't notice, but you and Seth did? Do."

She spins on her heal and hugs me.

"You can't say anything to any one. I haven't mentioned it to anyone."

"When do you go to the doctor?"

"Tuesday."

"I am going with you."

"You would do that?"

She bends her finger and knocks on my forehead with her knuckle. "Yes. After what you have done for my cousin and his son. I would do anything for you. My dad is running an investigation and when he has everything done, I think you are going to like the results."

Justin knocks not eh door. "We are all needed upstairs." He says.

We leave the bathroom after Trix gives me a breathe mint. She holds the door for me. "Kiss him like your life depends on it. Let him know that he is the only one that you think about."

"Trix." I say.

"Be a lioness." She winks and smiles.

Justin takes me in his arms and lifts me out of my wheelchair. He carries me up the steps. "Elevator troubles." He says.

I kiss him. I smile against his lips when Jacob brings my wheelchair out of the elevator. "I love you." I say.

"I love you too." He puts me in my wheelchair and then steps aside to get us a drink.

Jacob hugs me. Lindsey walks over with Astro. She hugs me.

"Thanks for bringing him." I say. I pet Astro on the head. I put my hand under his chin and scratch him. He wags his tail joyously.

"Oh sure." She says. She looks me over a few times. "You look beautiful. You are glowing."

Jacob looks at me. "You are glowing."

Lindsey looks over at me. She smiles. "Are you pregnant?"

Jacob looks at Lindsey and then at me. I look at Lindsey. I don't say anything to her. Lindsey takes my hand and pulls me aside. She walks over by the speakers where music is playing loudly. She squats in front of me.

"Are you pregnant?"

"I don't know." I tell her honestly.

"You need to make an appointment to go to the doctor." She says.

"I know. I have an appointment on Tuesday."

She smiles at me. "I will go with you." She says. "Just like last time."

"Lindsey." I close my eyes. My eyes sting.

"You didn't do anything wrong." She says softly. "You never told him?"

437

I shake my head.

Ivan walks up the stairs. He looks around the room and sees me. He rushes over to me and takes me in his arms. He holds me tight in his arms. He looks at Lindsey. "Hey."

"Hey yourself." She says.

He kisses me on the cheek. "Whatever is going on, don't let it stop you from enjoying the evening with all of us. We love you." He kisses me on the lips like he does. Its never passionate but this time its more than his usual kiss. He holds me closer to him. "I love you always." He says pulling away but still holding me in his arms. "If you think that I didn't know all those years, I did. Maybe you forget but you put me as your emergency contact. They called to tell me that your results were in and that you were pregnant."

When he says the words that he knew, my heart leaps in my throat. "That's why you left?"

He looks at me. "No. That's why I struggled to choose which way to go. I had to go. I loved that you loved me enough to stay with me no matter what. It meant the world to me. When I found out that you lost the pregnancy, my first instinct was to come back to you. I sent Lindsey to you."

Justin stands off to the side of the room watching me. He never takes his eyes off of me. Mark and Sebastian stand next to him.

"What's going on?" Sebastian asks.

Justin looks at him briefly but then looks back at me. "She keeps things from me."

"What do you think she is keeping from you?" Mark asks. He puts his hand on Justin's shoulder.

"She still loves Ivan."

"She will always love him. He will always love her. He is with Trevor." Sebastian says.

"I know."

Sebastian looks at Justin and Mark. "Did you know that she got pregnant?"

They both look at him.

"Ivan and her only slept together one time. That's all it took. She got pregnant. She was only pregnant for five weeks before she miscarried."

"How do you know this?"

"I have found out a lot about her by looking into her medical records. I also know that she was a straight A student always."

Justin looks at Sebastian. "Was he there for her when she lost the baby?"

"No." Mark said. "She came to me a few weeks later. She told me about it. She cried for weeks. She stayed with me. I got home from work one day and she was gone. When I found her, she was working on a cruise ship. I took a job working on the cruise ship so that I could make sure that she was ok."

Justin looks at both my brother and his his. Then he runs to me and takes me in his arms. "I love you."

I look at him. "I love you too."

Seth walks in the room and gets everyone to go to the tables. We have dinner together and then open presents that we never opened at Christmas. The night goes by quickly. We all laugh and have a great time together.

After dinner which was delicious, the food hits me like a punch in the gut and I rush into the bathroom and vomit. I clean myself up and leave the bathroom. Seth is waiting for me outside the door. He hugs me.

I look at him. "You must be thinking, I am never going to have Sebastian here again."

He looks at me. "Why do you say that?"

"Every time I am here, I cry."

He hugs me. "I don't think that at all."

"Sebastian hasn't spoken to me in a while now. I don't know if I hurt his feelings some how. Or if he is thinking that maybe he shouldn't have ever opened Pandora's box."

Seth looks at me. "That's not true. Sebastian has been working on something very important and none of us— him especially doesn't regret finding out about you. We feel grateful."

Jacob's words always burn in my ears that I was just a gold digger. I think that they might think that may be true. I look around the room and see Justin talking to a beautiful woman. I feel my stomach knot again. I push away from Seth and run into the bathroom again. I didn't think that I could vomit anything else, but apparently there is more. I feel weak. I leave the bathroom after again cleaning myself up.

This time when I leave the bathroom, Justin is waiting for me. He looks at me. "What's going on?"

I look at him. "I think I am pregnant." I tell him. I heave.

"I am taking you to the hospital." He says.

I look at him. "I know I am pregnant. I haven't taken any tests or anything. I go to the doctor tomorrow. But I was—" I close my eyes. "I was pregnant before." I squeeze my eyes shut. "I lost the baby."

Justin holds me in his arms. He rubs my back. "I know. My dad told me."

I open my eyes. "Your dad?"

"My dad saw your charts."

"What do you mean your dad saw my charts?"

He looks at me. "Sebastian, my dad is a doctor."

I close my eyes tight and squeeze the tears that are threatening to fall.

"I know that it was Ivan's."

I push away from him. I scan the room. I see Trix. I go to her. "Can you take me home?"

"Yes, of course sweetheart." She says.

Justin walks over. "Wait. Let me take you home. Don't run away from me."

I look at him. "I am not running away from you." I see the beautiful blonde walking over. "Who is she?" I ask.

She stops short before approaching completely. She looks at me and then at Justin. She finds Mark in the crowd. "I am their sister." She says. "My name is Belle."

I look at Justin. I have heard Edward over the years mention Belle. I honestly thought that Belle was a pet. I look at her and then back at Justin and I burst into a fit of laughter that I can not control.

Everyone looks at me. Tears stream down my face from hysteria. I try to stop laughing. I can not. I make my way to the elevator and laugh the whole time I am in in there. I go outside and when the fresh air hits me, I feel bile building. I vomit.

Justin runs over. "You have a lot to explain. Let me take you home." Astro is with him. "I think that a nice shower will do you well and rest."

I look at him. "I am sorry." I giggle and once I start up again I can't stop. But I explain my laughter. "I thought that Belle was a pet. Your dad would talk about Belle and it was always animated talk so I assumed that Belle was a dog or a cat." I look at Justin seriously. "I am sorry."

Chapter 29

I sit in the waiting room to my doctor's offices. I am with Justin. He took off work to find out if and how long I am pregnant. The nurse comes out the main doors and calls my name. I go with her. She looks at Justin.

"Once we do her bloodwork and she is in a gown, we will come back for you."

He goes to sit down.

"I asked if he could go in for the whole exam. I was told that he could be with me." I say.

The nurse looks at me. "Let me check." She calls another woman to go back.

I go back over by Justin and hold his hand. He holds my hand and smiles.

The nurse comes back. She calls my name again. We go with her. The doctor comes in and examines me. The technician does the ultrasound. The doctor looks at the images.

"Wow, you are very pregnant." She says. "You haven't had any symptoms until recently?"

"No." I say. "How far am I?"

"It seems that you are four months."

I look at her. "Does the baby show any signs—"

"The fetus appears to be healthy. She looks like a happy camper in there."

"She?" Justin and I ask together.

She looks at us. "You are having a girl." She says joyously.

I put my hand on my belly.

"We need to get you on prenatal vitamins." She looks at me. "We are going to monitor you every two weeks."

"Ok." I say to her.

We leave there and I look at Justin. He has been quiet since we found out that we are having a girl. I don't think he is happy about it. We have our own cars because he has to go into work.

"Are you alright?" I ask him.

He looks at me. "There have been no signs until now?"

"No. I have irregular cycles and I have had spotting."

He looks up at the sky and there is a rainbow shining brightly over us. "Look your dad is happy that you are having a girl." He says.

"Justin!" I say excitedly. "You really think so?"

"How could he not be happy for you? I am thrilled." He says.

"Really? Because I have been holding my breath. I didn't think you were happy about this."

"I am beyond happy." He kisses me and I am filled with warmth throughout my body. "I have to go to court today. Trix is going to be there. Do you want to come?"

"I would love that." I say.

"Are you hungry?"

"I am starving." I say. Because I had a morning appointment, they told me not to eat anything. My stomach grumbles.

"Ok, lets grab something to eat and then we can go bring your car to the house. You can come with Trix or Mark."

"I would love that." I say again.

An hour and half later, we are in the Fort Lauderdale Court House and I am watching Justin in action. He is great. He is a great prosecutor. He wins his case and the guy is sentenced to four years. The guy stands up and tries to jump on Justin. Justin jumps out of the way as police officers seem to appear out of no where. They restrain the criminal. Justin looks around the room to find out where I am. He is sweating.

Trix and Mark escort me out of the room. We go in the elevator and go downstairs to the second floor. That's the floor that has the covered walking bridge. We go to the parking garage and go to Mark's car.

Mark's phone rings. "Tell me you have her and you are all safe." Justin yells in the phone. He is frantic.

"We have her and we are all safe. We are in the parking garage." Mark says.

"Take her to my office."

"Ok. We will."

"Mark, I was so worried for her."

"She is fine." Mark tells Justin. He walks away from us. "I will be right back." He says to us over his shoulder as he walks away. "She was so brave. So much more than Trix. I will take her home."

"No my office." Justin insists. He screams.

"What is it?"

"I have always wanted her to come watch me at work and the one time she does—"

"Everyday isn't like that. And Justin, she is really fine. She never stopped talking while we were in the elevator how exciting it was. She is so excited that she got to see you doing your job. She keeps referring to you as a superhero. She is comparing you to Daredevil."

"What if he would hurt her?"

"Justin!" Mark snaps at him. "Do not play the what if game. It didn't happen. The guy went to attack you. He didn't go to attack anyone in the gallery. The police were on him so fast." He takes a deep breath. "Are you hurt?"

"No."

"Drive safely."

"You too."

Mark walks back over to his car and gets in it. He drives to Justin's office. I look at him with a big bright glowing smile. He looks at me. "This is Justin's office."

I get my legs out of the car and wait for him to bring my wheelchair to me. When he does, I get in my wheelchair. I look around and notice that his office backs up to my bookstore's new location. Mark smiles when he realizes that I know.

"Why didn't he just take the space next to my bookstore's new location?"

"There is no keeping secrets from you."

I turn around in a full circle and squeal with excitement.

Justin pulls into the parking lot. He jumps out of the car. "You told her?"

"No. She knows her geography." Mark says.

"Oh my god!" I yell with excitement.

"You aren't mad?" Justin asks.

"No!"

"Come inside. I will get you something to drink and eat." Justin says.

Mark looks at both of us. "I have to go home. I have to get ready for work. I have to meet with someone who wants me to build her a closet."

"Thank you for everything." I say to him.

He hugs me. "Always Little Mermaid. I love you always."

"Me too." I tell him and mean it.

Justin takes my hand and we go inside. The office has beautiful honey colored woods. I look around and see that Mark worked his magic for Justin.

In the distance a phone rings non-stop. Justin looks at me. "I have to get that."

"You don't have a receptionist?"

"No."

"Do you want one? I have some time before my bookstore is ready to open."

"You would want to do that?"

"Yes." I look around. "This is beautiful."

"Let me get that and then I will get you set up with a phone." He kisses me on the lips. He walks down the hall and into an office. He answers the phone.

I hear his voice but can't make out what he is saying. I sit at a desk in the front of the of the office and open the drawers. One has a computer in the drawer. I take it out and turn it on. Emails pop up on the screen.

Justin walks back over and looks at me. "Putting yourself to work already?"

I smile. "I didn't read anything yet."

He kisses me. "You can. That is just stuff that my last assistant did. That would be your computer so you are free to know all that is on it."

~~~~~~~~

I sit in my kitchen with my new roommates and we are enjoying breakfast that Seth brought for all of us from the Marina Beach. It is a healthy pregnant safe to eat meal. I pick up the note that he wrote and read it again.

'We are so happy for you! From all of at Marina B. We are so happy for you. Enjoy a pregnant safe breakfast. Love you. See you for dinner! Call me when you are done and let me know what you think.'

Trix smiles as she eats another piece of bacon. "I normally dislike bacon, but he makes it just the way I like it."

"Burnt!" Lindsey and I say laughing.

"I will tell him that you were not grateful for his thoughtful breakfast." She says laughing.

"I will call your dad and tell him that he needs to shoot you." I say smiling.

"Wow! The hostility of a pregnant girl." Lindsey smiles.

They both look at me as my small belly moves on its own. They both put their hands on my stomach and feel her move around and kick.

"That is so cool." Trix says. "Has Justin felt her move?"

"Yes." I answer. "She must have felt a little crushed when we were—" I laugh.

"I have never seen you so happy." Trix says.

"I have seen her this happy." Lindsey says. "My boyfriend has pictures of you this happy and maybe happier."

I look at her. "What are you talking about?"

"Jacob is a world renown photographer." She looks at me like I am an idiot. "The pictures that are hanging in your private den of you from the party in New York, Jacob took them."

I look at Lindsey. "I didn't know."

"He sold a picture that he took for over a million dollars. That's how he got the money to pay for—"

"Pay for what?" I ask her.

"I think I hear my phone ringing."

"Lindsey, your phone is next to you on the table. What are you talking about. What did he buy for a million dollars?"

There is a knock at the front door. Astro barks like a mad dog. He starts growling. I push away from the table. I go to the door. "Hey, buddy what's going on?"

I open the door. Lilliana and Julianna are standing there. Astro bolts from the door with his tail wagging. They both drop to their knees and pet Astro who flops himself down and then rolls on his back to show his belly to them. Aunt Grace stands behind them with Oliver.

Aunt Grace reads the shirt that I am wearing. "Baby bump?" She asks.

I look at her and smile. "I am pregnant." I say.

The two girls jump to their feet and hug me. "That's so exciting!" They say together.

I look at all of them. "Do you want to come in?"

"You have company and we should have called first." Oliver says.

"No. I mean yes, I have company but its my roommates. Trix and Lindsey."

"You live with an icon?" Julianna says with excitement.

"You know, we try not to remind her of that because then her head will swell big enough that we can float it in the Macy's parade." I say with a smile.

Lindsey walks up behind me. "Are you talking shit about me?" She asks with a smile. She looks at my family.

The girls both laugh. Astro jumps up on Uncle Oliver. Grace runs her hands over Astro. They all come into the house.

Trix cleans the kitchen up. She is putting things in the refrigerator. Julianna looks around and smiles. "It smells so good in here."

"Are you hungry?" I ask. "We have plenty of food. Seth brought breakfast for all of us." I look at Trix. "He thinks that I have to eat for six people."

We all laugh.

Oliver looks around. He sees that I have the mailbox that my dad made and that Oliver gave me in my backyard. He kisses me on the head. "Do you get mail out there?"

I laugh. "No, but it protects it from crazy neighbors."

"Are you still having problems with neighbors?" Grace asks.

"No. Unfortunately she and her granddaughter passed away." I get sad saying it so casually

"I am sorry to hear that." Grace says.

"Tell me, did you have problems with her always?" Oliver asks.

I look at Lindsey. "My cousins think that you are an icon. You want to show them all of your beautiful violins?"

"I will do just that." She says. She kisses me on the cheek. "You know maybe they don't know what an icon you are. I will tell them all about it."

I smile at her. "I love you, Gina." I say calling her by her last name.

She takes the girls by their hands and walks out of the room with them and into her room.

Trix makes coffee and gives me a bottle of water to drink. Oliver and Grace sit around the table with us. I look at both my uncle and aunt. "The truth is, I never had any problems with her until I started dating Justin. Justin and Mark moved into the neighborhood. It all started one day when I took Astro for a walk. She drove by and asked me about my boyfriend and I tried to avoid the one hundred questions."

"You never had problems before?" Grace asks.

"No. Well maybe a bit. She always insisted that mom was a bad mother because she owned the house and left me alone too long. The truth is, my mom sold the house and I bought it."

They both look at each other.

Oliver speaks first. "Your mother sold the house to you?"

"Well ultimately yes, but no. I bought it from the real estate woman. Mom was hurt when she found out it was me who bought the house, but she didn't even ask me if I wanted to move. When she was selling the house, I went to meet with the real estate agent and made an offer on the house."

"How did you afford the house?"

"I have been working since I was thirteen."

"How come?" Oliver asks.

"Grandma stopped coming around when I was twelve and when I wanted something, my mom would tell me that I had to work for it. I got a job tutoring older kids. They paid money to pass their classes."

"You did the work for them?" Grace asks.

"No. I tutored them. When they got higher grades then they expected, I charged more money." I laugh.

"Little hustler." Trix laughs.

I excuse myself to go to the bathroom. I pass by Linsey's room. I hear her playing the violin with my cousins. "When you are done with the music fest, we have cookies." I say.

Julianna smiles. "I love cookies."

"I remember." I say smiling.

"Where are you off to in such a rush?" Lindsey asks.

"The bathroom." I say.

When I return to the kitchen no one is in there. I look outside by the pool and see that the girls are swimming. Oliver and Grace are sitting in my gazebo. Lindsey is sitting on the side of the pool with her legs in the water. Trix is out there too. Astro runs circles around the pool.

I go out side to join them. Astro trots over to me and puts his head on my legs. I pet him. Oliver walks over. "Your dog is devoted."

I look at Oliver. "Its nice to be loved by someone."

"I feel so sad that I was so stubborn and didn't come meet you and Sebastian sooner."

"Did grandma ever tell you about me?"

He looks at Grace and then back at me. "When she did, Grace bought that farm that you volunteered at. She wanted to get to know you."

"Did Francesca ever go to the farm?"

"Why do you ask?"

"Because I am wracking my brain trying to remember where I know her from. I know that I met her before, but she told me another name."

We hear the fence open. Astro runs over to the fence to greet Justin. He pets Astro on the head. He bends and kisses on the top of his head. Then he runs over to me. He kisses me and gets his hand knotted in my hair. He pulls my head back a bit and deepens the kiss.

"I have been calling your phone. When you didn't answer I drove by the house and have been knocking at the door for the last ten minutes."

"I left my phone in the house." I tell him.

"I know."

"Why didn't you use your key?" Lilliana asks.

He smiles at my young cousin. "I don't live here."

She smiles shyly. "I thought you lived together."

"Well we almost do." I say smiling at my cousin and trying to make her feel less embarrassed. "I have a key to his house."

Justin smiles. "You have a key to my house?" He asks just loud enough for me to hear him only.

I smile. "I do." I say just loud enough for him to hear me.

"What are you two doing?" Grace asks in her motherly tone.

We both laugh. "Nothing." We say together.

Trix comes over and kisses all of us and then runs in the house to leave. "I have to go." She says.

"See you later." I say.

She turns quickly and looks at me. She asks me to join her in the house. I excuse myself and go inside with her.

"You ok?" I ask.

"I am going to sleep over at Seth's." She blushes.

"Have fun." I say to her.

"You don't think badly of me?"

"Are you kidding?" I ask her. "You are an adult."

"Listen, if my dad calls can you tell him that I am sleeping."

"Of course." I tell her. "Sleeping with your boyfriend." I tease.

She slaps me playfully. "Bitch!" She says.

Lindsey walks in the house. "How long do we have to entertain them?"

"If you have plans, go. You are not obligated to entertain my — my family." I say.

"Its just that Jacob asked me if I wanted to go have lunch with him and then go out of town for a few days."

"Lind, you can go. You don't need my permission. Go have fun." I tell her.

"What will your family think?"

"What do you care?" I ask.

She hugs me. "I love you. I will text you later."

"I will text you later too." Trix says.

They both leave and I go back outside with my family. They stay for a few more hours. I make lunch for them. Overall it seems like things weren't said. Important things were not stated. I had so many questions to ask but I held back because my young cousins were around.

They leave shortly after lunch. They left my house in a total mess. The patio area around the pool has towels thrown all around. There are pool toys in the bottom of the pool.

I look at Astro. I kept him out of the pool while the girls swam but now I let him go. He jumps in the pool and dives for the toys. He comes up and brings them to me. Then he dives again for the others.

Justin stands next to me. "I would have gotten them out with the net."

I look at Justin. "Astro wanted so badly to swim with the girls. Liliana would have been fine. Julianna would have had a problem. She likes animals from afar."

"You doing ok?" He asks.

"I just feel like their visit had a purpose that went missed."

"The purpose was to see you, my love." He says.

"I have so many questions." I say.

"Invite them back." He says.

Our phones ring almost at the same time. Justin looks at his phone and I look at mine. He takes his phone and steps back in the house.

I stay out with Astro. "Hi Piper." I say.

"Are you home?"

"Yes."

"I am coming over. I have to pee." She says.

We both laugh. "The door is open." I tell her.

"You are keeping your door open again?" She teases. "Where are the roomies?"

"Off on dates with their boyfriends."

"How are your brothers doing?"

"I don't know. Seth stopped by this morning with breakfast, but I didn't see him. For all I know, he could have cooked in my kitchen and cleaned it up before he slipped out." I laugh.

"Have you spoken to Savannah?"

"Not today." I say to Piper.

"She called me earlier." She says. "Oh, I am here. Can I just come in?"

"Of course." I tell her. "I am in the backyard with a wet Astro.

"I will come out when I finish." She says.

Astro dives in the pool again only this time its to retrieve one of his balls that I throw for him. He gets it and comes back to me with the ball. I throw it again in the pool and again he jumps in to retrieve it.

Piper walks out of the house and stands in the shade. She smiles at me. "How far along are you?"

"Four months."

"I just found out that I am three and half months." Piper says.

We embrace each other.

"You know, Sav is really going to lose her shit over us both having babies before we are one married and two that we are having them almost at the same time." She hugs me. "How are you feeling?"

"I have all day sickness." I tell her.

"I have night sickness." Piper says.

"Do you know what you are having?"

"Not yet." She says. "You?"

I smile brightly. "I do know."

She smiles at me as she grabs a towel from the bench seat and grabs Astro to dry him off. "Well?"

"If you guess I will tell you if you are right or wrong."

She looks at me.

"Pipes, you can only go one or the other."

"You are having a girl?"

I smile brightly.

"You are having a girl!" She yells.

"I am having a girl." I say with excitement.

"That's so great." She says. She rushes over to me and hugs me. "I will find out in a week or two." She goes back to drying off Astro.

"You don't have to do that. I have to give him a bath." I tell her.

She walks over to where she knows I keep his doggy shampoo and takes it out.

"Piper, you don't have to do this."

"I want to. I miss being around him and you all the time." She says.

"You can come anytime you want."

"You have roommates now."

"Piper, there is always room for you."

"Eric asked me to marry him." She says as she puts a dapple of soap on Astro. She sits on the ground and rubs the soap all over his body. He loves it.

"When? How?" I ask joyously.

"He took me to dinner and I met his parents. They are wonderful. They told me how much they already knew about me because of Danny. They told me that they love me already." She looks up at me. "Do you know how much that means to me?"

"I do know. Congratulations."

"Eric wanted you to be there, but he couldn't wait any longer. He didn't plan on doing it without you there." She says.

"Piper, I am so happy for you. I know how much you love him and Danny. I know how much they love you. I am happy for you." I get towels ready to dry Astro.

Piper takes Astro over to the outdoor shower head and rinses him.

Justin walks back outside wearing swim shorts. "I was going to do that." He says to the two of us.

"Its ok." Piper says.

Justin walks over to us and hugs me. "Do you know a Sabrina White-child?"

"The name sounds familiar." Piper says.

I don't answer right away. "Sabrina White-child?" I look at Piper. "Sabrina White-child. That's the name Francesca gave us when we met her on the ship."

"Francesca?" Justin asks.

"I have been wracking my brain trying to think back to what name she used when she introduced herself to me." I look at Justin. "Why are you asking us about Sabrina White-child?"

"Because she has been arrested and is asking to talk to you."

"Me?" I ask.

"What the hell does she want?" Piper asks. "Let me make a phone call." She says. She goes in the house to make her call.

I look at Justin. I take a clean towel and dry Astro. "Come on love." I say to Astro. "Lets go get the blowdryer." When I mention the blowdryer, Astro's tail wags. We go in the house and into my bathroom. I plug the blowdryer and set it to low and hold it over Astro. He sits and lets me blow his fluffy hair all over the place.

Piper hearing the noise comes into the bedroom. She walks into the attached bathroom and sits on the counter. She looks at both Justin and then at me. "She is being held at the women's detention center. She can have two visitors. She will be held until tomorrow and then released."

"Why is she being held in the women's detention center?" I ask.

"A DUI." She says.

Justin nods his head. "You are amazing." Justin says to Piper.

"This is my job. I am taking a few weeks off but I will still be able to do it wherever I am." She says. She stands and pushes Justin out of the bathroom. "I have to pee. Get out."

Justin looks at both of us and laughs. "Why does Astro get to stay?" He smiles.

"He has seen us naked. You haven't." Piper says. Then she laughs. "Well you haven't seen me naked." She closes the door and sits on the toilet. She pees.

She takes the blowdryer and finishes drying Astro. He lays flat on his back wagging his tail.

Justin comes back in the bathroom an Astro stands on his back legs and puts his front paws on Justin's shoulders. "I love you too." Justin says to Astro. "Come on, lets go get a bone." He leaves the bathroom with Astro trotting after him happily.

We follow them out of the bathroom. I go outside and pick up the towels and put all the pool toys in bench that I keep all the pool stuff in. I bring the towels in the house and put them in the washing machine.

"You don't have to do that." Justin says.

I look at him like is crazy. "Um, if I don't wash my clothes and towels, who else is going to do them? My uncle, aunt and cousins came to visit an left my yard like there is a maid who is coming to clean up after them. Only thing is, its just me. My house, my mess."

"Do you want to go see Francesca?" Justin asks.

"Yes, but I have to get changed." I say.

"It doesn't have to be today. She is going to be in holding for at least three days."

"They Baker Acted her?" I ask the same time that Piper does.

"Yes."

"Why?"

"She got violent with a cop and wouldn't stop slapping herself in the face."

My heart sinks. I look at Piper. She looks at me. I run into my room and get changed quickly. I pull my damp hair into a pony tail and put on a black sundress with yellow and pink flowers on it. I put on a pair of sandals that match the dress. I go back into the kitchen.

"I am ready to go." I say. I put Astro's leash on him. "Lets go."

"Whats going on?" Justin asks.

"I have to see her." I say. I put Astro's working dog harness on him.

~~~~~~~~

I sit in a large room with Astro next to me. Everything in the room is white. The walls. The chairs and tables. The floor and ceiling. The only things in color in the room are Astro, me and Piper. Justin didn't come in with us.

A female guard leads Francesca into the room. She has bruises all over her face. There is scab over her left eye. Her hair is matted. She is wearing a pink jumpsuit. She looks awful. The guard stops and looks at me.

"The dog needs to go." She says.

"The dog is approved." Another guard says.

"Do not touch each other." The first guard says to all three of us. "I will be over there listening to every word."

I look at Piper. I reach for her hand.

"Excuse me. What did I just say?" The guard snaps.

The second guard looks at us. "I will watch them. Why don't you go change your tampon." She says.

The first guard looks wounded. "Bitch!" She says and then walks away with attitude.

The second guard looks at the three of us. "I will be over there. Just don't do anything stupid." She looks at Piper. "How did I get the pleasure of working when the Attorney General shows up."

"Its nice to be recognized." Piper says. She smiles.

"I am sorry about my colleague."

"Listen, don't say that you know who I am. I am here just to see my friend." She says.

We sit with Francesca. For a full five minutes no one says a word. She looks at me. I look at her. Piper breaks the silence. "Why didn't you tell us who you were?"

Francesca looks at Piper and then at me. "I had to come find you. I needed to know who was taking my grandma away from me. She would come back from Florida talking about Sebastian this and Sebastian that. At the time, I didn't know that she was talking about two different people. She would tell stories when she camee back to us and tell my mom all about you. Both of you. She had pictures of just you. When you graduated college, she was there and took pictures of you."

"Where did you tell your parents you were for an entire summer?" Piper asks.

Francesca looks at Piper. "I told them that I was going to Paris."

"They didn't ask to see pictures?" I ask.

"They did. I showed them pictures of every place the ship docked. They didn't question anything because they know that I don't like crowds."

"Why did you act like did?"

"I didn't want my mom to know that I lied to her."

"Francesca this is so crazy." I say.

"I know." She says. "The only other person who knew that I knew who you two were is my sister. I am sorry that we were so rude to you. I really need to tell my mom and dad. Grandma knows that I lied."

"How did she find out?"

"She found my fake ID. She asked me who Sabrina was and I tried to lie to her but she somehow knows when I am not telling her the truth. She told me that I have to tell my parents immediately or she is going to tell them and then I am going to be cut off completely."

I look around. "I have to go to the bathroom." I say.

The guard looks at me. "Let me show you where you can go."

I go into the lady's room and come out a few minutes later. The first guard is standing blocking the door. She won't let me out of the bathroom. I send Piper a text message. Piper comes to find me.

"Whats going on?" Piper asks.

"Nothing." She says.

"Then let my friend out of the lady's room."

"Your friend left."

"No. She texted me that she is stuck in the bathroom."

"Can't someone play a joke?"

"Not here. Not now." Piper says.

We leave shortly after with Francesca with us. We take her back to my house. Once she is in the house in a spare bedroom, I call Sebastian.

"Hi." He says.

"Hi." I say.

"Can I ask you a question?"

"Yes." I say.

"Why haven't I heard from you sooner?"

I smile. "I need you and Jacob and Seth." I say.

"Where are you?" Concern radiates thought the phone.

"I am home."

"Are you ok?"

"I just have a lot to tell the three of you." I say. "Can you come?"

"We will be there immediately." He says. I hear him smile through the phone.

"Am I taking you away from anything?"

"Nothing." He says. "Sit tight, we will be right there."

Not even fifteen minutes pass and my three brothers are walking into my house. Lindsey is sitting on the couch with Astro. Trix is sitting on the floor stretching. Francesca is sleeping on the couch. Piper is standing next to me with her hand on my shoulder.

Sebastian takes me in his arms and hugs me. I hug him. He sees Francesca. "Is everything ok?"

We tell them what has been happening. With the visit from Oliver and Grace starting the day off. Then that Justin received a call about Francesca aka Sabrina. I tell them that Piper and I went to the women's correction center.

Justin and Mark knock on the door. Piper lets them in. Justin hugs me. Mark sees Francesca sleeping.

"Hey, isn't that Sabrina?"

"You know her?" Justin asks.

"She was the one from the cruise ship. She worked with us." Mark says.

"That's Francesca." Seth says.

Mark looks at me. "What's going on?" He asks.

"That is Francesca. She told us that her name was Sabrina."

Mark looks at Justin and my three brothers. "It was my job to look into people's backgrounds. Sabrina came from England."

"No. New England maybe." Trix says.

"Why is she here?" Justin asks.

"She was being—" Piper starts. "Lets go talk in the kitchen."

"She had pictures of me from grandma when I was little until recently." I say once we are in the kitchen.

There is a knock on the door. I open it and Oliver is standing there with Scarlett. They both hug me.

"Thank you for calling me." She says. "I have been frantic."

"Please come in." I say.

Before I close the door, I watch a car pull into my driveway Savannah runs to me and hugs me. "Are you ok?" She asks.

"I am fine." I tell her. I feel better that she is with me.

458

"How did everything go with the doctor?"

"I am four months pregnant." I say. I expect her to recoil from me. I expect her to be upset. Instead, she throws her arms around me and hugs me tighter. "I didn't know I was pregnant."

She looks at me. "Four months?" She asks.

"Yeah."

"Do you know what you are having?"

I whisper in her ear that it's a girl. She hugs me again.

"Your dad must be smiling down on you."

I hug her.

Piper walks over. "Having a private party and didn't invite me." She says. She hugs us both.

We go into the living room where Francesca sleeps on the couch. Scarlett gets on her knees in front of the couch and rubs Francesca's arm where there is a big bruise. Finger prints where someone grabbed her.

Francesca opens her eyes. She quickly closes them. She opens her eyes again. "Mom!" She cries and jumps off the couch and hugs Scarlett.

We all sit around the room and listen to Francesca tell how she found out about Sebastian and me.

Justin holds my hand the whole time. Mark has his hand on my shoulder. Sebastian, Jacob and Seth sit close to me.

"Grandma would show me pictures of my cousins." Francesca says. She would show me pictures but she would only say Sebastian one time." She looks at Scarlett. "I am sorry I lied to you and daddy." She looks at all of us. "I am sorry I mistreated you when you were in New York." She looks at me. "I knew the second that you saw me that you recognized me."

"I did." I tell her.

"I am sorry for all the heartache I caused." Francesca says.

I look at everyone. My whole family minus my mom is sitting in my house. I feel love coming at me from everyone there.

Chapter 30

Justin runs his flat hand on my growing belly. I stretch and he slips his hand between my legs. I open my eyes and smile.

"Stop teasing and get inside." I say.

He smiles at me. "I am enjoying teasing you."

"I have t a lot to do today." I tell him.

"What do you have to do?"

"I have a hard ass new boss that expects me to book his appointments so he can get beat up in front of his girl friend in court." I tease him.

He pushes his finger into my core. I gasp. He pulls his finger out and then pushes in. It doesn't take long for my orgasm to build. My toes curl. I gasp.

"Just— please." I beg.

He gets on top of me and thrusts inside me. I cry out. He goes deeper. He takes my hands and holds them as he climaxes.

When we finish having mind blowing, toe curling, earth shattering sex, we sleep wrapped in each other for hours.

When I wake up, I kiss Justin's shoulder. I smile devilishly and put my hand flat on his low belly. I run my nails over the sheet adding pressure to him. His eyes open and he tickles me. I laugh into his chest.

"You don't play fair." He says.

"Me?" I ask with a shriek.

"I can't play right now. I have to prepare for trial."

"When I told you I have a big day to prepare for, it didn't stop you. I want to play." I say whining.

"It will give you something to look forward to." He says.

I sit up and get out of bed. I go into the bathroom and shower. Justin opens the shower door. "Nope!" I laugh.

Mark knocks on the bathroom door. "Are you two decent in here?"

"I am in the shower." I yell.

"I am coming in." He says.

"Oh my god! I am naked." I say.

He comes in. Justin is standing at the sink shaving. Mark walks in. He hits a light switch and the shower doors frost over so he can't see me. He can see my head but not my naked body.

"I need to tell you both something. I am going to ask Savannah to marry me."

"Oh my god! That's great." I say. "Congratulations!"

Justin doesn't say anything but looks at his brother through he mirror. They exchange a look.

Mark looks at Justin. He puts his hand on Justin's shoulder. "When are you going to tie the knot?"

"We haven't talked about it lately." Justin says.

I make like I am not listening to the two of them. I start singing Like a Prayer. They both continue talking. I turn the water off and Justin hands me a towel. I dry off and then get in my wheelchair. I kiss both of them on their cheeks and leave the bathroom. I take my clothes into the guest bedroom and get dressed.

When I find the two of them, they are making breakfast. Mark hands me a bowl of fruit. I eat it. Justin puts a plate of scrambled eggs and toast in front of me. I eat breakfast. They feed Bob and Astro together.

Mark stands next to me with his hand on my shoulder after Justin leaves for work. He had to go to court. He sits with me at the table. I open up the laptop so that I can book Justin's clients.

Mark looks at me. "What do you think about me marrying Savannah?"

I look up from the computer screen. "Mark. You have. Loved her since we were children."

"That's not what I asked you."

461

"Mark, I love you. I want you to know that if you marry her and it doesn't work out, I am on your side no matter what. I am willing to lose my best friend because that's how strongly I feel about you."

"Sebastian, I value your view."

"Mark, I love you enough to keep my views quiet."

He grabs me in a tight hug. "I want to marry her, but I don't want to loose you."

"Loose me?" I hold him close. "Why would you loose me?"

"If I marry her? Will I loose you?"

"No. Of course not. I am going to be your sister. I am going to marry Justin."

He holds me closer to him. He closes his eyes tightly. "I love you."

"I love you." I put my hands on his shoulders and look up at him. "Why didn't you tell me that I always dreamed of Justin? You know all my secrets. Why didn't you tell me that Justin was dream guy?"

"He wasn't ready. If you would have known him growing up, we wouldn't be here right now. Justin has turned into a great guy, but he wasn't always a great person and he wasn't ready for you."

"Mark?" I look at him. Tears stream from my eyes.

"Losing the baby was not your fault. No one ever blamed you." He kisses me on the forehead.

"It meant the world to me that you came."

"I had to."

"Why?"

"Sebastian I have loved you since I met you. Every time Candy had you over for whatever reason, I changed my plans so I could be close to you."

"Oh my god, Mark."

"I am happy that you and Justin found each other. I love that you two are going to have my niece and that you are going to get married. I love that you are going to be my family."

"Mark, you have always been my family." I hug him. "Marry her. She loves you. She has always loved you. She was so happy that your parents were together because then she could always be around you. You are her sunrise and sunset. She loves you. She always has. She always will. She's not perfect but she loves you."

"She told me about that guy when she was in college."

"She never dated anyone in college. She was homesick for you. She stayed in her room. When you came to visit her that was the best day of her life. She was sad when you left her. She was devastated because you were dating that one girl."

"I had to."

"Why?"

"Because I had to get you out of my mind."

"Me?"

"If you were with anyone else other than my best friend and little brother, I would steal you away and I would be planning the wedding of my dreams to my Litter Mermaid."

"Mark." I choke. "Why didn't you ever tell me?"

"I didn't want anything to ever ruin our relationship."

"Me either. But don't think that the times that you just showed up to be there for me when no one else was went unnoticed. It never did. It meant the world to me."

"It meant the world to me too." He looks at me. "Have you spoken to her lately?"

"No."

"Why?"

"I guess I am stubborn. I am waiting for her to call me."

He smiles. "My Little Mermaid."

"My bookstore is going to open soon."

"I know."

"You and your cousins are always in my heart. And the new location! I have always wanted to bookstore to be there."

"I know." He says. He stands and picks up Bob who has been rubbing all against him the whole time that we were having our heart to heart. "It became available and Sebastian, Jacob and Seth reserved the spot."

I close my eyes.

"Sebastian? What are you thinking?"

"I wish I knew about them sooner."

"They do too."

My phone dings. I look at it. Savannah sends me a text message that she is at my house. I get Astro and my stuff. I hug Mark tight. He kisses me on the cheek close to my lips like he always has done.

I put my belongings in my car and get in. Astro gets in the car. I leave Justin's house and within minutes I pull into my driveway. I get out of the car.

Savannah gets down on her knees in front of me and hugs me. "I am so fucking sorry." She says.

I laugh.

She looks up at me. "Why are you laughing?"

"If you are fucking sorry, you are really sorry." I laugh again.

She laughs too. "Where were you?"

"I stayed at Justin's house last night. My house doesn't feel like my house much any more."

"Tell them to go."

"Its not them. Francesca is staying in my fucking den."

"Why?"

"She is working off her debt to society."

"Why stay at your house?"

"My house is the closest to her mandatory volunteering."

"Fucking wonderful." She says. "Why is she here?"

"She is Sabrina."

"You are fucking kidding me?"

"Nope. I knew that she looked familiar to me."

"I know."

We go into the house. Lindsey is standing in the middle of the room playing the violin. She plays songs from Phantom of the Opera. She plays with her eyes closed. She looks beautiful in a pale pink dress that hugs her body to her hips and then flares out.

Astro sits in front of her waiting for her to stop playing and then he throws himself down at her feet.

She opens her eyes. "Oh hi." She says.

"Hi."

"Trix left and took Francesca with her. I am going to be preforming later."

"Where are you doing that?" Savannah asks.

Lindsey looks at her. "You finally pulled your head out of your ass."

"Hi Savannah, how are you doing? Its nice to see you." Savannah says.

I look at the two of them.

"You are such a bi—" Savannah says.

"Both of you, cut the shit!" I tell them. I go into the bathroom and come out moments later.

"You want to fight?" Lindsey asks Savannah. "Get your violin and lets do it."

"Both of you stop." I say.

"Let me get it. I have it in the trunk of my car." Savannah says. She leaves and Lindsey locks the door.

I look at Lindsey. "She has a key."

"Yeah well, she will have to find it." She says holding up Savannah's key ring.

I smile at her.

"Did you have a good night?" She asks. She takes her bow and waves it in the air.

"I had a great night. I sleep better when I am with him." I say.

"I sleep better when Jacob is close by." She says.

"Is he still asking you to live with him?"

"He wants me to. Charlotte doesn't think too much of me."

"Why do you say that?"

Lindsey puts her violin down and sits on the floor with Astro. "I was there the other day having dinner with him. Charlotte came over. I went outside by his pool and stayed out of sight. I heard her telling Jacob that he can do so much better than Gina."

I look at her and smile.

"Why are you smiling?"

"Gina is the name of one of his boats. He is selling it cheap. She was telling him that he needs to demand more money. They weren't talking about you."

Lindsey hugs Astro. "Are you sure?"

"Yes."

"Should I be embarrassed?"

I move closer to her and put my hand on her shoulder. "No."

"Do we have to let her back in?" She asks with a twinkle in her eyes. She asks as Savannah knocks on the front door.

I roll my eyes. "You know we do."

"Just so you know, I hate her."

"I know you do."

"I will be nice for your sake."

"I know you will. That's why I love you."

"I love you too." She says.

Savannah bangs on the door. "Let me in!" She yells.

"I will do it." Lindsey says.

"Um no fucking way." I say laughing.

She rubs my belly before I can get away from her. "You hear your mommy's language? You can't use that word little one."

I laugh. I open the front door.

"Why would you lock me out?" She asks.

"The door is set to lock automatically." I say.

Lindsey takes my phone in her hand and goes on the app that allows me to lock and unlock the door from my phone. She locks the door.

Savannah spins around. "Oh is that something new?"

"Yes." Lindsey and I say together.

"Sebastian and the guys installed it to a make sure that I am safe." I say.

"We." Lindsey says.

I look at her. "Oh yes, I am sorry. To make sure that we are safe."

The two of them get into a fierce argument and go outside in the backyard to yell at each other. I can hear them through the closed doors. I sit at the piano and I play the scales soft at first and then get louder with every octave I play. I play Moon Light Sonata as fast and furious as I can.

I don't hear them come into the house. I don't hear the hum of their violins finding the notes. I play louder and faster. They match my pace.

None of us hear Trix return with Francesca. They stand watching the three of us. Lindsey stands with her eyes closed. Savannah play with her back to Lindsey. Trix takes out her phone and records us.

I play Phantom of the Opera songs next. I start the first song off quietly. Lindsey and Savannah let me set the pace and the volume. They step away from each other. They still don't notice that Trix is back.

I play the first two songs the way they were meant to be played. The next one I speed up the tempo and they match me. Lindsey knows my style as we played a lot in college. Savannah knows my style too because we would play together as children.

My brothers stand outside and listen to the music battle that is taking place inside my house. Sebastian listens to the piano getting louder and louder as I play Memories from Cats.

Seth looks at Jacob and Sebastian. "I can almost hear her crying as she plays."

"I would have loved to have been at her college when she gave the performance of a lifetime." Sebastian says.

"We have heard her play." Jacob says. "But this. Whatever is going on inside that house, there has got to be tears involved."

"Should we go in?" Seth asks.

Justin pulls into the driveway. He can hear the music battle going on the second that he opens his car door. He joins Sebastian and the others on the driveway. Justin takes his phone out of his pocket and calls Mark. "I need you to come to Sebastian's."

"Is everything ok?"

"No. Savannah is over and they are having a music battle. I don't know who is playing louder."

"Oh shit." He says. "I am on my way."

"Should we go in?"

"No." Mark says. "I am on my way." He says again.

"What should we do?" Justin asks. "Mark. I have to tell you, this is the most beautiful thing I have ever heard. Its such raw emotion. We can feel the tears."

"We?"

"Sebastian and the others are here."

Mark pulls into the driveway. He hears the music collaboration. He jumps out of the truck and walks up the driveway slowly.

"How long do you think this will last?" Seth asks.

"Not sure." Justin says.

Inside the house, Francesca stands next to Trix. "This shit has got to stop."

"Francesca, I swear if you do anything to stop them, I will arrest you and lock your ass up."

"What is this? Its so loud in here."

"This is nothing. They can each get louder." Trix says.

"What is this?"

"This is how they fight."

"Why don't they fucking fight like everyone else?"

Trix looks at Francesca. "Someone has to give." She says. "This is a fair fight."

I can tell the differences in who is playing. When Savannah stops, I hear it. She screeches the last E and then stops. She finally sees Trix and Francesca standing there. Trix puts her finger to her lips.

Lindsey sits on the wheel of my wheelchair and she plays softer. We take it down and we both play softer. We play so soft that everyone thinks its all over. We play Cannon in D. We finally end.

Trix claps her hands. "That was amazing."

I look at her. "How long have you been here?" I ask.

"We have been here a while." Trix says.

"You should have told us." Savannah says.

"No way."

Francesca doesn't say anything.

Justin and the other guys come in the house. Lindsey and I put our heads together. Savannah gets on her knees next to me. She hugs me. I hug her. Every eye is on the three of us. Trix stands leaning against Seth bent over in a fit of laughter.

"Oh god, you bitches don't know how to fight!" She says.

I look at Trix and laugh. "I love you." I tell her. The whole room erupts in laughter.

Anastasia sits in Sebastian's kitchen at the table with photo books laid out. We all sit at around the table with her looking at pictures of my dad. I sit at the table crying. With every turn of the page, more tears fall. He stands in one picture holding Sebastian's hand. In the other hand he holds a balloon that reads, IT'S A GIRL!

I look at Anastasia. "I thought that he died before he knew that I was a girl." I say.

"He believed in his heart of hearts that you were a girl." She says. She looks at Sebastian. "When your momma was pregnant with you, he knew in his heart of hearts that you were a boy. When you arrived he popped a bottle of champagne. He held you for three whole days before anyone else could hold you."

Sebastian and I share a look and then hug each other.

"I remember him being happy that your mom and him were going to get married and that you were soon arriving. He couldn't wait." Sebastian says.

I look at Anastasia. "Do you have any recordings of his voice?"

Charlotte is standing in the kitchen. She hears my question. Jacob is standing with her. He looks at her and then back at us at the table.

"I will have to see if I can find anything. I am sure that I have something." Anastasia says.

"If you find anything, I would love to hear his voice." I say.

Jacob looks at Charlotte. "What aren't you saying?"

"I have recordings of him. He loved to make videos with Sebastian. I could alter some of them so that she knows that he was excited for her."

"You can't do that." Seth says.

"It was just an idea."

I sit in my car at a red light. I am deciding weather or not to go home. Astro barks at me and I look up at him in the review mirror. I decide to go to the bookstore. Its going to be opening soon, but I don't have a date set yet.

I pull into the parking lot and get out of the car. I get Astro out. I take the keys and go into the bookstore. I haven't been in here often enough. I have been avoiding coming to the new location, but when

I go inside, I am overwhelmed with how beautiful it looks. There are some things that are the same. But overall, its nothing like the old store.

The piano sits on a stage in the corner. I go to it and I start playing. I get lost as my fingers travel over the keys. The keys to a piano I have loved the moment I saw it. Its like returning to the most intimate lover I have ever had.

I don't hear the door open or Justin walk in and say my name. He stands in the middle of the room watching me. Seth walks in. He stands next to Justin.

"Does she always cry when she plays the piano?" Seth asks.

"No." Lindsey says as she walks over to join them. Astro walks over to them and lays at their feet.

Jacob walks in. When he sees me at the piano crying he doesn't stop to watch me with the others, he walks over and joins me at the piano. He sits with me and he plays with me.

Lindsey watches. She smiles. She puts her hands on her chest hugging herself.

Mark and Savannah walk into the bookstore.

"We saw the lights were on and thought that we would check it out." Savannah says. She watches Jacob and me playing. She looks at Lindsey. "Whats going on?"

"I guess they speak the same language. Its like us when we fight." Lindsey says.

"Doesn't that upset you?" Savannah asks.

"No. He is going to marry me and she is my sister in my heart. So family."

Eric and Piper walk in with Danny. Matt and Tristian come in too with Sebastian and Trix. They all stand in the middle of the bookstore.

"How long has this been going on?" Piper asks.

"She has been playing for a long time." Justin says. "I don't know that she knows that she set the alarm off. I am the on the call list so they called me after they called her and couldn't reach her."

"Has she been crying the whole time?" Eric asks.

"Since I got here." Justin says.

Ivan and Trevor are in town. They come to the bookstore.

Ivan watches me. He looks at everyone. "Was she talking about her dad?" he asks the room at large.

Sebastian and Seth look at Ivan. "Yes." They say together.

"How did you know?" Sebastian asks.

"I know her. I love her." He looks at Justin. "Differently than you do. But I will always love her."

Mark looks at Ivan. He knows exactly what Ivan is saying because that is exactly how he feels about me.

Sebastian looks at Jacob. "I didn't know he could play like that."

Lindsey looks at Sebastian. "I met him in a music class. A classical music class. He was classically trained. Larry would sit in the back of Jacob's class and would applaud loudly when Jacob had played a flawless piece. When he didn't, Larry would walk over to Jacob and slap him in the face in front of everyone."

Sebastian looks at Lindsey. "I didn't know that."

Seth watches. "Are we going to stop her? Are we going to stop them?"

Peter walks in the bookstore. He walks over to everyone. "What's going on with our girl and Jacob?"

"From what I have gathered, she was talking about her dad. Whenever she really thinks about all that he has missed. Everything. It makes her really sad." Ivan says.

"She should be a concert pianist." Peter says.

"When she was in college and I left her and her professor told her that she was showboating and needed to stop making it about her, she vowed that she would never be a concert pianist." Ivan says.

Piper hugs him. "I didn't know that you knew that."

Ivan hugs her back. "I know everything about her."

Jacob stops playing and takes me into his arms. He hugs me and holds me. I cry harder than I have been crying. Sebastian and Seth walk over and join in the hug. Ivan, Mark and Justin join us. Ivan takes me in his arms along with Mark. Mark rubs my back.

Matt takes Tristian by the hand along with Danny and gets them books. They each take a copy of The Call of the Wild off the shelf and they sit together reading.

Matt walks back over to the group of people who mean the most to me. "I haven't seen her like this in a long time."

"She used to do this in the other bookstore?" Justin asks.

"Not all the time." Matt says. "When there was only a few people in the store and my mom forced her to work the midnight shift. She would sit there and play the most joyous songs on the piano. Then the mood would change when she would play a lullaby. She would start playing and wouldn't stop. Then she would cry. Then she would go in the bathroom, clean herself up and go teach all day. I watched her one time play until she fell asleep."

"She would do that a lot when we were growing up." Piper says. "Her mom would carry her to bed."

"What was she talking about her dad?" Peter asks.

Oliver and Blake walk into the bookstore. "Whats going on?" They ask together.

"Did Francesca do anything to upset her?" Blake asks.

"No." Savannah says.

"She asked if there are recordings of Sebastian's voice." Seth says.

Oliver looks at Seth. "She wants to hear her father's voice?"

"Yes." Piper says. "She has always wondered what his voice sounded like."

"I will get her what she wants." Oliver says.

Justin walks around the bookstore. Blake follows him. "You ok?" He asks him.

Justin looks at Blake. "All these people love her. I just don't feel like I come first. Ivan and Trevor say that she is the love of their lives. My brother says that about her too. I know she loves me, but what if I am not enough."

Blake embraces Justin. "You know what you do that no one else does?"

"No."

"Stay. And she sees that. She loves you. There is no doubt in my mind that she loves you."

"Blake, I mean no disrespect to you, but you really don't know her."

"That's fair. Hurtful, but fair." Blake says.

"She wants to know about her dad. Did you know her dad? Can you tell her anything about her dad?"

"I didn't know him well enough. I know that he always welcomed people."

"Would he approve of me?" Justin asks.

Scarlett walks in the bookstore. She walks over to Blake and kisses him like there is no one else around them.

Francesca and Bianca look at them. "Oh my god stop!" Bianca says.

Francesca looks around at everyone. "She has a wealth of support." She says it quietly but Blake hears her.

"What?"

Francesca looks at Blake. "I have seen her where she has been totally alone."

Scarlett looks at her daughter. "I am glad that you know her." She looks at me. "I feel like my brother would be very disappointed in me that I didn't get to know his children."

"She wants to know about her dad." Justin says.

"I will get her the videos that I have of him."

"Go to her." Bianca says to Justin. "Take her in your arms like you did in New York."

He looks at me. "She is surrounded by the ones that she loves." He watches me. He notices that my color fades. He runs over and grabs me just before I faint. He lifts me into his arms and carries me into the private room in the back. He closes the door behind him. He holds me on his lap. He runs his hand through my hair. He kisses me tenderly.

I open my eyes. I hug Justin. "I am sorry." I start to say.

"Why?"

"I took you away from your work."

"Sebastian, you didn't take me away from anything. I heard you playing and I came in. You set off the alarm."

"What?"

He stands and walks over to the couch and sits me next to him. "I got a call from the police saying that the alarm was going off and that you weren't answering the phone."

"Everyone is here."

"They all came for you."

I move closer to Justin. I hug him. "I think my dad would have loved you. I think that he would have loved Sebastian and me."

He holds me again on is lap. "I love you."

"I love you too." I tell him.

"Lets go back out there and be with everyone who loves you. I will share you right now, but tonight there is only one soul I will share you with and that is Astro."

I smile.

He carries me back out to join everyone.

Eric hugs me. "We ordered pizza because the boys are hungry."

"Oh good. I am starving." I tell him. I hug him. "Thanks for coming.

He bends his finger and taps his knuckle against my forehead. "You set off the alarm. You set everyone off in a panic. Peter called me. I raced over here and came into the most beautiful sound I have ever heard in my life. It sounded so beautiful and so emotional." He looks at Danny and Tristian. "They were crying in the parking lot. Sebastian, your music, you as a whole person move all of us who know you."

Piper walks over and hugs us both. "Eric, you are such a romantic." She says.

"I love you all so much." I tell them.

"We love you too. Unconditionally." Piper says.

"I love you unconditionally." I tell her.

She kisses me on the cheek. "Go love him unconditionally." She says pointing to Justin. She puts her hand on my belly. I put my hand on her belly. "My belly is better than yours." She says. We both burst out in a fit of laughter.

"Piper, I love you!" I tell her.

"I love you too." She says.

Peter walks over and hugs me first then he hugs Eric. "My children, I have to go." He says.

"Stay and have pizza with us." Eric says.

"I have to go pack." He looks at me. "I am going to Paris tomorrow to meet your mom. Does she know that you are pregnant?"

"I told her. She told me she will try to get back for the delivery." I say.

He looks up at the ceiling. Then he looks back at me. "I promise you that if she is not here, I will be here no matter what. I can't wait to meet my granddaughter."

I hug him. "Peter, thanks for everything." I look around my bookstore that is only a week or two from opening its doors for business and I see all the hard work and dedication that went into relocating and reopening my store. I hug him and he leaves with tears in his eyes.

Chapter 31

I am at the bookstore with the front door perched opened. I can smell all the different fragrances coming from Seth's new restaurant. He still has the Marina Beach but he wanted to be closer to me so that if I needed anyone he is just two stores away. I can smell garlic bread baking and tomato sauce cooking.

Justin moved his beautiful office into the space next door to my store. The new office isn't as beautiful as the other one but he likes that he is right next door. He doesn't do trials as much because that takes him away from me.

Mark took Justin's office and turned it into a workshop so that he is closer to me too. He comes everyday to check on me more than once a day.

Savannah works as a consultant and opened her new office across the street from my store. Its in the same plaza. She stops in everyday to see how I am doing. She and Mark have stopped seeing each other. She was sad for a while, but she met someone who is remarkable and loves her. Actually, Dylan Landings came back into her life. She dated him when they were in college.

Dylan walks into the bookstore. He finds me behind the counter. He walks over and kisses me on the cheek. "Hi." He says.

"Hi." I smile.

"Savannah wanted me to come over and have lunch with you because she can't."

"Oh, you don't have to do that." I tell him.

"I wanted to ask you if Mark is ready to meet someone?"

"I am not sure." I say. "When they broke up a few months back, he took a job that took him away from us for a while."

"He isn't back yet?"

"No. We expect him back in a few weeks for the birth of the baby." I say.

"Do you talk to him."

"Everyday. A few times a day."

"Well my sister is looking forward to meeting all of you. She is looking forward to meeting you especially."

Since Savannah and Dylan started dating, she has been so much nicer to all of us. She smiles more. She sings all the time. That's what she does when she is the happiest. Although her and Mark were together what seemed like forever, when they went to couple's counseling they had found out that they fought more than they didn't. She returned the ring that Mark's grandma gave him to give to her. He tucked it away in a secret place and vowed that he would only give it to his daughter if he had one.

Dylan looks at me. "You feeling ok?" He asks. "I can call my brother. He is on alert. He told us that he thinks the baby is coming any time now."

I look at him. "I am feeling fine."

"You don't look like you are." He says.

"I just have been having cramps."

"Are they labor pains?"

Justin walks into the bookstore. "You still having cramps?"

"Yes." I say. "Its not severe."

"The doctor said that I should bring you for a check."

"Justin."

Dylan looks at Justin. "Its too soon for you have to gotten my text message."

Just then Justin's phone pings with a text message alert. He takes the phone out of his pocket and reads it. He smiles. "Thanks for looking after her."

Justin insists that we go to the doctor. So he takes me to my doctor. We go into the office and she tells me that I am in labor. She tells me to go the hospital.

Justin takes me to the hospital. He calls everyone. They all show up. My aunts and uncles. My cousins. Our grandmas are there.

Justin helps me on the bed.

They check to see how dilated I am. "The baby is crowning." The one says.

Justin holds my hand. "Are you in any pain?"

"No. I am uncomfortable but not in any pain." I say. My breath catches.

"Are you ok?" Justin asks.

"I am ok." I say.

An hour later, I am holding my baby girl in my arms. She is beautiful. She has ten long fingers and toes. She lets out a little whimper. She is so beautiful. Justin sits on the bed with me.

"She is just as beautiful as I thought she would be." I say.

"She is stunning." Mom says from the door. "Peter told me that if I didn't get here in time for the birth of my granddaughter that our relationship was over."

I look at Justin. He leans close to me and I put my head on his shoulder. "It's always about her."

He kisses me on the lips.

"Come meet your granddaughter." I say.

Mom walks over and takes her from me. "What is her name?"

"We didn't name her yet." Justin says.

"Do you have any ideas?" Mom asks.

Jayne walks in. She walks over and kisses me on the cheek. She hugs Justin. She looks at the baby. "Oh my, she is beautiful." She says.

She sits on the bed with us. My mom cradles my daughter closer to her. Jayne watches her.

Jayne looks at the two of us. "What are you going to name her?"

Mom hands her back to me.

Justin puts his hands on me and the baby. He kisses the baby's forehead. "What do you think?" He asks me.

I kiss him.

"You both are killing us." Mom says.

"Valentina." I say.

Justin kisses me passionately. "That's the name I wanted."

Mom looks at me. She sits on the chair. "That's what we were going to name you." She says. "I named you after your dad like you know, but we had picked Valentina for you."

Goosebumps cover our arms. I close my eyes and breathe in my baby. I open my eyes and look into my daughter's eyes.

The nurse walks in. "We are going to take the baby for now."

"No. I want to keep her with us." I say.

"Are you going to nurse her?" The nurse asks.

"No."

"We have to feed the baby."

"I don't know who you are and I want to keep my baby with us." I get loud.

Peter walks in with the nurse that I know. The two nurses chat among themselves. The one that I know walks over. "Did you pick a name for baby Case?"

"Yes." I say.

"What did you decide?"

Trix walks in with Seth. They walk over and kiss me. She puts a big pink bag on the bed with pink balloons. She looks around the room. There are pink flowers everywhere. "Just so you know, Anastasia is coming. She stopped at the gift shop to get you something nice." When she says 'something nice' she does air quotes. She rolls her eyes.

I hold out my hand to her. When she takes it, I pull her towards me. "She's going to be your grandma when you marry Seth."

"I know." She says and flips her bright pink hair.

Seth takes her into his arms and kisses her. "She is technically the Sebastians grandma." He smiles against her lips.

"And she will kick your ass for saying such a thing." Jacob says. He walks in with a pink gift bag, balloons and flowers. He kisses everyone in the room. He looks at Valentina. "Can I hold her?"

"Of course you can." I say.

He cradles her in his arms. "She is stunning." Jacob says.

A nurse walks into the room. She looks at me and sees that I appear to be tired. "Ok, only the daddy can stay. Everyone else needs to go." Once everyone has left the room she hands me a bottle to feed the baby.

Justin sits with his shirt off and the baby laying on his chest. He feeds the baby while I sleep. Valentina makes a whimper. Justin stands and walks around with her and she closes her eyes. She falls asleep. He puts her down in the crib that they brought in for her and she cries immediately. He picks her up and sits back in the chair with her and she falls asleep again.

An hour later, Justin's parents are back in the room with us. His mother is holding Valentina. She sits quietly talking to her. Justin sleeps in the other bed in the room. Justin's dad walks around the room looking at the cards and the flowers.

He walks over to me. "I think you need to get out of the bed." He says.

"I think so too, but I am waiting for my doctor to clear me."

"I am clearing you." He says. "I will help you. I think that you need to go for an outing." He helps me get my legs off the side of the bed. Then he helps me when I stand up. He gets my wheelchair for me. When I sit in it, he walks around to help me put my feet on the hangers. He walks back around my wheelchair and pushes me out of the room. Before we get into the hallway he slips his white coat on.

"Where are you taking me?" I ask him.

"We are going to see the garden. You need fresh air."

When we go outside into the atrium its beautiful. He sits on a bench. He looks at me and smiles.

"Are you happy?" He asks me.

"Thrilled." I say.

"Justin told me that he is so excited to be a dad. He also shared with me that he sad that you aren't married yet."

"Edward, I would marry him any day. He thinks that I want all the wedding hype, I don't need that. I just want to be his for the rest of my life."

"He wants you to have a memorable wedding."

"Anyway it happens will be memorable." I look away from him. I blink away my tears. "Edward, you have known me almost my whole life, if you were my —"I choke. "If you were my dad, would you be proud of me?"

"Words can't be spoken of how proud I am of you." He says. "I am proud of all four of you." He hugs me tight to him. "Your dad, would be extremely proud of you and Sebastian."

I burst into tears.

"I never missed one of your recitals. I never missed your graduations. I was late to your high school graduation, but I was there to see you, my sweet girl cross the stage."

"Thank you." I say.

A nurse comes running out of the main doors. "You are not allowed out of your room!" She yells at me. She looks at Edward who is clearly identifiable as a doctor. "Oh I am sorry. They told me that the new mom left the hospital with some guy." She crosses the distance. "Its time to feed the baby again."

"I will take her back to the room." Edward says.

"I can let the dad feed the baby."

I smile. "Thank you. I will go back to the room and feed my little princess. Her daddy already fed her and changed her twice."

"How sweet." The nurse gushes.

We go back to the room. Justin is holding Valentina. When I enter the room, he hands her to me. He kisses me on the lips.

"I opened my eyes and my mom was holding the baby and you weren't anywhere. I panicked. I scared my mom." Justin says.

"Your dad told me that I had to get out of bed. He demanded it." I take Justin's hand. "You were sleeping and I didn't want to disturb you."

"Where's your mom?" Jayne asks.

"I am not sure." I say "She didn't say goodbye but that's like her." Jayne looks at me. "You know she loves you."

"I never said that she doesn't love me. I know she does. I just also know that she loves her life and wants to live it at all costs."

Justin kisses me.

Mark walks in the room with Paige. She is a nurse. She walks over and checks the baby's color. "She looks a bit jaundice. It seems like your little one is going to have to go into the tanning bed." She jokes.

I smile at her.

"Don't worry. This is all normal." She takes the chart. "Let me go check with your doctor and make sure that we are all on the same page." Her long hair shuffles around her shoulders as she talks. Her long ponytail is thick and it swishes from one side to the other as she talks. Its almost like a clock's tick tock. I find it a bit annoying.

"Thanks Paige." I say.

Before she leaves the room, she kisses Mark on the cheek close to his lips. "I will be right back."

I look at Mark. "I like her a lot." I say but don't really mean it.

"Me too."

"How did you meet her?" Jayne asks.

"I built her a closet the size of my house." Mark says.

Justin looks at Mark. "Do I not live there anymore?"

"Relax. You do."

"Are you two going to live together?" Jayne asks Justin and me.

I bury my face that is glowing with embarrassment into my daughter.

"We do live together." Justin says. "I am still helping Mark out with the house. I still have clothes there and some of my belonging there."

"I thought that you were going to move into Sebastian's house."

"I have roommates." I say.

"Oh, it was my understanding that you owned the house." Jayne says raising an eyebrow.

"I do. My friends needed somewhere to live and I have the room for them."

"Have you thought of selling your house and buying one that the two of you own together?" Jayne asks.

Edward reads the room better than anyone. "They have a child. They are not married and they each are paying for their own way right now."

"I love my house." I say quietly.

Paige walks back in with the doctor. Valentina appears orange against the little white blanket that she is swaddled in. He takes her from me. "We will bring her back in a little while." He says.

A few days later, I am home and Justin is with me. Trix and Lindsey are staying with Seth and Jacob. Its nice to have quiet in my house again but I truly miss my friends who will soon be my family.

Justin has set up with Mark and Edward cribs that I can easily get Valentina in and out of. Astro has been really great since we brought her home. But It has been just him and me for a long time so I can read him like a book. I know that he misses his time with me.

Justin has taken time off of work to be with us. He doesn't live with me full time yet, but we are making it work. He stands in the kitchen making lunch for us. Actually warming up lunch that Seth brought for us.

I sit on the couch with Valentina on my lap. Astro lays on the couch with me. He is curled up touching me. I put my hand on his head and fluff his ears. Justin brings over the plates and puts them on the coffee table. He gives Astro a chew toy. Astro looks at me.

"Its ok." I say. I pet him.

"He has always been a fan of mine, but lately he doesn't like me."

"He loves you, Justin. Its just that its been him and me all this time. I play with him as much as I can. I think that he would love to go to the dog park and run. I think he misses Bob."

Justin kisses me. "I miss Bob."

"Can you take her for a minute? I have to change positions."

Justin takes her. "Have you heard from any of your girls?"

"No." I say.

"What do you think of Paige?"

I look at Justin. "I am trying to give her a chance but I don't see what he sees in her. I don't say that to be mean."

"I don't see it either." He holds Valentina close to his chest. "I know that he is over Savannah."

"I don't know that to be true."

"She seems over him."

"Justin, she is good at making people see what she wants them to see."

"I thought that you didn't want him to marry her."

"If she isn't the right person for him. I don't. They are each other's fall back. They are comfortable. With each other but overall do they love each other, I am not sure."

"I miss my brother being happy."

"I miss Mark being happy too. I miss Savannah and Piper. I miss my friends."

"Do you miss your brothers?"

"I do. I think my mom spoke to them and told them to stay away."

"You should call them."

"I don't want to interfere with their lives."

Justin gives Valentina back to me. "You get the opportunity to interfere in their lives. They want you to."

I feed Valentina and then Justin changes her. He gives her a bath in the sink and then puts her in our room for a nap.

I have been home for three weeks without leaving the house. I have been going stir-crazy. I love having Valentina, but the house is so quiet. Its been three weeks without seeing any of my friends or even receiving phone calls from them.

When Justin has to leave for work his dad comes and stays with Valentina and me. I love that but he makes himself busy. He cleans my pool. He does my laundry. He cleans my house. He mows the lawn.

My bookstore has been up and running for weeks now and I haven't been there once. Matt is running it and doing a great job. Matt emails me a lot during the day and I respond to them almost immediately. He doesn't call because he doesn't want to wake the baby.

Edward comes in from the backyard of my house. He looks at me. "You doing ok?"

"No." I say.

"Are you not feeling well?"

"I feel fine. I miss my friends and my family all around me. I miss noise. I hate silence. She's not going to break if there is noise around."

"Sweetheart." Edward says.

"I need to take a shower."

"Go, I will be here if she wakes up from her nap. I love that I have a grand baby. This makes me very happy. The time spent with you and her."

I go in my room and close the door. I take a quick shower and then get dressed. I do my hair and put makeup on for the first time in weeks. I take my phone off the dresser and look at it. I have twenty-five text messages.

Ivan: Hi love, hope you are doing well. Trev and I will be in town by the weekend. We want to come visit you and your princess. Love you

Savannah: Hi girlfriend-sister I need to talk to you ASAP!

Piper: I am in labor!

Lindsey: I miss you. I love that I am spending quality time with my MAN!! Xoxo! But can I come home?

Trix: Hi sweetie, my dad is making me crazy. He wants to come see you and the baby. Let me know what works. I don't think I can take him calling me a thousand times a day. Help me. Help me. Help me.

Seth: Your mom told us to stay away. I have a niece that I am dying to hold.

I stop reading and scream. "I fucking new it!"

Edward comes in my room. "Are you alright?"

I show him the phone. "I fucking new it." I say again.

He holds Valentina closer to him and covers her ear that is closest to me.

I laugh at him. "Edward, what are you doing?"

"Don't use that language in front of the baby."

I laugh. "You are crazy. Is the baby going to remember that I said fuck when she was almost a month old?"

"Take your time, I am going to dance with my granddaughter."
Edward says.

There is a knock on the front door. I race out of my room to go
get the door. Peter stands there with flowers and two gift bags. He has
a big teddy bear too. When I open the door he comes in and puts the
teddy bear on the floor for Astro. Astro circles it three times and then
pulls it across the floor and then lays on top of it.

Peter hugs me. "Hi sweetheart."

"Hi." I say cheerfully. "Astro loves you the most grandpa."

Peter hugs me. "Can I hold her?"

Edward walks over and hands Valentina over to him. He kisses me
on the cheek. "I have to go. Candy is coming for dinner."

"Edward, thank you for everything. Love you."

"I love you too." He kisses Valentina on the head. "Tell your daddy
to call his daddy." He says.

"I will tell them both to call you." I say.

Peter sits on the couch with Valentina. He never stops smiling. He
looks at me. "How are you doing?"

"Good. Not good. Good."

"Ok. Whats going on?"

"It seems that mom told everyone not to bother me."

Peter looks at me. "I told her not to do that."

"She told my brothers to stay away."

Peter closes his eyes. "Call all your friends and the friends that are
your family and get them here. Its too quiet around here."

"Piper is in labor." I say. "If you want to go be at the hospital for
the birth of your grand baby, I am ok."

"Eric is like my son."

"Go. Be there for the two of them." I reach for Valentina and he
puts her in my arms. I kiss him on the cheek.

"Love you. If you need anything at all, I am a phone call away."

Valentina sleeps in the crib in the family room. I have the television on the Hallmark channel playing one love story after another. I set my iPad up so I can read all my text messages. I respond back to Piper.

Me: So happy for you. So sad that I can't be there. Love you.
Piper: She's here!
Me: Congratulations
Piper: love you ♥
Me: love you too always

Lindsey unlocks the front door. She comes in with her bags. She greets Astro and brings him outside so he can run around and play for a bit. Jacob is with her and he runs chasing Astro. Astro loves it. He jumps on Jacob. Then he squats and does his business. Lindsey walks over to the mailbox and takes a dog bag and picks up the poop.

They come in and Astro lays on the teddy bear. Lindsey looks at it and laughs. "What the hell is that?" She asks.

I laugh. "What the hell does it look like?"

"Why would you get him a teddy bear that big?"

"You think that I got him that teddy bear? I didn't. Peter was here and he brought gifts for us. All of us."

"Nice." Lindsey says.

Astro rolls on his back with his paws up and throws his head back biting the teddy bear's nose. Jacob sits on the floor next to the big bear and pulls Astro unto his lap. He rubs his hands all over Astro. Astro loves every second of the attention.

Lindsey walks over to the crib and lifts my sleeping daughter. Valentina opens her eyes and then closes them. "She's a living doll." She says.

Ivan and Trevor come with flowers and bags full of presents. Ivan takes me in his arms and holds me tight. I melt into him. Trevor hugs both of us.

The door opens and Justin walks in from work. I can feel his eyes on us. He surveys the room and sees that Jacob is sleeping on the floor using the big teddy bear as a pillow with Astro curled up with him.

"Wow, it's a party." Justin says.

Ivan straightens and hugs Justin tightly. "Congratulations daddy."

"Thank you so much." Justin says. "How is fatherhood treating you?"

"All I can say is thank god for grandma." He looks at Trevor.

"Its ok. My mother loves having the twins. She loves keeping them when we need to travel."

"Have you been traveling?" Lindsey asks.

Ivan looks at all of us. "I am in an expedition dancing. It will be touring at the end of the summer in Fort Lauderdale. That's why I signed on to do it." He looks at Lindsey and me. "I want to dance to the two of you playing."

"I am so there." Lindsey says.

"Me too." I say. I can't help but smile.

There is a knock on the door. Trevor is closest to it so he opens the door to Matt and Tristian. Danny is with them too. They run to me and hug me tight. I hug them back.

"We miss you so much!" Danny says.

"I miss you too." I tell them.

"Are you coming back to us?" Christina asks.

"Maybe in the fall." I say.

Matt hugs me. "The bookstore is doing so well. It totally helps that we offer free WiFi." I smile at him. He looks at Valentina. "She is beautiful."

"Thank you so much."

"Does she sleep well?" Trevor asks.

"She does. She is really an easy baby. She cries a bit but mostly she is really good and seems content." I say.

Ivan looks at Justin. "Are we overwhelming you by all of us being here?"

"No." Justin says. "Sebastian has been stir-crazy because its too quiet." Justin takes the throw blanket off the couch and covers Jacob with it.

Lindsey looks at all of us. "Jacob's apartment is being sprayed for ants. He just got back from a long trip and we couldn't go to his apartment."

"You can stay here." I say.

"No. We are going to stay with Seth and Trix."

"Your room is still your room." Justin says.

I look at Justin. "Piper had the baby."

Everyone gets excited. Jacob opens his eyes. He jumps up. Astro jumps up too and barks. I hold out my hand to Astro. He trots over. Jacob looks around the room and embarrassment creeps up his cheeks. "I fell asleep."

"Its ok." I say.

"We just got back from a really hard cruise and I can't go to my apartment." He rushes.

"Jacob, you are welcome here any time. All the time."

"No. Your mom told us to stay away from you or she was going to get a restraining order."

"What?" Justin and I ask together.

"She told Sebastian that he if calls or comes here she will have him arrested for identity theft."

"Get him on the phone." Justin says.

Jacob takes his phone out of his pocket and then hands the phone to me. When Sebastian answers I burst into tears. Jacob takes the phone. "Come to Sebastian's house."

"I can't do it."

Justin takes the phone from Jacob. "Come over and see your sister. If any legal issues occur, I will take care of them."

"She's going to have me arrested for identity theft." Sebastian says.

"Come over. We all need to see you."

"I am with Seth and Trix."

"You all need to come and hold your niece." Justin walks out of the room. "Your sister is suffering from depression because she misses all of you. And your mom."

"Linda told us."

"Sebastian, I swear that nothing will happen."

"Ok. We are coming."

"She needs you."

They are at the new restaurant. Peter goes into the restaurant. He walks over to Sebastian and Seth. "I heard that Linda claims that she will have you arrested if you go see your sister. Go see your sister. She misses you guys terribly. She going crazy being in the house. She loves Valentina. She just needs to be around people her own age. You need to go to her. You need to stay as long as you can and then keep going back."

"Linda made it clear at the hospital that if we went into the room to see Sebastian, she was going to have all of us arrested." Seth says.

"She probably thinks that we don't want to be around her." Sebastian says.

"Well then go to her." Peter says. He looks at all of them. He takes Trix by the hand. "Piper and Eric had a girl."

They all cheer.

"Go spend time with your sister and your friend. She needs you all. Trix call your dad and bring him with you."

"I will." She says.

Almost an hour later, my house is back to what I am used to. It's loud with a lot going on. Conversations are taking place in every inch of my living room and kitchen. Seth and Jacob are in the kitchen making dinner for everyone. Homemade pizzas. There is laughter and pots dropping. Spoons clank against the pots and counters. Valentina sleeps through the whole thing.

Savannah plays the violin softly with Lindsey. My house is full of music. It comforts me. I sit on the couch holding my daughter. I snuggle into the couch surrounded by Justin and all the people that I love. I close my eyes and sleep like I haven't done since before I got pregnant.

Justin takes Valentina and puts her to bed. He comes back and he covers me, Sebastian, Jacob and Seth. Savannah and Lindsey are sleeping on the other couch with Trix.

Ivan and Trevor go in the kitchen with Justin. They clean up the kitchen. They sit at the table and Astro sits with them. He puts his head on Justin's lap.

"I am going to take him out. You want to come with me?" Justin asks both of them.

"Yes." They both say staggered from each other.

Justin puts Astro's leash on him. He opens the door and they walk outside. There is a police car circling the neighborhood. The car pulls into my driveway. Ivan and Trevor take Astro from Justin.

Trix walks outside. She looks at the police officer who is sitting in his car. She walks over to the car with Justin.

"Can we help you, officer?" Justin asks.

"There was a complaint made about too much noise coming from this house." He says and rolls his eyes at how stupid that sounds because its overly quiet. He hears Valentina cry. "Sounds like we woke the baby." He looks at his partner. "Lets go."

"Are there all men living in that house?" The other officer asks.

Justin looks at the two officers. "These two are my brothers and my wife is in the house with the baby." He looks at Trix.

"I will take care of this." She says.

Chapter 32

Jacob and Lindsey sit in his apartment on the balcony having breakfast. Lindsey is sitting with her phone in her lap as she pops scrabbled eggs in her mouth. Jacob sits across from her at the table. He stares off at the horizon.

"Babe, are you alright?" She asks.

He looks at her. "I am fine."

"What's going on?"

"Nothing." He says.

"Honey, I can sense that something is wrong. What is it?"

Jacob looks away. He stands up and walks to the railing and puts his hands on it. "I sold something for a lot of money."

"That's great."

"Well not really. I mean it was meant to be sold but it was the only copy that I had of it and—"

"And?"

"And I want it back."

"What was it?"

"A picture."

"You sell a lot of pictures."

"I meant to make a copy of this specific one and I didn't get around it."

"Don't you have the prints?"

"I can't find it." He says.

She stands and walks behind him. She puts her arms around him. "Don't you know who the buyer is?'

"No. It was a blind sale. The buyer wanted to stay unknown."

"Can't you track it by the payment?"

"No. It came from a LLC." He says.

"Can you recreate it?"

He turns to her and takes her in his arms and kisses her face over and over again. She laughs at him.

They both sit down and finish their breakfast. Their phones rings almost at the same time. Lindsey looks at it and sees that its me. Jacob holds his phone up to show that its Sebastian calling him. They both answer their calls. Lindsey brings the plates into the kitchen.

"Hi." She says into the phone.

"Hi." I say.

"What's going on?"

"I am planning the Christening for Valentina and wanted to make you the Godmother."

"Oh my god!" She says. She squeals with happiness. "What does that mean for Savannah and Piper?"

"Piper is going to make Savannah a godmother too."

"She didn't ask you first?"

"I am the godmother to both of Ivan's babies."

"What?" She asks. "He made me the godmother of the twins." She says.

"I know. I was there." I say laughing.

Jacob talks to Sebastian. "All I know is that with the baby and the bookstore and all that she does, I miss seeing her. You haven't seen her in weeks."

"I know. I feel terrible about it."

"What can we do to make this better? Seth sees her everyday. Sometimes more than once a day. I just don't want to overwhelm her."

"That's how I feel, so I stay away. Linda was scary when she threatened us." Sebastian says. There is a knock on his his door. Astro, his cat, runs to the door. He meows and jumps around. "Hey, hold on once second, there is someone at my door."

"Call me back." Jacob says.

"I will." Sebastian says.

He walks to the front door. He opens it. "Hi." He says.

"Hi." I say back. "Want to hold Valentina?"

"Yes." He says and takes her from me. "I didn't see anyone drive up the driveway."

"That's because I didn't. Justin dropped us off for a visit." I say.

He hugs me warmly. "Come in."

"I miss you." I tell him.

"I miss you too."

When I enter the house, Astro jumps on my lap. "Hi Astro." I say. The cat rubs his face against my chin. "Its nice to see you too." I tell him.

"Can I get you anything?"

"No."

He holds Valentina up to look at her. "She looks like you did when you were a baby."

"That's what I keep hearing." I say. "I don't really see it." I pet Astro. "Thank you for saying that." I look up at Sebastian. "Why are you stating away?"

"I got served at work." He says.

"You were what?"

"Linda had a restraining order served to me at work. The orders say to stay away from you."

I look at him. "Don't." I tell him.

"Don't what?"

"Stay away. She did that to grandma. That's why she stopped coming to Florida to see me. You. Us." I look away. "Please don't stop coming over and seeing me. I missed out on too much of you my whole life."

"She attached a note." He says.

"Can I see it?"

"Yes." He walks to his home office and gets the letter. He comes back and hands it to me. He is still holding Valentina in his arms. She has fallen asleep.

"She must love you."

494

Unconditional Love

"Why do you say that?"

"She's sleeping. She doesn't do that often."

"No?"

"She likes to sleep in Justin's arms. She doesn't like to lay flat. She did but then my mom came to visit and disrupted everything. My mom thought it was better to let her cry it out. Since then she screams when we put her in the cribs."

"Sebastian, why didn't you pick her up?"

"I did. My mom ran over taking her from me and put her in the crib forcefully. I picked her up again and my mom yelled at me that I was spoiling her."

"What did Justin do?"

"He brought her in our room and slept with Valentina on his chest."

"What happened after that?"

"My mom and Peter left. My mom came back the next day and pulled the bottle out of Valentina's mouth. When she started whaling, mom took her from me and put her in the fucking crib. Valentina screamed and I picked her up. Mom yelled at me that she needed to self sooth. Trix came in and threw mom out."

Sebastian puts his hand on my shoulder.

"How can I ever repay the money to Jacob for my bookstore?" I ask.

Sebastian steps back. "You don't have to pay him back."

"I do. I know that he sold something to get the money for my bookstore." I hoist Astro in my arms and kiss the cat on his forehead. "I know that my insurance didn't pay enough for the location."

Sebastian looks at me with his cat. "Don't spoil him." He says and laughs. "The more kisses you give him, the more he will want me to do the same."

I put my forehead to Astro's forehead and he purrs loud enough for both of us to hear him. "I have to pay everyone back. Mark did the most beautiful woodwork again. Only this time it tops what he did in the last one. He carved mermaids into the wood like we talked about years ago when—" I stop talking.

"When what?" He asks. He lays Valentina on the couch and barricades her with pillows. She sleeps soundly. He walks over and takes Astro from me. He sets Astro on the floor. He sits on the arm of the couch and takes me in his arms. "When what?" He asks again.

I start crying. "I got pregnant in college. Ivan and I had sex a few times. No one had ever showed me that kind of love before. I knew he was gay but it didn't matter to me. I loved him unconditionally. I found out that I was pregnant and he left. He left before I could tell him. I carried for a while and then I broke out in the worst sweat of my life. I was sick to my stomach and bleeding. Lindsey brought me to the hospital with her boyfriend at the time. He carried me in his arms the whole time. He held me when they told me that I had lost the baby. Lindsey and him brought me back to the dorm. Lindsey stripped the bed and her boyfriend never put me down. He held me they way I wanted to be held by Ivan. Mark called and Lindsey told him that I needed him. He came immediately. He held me in his arms for weeks."

"You didn't do anything wrong. Not all pregnancies last."

I wipe the tears from my face. "I called my mom and told her that I needed her. She was in Italy traveling to France and then Spain. She told me that I knew it was her travel time and she would be there when she could get there." I reach for Sebastian and he takes me in his arms again. "She never came." I cry. "I never told her about the baby."

"Hey, look." He says. "You have a beautiful daughter. She was meant to be here. She was meant to be yours." He kisses my forehead.

"Mark stayed with me for weeks. He took me home. Edward and Candy were there too. Mark would call me Little Mermaid all the time."

"I want to call you that too."

"You can. Its fine. Can you tell me about dad?"

We sit together on the couch. Valentina sleeps the whole time. Sebastian looks at me. I smile. "What?"

"I want to hold her." He says.

"You can hold her." I tell him.

"Tell me about Craig Harrison." He says.

I tell him about Craig Harrison. My husband. I married him when I was in high school. He died shortly after. I did it because I felt in my heart that it was the right thing to do. I tell him that I went to school and focused all my time and energy on learning. I played the piano as therapy sessions. I started playing twenty-five minutes a day and then before long, I was playing more than I was doing anything else.

"Tell me about Trevor." He says.

"I was trying to get over constant losses in my life. I lost Ivan to Europe. I lost the baby. I lost my scholarship." I laugh.

"Why is that funny?"

"It just is. I sat out of school for my suspension. I was falling apart. I met Larry and he gave me a job. I worked my ass off for him. I worked long hours I worked longer than I was scheduled to do. I worked so hard I fainted at work. Larry sent me home. I was driving when I saw Trevor's car flipped over. I called for help and then I got out of my car and I stayed with him. I held his hand until help came. They had to use the jaws of life to get him out of the car. They put him in the ambulance and he wouldn't calm down. They got me in the ambulance and I held his hand. He was in the hospital for days, I never left him. I worked from the hospital room. When he was released he had no where to go. I was able to go back to school so I brought him back with me. One day Trevor was gone and my scholarship money was somehow reinstated."

"Wow."

"I have to tell you, I know that I cry a lot but the happiest day was finding out that I have brothers. I love you guys. I love that I am not an only child anymore."

"I hate that Larry didn't tell us about you."

"I feel the same way."

Valentina opens her eyes. I reach for her but Sebastian beats me to it. "Hi sweet girl. I am your uncle. My name is the same as your mommy's which is going to confuse people." He kisses her forehead. "You are my first niece."

There is a knock at the door. Jacob doesn't allow Sebastian to come answer it. He walks right in. "Asher!" He yells. "I can't find her. I have been everywhere looking for Sebastian—" He walks fully in the room and runs to me. He hugs me. "I have been in a panicked state of mind for the last twenty minutes. I have been calling your cell phone. I went to your house I have been calling everyone. Lindsey said that the last time she saw you was at the bookstore. I went there."

"I am ok." I tell him. "Justin dropped me off here because there is a problem at my house."

Sebastian looks at me with worry. "Whats going on at your house?"

"Francesca has barricaded herself in my house and has threatened to do harm if anyone comes in."

Sebastian reluctantly hands Valentina to Jacob. He takes her and sits right in the same spot that Sebastian was just sitting. Sebastian walks across the room and gets his cell phone. He punches in numbers. "Blake, go get your daughter! She has worn out her welcome." He clicks the phone to end the call.

Jacob sits next to me. He holds my daughter in his arms. "The little thing radiates love." He kisses her forehead.

"How do I repay you?" I ask.

They both look at me.

"You don't have to repay anything. We owe you so much more than a bookstore." Jacob says.

"You don't owe me anything." I say.

Jacob kisses Valentina on the forehead again. "I called you a gold digger. I have to make up for that."

"No." I say.

Sebastian looks at the two of us. "Mom is coming over. She doesn't want to intrude."

"Because of me." I say.

"She doesn't want to intrude on our time together."

"She can come. I could use a mom. It doesn't have to be mine. My mom is making my life harder than it has to be because I am not married. She—" I stop talking.

Jacob stands and hands the baby to Sebastian. He stands in front of me. "She what?"

"She called me a s—"

"Your mom called you a slut?"

"Yeah."

"Why does she do that?" Jacob asks.

"Because she can." I say. "Maybe she is right. I have been intimate with a few guys in my life."

Charlotte comes to the house. She comes with Seth and Trix. When they come in the house, Justin is with them too. Mark comes as well.

Lindsey comes over too. She brings my Astro with her. The second that Astro sees me, he runs to me and leaps on me licking me in the face. I kiss the top of his head. Lindsey makes her way around the room hugging everyone as does everyone who just got to Sebastian's house.

There is a knock on the door. Sebastian walks to the door. He opens it to Anastasia. She hugs Sebastian.

"You have a house full of people." She says.

"I have a house full of family." He says.

"Where is your girlfriend?" Anastasia asks.

"Amanda? She took a job transfer. She now works in New York." He says with a hint of sadness in his voice.

"Do you date?" She asks him.

"I have in the past. Lately I haven't, but I am not looking for anyone now."

She looks around. "Your family is here."

"My family is here."

"Sweetheart, everyone has someone." She tells him.

"I know." He walks over to Seth and takes Valentina from him.

"Hey! I was holding my niece."

"You had her too long." Sebastian says.

Justin looks at them and smiles.

Justin takes his phone out of his pocket and walks into the kitchen to answer it. "Hi Rachael." He says.

"Hi. I don't mean to bother you at home with your family, but I needed to run something by you."

"Sure." He says.

"My team is investigating Larry Jenson and we keep coming back time and time again his ties with Sebastian. The problem is that when we look into Sebastian Timely we come up with two of them."

"I know." He says.

"They both have ties with Larry?"

"Yes."

"How is that possible?"

"He is the step father to Sebastian."

"Your Sebastian?"

"No."

"When do I get to meet him?"

"You will have to turn over the case to Jack."

"As soon as possible. I keep hitting a wall in my investigations." She stops talking and then takes a deep breath. "Linda has filed a restraining order against Sebastian from seeing Sebastian."

"I know."

"What are we going to do about that?"

"We can work it out tomorrow. I am with my family right now."

"Oh sure." She says.

Justin returns to the family room. Mark is now holding Valentina. Mark looks around the room. "Paige and I broke up."

"Sorry to hear that." Justin says.

"Yeah well." He looks at me. I look at him and then look away. "I miss my Savannah."

Trix looks at all of us. "Dylan left Savannah."

Mark's head jerks up. "What? They were so in love with each other. They were picking out wedding rings."

"He treated her badly." Trix says. "She changed jobs and he called her stupid for that."

"What is she doing now?" Mark asks.

"She's the top manager in a department store." I say.

Mark looks at me. "You knew?"

"Of course."

Mark walks over to Justin. He gives Valentina to him. He kisses Justin on his cheek. He kisses the baby. He walks over and hugs me. "What store?"

"Macy's in Boca Raton." I tell him.

He hugs me again. "I need her. Its like a I can't breathe without her."

"She says the same about you." I tell him.

Mark takes his keys off the table and walks to the door. He turns to say goodbye to everyone and then opens the door. Savannah stands in front of him. He takes her in his arms.

"Mark!" She cries.

"Savannah, I was just coming to get you." He kisses her over and over again.

Justin gets Valentina in the car seat. He puts my wheelchair in the trunk of the car. He drives us home. Lindsey and Trix are staying the night with me. Justin goes into my room and climbs into my bed with Valentina.

I sit in the kitchen with my friends. Savannah comes over as well. We sit having coffee. Piper comes over with both Danny and the baby. She places Erin, her daughter, in my arms. She kisses me on the forehead. "Meet your niece." She says.

"She's stunning." I gush.

"She's so pretty." Danny says.

"Your little sister is beautiful." I tell him. "She is very lucky."

Danny looks at me.

"How could she not be? She has the best big brother in the world. You are the sweetest boy."

"Did you tell Aunt Sebastian that you already changed poopy diapers?" Piper beams.

"You promised not to tell anyone." Danny whines.

"No. I promised not to tell grandma." She says kissing him on his nose. "But my best friends in the whole wide world, well we have no secrets. Besides you told Tristian."

"I am so proud of you." I tell him. "When I am not holding your baby sister, I am going to hug you tight."

"Can I watch TV with Astro?"

"I am sure that Astro will love the attention. He misses watching television."

"He doesn't get to watch anymore?"

"He does get to watch television, but Aunt Lindsey lives to play the violin and Astro loves listening to her play for him." I say.

"That was my favorite part of going to the bookstore. When you thought that no one was around and you play the piano. Astro would sit behind you with eyes on you the whole time. He would let Tristian and I pet him, but he never took his eyes off you." Danny says.

I look at Piper. She takes Erin from me. I grab Danny in my arms and hug him. I kiss him on his cheek over and over again. He laughs. "Danny, I love you." I tell him.

"I miss you." He tells me. He hugs me.

"Go watch anything you want with Astro. Remember no scary movies, he gets nightmares." Piper says. She kisses him on the cheek.

"Ok, mommy." He says. He runs off with Astro.

We look at her.

"The adoption went through. He is mine." She tells all of us.

"Congratulations." We all say.

She looks at everyone and then turns to me. "The adoption went through the day that Erin came. The judge came to the hospital to let it happen before Erin was born."

We sit and chat. Lindsey looks around. She stands and then sits.

"Lindsey, whats going on?" I ask.

"Jacob." She stands. "He is really sad lately."

Savannah looks at her. "Why don't you live with him permanently?"

"Its not about living with him. Besides, I promised my parents that I wouldn't live with him full time until we are married."

"Your parents would never know." Piper says.

"My mom knows all." Lindsey says.

I look at her with concern in eyes. "What's wrong with Jacob?"

"He sold a photograph before he wanted to. He didn't have a chance to duplicate it." She says.

"Why doesn't he ask the buyer for it back so he can make a duplicate?" Trix asks.

"Because the buyer wants to remain unknown." Lindsey says.

I look at her. "I will be right back. I have to go to the bathroom." I go into the bathroom I close the door. I call Ivan.

"Hi Love!" He says.

"Hi."

"Everything ok?"

"Did you privately buy a picture from Jacob?"

There is silence.

"He wants to make a print of it."

There is more silence.

"Ivan. Just let him know that you have it. Let him come to you and make a print of it and everyone will be happy."

"How do you know you I have it?"

"Is it a picture of me?"

"Its breathtaking." Ivan says.

"Let him know its you that has it. Let him make a print of it."

"I will contact him." Ivan says.

"Call him now." I tell him.

"I love you." He tells me.

"I love you always." I tell him. "Call him."

"I will call him right now."

I go back into the kitchen.

"You ok?" Savannah asks.

"I am." I say.

"Can I talk to you, privately for a minute?"

"Yes."

We go outside to the backyard. She sits on the bench seat. "Sebastian, I miss Mark so much. I tried staying away. I tried listening to everyone and giving him space and letting him try to find his way without me. The truth is, I am lost without him." She gets up and walks by the pool. She walks around the pool and then back. "I know I behaved badly. I am sorry." She walks back over. "Sebastian, I feel like I can't breath without him." She sits on my lap. "I don't want his grandma's ring. I don't want expensive things. I want him. I need him." She stands up and then gets on her knees in front of me. "I need your approval."

"You don't need my approval." I tell her.

She hugs me. "I know that you told him that you are willing to say goodbye to our friendship if I break his heart."

"Savannah, I have never held that back from you. I love you. I love him too. I have loved you since we were in second grade. I have loved him since Candy Kiss started dating Edward. The second that I set eyes on Mark, I have loved him. Whenever I needed a big brother that I didn't have, he was there."

"Will you stop loving me if I go back to him?"

"No. He loves you too. He misses you too. He needs you just as much as you need him."

Savannah hugs me tighter. "You are blessed."

I look at her. "You think so?"

"I do. You are loved unconditionally from Ivan, Trevor, Mark and your brothers adore you. Justin loves you so much."

"I don't always feel that Justin loves me." I tell her.

"Sweetheart, I wish you could see the way he looks at you. He radiates love just looking at you."

"We haven't spoken a word about getting married in weeks." I look at the French doors that lead into my bedroom. Justin is in my bedroom with our daughter. "I don't know if he wants to marry me."

"Talk to him about it."

"It makes me nervous because I don't want to know the answer if he doesn't want to."

"Sebastian, when we were young, after he kissed you for the first time. You said that you wanted to marry him. You didn't know his name but you have always dreamed of marrying him." She looks at me. "Marrying his isn't betraying Craig."

I look at her. "What?" I feel my blood boiling. I am getting madder by the second.

Trix comes outside. "I don't mean to interrupt, but Justin is requesting that you come into your room."

I look at Trix. Its like she knows that I am beyond mad. "Sure." I say. I open the French doors and go in my room. I close the doors behind me.

Justin takes me in his arms. "I can't wait to marry you. Lets plan a wedding that will make everyone you know jealous." He kisses me like he hasn't in a long time. He takes me in his arms and kisses me so passionately my toes curl. He senses my anger. He kisses me deeper. I relax a bit but my anger boils again.

He pulls back. "What's wrong?" He asks.

I rush into the bathroom and vomit in the toilet.

He comes in. "What's wrong?"

"I am so fucking mad." I say.

"What happened?"

"I love her. I hate her. She has to get out of my house. If your brother marries her, I will never see him when he is with her." I say and then turn to throw up again.

Justin leaves me in the bathroom and goes out to the kitchen. He stands staring at Savannah.

Lindsey and Piper get up from the table and come in the bathroom to be with me. Lindsey stops and picks up Valentina.

Justin looks at Savannah. "I am so sick of your shit." He says.

She blinks and tears come in force. "What?"

"What did you say to Sebastian?"

She blinks again. "I told her that marrying you wasn't a betrayal to Craig."

Trix looks at her. "Did you lose your mind?" She yells. Trix's outburst startles Justin. She puts her hand on his shoulder. "Savannah, what is wrong with you?"

She cries her eyes out. "I didn't mean to say it. That's not why I asked if we could talk alone. I wanted to tell her that I—" she looks at Justin. "I feel like I can't breath if I am not around your brother. I love him. I need him."

Justin looks at her. "You know, Mark loves you. But you know every chance you get you hurt his Little Mermaid, he will resent you. He loves her."

"She's hard to compete with." Savannah says without thinking.

Trix looks at her. "You jealous bitch."

"Every guy she meets falls in love with her. She becomes the love of their lives. No one has ever said that about me." Savannah say.

"You hold that against her?" Justin asks.

"I don't." Savannah says.

"It seems like you do." Trix says.

"Someone runs to Mark and tells him what I do and or how I act." Savannah says.

"She doesn't. She protects you." Piper snaps. "You make me sick. You literally made her sick to her stomach. She's in there throwing up because you told her that she is not betraying Craig." Piper steps closer so that she and Savannah are face to face. "You went that far back."

"I didn't plan on bringing him up."

"Why? Why would you do that?" Piper asks.

"I was asking her for her approval."

"Why?" Justin, Trix and Piper ask at the same time.

"Mark is my air." She says.

"You suck the life out of him." Justin says softly. "You drain him. But for whatever reason, he loves you. He is miserable if he isn't with you." He looks at her. "Stop hurting them. If you love him— love him. But this crazy act that you do when things don't go your way, stop that."

She inhales sharply. "You have never liked me." She accuses Justin.

"You never gave me a good enough reason to like you. I see how you treat people and I never wanted to be involved in your drama. My dad fell for it. Your mom fell for it. She still falls for it. She loves you and makes it so that its everyone else's fault, but its your fault. If my brother marries you, I will be nice to you because I love my brother and he is all I have. And you are Sebastian's friend, but know this. We. Will. Never. Be. Friends."

She gets her purse and runs to the door. She leaves quickly.

Justin looks at Trix and Piper. "Maybe that was harsh."

"No." They both say at the same time.

"No one ever stands up for Sebastian to Savannah." Piper says. "You know Mark loves you." She looks at Danny who is sleeping on the couch. "I have to get my children home."

"Let me help you carry him out." Justin says. He walks over to the couch and picks Danny up. Danny wraps his arms and legs around Justin without opening his eyes. Justin puts him in the car and kisses the top of his head. "Call her and let her know that you are home." He tells Piper.

"Ok, dad." She says. She hugs Justin. "Thank you for loving her. Never stop loving her. She loves you."

"Piper, you know I have always loved her. I always will."

"Tell her that." Piper says and kisses him on the cheek. "Call Eric and let him know his family is coming home."

"I will." Justin walks back in the house and gets Astro. He walks around the block to his house and walks in. He hugs Mark tight. They sit for a while with Bob and Astro at their feet talking. Justin tells Mark what he told Savannah.

"She always tries to one up my Little Mermaid." He scoops Bob up in his arms. "The truth is. I don't want to live without her."

"Well then don't." Justin says.

"I can't lose you. I can't lose Sebastian."

"You will always have us." Justin tells him.

"You have to marry her." Mark says quietly into Bob's fur. "The sooner the better. I have to move on. You have to marry her." Mark looks at Justin. "I have always been the one that she comes to when she really needs someone."

"Tell me about Craig." Justin says.

Mark looks at his brother and tears fill his eyes. "She loved you. She dreamed of you. She wrote journals that she would marry you. Mom took you away from dad and me. And her. Craig showed her love that she never knew. He was dying. For three years that's all we heard was he was dying. He asked her to marry him. She never hesitated. They said 'I do' and he passed out. He was in the hospital for weeks. She never left his side. She was with his mom. They never left. Two weeks later he died. It seemed like months. It seemed like time stood still. He was dying for so long. When he was gone, I went and got her. I brought her home. I held her while she cried. I was with her at the funeral. I held her hand while she spoke about him.

"She graduated top of her class in high school. I was there. I stayed with her the night that she moved into the residential hall at school. I was there for her. Savannah was there for her too. The best thing that happened to the two of them was going to different colleges. There was so much hurt. Savannah didn't say that she applied somewhere else. But absence makes the heart grow founder. I believe that." Mark looks at Justin. "Do yourself a favor."

"What's that?"

"Ask to see Jacob's portfolio."

"What?"

"Just trust me. He has captured all her big moments. He didn't know that he was taking pictures of his sister." Mark laughs. "Larry would bring Jacob with him. Jacob never went anywhere without his cameras."

"You know so much."

"I know a lot of things when it comes to my Little Mermaid."

Justin stands. He takes Astro's leach. "I love you."

"I love you too."

"Are you mad?"

"For being honest?"

"Yes."

"No." Mark hugs him. "Go hold her all night long."

Chapter 33

I sit at the counter of the bookstore working. I have wedding magazines open in front of me. I am looking at dresses and flowers. I am looking at color schemes and locations. Do I want a clubhouse wedding? Do I want a backyard wedding? Do I want a country club wedding? All things I write down. I rip the pages out of a couple magazines.

Justin is in the back room with Valentina. He contacts Jacob. "Hey, I have a client who wants to see your portfolio." He says leaving a message. "Call me when you get this."

Matt is working stocking the shelves with the new books that came out as it's a Tuesday. Music plays softly in the background.

I hum along with the song that plays. Life Will Go On by Chris Isaak plays next and I sing along with the radio.

Matt walks over to me. He pets Astro's head. "You look great."

I smile at him. "Thank you."

"Its nice to be working again." Matt says.

"I totally agree."

"Its safer that we close and that we are not open twenty-four-seven any more."

"I do miss the over nights." I say.

"I think like we discussed that we stay open twenty-four hours on Friday and Saturday nights. I like that. We are really busy those nights. And the piano bar and open mic night brings our customers back. The regulars agree that we shouldn't be opened twenty-four hours." Matt looks at what I am working on and then back at me. "They only came to make sure that you were safe." He smiles. "Wedding planning."

I look up from what I am working on. "I am grateful."

"They are too."

Justin walks over to me. He hands Valentina to me. "I will be back in two hours." He says.

"Justin, you don't have to come back for us. Seth is going to help me get home. Trix is coming over too." I pull him close for a kiss. "Where are you going?"

"I have a meeting in Jupiter."

"Are you going to jump on your rocket and pass by Mars?" Matt teases. He takes Valentina from me. "She is such a great baby."

"Ha. Ha. Very funny." Justin says.

I look at Matt and than at Justin. "Are you going to Jupiter with Jacob?"

He kisses me on the lips. "I love you. I will see in you in a bit." He runs to the door.

Matt look at me. "Go after him and kiss him in the parking lot where everyone can see your love. I have the baby."

When I move, Astro moves with me. "Go get him." I say to Astro. I rush to the door and go outside. "Justin!" I call.

He is on the sidewalk with Seth and Jacob. The three of them run over. "What's wrong?" They all ask at the same time.

I take Justin's hand. "I love you."

He straddles my wheelchair putting his one leg between my legs. He leans in and kisses me like we are the only two people living on this corner of the earth. He kisses me until we are both breathless.

"Be safe." I tell him.

He steps back grinning. I turn and go back into the bookstore. Astro trots in next to me.

Justin runs in the bookstore. He takes my hand in his and leads me to a corner of the bookstore that we can totally be alone. "You make it difficult for me to leave you. I have to go to this appointment."

"Go." I say breathlessly. "I don't want to keep you from your work." I grin at him.

"You are killing me." He smiled against my lips.

"The longer you stay here with me, the longer it will take you to go there and come back to us." I laugh.

"Sebastian!" He says.

"What? I am trying to get you to leave for your appointment."

"I have to go."

"Then go."

He takes my hand and puts it on his chest. "My heart is racing for you."

I smile bigger.

He hugs me.

Jacob walks in the bookstore. "Justin! We have to go."

"I will be right there." He says.

I kiss him. "Go."

"You make it hard for me to leave you." He says kissing me.

Jacob walks over. "Come on. If we don't go, I won't get my thing back."

Jacob's words strike me as funny and I burst into laughter. "You leant your thing out?" I ask in a fit of laughter.

The two of them laugh with me.

Matt walks over. "Sebastian, a customer is asking for you." He leans in so I can kiss Valentina. She snuggles into him.

"She loves her Uncle Matt." I say.

Justin kisses me one last time. "I will be back."

"Love you." I say.

"Love you." Justin and Jacob say together. They leave.

I go to find the customer who has been looking for me. Ginger stands at the counter with her three daughters. When I greet them, the four of them hug me. Ginger smiles, but I see sadness in her face.

"What's wrong?" I ask.

"Daddy left us." Meg says before Ginger can stop her.

"What?" I ask. I look at Ginger.

Trix walks over. She hugs all of us. She reaches her hands out for the girls. Meg takes her youngest sister's hand and Sara takes Trix's hand. "Is it ok if they have a cookie or a brownie?"

Ginger looks at Trix. "They can have whatever you give them." She reaches in her purse. "Let me give you some money."

"Stop it. Seth's restaurant is just a few doors down." She shakes her bright pink hair. "Stop it. I will take them next door. They are in good hands." She looks at Astro. "Come Astro. Uncle Seth wants to try his dog cookies on you." She looks at me and winks.

"Love you." I tell her.

"I love you too." She leaves with the girls and Astro.

I look at Ginger. "Lets go talk."

"I don't want to take you away from your work."

I look around at the bookstore that is almost empty. "Matt can cover." I say.

Matt walks over and gives Valentina back to me. "I prepped her bottle." He says handing it to me. He walks away. He turns back. "Just one thing, I put the stuff that you were working on in the office."

"Thank you." I say to him.

Ginger runs her fingers through her hair. "Jack is seeing someone named Racheal."

I almost laugh. I bite back my laughter. "Who?" I ask her.

"She's a detective. She works for law firms. She calls him all hours of the night. She—"

"She is not having an affair with your husband."

Ginger looks at me. "How do you know that?"

"Racheal is married. She is a young detective and is trying to get to the bottom of a case that Justin is working on. She needs to be off the case as soon as possible."

Ginger looks at me. "You know this for sure."

"I do." I tell her.

"I am not home when he gets home from work. My job keeps me away from him. I just thought he got bored waiting for me."

"You should tell him that." I say. I look at her. "Ginger, Jack loves you."

"I love him too."

"Why do your girls think that he left you?"

"That was the last conversation that we had. He said he was leaving."

"Did he have to go to work?"

"Yes." She says.

"Ginger, don't doubt his love for you." I tell her.

"Tell me about Savannah."

I roll my eyes.

"That good."

"The truth is, I haven't spoken to her."

"Ok we don't have to talk about it."

"I love her. I am so mad at her. I will get over it."

"You shouldn't have to get over it." She looks away. Then she looks back at me. "Are you sure that Jack isn't cheating on me and the girls?"

"Yes."

"I am going to call him."

"Call him." I tell her. While she goes off and calls Jack, I put the front carrier on and slip Valentina in it. She likes being in it. "What are we going to do?" I ask her. "We are going to plan a wedding to Daddy." I look at her. "I love your Daddy."

Ginger comes back over with a big smile on her face. "Thank you." She says.

"Glad I can help."

"Jack wants to know where Justin is."

I look at her. I know that Jack and Justin do the same job, but they never need to know what the other is doing. They have different practices. I know that Racheal is the detective that looks into their cases for them, but Justin doesn't ever report to Jack.

"He had to go with my brother somewhere."

"What does it feel like to know that you are no longer an only child?"

"It feels great knowing that I have siblings."

"Technically—"

"I am not an only child anymore. That's it." I say.

"What does your mom think?"

"My mom, is my mom. She is mad I go to them. She is mad that I welcomed them with open arms."

"Do you trust them?"

"With everything I am."

"That's so great."

She looks at her watch. "I have to go get my girls."

"Come in anytime. It was good seeing you."

"You too." She says.

~~~~~~~~~~~

Piper and I are at the park with Danny and the two babies. Danny and Tristian run around chasing each other. Both babies are sleeping in the strollers. Danny runs over. He hugs Piper and them me. He than takes off running back to Tristian.

"How is everything going?" I ask.

"If it wasn't for Danny, I would be so bored." She says.

"I know."

"Don't get me wrong, I love having Erin. I am just so bored. My bosses won't let me work for another three weeks."

"Help me plan my wedding." I tell her.

"You are going to have a big wedding?"

"We have a big family."

"Did you set a date?"

"March twenty-first." I say.

"That is just a couple weeks away."

"I know."

"Do you have a dress?"

"Oliver and Blake are going to make my dress."

"Oh you will look beautiful. You always look great in Oliver's dresses."

"I always feel beautiful in one of his dresses."

"What color are you going to have all of us wear?" She asks. "Don't pick peach. I don't look good in orange."

I laugh. "No worries."

"So what color?"

"I think periwinkle."

"I love that."

"I know."

"Who is going to be in the wedding party?"

"You, Lindsey, Trix and I am still thinking if I want Savannah there."

"Put her on a gag."

"Yes." I say.

Valentina cries. I reach in the stroller and lift her out.

Piper looks at me. "You should have Jacob take the pictures. He has been taking pictures of you before he even knew who you were."

"I remember him. Larry was so mean to him." I lift Valentina up and look at her. "I don't know if he remembers but one time Larry was so mean to him and had slapped him in the face, I am not sure why, but I found him and held him while he cried."

"He told Eric the same thing just the other day." Piper looks around. She doesn't see Danny. She stands quickly and turns scanning the park. Tristian runs and hugs her. She hugs him. "Where is Danny?"

"Right there." He points to a sand castle and Danny is putting a white flag on top.

Piper kisses Tristian on the top of his head. She fluffs his hair. She runs over to Danny. She dances with him for a moment and then picks him up and spins him around. "Sebastian!" She yells.

"What?" I ask.

"Should we do it?"

"Do what?"

"Knock over the castle." She says smiling.

"No!" Danny yells. "I made it for you."

I hand Tristian my phone. "Go take pictures of it."

Tristian hugs me. He runs off and takes pictures. He clicks some of Piper and Danny. He then stands facing me and takes some of me and Valentina. He runs over to Piper and says something to her. She looks at me and nods her head. She nods her head at Danny too. Tristian and Danny run over. Danny pushes the stroller over to Piper. Tristian holds his arms out for Valentina.

"What's going on?" I ask.

"We have decided that we can not knock over the castle without you." Tristian says.

I hug him.

Trix walks over. She hugs her nephew tight. "I came to get you. Your dad is ready to go home."

"Wait!" He says.

"What's going on here?" She asks. She loops her fingers in loops of her pants.

"We are going to knock over the sand castle." Tristian beams at her. "We want Aunt Sebastian to do it with us." He says brightly.

She reaches and takes Valentina from me.

Seth runs over. "What's going on?"

"We are going to knock over the sand castle." Tristian says.

Piper and Danny are running around. She is holding Erin. She sits next to castle with Danny next to her. "Are they coming?"

Seth scoops me up in his arms and runs over to the sand castle. He looks at Danny and Tristian. "Ready?" He asks the two boys.

"Yes." They yell.

Jacob runs over with his camera in hand. He snaps constantly. Trix moves to stand next to Jacob. She is holding Valentina. She looks at the sleeping baby in her arms. She sets her in the stroller and takes the camera from Jacob.

He looks at her.

"Go have fun with your sister."

Piper looks over and smiles at the two of them. She holds up her hands. "Ready. Set. Stomp!"

The boys stomp their feet around the castle.

Piper looks at both of them and smiles bigger and brighter. "Good listening." She looks around. "Ok, ready. Set. Sit." She says and we all sit on top of the castle.

I am still in Seth's arms. Jacob takes me in his arms and he runs around the park. He puts me on a slide. Seth runs over and the two of them go down the slide with me between the two of them. Seth takes me on his back.

Trix stands taking pictures. She takes her phone out of her pocket and group texts Justin, Mark, Matt and Sebastian. She tells them to come to the park. She then sends Lindsey a text message telling her to come to the park too.

One by one they show up. Sebastian gets there first. He stands in the parking lot taking it all in. He gets his phone out and takes pictures of Seth running with me on his back. Jacob is running after us and all three of us are smiling brightly.

Justin pulls into the parking lot and parks next to my car. He walks over to Sebastian and they embrace. "How is the bank?"

"Still standing." He says. "How was your day?"

"Trial prep is a bitch sometimes. My client won't cooperate. I would like to drop her on her ass but I am doing this case for a friend."

Sebastian looks around.

"Do you miss Amanda?" Justin asks.

"Not really. I mean we were dating on and off for years. She is dating the manager of the second branch in New York. She ran into him at the party and they shared an elevator that led to a cab that led to the rest of the night."

"Are you seeing anyone?"

"I really like your friend."

"What friend?"

"Racheal." Sebastian says.

Justin turns to him. He takes out his phone.

"What are you doing?"

Justin puts the phone to his ear. "Are you busy? Good. Come to the park. Yes that one. See you soon."

Sebastian looks at Justin. "What did you do?"

Lindsey gets there and out of her. She kisses Sebastian and Justin on the cheek. She runs over to Trix. She kisses her on the cheek too. She picks up Valentina and kisses her. She goes in the diaper bag and takes out a blanket and a fresh diaper. She lays Valentina on the blanket on the park bench and changes her diaper. She lifts her up again and reaches in the bag again for the bottle.

"I would have done that." Trix says.

"I got it. Thanks for you texting me." She looks at all of us. "How long have they been running around like that?"

"About a half hour. They haven't put her down."

Eric pulls into the parking lot. No one had told him to come. He gets out of his truck. He runs over to Justin and hugs him. He hugs Sebastian next. "Whats going on here?"

Piper sees Eric she runs over. He takes Erin from her. She kisses him. She turns and watches Danny and Tristian still running around.

Danny sits with Tristian and they make a bigger sand castle. Eric, Piper, Justin and Sebastian watch the boys. Justin takes his jacket off and puts it on the hood of his car. He then runs over to Danny and Tristian. He helps them build the castle.

Mark pulls into the parking lot. Savannah is with him. She stands back watching everyone. She takes out her phone and takes pictures. Mark watches and Savannah takes his hand. He pulls Savannah against his chest. She turns in his arms and hugs him.

"Is my love enough?" She asks him.

"You are enough for me." Mark says. "I have loved you my whole life."

"I have loved you my whole life." She repeats. "I am sorry I have crazy moments."

"We need to work on that." Mark says kissing her.

"All I want is to be apart of that group over there again." Savannah says blinking back tears.

Justin waves to Mark and waves him over. Savannah steps back. Mark runs over to Justin and the boys.

"What are you doing?" Mark asks.

"We are building castles that we are going to knock over like the last one."

"You did this before?"

"We did this." Tristian says. "Aunt Trix took pictures of us."

"We will have to look at them." Justin says.

Danny gets up from where is in the sand. He jumps in Justin's arms. "You should go play with her like they are. She is so happy to be part of the group."

Justin sets Danny on his feet and kisses the top of his head. He ruffles Danny's hair. Justin runs over to us. I reach for him and Jacob runs in the opposite direction to make Justin run after us. Justin grabs Jacob and tackles him and me.

He takes me and sits me on the tire swing. He climbs behind me and holds me between his legs.

I lean my head back and kiss Justin. He kisses me.

"What did you do today?"

I look away.

"What happened?"

"We came to the park."

"Sebastian. What are you not telling me?"

"I went to look at a venue for the wedding."

"And?"

"They weren't nice to me."

Justin puts his finger under my chin and makes me look at him. "What venue?"

Seth and Jacob stand next to the tire swing. They call Sebastian over. Sebastian walks over with Eric and Mark.

"What Venue turned you away?"

I look at all of them. "Lavenders."

Mark and Justin look at each other. Mark looks at me. "You went to Lavenders?"

"Yes." I say.

"And what happened?" Justin, Jacob, Sebastian and Seth ask.

"When I went in I met with the manager. I had called ahead and told her the dates that we are interested in. She told me over the phone that they had many openings. She told me to come meet with the staff and we could pick the perfect date. When I got there she never let me go inside. She told me that there were no dates available. She told me that she didn't deal with—" I choke on my words. Justin stands up and ducks under the tire. He stands and takes me in his arms.

"We will find another place." He says.

"I really want Lavenders." I say.

"Why?" Seth asks. "You can do the wedding at the restaurant. I have three of them that we can use."

"My dad was going to marry my mom at Lavenders." I say so quietly.

Justin looks at all the brothers around us. "You want Lavenders, we will get it."

Sebastian and Jacob exchanges looks with each other and with Mark.

Sebastian looks at me. "Do you have pictures of it?"

"On my phone." I say.

He lifts me and carries me back to my wheelchair. I look at Trix and smile. She hugs me. She is once again holding my daughter in her arms.

Trix's dad pulls into the parking lot with his wife. They both get out of the car and walk over. They hug everyone. Trix's mom looks at me. She smiles and hugs me again.

"Its good to see you." I tell her.

"I heard that you had an appointment at Lavenders."

"I did. Then they told me that they had nothing available." I say.

"That's what I heard." She says.

"That's unacceptable." Trix's dad says.

Jacob looks at me. "Tell me something."

"Anything." I say.

"What makes this place so special?"

"When I was young, my mom would take me there for my birthday. They have a beautiful auditorium. I played the piano there when I was young. There is a beautiful window that overlooks the most beautiful grounds with an exceptional garden and waterfalls. There are purple flowers everywhere. It was my favorite place." I get my phone out of my purse and show him pictures. "I went to a wedding there and I always wanted to get married there. Its been my dream to get married there since I was ten years old."

He kisses me on the forehead. "Forward me those pictures." He says.

I look at him. "You took pictures of me playing the piano there."

"You have me confused for someone else."

I look at him. "I have done some searching and I know that Larry always knew who I was. I know that he brought you with him. You played the piano with me that one time."

"Sebastian, please stop."

"Why? Why deny it?"

"Just don't talk about that now." He says.

Lindsey walks over. She stands on her toes as she kisses Jacob on his lips. "Can you take me home? I have to practice. Tomorrow is the big concert."

I look at her. "I am ready." I tell her.

"I am ready." Piper says.

We all look at Savannah. She looks at us and smiles. "I am ready."

Jacob and Lindsey leave. Then pretty soon we all leave.

When we get home, Justin gives Valentina a bath. He puts her in pajamas. I get her bottle ready and feed her. Justin takes her from me and burps her.

"Play for me." Justin says.

"What do you want to hear?"

"Fur Elise." He says.

I go to the piano and I start playing. Astro lays on the couch next to Justin and Valentina. They listen to me playing. Justin's phone chimes with text messages. He lays Valentina in the portable crib and walks out back. He takes Astro with him.

Justin calls Jacob. "Hi. Whats gong on?"

"Hi." Jacob says. "You are the phone with all of us. And Mark too."

"What's going on?"

"It seems like our family bought something very special for our sister."

"Oh my god." Justin says.

"Listen, she wants Lavenders for her wedding. Your wedding. She got it. The owner was extremely willing to sell." Sebastian says.

"When she finds out, she's going to be emotional." Justin laughs.

"What's she doing now?" Seth asks.

"She's playing the piano."

"Once she gets started, she could be there all night." Mark says.

"I love it." Justin says.

I open the back door to let Astro back in. I walk over to Justin and put my hand in his hand. He looks at me. I am wearing a bathing suit.

"I love you all. I have to go." Justin says. He clicks end and puts his phone down. He lifts me in his arms and jumps in the pool with me.

We swim together for a while. Justin sits on the steps of the pool. I stand in front of him and puts my hands on his knees. I step closer. With the support of the water, I can walk in the pool on my own. I put my hands on Justin's shoulders and kiss him on the lips. He wraps an arm around my back. He slips his other hand between my legs and holds my mound. I deepen the kiss. He then pulls my bottoms off of me and slips his fingers inside me.

I hum against his lips. He deepens the kiss the time. I pull back to gasp for breath. I feel all my nerve endings coming to life at his touch. He pushes deeper inside my folds. He stands and steps behind me. Justin then sits back on the steps of the pool and pulls me on his lap facing him. He thrusts into me. I sink down on him. I put my hands on his shoulders and push myself up and then sink back down on him. I do this time and time again. I squeeze my eyes shut and shake in his arms. He kisses my lips to silence his moans and my own.

"I love you." I say.

"I love— you." He says and he holds me still on his lap and then puts his hands under my legs and lifts me a bit and then pulls me down on him.

I see stars. My body quakes again. When we finish, Justin stands and takes me in his arms. He carries me in the house and puts me in the shower. He goes back outside for my wheelchair. He joins me in the shower.

Justin carries me to our bed and he lays me in the middle of it. He climbs into the bed. I curl on my side. He curls behind me and we fall asleep in each other's arms.

"Justin?"

"Hmm."

"I am sorry that I went looking for the venue without you."

"Don't be. I would marry you in a courthouse."

It starts raining. A hard dirty rain. Justin pulls me closer to him.

"Are you mad?" I ask.

"No. Of course not."

"Justin?"

"Hmm?"

"Justin?"

He opens his eyes. He sits up and takes me with him. "What's going on?"

"What do you picture for our wedding?"

"I think whatever you want is what I want."

"I want you to tell me what you want. This wedding is not about me. Its about us."

"I just want our brothers to stand next to me as we marry."

I smile. "I would love that." I say.

"Can I ask you a question? I am going to change the subject."

"You can ask anything."

"Are you going to be ok with Savannah playing with you?"

I look at Justin. "As mad as I get with her, I can't deny that she makes us who we are."

"Are you ok with her dating Mark again?"

"I love him. She is his choice. I can't. I won't stand in the way of that." I pull Justin closer to me. "I love you."

"I have loved you since the second that I saw you in the interview room. Then when you passed out, I held you in my arms. I kissed you a few times on the lips. I remembered knowing you." Justin says.

"You kissed me on the lips when I passed out?"

"Yes."

I kiss him. "I should never had said anything about Lavenders."

"No, I am glad that you did."

"I just have a feeling that—" I stop talking as Justin kisses me. I pull back. "Are you trying to stop me from—" he kisses me again. "Justin!"

"You are going to love Lavenders on our wedding day. What color am I going to wear?"

"Black and periwinkle." I say. He kisses me on the lips and then lays with me in his arms.

Chapter 34

Sebastian comes to my house first thing in the morning. Jacob and Seth are with him. Lindsey stands holding Valentina. I am in my room with Justin.

"Come on, my brothers are here. What are we waiting for?"

"Mark to get here." Justin says.

"Justin, Valentina needs to eat."

"Sebastian, Lindsey is going to feed her."

"Why won't you let me out of my room?" I whine.

He kisses me.

"Justin! What's going on?"

Astro barks.

"He has to go out." I say.

There is a knock on the door. Justin opens it and Seth reaches in with Astro's leash. "I will take him.

"Seth!" I say.

"What?" He asks.

"Take me with you."

"I can't." He says.

"What's going on?" I ask.

"Come Astro." Seth says. He looks at Justin. "I will let you know when they are here."

"Thank you." Justin says. Justin closes the door.

"I am getting annoyed." I say.

"Come on. I know you hate waiting but this is going to be so worth it." Justin says.

Ten minutes later, Justin's phone rings. He answers it. He looks at me and walks to the door. He opens it. He takes my hand and leads me out of our room.

He walks slowly down the hallway and I hear the clicks of Jacob's camera. The flashes nearly blind me. Oliver and Blake are standing in front of me holding the most magnificent dress I have ever seen. Ivan and Trevor are standing with my uncles. Mark holds up a suit for Justin.

Lindsey is holding Valentina. They are both in periwinkle dresses. My mom and Peter are standing hand in hand.

"What's going on?" I ask.

"Well the truth is that we didn't pick a date to get married." Justin says. "And you are now the owner of Lavenders."

"I am what?" I ask.

Sebastian looks at Justin. "You ruined our wedding gift."

"You bought Lavenders?" I ask.

"We are going to revision it for you. But today, its your wedding venue." Mark says. "The second I saw the inside of it, my mind has been spinning."

I hug him. "Everyone is here?" I ask.

"Not everyone. But everyone that you know is at Lavenders waiting to see you marry your Prince Charming." Savannah says. She is referencing my diary from when I was young. She smiles as Mark takes her hand in his. They lace their fingers together.

Scarlett looks at me. "Sweetheart, can I talk to you privately?"

"Yes." I say. I go back into my bedroom and close the door behind us.

She crosses the room and sits on the loveseat by the French doors. "Come here please." She says quietly. She has a box with her. She sets the box next to her on the loveseat. "Open this later. The contents will make you cry. I hope that they will be happy tears."

I look at her.

"Its my gift that I have been working on for a while. I have a similar one for Sebastian. It's something that you asked for." She opens her purse. She takes out a blue box. "Here is your something borrowed and something blue." She gives me the box. "Before you open it, its borrowed because you are going to keep it and give it to your daughter on her wedding day. You are going to tell her that its borrowed and she is going to keep it to give to her daughter."

I smile.

"This is something that was your dad's." She says. "He planned on giving it to your mom for their wedding." She closes her eyes. "I should have given it to her for you years ago." She puts her hands around my hands. "Ok."

I open the box and it's a blue dragonfly on a cluster of stars pin. It's the most beautiful thing I have ever seen. "Oh god, this is beautiful." I say.

"He made it."

I blink my tears away. "I may never give this to anyone." I smile.

"You will want to give it to Valentina for her wedding day." She hugs me.

I smile.

"Why are you smiling?"

"I can't wait to wear the wedding dress. Aunt Scarlett, I have loved wearing their dresses. I always felt so pretty and confident."

"We know."

"What?"

"Jacob has a ga—" she stops talking.

"What?" I ask.

"Its time for you to get dressed."

"I want to put the dress on at Lavenders."

"Of course." She says. "I will be right back." She says kissing me on the cheek. She leaves my room. She comes back with a box. She walks back over. She sits back on the loveseat.

I open the box and gasp. "Oh my god!" I take the dress out of the box. Its stunning. Its periwinkle. "When did Uncle Blake do this?" I ask.

She looks at me. "How do you know that Blake made this?"

"He always made my favorite dresses." I hold it up and look at it.

"Tell me how did you start wearing Blake and Oliver's dresses."

"Ivan. I was called up to replace someone who was supposed to play the piano. She got sick and was in the hospital. I didn't have anything to wear. Ivan came in with a dress. He told me to just try it on. I did and it fit alike a glove. It was the most elegant dress I had ever worn. I played the best I ever played." I say.

"Ivan showed us." She says.

"Ivan is so special." I look at the dress again. "Ivan wore their designs too and he danced with confidence. I loved watching him dance."

"Wow. You should be the spokesperson for their line."

"I could sell it." I tell her.

I put the dress on and I smile. Justin comes in our room. He looks at me. "Wow." He says.

"Can you pick me up?" I ask him.

He scoops me up in his arms. "Like this?"

"Yes." I say. "Can you spin around a few times."

He does and the dress twirls around the two of us. I hear Jacob's camera click. I look at him and smile. He smiles back. Justin kisses me and Jacob captures every second.

Sebastian walks in the room. "Ok, we have to go." He says. "All the guys are going now."

Justin sits me back in my wheelchair and kisses me. "I love you."

"I love you too."

Jacob walks over and fans the dress out. He snaps pictures of me. He leans in and kisses me. "I love you."

"I love you too." I tell him.

Sebastian hugs me. "You look gorgeous."

"I feel gorgeous." I say.

He looks at Scarlett. "Give us twenty minutes and then you all come."

"I know the agenda." She says ands smiles.

When they leave, I look at Scarlett. "Who is going to walk me down the isle?"

There is a knock on the door. My mom walks in the room and gasps. "Oh my god, you look beautiful." She smiles. "You are always beautiful but you are glowing. You radiate beauty. Your dad would love to see you today." She says.

I put my hand to my chest. Scarlett stands behind me and does my hair. She makes big beach curls.

Trix walks in the room. She looks at me. She takes her phone and clicks pictures. "Oh my god, Sebastian you are beautiful." She says.

I hold my hand out to her. "Thank you."

"We have to go. My dad is going take you."

I smile. "Who is going to a walk me down the isle?"

"You will see." Trix says.

When I come out of my room, Astro is sitting on the couch and he is has a black vest with periwinkle. I hold my had out for him and he jumps off the couch and trots over. I hug him. "Look how handsome you look." He licks my cheek.

Lindsey holds Valentina. Trix walks over and takes her from Lindsey. "Everything ready?"

"Everything is ready." She says.

We leave the house and everyone gets into the waiting limo. Trix's dad is driving us. When I come out of the house, he kisses me. "You are breathtaking." He tells me.

"Thank you ." I say.

"Are you aware of how proud I am of you? My daughter. My nephews. We are better people because we know you." He says.

I gasp.

"We love you."

"I love you all too."

He helps me in the car and kisses me on the cheek.

We get to Lavenders. Trix's dad pulls into the lot and right up the front doors. Everyone gets out. I get in my wheelchair. Ivan meets us at the door. He drops to his knees and hugs me.

"You are stunning." He says.

"I love you."

He lifts me in his arms.

"Put me down. You will wrinkle."

"I will not wrinkle." He brings me into the bridal suite.

The wedding dress hangs with the pin on it. I gasp when I see it.

"What's wrong?" Ivan asks.

"My dad made that." I say pointing to the pin. "He made it for my mom."

"A dragonfly?" Ivan says. He puts his forehead to my forehead. He closes his eyes. "I should have been there."

"Ivan." I say. I kiss him on the lips. Not a romantic kiss. "I never blamed you."

Trevor walks in. "No time for sadness. We have to get you married." He says and kisses both of us. He brought my wheelchair in. He takes me from Ivan and sits me in my wheelchair. "Ok, dress off." He takes the dress when I take it off and he hangs it up. "Wow, they outdid themselves on this one." Trevor hands me the wedding dress.

I put it on. I go over to the couch so that I can stand up and hold on to something sturdy. Trevor zips up the dress. He stands back and gawks.

Piper knocks on the door. "Can I come in?" She asks.

"No." Trevor says. "We want her to be a surprise to everyone."

She sticks her head in the door. "Trevor, you know that her bridesmaids are the ones who are supposed to get her ready? You are supposed to be with the groom."

He kisses her on the forehead. "Go make sure that everyone is ready."

"Everyone is ready." She says.

"Moonlight and then Cannon—"

"Trevor, I know. I planned this." She says.

Trevor steps out of the room with her. He looks at her. He takes the material at her shoulders and pulls it off her shoulders.

"Trevor, what are you doing?"

"You are not wearing this right."

"How the hell would you know?"

"Its my design. This is the different dress. This is the special one."

"Why did I get the special one?" She asks.

"Because."

"Trevor don't be five." She smiles.

"Because when Sebastian and Justin say 'I do' you and Eric are going to join them."

"Am I getting married today?" Piper asks him.

"Yes."

"No."

"What?"

"I don't want to ruin her day."

"She wants this to happen. Why do you think she picked periwinkle?"

"She knows its my favorite color."

"She knows you don't want to get married in white."

Piper smiles. "Can't I go hug her?"

"No." Trevor says and kisses her. "Your violin ready?"

"Yes." She says.

"You look stunning." Trevor says.

"She does look stunning." Eric says and kisses her. "Erin is with your mom."

"Ok." She kisses Eric. "Where is Danny?"

"He is with the groomsmen having the time of his life. He feels so special being one of the guys."

"Sebastian loves him." Trevor says.

"Danny and Tristian both feel like they are on cloud nine."

Piper kisses Eric and then turns on her heals and picks up her Violin. Eric picks up a violin of his own and he starts playing. Piper turns and smiles. She turns back around. Lindsey comes and stands next to Piper. Savannah walks over. Her violin is up and ready.

Linsey and Piper play Moonlight Sonata. Savannah plays Fur Elise. The combination of the two melodies marry and sound lovely. Eric leans in and kisses Piper on the lips. He plays the traditional Wedding March.

The bridal doors open automatically. Mark stands right outside the doors. He takes my hand. Trix hands me the bouquet of flowers. She pulls one of the curls away from the pin so that it shows.

Jacob gets on his knees and snaps pictures. He smiles. When I pass by him, I take his hand and squeeze it. He takes pictures of Eric, Lindsey, Piper and Savannah.

When we get half way down the isle, Mom joins us. She leans in and sees the pin. She puts her fingertips on it. She gasps. She smiles. "He is with you." She says.

Peter walks down the isle with us. He takes Mark's place. Mark joins Justin. Justin looks at me and tears fill his eyes. Charlotte is holding Valentina. Sebastian stands next to Mark and his brothers. Ivan and Trevor stand next to them. Right next to Justin is Danny and Tristian. They each hold periwinkle pillows.

When I walk down the isle, Blake and Oliver both look at me and beam. This is the best dress that they have created. Scarlett beams too.

Anastasia is standing under the lavender canopy. It's the first time that she has seen me. She smiles. The music stops after Canon in D stops. They come join me. Mark steps back and Eric joins the groomsmen.

Trix takes the flowers from me.

Mom kisses me on the cheek. Peter kisses me on the other cheek. "I love you." They both say.

"Your dad is beaming up in heaven." Peter says. He kisses me again. "One from him."

Anastasia looks at Justin and me. "Take each other's hands. Take the rings. And repeat. With these rings, I thee wed."

"With this ring, I thee wed." Justin says. I follow him. Eric follows me and then Piper follows Eric.

Anastasia looks at the four of us. "You may kiss your brides."

Justin kisses me like his life depends on it. I giggle against his lips. He smiles and kisses me deeper.

"This is why they have a baby." Mark says.

We laugh.

Everyone cheers.

Jacob takes pictures of all us. Peter takes the camera so that Jacob can be in the pictures as well.

We all go outside and take pictures in front fo the waterfall. Justin pushes me as I am holding Valentina in my arms. Ivan and Trevor sit on the ground. Everyone sits on the ground with the waterfall behind us.

Peter takes Jacob's camera. He hugs Jacob tight. "You know, if you ever need a dad to talk to, I am here for all of you."

Jacob hugs Peter.

A woman walks over. She finds Sebastian. "Hi, do you think I could be in the pictures?" She asks.

Sebastian looks at her. "Amanda?"

"I was never in a relationship with anyone in New York. I thought of you everyday. I missed you every day. Jacob sent me pictures of you so it was less agonizing."

He pulls her on his lap and kisses her.

Justin lifts me out of my wheelchair. Trevor helps me get me on the ground. Trevor kisses me. Everyone sits for the wedding the pictures.

Justin kisses me like we are the only two people on the earth.

"I love you." We both say together.

When we get home, I open the box that Scarlett left for me. Inside is recordings of my dad. I watch them with my brothers and Justin. They all hug me.

Justin kisses me on the lips. "Love you forever and always."

Epilogue

Three years later.....

Justin and I have Valentina and a son Named Asher Douglas. We still live in my house. Savannah and Mark still live three streets behind us. They are married and have a son. Piper and Eric bought the house next to my house. Danny is the best big brother to two sisters. He can't get enough of them.

Seth married Trix. They run the two restaurants and are constantly coming over to Lavenders to see me. Trix is expecting twins. One of each will be coming in the summer. She can't wait to not be a beach ball.

Jacob uses the top floor of Lavenders as his gallery. He displays all the pictures he took of me, Sebastian and Seth. His gallery brings in a lot of people. Lavenders is adding on a restaurant which Seth is going to run. Lindsey uses the quiet rooms to give music lessons.

Sebastian and Amanda are married. They now have several banks. They both work at the big branch office which shares a parking lot with Lavenders. I see them every day. There hasn't been a day that has gone by in three years that they have missed. Sebastian and Amanda are raising her niece and nephew.

Matt is running the bookstore and its doing well. I still work in the bookstore one or two days a week. I usually cover the Friday schedule. There was a girl named Amber who I hired to help in the bookstore.

Matt and Amber have been a couple for the last two years and she loves Tristian as mush as we all do.

My mom moved to Paris and hasn't been back in two years. Peter lives here still. We have dinner with him two or three days a week. He loves being with us. Peter comes to be with the children almost every day. He loves my children as if they were his own grandchildren. He also loves that he he can leave either Piper's house first or my house first and go right next door to see the other set of grandchildren.

Scarlett and Blake come to visit as much as possible. Blake does come more often then Scarlett does. Francesca has been band from coming to my house or anywhere around me. We have decided that its best if she never comes near me.

The whole family will be coming to see Lindsey, Piper and me playing our instruments while Ivan dances for the last time. Jacob is going to play the piano with me at one point in the evening.

Lavender is all set to welcome everyone. The auditorium is breathtaking. Mark has gone to extremes to make it the most elegant hall. I love being on the stage. The piano was delivered from my grandma in Paris. It was the best gift that she ever gave me.

We all get there early. Seth is catering the event. Trix helps him set up the dining room. We all help set up the room. There is music playing and we are singing together. Justin pulls me aside and dances with me.

Sebastian walks over and takes me away from Justin. "I need to dance with my sister."

Trevor walks over to Justin. "Can I talk to you?"

"Of course." Justin says.

"Ivan wants to dance with her." Trevor says.

Jacob walks over. "We've got it all worked out."

Trevor looks at Justin and Jacob. "He did once before with other dancers."

"I know, I was there." Justin and Jacob say together. They exchange looks and then look back to Trevor.

"We have it all worked out." Jacob says again.

"Only difference is, when I bring her down to kiss her, I am going to hand her off to you." Ivan says to Justin.

"God!" Jacob says.

Everyone stops and looks at him.

"What's wrong?" Justin asks.

"He is torn." Lindsey says. "He is thinking how he can be two places at once. He wants to be apart of the whole stage thing that we have planned for tonight, but he also wants to capture the moments that he knows will happen and that only he can take."

Jacob takes her in his arms and hugs her intently. He kisses Lindsey so passionately.

Seth walks over. "Give your camera to mom. Let her take the pictures. She will capture the images just as you do. You learned from her."

Jacob hugs Seth tight. He kisses Seth on the cheek over and over again.

"Stop! You are going to make me blotchy." Seth says.

Sebastian runs over and hugs both his brothers. He alternates kissing Jacob and Seth over and over again.

"Stop." Seth says. He tries to squirm out of Sebastian's hold.

Charlotte walks in and takes pictures of her sons. She looks at me. I am watching them. I can't take my eyes off of them. Charlotte watches her sons all look at me and then run over to me and they all start kissing me at the same time. She snaps picture after picture.

Piper walks over and hugs Charlotte. Piper blinks tears out of her eyes. Charlotte hugs her tighter. "I have to tell you, I will never regret meeting Larry and telling him about my friend who needed a job." Piper says.

Charlotte hugs Piper again. "Does she know what a wonderful friend she has in you?"

"Oh my god yes. We have loved each other unconditionally our whole lives." Piper reaches her hand out for Danny when he walks over. She hugs her son close to her. "Did you tell Aunt Charlotte what you have been doing lately?"

Charlotte looks at Danny. "What have you been working on?"

"Tristian and I are going to dance with Uncle Ivan."

"I am so glad you told me." Charlotte says. "Excuse me." She says. She walks over to all of us. "How can I help?"

"You being here is help enough." I say. "I can't tell you how grateful I am that you have been in my life."

She hugs me. "I am grateful too to have you in my life. You have made my sons better people."

"I like to think that I was a good person before I knew that I had an identity clone." Sebastian says.

We laugh.

Mark walks over. "Little Mermaid." He walks over and hugs me. "I need some private time with you." He takes me by the hand and we go upstairs to practice dancing.

Justin walks over. Mark and Justin both sit on chairs next to me. They tie their legs to my legs. They both stand and take me with them and they dance with me.

Jacob takes pictures of us.

I put my arms around their shoulders and they lift me. Mark detaches his leg from mine. Justin takes me in his arms and then they both lift me up and then bring me down on each of their knees. Justin kisses me.

"You are going to be beautiful tonight." Jacob says.

Blake and Oliver walk in. They are awestruck by our place. They each carry garment bags. Trevor shows them where to take them. Then he helps them with the rest of them.

"Can we see the gallery?" Blake asks Jacob.

"Sure." He says.

They go upstairs with Jacob. He lets them walk around. Jacob sits at the piano up there and he plays. His fingers glide over the keys effortlessly.

"Where did you learn how to play?" Oliver asks.

"I went to college on a music scholarship." Jacob says.

"You should play with the symphony." Blake says.

"I am not that good." Jacob says.

The elevator doors open. I cross the room and sit on the piano bench with Jacob. "Start whenever you are ready." I say.

We play a duet together. When we finish, I hug him. "You are that good. You are better than that good and you know it." I hug him again. "Your dad should never had told you otherwise."

He hugs me. "I love you."

"I love you too."

Trevor comes upstairs. He walks up the steps. "We need you both to come downstairs and get changed. We are getting ready to let guests inside."

An hour later, I am sitting at the piano playing Moonlight Sonata. Savannah, Piper, and Lindsey are playing violins with me. My dress is flared around me. My uncles have made me a dress that is second to the wedding dress that they made for me three years before. I play music with my friends like there is no one around us.

They start playing Dance of the Sugar Plum Fairy and that's when Mark lifts me off the piano bench. He dances with me like he danced with me our whole lives. He passes me to Ivan. Mark steps aside and watches us. Ivan holds me in his arms and when he takes us down the ground, Justin takes me in his arms and kisses me. They both hold me in their arms. Mark joins us along with Trevor. Each of them carrying one of my children. My friends who have become my family join me on the stage. Its like we have recreated my wedding pictures with the waterfall behind us. We all embrace.

The audience erupts in applauds. They all stand and cheer louder.

The show isn't over yet. Justin lifts me in his arms and carries me to my wheelchair. He dances with me and spins me around. Ivan takes my hand and he dances with me too. Sebastian takes my hand and leads us to the piano. He sits next to me and we play Heart and Soul together. Lindsey stands with her violin and Jacob behind her holding her. Eric holds Piper in his arms. Mark holds Savannah. When we play the last note, they kiss us.

"I love you." We all say to the loves of our lives. "Unconditionally."

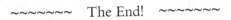 The End! ~~~~~~